Concealed From Sight

Also by Art Burton

For Hire, Messenger of God
A murder mystery

Caught in the Line of Fire
A murder mystery

Hobos I Have Known
A collection of short stories

Check out: users.eastlink.ca/~artburton

Concealed From Sight

By Art Burton

For Connie

Acknowledgements

Once again, I have to thank, my editor, Bev Dauphinee, for her patience and suggestions and for all those thousands of useless words that ended up in my trash bin. It was painful but necessary. Sometime or other, I might actually learn all those rules of grammar and spelling. You were a blessing.

Jim Ettinger stepped up once again to be the initial proof reader. Thanks Jim for you knowledge and keen eye.

Teri Cryne also served as an early reader. Her enthusiasm was encouraging and kept me fired up to continue the process.

Stephen Lowe and Gwen Frankton offered some great ideas for the cover. One of Stephen's pencil sketches led to this final design. Stephen gets the credit if you like it, but none of the blame if you don't as he didn't actually get to see my final decision except maybe on Facebook. Thanks to all those Facebook friends who took the time to make comments. I'm a controlling person at heart and always have the final say, but I did consider your suggestions.

And as always, there are not enough words to thank my wife, Flame. Writing is a solitary profession in the early stages and a consultatory one as you prepare for publication. She was there for me all through the process.

CHAPTER 1

Late April

CONNIE WILSON PEERED from her farm kitchen doorway. Her hands, encased in blue rubber gloves, held a damp, red-and-white checked dishcloth she unconsciously kept wringing and wringing, although it was long past giving up any additional moisture. Her gaze shifted between the road leading to the village of Raymond's River to her left and the road that should be bringing her husband, George, home from his work site at Mary Jane Falls to the right. Neither carried any vehicles at this moment.

She knew the red, half-ton truck of Brian Cosh should be cresting the hill from the village at any minute. Brian served as chief of the local volunteer fire department in Raymond's River. Connie had called him ten minutes previously, panic in her voice, tears in her eyes.

Behind her the supper table was prepared for the evening meal, two place settings, one at each end of the chrome-and-red Formica table. On the now flameless propane stove, overcooked hamburger patties sat marinating in their own fat. A slimy heap of fried onions occupied one corner of the pan. Half of a freshly peeled onion sat on a chopping board on the kitchen counter, the same counter the now dry dish cloth had left spotless from being cleaned three times since the phone call was made. The smell of the onion sat on top of the regular kitchen odours and tickled her eyes.

A degree of relief flickered through her body as the chief's truck broke into view at the far corner of her property. She looked down at the over-wrung dishcloth, threw it towards the sink and wiped her hands on the flowered, yellow-and-green apron tied around her waist. That, too, came off and landed on a chair in the corner. A smile slowly spread across her face. She left the door open and walked over to the counter, pausing only long enough to put a low heat under the frying pan on the stove. Without apparent thought, she picked up a sharp kitchen knife and skillfully sliced up the remaining onion. Busy work. She slid the results onto one of the plates on the table and turned back to the door.

Brian came running up the outside steps, two at a time, and stopped in the opening.

Tears were welling in the corner of Connie's eyes, again. "Oh, Brian. I didn't know who to call. Thank you for coming so quickly." She rushed towards the big man.

Brian took off his black baseball cap and quickly took note of the distraught woman coming at him. Her long, blond hair had only been half-heartedly brushed. The tips clung together in matted clumps. Dark rings circled her ocean-green eyes. Tears flowed like the incoming tide down her pale, drawn face. The eyes begged for more sleep.

Wrinkles creased her white, cotton blouse. Her blue jeans were spattered with mud around the cuffs. Her feet were dressed in light pink crocs. No thought had been given to her wardrobe when she dressed that morning, if indeed she had dressed that morning. Her clothes looked more like she had slept in them. This was not the always well-turned-out Connie Wilson that Brian knew. The shock of her appearance registered on his face.

"Connie, what's wrong?" He stepped into the kitchen and Connie fell into his arms. He could feel her tears soaking through his own checked, flannel shirt. He put a comforting hand around her back and held her for a few seconds while he quickly scanned the kitchen, taking a fleeting look through the window towards the barn. "Has something happened to George?"

Connie stepped away from him and extracted a crumpled Kleenex from her jeans pocket. She wiped at the tears streaming down her face. This only served to divert the salty flow towards her ear.

"He hasn't been home since yesterday morning." She struggled to control the hitch in her voice. "I don't know where he is. I've been going crazy here waiting for him."

The chief stood silent for a minute. She could see the internal debate going on in his eyes. Then he guided her towards one of the kitchen chairs and, with a gentle pressure on her shoulders, encouraged her to sit down.

"Wa-was he drinking?" Brian had to force himself to verbalize the question.

Connie lowered her head and studied the table top. "Not when he left here yesterday morning. He was going to work. He's yarding firewood from the Millicent place up by Mary Jane Falls. I drove by last night when he didn't come home for supper and spotted his porter out by the end of the road. His half-ton was nowhere to be seen."

Again the chief remained briefly silent. "He has stayed away all night before, hasn't he?" It wasn't really a question. Brian knew full well the answer was yes. Brian and Connie were close first cousins. There were no secrets.

George occasionally succumbed to binge drinking. He didn't drink often anymore, but when he did, he drank a lot. Brian knew this. Connie knew that Brian knew this. She had never asked for his help on those other occasions. She could see the question in Brian's eyes. What's different this time?

Connie nodded. "You know he has, Brian." She hesitated. "But he's always came home the next day." Her eyes drifted over to the meat on the stove. "He's always home by supper time and God help me if it's not ready." The last part of that statement had just slipped out uninvited.

Brian noticed the congealed fat in the bottom of the frying pan was starting to bubble around the edges. His eyes travelled to the onions on the plate in front of Connie. He looked back into her eyes, encouraging her to continue.

"When he wasn't here by six, I didn't know what to do. I did the chores myself last night and again this morning. I spent most of the day preparing for tomorrow night's supper at the fire hall. At least that kept my mind occupied for a while."

Without apparent thought, she pulled the rubber glove off her right hand. Underneath a flesh-coloured, Elastoplast Band-Aid crossed her palm and the fleshy part of her thumb. The edges were turning up from wear.

Brian reached for the hand. "You've cut yourself. Let me see."

Connie pulled her hand away from his and stared absently at the bandage. "It's nothing. I scratched my hand on a nail in the milking parlour last night." She laughed. "Carelessness." She pulled off the other glove and threw them both into the sink.

The fleeting smile disappeared. "Even when he's drinking, it isn't like George to neglect the animals for any longer than one day. No matter how bad he feels, he's always here to take care of the milking. That's why I called you. He should be home by now."

Brian looked out the kitchen window at the cows milling around the barn door. His farmer's eye could see they were due to be milked. He pulled the other chair closer and sat down. His callused hand enveloped Connie's almost equally rough, working woman's hand. He surreptitiously examined the dressing. It was clean and showed no trace of dried blood.

"I'm sure he's all right. We both know he doesn't drink and drive anymore. Not since that DUI two years ago when he wrecked the truck and…" He let the sentence drift off into nothingness. "He's probably just sobering up somewhere."

Like most drinkers, George had pictured himself as being invincible. Even when he could hardly stand up and stagger to his truck, he always felt able to drive once he got there. That all changed the winter before last. A combination of slippery roads and too much alcohol had led to the death of a small boy in a horrific motor vehicle accident. Most people, including the courts, said the road conditions were the main cause of the collision. The accident reconstructionist said that under the circumstances, a completely sober person would not have been able to avoid the accident. George's drinking had no bearing on the outcome. Still, George was found guilty of driving under the influence. He was slapped with a hefty fine and lost his licence for a year.

The boy's family thought a great miscarriage of justice had taken place. They believed George should have at least gotten jail time. The grandmother, interviewed outside the courtroom, said she would not accept that justice was done until George was rotting in his grave. A silent contingent of people in the community still shared her view; their condemning stares never allowed George to forget how lucky he had been before the courts.

He did not let himself off easily, either. Despite what the experts said, every time he replayed the accident in his mind, he could see hundreds of things he could have — should have — done differently. Things that came naturally to a sober man. Every one of those differences led to a non-fatal conclusion to the event. In his mind's eye, the roads were never as slippery as the reality had been.

Connie often woke up in the wee hours of the morning to see George thrashing in his bed, tied up in the blankets, soaked in sweat, reliving the event. It was not his conscious mind that insisted on reliving that day; it was his unconscious mind that wouldn't let go. Like those critics in town, it contained no forgiveness.

George had not allowed himself behind the wheel of his truck after even one beer since that terrifying day. Now, most, but not all, of his drinking took place at the end of the day in the comfort of his own living room. Every five or six months, some devil-induced spell grabbed hold of him and he drank himself into oblivion.

Connie forced a smile to her lips. She hungrily clutched at the straw Brian held out to her. "Do you really think so? Where would he be? Why hasn't he at least called?"

Brian had no answers for that. She could see him running through the list in his mind of people with whom George might be drinking. People who wouldn't encourage him to call home. The list wasn't short, especially if George was the one supplying the liquor.

There was an element in Raymond's River and surrounding area that could smell out free booze. That element also had the ability to draw out every last drop of the free stuff before releasing the buyer back to his family. This list of candidates would require a closer look before Brian started fearing the worst.

"Was anyone working in the woods with him?" He hoped to refine the roster.

Connie shook her head. "I don't know. Sometimes he had help; most times, he worked alone. Depended on exactly what he was doing. I worried about him working out there by himself with all that dangerous equipment. Sometimes I would go out and help him. It wasn't that he needed, or even wanted, my help. It just gave me peace of mind to know that he wasn't alone if something went wrong. But he was always careful. I saw that and felt a little better."

Brian tried to visualize Connie handling a roaring chain saw. Surprisingly, he could.

"You say you found the porter out at the end of the woods road. Could he have still been back there working?"

"No. The road was too chewed up for anything but a big-wheeled vehicle. He brought the logs out to a work area he had developed at that spot. That's where he chunked and split the firewood. The porter contained a full load of logs. He must have been alone. If he has help, it's with the splitting. There was no pile of split wood. The old gravel truck he uses to deliver the wood was still there, empty. He must have delivered his first load early and came back to do a little more."

"Or something interrupted him early in the day."

A surprised look appeared on Connie's face. "I never thought of that."

"Who usually works with him?"

"It's all under-the-table stuff. There's a bunch of cronies that hang around Winston's service station. He just asks whoever is available when he needs them. Anyone willing to work long enough to get a bottle. You know who I mean."

Brian nodded. He knew all too well. These were not the most contributing citizens of Raymond's River. He had used their services on a few occasions himself.

"That's a starting point. Let me make some calls," he said. "I'm sure someone knows where he is or has seen his truck parked in a neighbour's driveway." His voice sounded reassuring. He looked at his watch. "It's 6:30. There are still a couple of hours of daylight left. I can get some of the firemen to drive around and look for his truck." He seemed hesitant to add any more but finally said: "We can't start a real search until we know where to start looking."

Tears leapt to Connie's eyes again. "Brian, I'm scared. What if something bad has happened to him? He hasn't had a drink in weeks. What if his truck went off the road somewhere and he's pinned under it?"

Brian squeezed her hand a little tighter. She winced. "Sorry," he said and loosened his grip. "Let's not let the devil be using your mind as a playground. I'll have my men take a look around first. I'll get them to check the ditches between the Millicent place and here. My experience is that these things usually work out all right."

"Sh-should I call the Mounties?"

"Let me do that. Strictly speaking, he's only been missing since supper time last night." He managed a smile. "I'll make a few calls from here to get things rolling."

"OK," Connie said. "I trust you." She looked over at the stove. "I'm not going to eat those burgers. Would you like one? I know you like your onions raw." She indicated the freshly cut pile on the plate in front of her.

Brian shook his head. "I've had my supper, but you should eat. You've got to keep your strength up."

She slowly shook her head. "No. I'm not hungry. I'll eat when George gets home."

"It's important that you don't let yourself become run down. No offence, but you look like hell." He flashed a quick smile, not returned. "I'll send someone over to help you with the milking tonight."

Connie started to argue, but then sat back in her chair. "That would be good," she said with a sigh of resignation.

CHAPTER 2

BRIAN COSH STOOD in the bay of the Raymond's River Volunteer Fire Station. Surrounding him were twelve fellow volunteers. Several of these men and women were farmers. Their evening chores were only partially completed when he called. Those remaining chores would have to wait.

The radio message that had assembled these people had advised them to keep an eye out for George Wilson's truck on the way to the station. No one had seen anything. Now they were organizing a more coherent search.

"Well, Chief," John Haydon, one of the captains, said. "I see two places for immediate attention. Winston Fleet's service station. Winston can tell us if George was in there yesterday looking for help and who he might have gotten. And the liquor store. They can tell us if George was in there on either day stocking up."

Even though it had been months since George had done any serious drinking, his image of always having a bottle at hand was firmly planted in everyone's mind.

"Don't forget Cal Lindsay's place," another man volunteered. "Cal is still in competition with the liquor store, especially after hours. George is no stranger there." This sounded like experience talking, not mere speculation.

Brian nodded. All three suggestions had merit. "John, you start with your ideas. You can call Winston, but you had better go to the liquor store in person. Make sure whoever you are talking to knows who George is. We don't want to start off with misinformation. If Lisa Tingley is working, she'll know not only if George was there but everyone else in the community who has bought any liquor in the last couple of days. As for Cal, he might be reluctant to offer any official information. That's not the business he's in. Maybe I'd better drop in to see him myself."

It would be understandable that Cal Lindsay would be hesitant about sharing his list of clients. Brian didn't know exactly what would be in the job description of a successful bootlegger, but he was sure that discretion found itself near the top of the list. Brian figured that if this search went badly, he would have a better chance of getting information from Cal than a uniformed police officer. Unconsciously he felt for his wallet. It went without saying that a purchase would be required before any serious discussion took place.

"I'll explain to Cal how worried Connie is. They went to school together, even dated, as I recall. That might soften him up enough to cooperate. With luck, he might be able to tell us not only if George was there last night, but who he was with."

"Cal worked for me today," John said. He looked at his watch. "We're getting the fields plowed up in preparation for planting. He still had a couple more rows to do when I left. He might be home by now."

"OK, maybe I'll swing by your place first," Brian said. He turned to face a big, wooden map nailed to the wall. Each house in the community was represented by a red pin. "Jerry, Bruce, you two check the route from the Millicent place to George's house." Brian traced the route with his finger.

"Rodger, Barry. You start at the house and work back the other way." Again his finger followed the roadway indicated on the map. "We don't have much daylight left. Be thorough, but keep the time in mind."

He turned to the remaining men and women. "Let's start phoning at least a couple of people on each of these roads. Have them look out towards their neighbours and see if they can spot George's truck. It's a silver-and-black Dodge. Oh-eight, I think."

He pulled a piece of paper from his shirt pocket. It was the list he had made with Connie's help of George's drinking buddies.

"Here's a list of possible houses where he might be. You four drive over to these places. Any of them would lie to us if there's still more booze to be had. We want to verify for ourselves that he's not there. Knock on the doors and go inside. Don't take no for an answer."

"Somebody should be with Connie," Brian's wife, Mary, said. "I can do that. If George comes home, she may forget to call us." She gave a little shrug of her shoulders. "Or George won't let her call. He might be too embarrassed if he's been drinking again. One would have thought that he'd learned his lesson a couple of years ago."

Brian's look at Mary would have caused flowers to shrivel on sight. There was no mistaking which side of the DUI sentencing debate Mary supported. "Good idea," he said, "but don't go over there with that judging attitude. That's not what Connie needs right now. You can help with her chores."

Mary nodded. Her entire life had been lived on a farm. She was as familiar with the interior of a barn as the interior of her kitchen.

"Are we calling in the police, yet?" John asked.

"It's only been a day so far. I'll give them a heads-up but I doubt if they'll get involved until tomorrow. George is an adult. We all know this isn't the first time he's stayed out all night. They'll be reluctant to jump in too soon and I don't really want to cause George any undue embarrassment. Maybe I can persuade them to send some patrols through the area."

The chief again looked around at the eager faces. "If we don't have any luck in the meantime, we'll reassemble here as soon as it starts to get dark. Let's say 8:30. That doesn't give us much time, but who knows, we might get lucky. We'll pool our information and decide where to go from there. If there are no other questions, let's get started."

Everyone moved to tackle their respective tasks.

Ten minutes later, Brian stood on the doorstep of Cal Lindsay's bungalow. The road in had been rutted and muddy from the spring rains. The house itself had faded yellow clapboard siding, popular back in the 1970s when the house had been built by Cal's father. Cal was following the family tradition of selling liquor to the locals without the blessing of the government.

Brian knocked lightly. He and Cal were acquainted with each other, had played ball together in their youth, but Brian was not a customer. The door swung open and surprise registered on Cal's lined, weather-beaten face. Most of Cal's sales took place in the dark hours of the night. When the sun was shining, Cal helped out the various farmers in the area, working in their fields and wood lots. He was a skilled machine operator.

"Chief Cosh," Brian said. "What's this, a fire inspection?"

Brian laughed uneasily. He was unsure of the proper procedure for making a purchase. "Wonder if I could get a pint of whiskey?" he asked.

Cal stepped forward and looked over Brian's shoulder into the yard. The surprised look was replaced with one of suspicion. "Are you alone, Chief?"

Brian turned and followed Cal's gaze into the yard. "Yeah, Cal. I'm alone."

Cal made another quick sweep of the surroundings, stepped back and opened the door wider. "Come on in and sit down."

Both men went to the kitchen table, a solid maple model, and sat. In one corner was a stack of empty beer bottles in cardboard cartons. Otherwise there was no product in sight. An oversized Kenmore fridge stood next to the double sink. A white, propane stove sat in the opposite corner. Brian counted six chairs crowded into the area, a lot of seating space for a man who lived alone. Everything was clean and tidy.

"What are you doing here, Chief? The liquor stores are still open in Raymond's River. I doubt that you've been cut off by the good people working there. Even Lisa Tingley hasn't got that much power yet."

Brian's face took on a pinkish hue. His sham had been overly obvious.

"I was wondering if George Wilson had been by in the last couple of days and who he might have been with."

"George? Haven't seen George in a dog's age. Guess he's on the wagon again. Bad for business. Means I'll have to run my old truck for another year." Cal smiled.

Brian looked conflicted. On one hand, he had hoped that George wasn't out bingeing. On the other, if he wasn't drinking, where was he?

The smile on Cal's face did a slow fade. "Why are you asking, Chief? Has something happened to George?"

Brian nodded. "He hasn't been home since yesterday morning. Connie's worried. We're thinking that falling off the wagon is the lesser of two evils."

Cal's head unconsciously bobbed up and down. "Otherwise he might be hurt somewhere." Understanding dawned in Cal's eyes. "Or dead." He slowly shook his head, trying to dismiss the consequences of that statement. "Can I get you a beer, Chief? On the house."

Brian shook his head. "No thanks, Cal. I might have a long night ahead of me."

Cal went to the fridge and got himself a bottle of Moosehead. From the overhead freezer, he picked out a frosty stein. Fastened to his belt on a key chain was an opener. He flipped off the cap and expertly poured the beer, leaving a proper head of foam.

He sat down again without drinking any of the beer. He stared intently into the chief's eyes for several seconds.

"Even though Connie disapproves of what I do, we're still friends. If I were to casually mention the names of a couple of people who made purchases in the last day or two, could you forget where you heard them?"

"My only goal is to find George and get him home, Cal. Nothing else is coming into play here." As Cal rhymed off the names, Brian mentally compared them to his own list. Cal gave him a couple of new leads.

"What can I do to help, Chief? Have you organized a search?"

"We're making a run through the village and placing some phone calls. There are some houses that are getting personal visits." He gave Cal a knowing nod. "If he hasn't shown up by morning, we'll have a more comprehensive search underway."

Cal nodded. "Count me in. I'll swing by the fire hall early."

Brian carefully picked his way down the driveway again. He was thinking that he should have followed through on his purchase. Before this night was over, he was going to need a good strong shot of Hiram Walker.

He keyed the mike on his truck radio. "Any word from John yet?"

"That you, Chief? John said no one remembers seeing George at the liquor store. In fact, he hasn't been there since Christmas, according to old Lisa Tingley. If she says a thing, it must be true. I guess you didn't have any luck with Cal?"

Lisa Tingley was approaching seventy-five. She had retired once from her government job at the liquor commission when she turned sixty-five. She then reapplied for her own job and, being most qualified, won the competition. Definitely the most qualified and if anyone mentioned her age, that would be violating her Charter rights. Under current rules, she would never be forced to retire again.

"Not really. I'm gonna check out a couple of other places that weren't on my initial list. I guess it's a good thing that we haven't heard back from Jerry or Bruce checking the ditches."

"Chief, what are we gonna do when it gets dark?" The voice sounded worried.

CHAPTER 3

CORPORAL SCOTT BOWEN pulled his RCMP cruiser into the Raymond's River Volunteer Fire Station parking lot. Several pickup trucks and a couple of SUVs were already there. The sky to the west had turned a vibrant red as the sun dipped below the horizon. Despite the layers of clouds that were reflecting this light, tomorrow should be a fine day.

"Red sky at night, sailor's delight," Scott muttered to himself. He was visualizing in his mind what the conditions for a full-scale search would be if this George Wilson character hadn't wandered back home by then. Scott was the search commander for this area of the province.

Chief Brian Cosh had contacted him about forty-five minutes previously and explained the situation to him. As the chief pointed out: "You've got to be patrolling somewhere. Why not swing by here?"

Scott knew that Brian was a straight-shooter. He was not prone to panic. Although it was too soon to open an official file on George Wilson as a missing person, Scott could have a look at what the local people had done to date. He joined the volunteers milling about inside.

Most had returned from their assigned tasks. One look at their faces broadcast the lack of good news. George and his vehicle had been sucked into the vacuum of space.

"There's two ways to look at this," the fire chief rationalized. "George has been on the wagon for several months now, so it's unlikely he's drunk somewhere, or..." and here he allowed a bitter smile to come to his lips, "…he's been on the wagon for several months now and he's long overdue to go on a bender."

Scott considered this statement for a minute. "You know him better than I do; if the latter is true, where would he do his drinking?" Scott had gone straight to the second choice. It wasn't that he always looked for the bad in people; it was just that George fit the demographic. Scott remembered the fatal accident from a couple of years back and the outcry from the verdict.

The chief shook his head. "That's the thing. We've looked in all those places. Talked to all his known acquaintances. No one has sold him any booze that we can find out about. All of his drinking buddies are accounted for."

"They haven't seen him in the last couple of days? Didn't forget that he was sitting right beside them at the local pub? That happens." Scott gave his head a nod to emphasize the point.

Brian gave an equally emphatic shake of his head. "Personally had a fireman drive up to their houses and knock on their doors. He's not with any of them. In fact, most of them don't remember seeing George around for quite a while."

"His marriage? Any problems there?"

Brian looked shocked by the question. He thought back to Connie's statement that supper had better be ready when George got home. "Who ever knows what goes on behind closed doors? I've heard of no problems and I know them quite well. Connie's my cousin." He looked around at the other firemen who were close enough to be listening to the conversation. They all shook their heads.

"You guys wouldn't notice if it was happening in the seat beside you." Scott looked over their heads. "Don't you have any female firefighters?"

"Jennifer's in the radio room. My wife is with Connie." Brian scanned the others in the room. "Donna Chambers must still be making phone calls in the office."

Scott looked at his watch. Light was no longer coming in through the hall windows. "I can't fault anything you've done so far. It looks like night's setting in. What are your plans?"

"No sense driving around in the dark. We're better off getting a good night's sleep and starting fresh in the morning. I've still got my chores to finish. Cows'll be getting antsy by now." Many of the others nodded in agreement. They also had chores to get finished before any thoughts of a good night's sleep became a reality.

"I'll put out an all-points bulletin on George's truck. I can at least do that much tonight. Who knows? We might spot it in the city or one of the other towns around."

"Good idea," Brian said. "He may have gone to one of those places for parts or something for that old porter. It's always breaking down on him."

"Porter?" The Mountie gave him a quizzical look.

"Some people call it a tree farmer. George's was parked at the end of the woods road where he was working. Still loaded with logs. That's why we don't think he is in the woods."

Scott nodded. "Oh, sure. A tree farmer. That's where his truck should have been if he was working?"

"If he went into town looking for a part, he may have had an accident. You should check the hospitals, too, although I can't image George not having ID on him." Brian's face dropped. "Or he may have been robbed and beaten up in one of these places."

"Unlikely," the corporal said, "but I can check that out as well. Right now, I'd like to talk to the wife. It looks like it's going to be an organized search in the morning anyway. I may as well lay some of the ground work tonight."

"OK," the chief said. "We'll meet back here around first light. By then we'll have finished our morning chores. Those of us who have 'em will bring our four-wheelers."

Scott reached out and shook Brian's hand. "Call it in to headquarters as soon as you determine he hasn't shown up overnight. That will get a case file opened. I'll meet you here."

CHAPTER 4

CORPORAL SCOTT BOWEN woke up to the erratic sound of rain beating on his bedroom window like a snare drum being played by a five-year-old. "So much for the sailor's delight," he said to the still dark room. He reached out and touched a button on the top of his clock. Foot-high red numbers flashed on his ceiling: 5:37.

He groaned and pulled the pillow over his head. Why did I want to get up this early? He had been on patrol duty until midnight and crawled into bed shortly after one, a mere four and one-half hours ago

Then he remembered what he had been doing last night. He threw the pillow to the foot of the bed and swung his feet onto the floor. A shiver shuddered through his body as he touched the cold floor.

"I hope George Wilson is someplace safe," he said. "If he's outside in this, he'll be dead from exposure."

His black-and-tan shepherd opened his eyes from his position on the floor at the foot of the bed. He gave Scott an "are you talking to me?" look and struggled to his feet. He limped over and nudged his master with his cold nose.

"Sorry, old-timer. Didn't mean to wake you." Scott ruffled the short fur on the dog's head. Old-timer's real name was Roscoe. He was retired from the police service after a short but distinguished career. On his last day on duty, he had taken a bullet to the chest. The shell had passed through his body without doing any fatal damage until it hit his back hip. It shattered this joint, giving him a pronounced limp and slowing his gait to a walk.

Scott had been the dog master and the bullet had been intended for him. If he wanted to stay with the K-9 unit, he would have to give up Roscoe and take on a new animal. Scott refused to do this. He moved on to other policing opportunities, and Roscoe and he had been room mates ever since.

"I may have a job for you later on," Scott said to the dog. Roscoe couldn't run and couldn't jump, but he could still search. Nothing along the path of that bullet had affected his keen nose. Scott thought it would be a crime to waste that talent, and fighting crime was what Scott did for a living. On his own time, he had taken Roscoe back to school where he received more intensive training as a search dog, for both the living and the dead.

He padded over to the window in his bare feet and looked out at the street lights. The wind was coming straight from the west. A fast-moving Alberta clipper was charging through the area. The weather man had predicted this rainfall, but still there was a red sky last night. Some things should be sacred.

He knew he should call someone. If George Wilson was asleep in his own bed, Scott should be doing the same thing. Chief Brian Cosh would be up by now and doing his morning chores. Did the number the chief had given him last night ring in the house or the barn? He hated to disturb the man's family before six in the morning.

Connie Wilson would have had a fitful night and probably not slept much. He didn't want to wake her if she had finally succumbed to the sandman.

He had left word at headquarters to call him when or if the report of the missing person came in. He watched the windswept rain dancing down the street under the outside light. The best option, he realized, was to make himself a cup of coffee, a strong cup of coffee, and wait. No one would be searching before daylight and daylight would not be an early visitor this morning.

He was working his way through his second cup of black brew when the phone rang. On a pad in front of him, he had been going over the search procedures. He acknowledged that much of the preliminary work had been done by the fire department. Now they were getting down to the short strokes.

"Brian Cosh here, Corporal. You told me to call you as soon as I knew anything."

"Good news or bad?"

"Bad. Connie called me to report that George still hadn't shown up. The rain woke her and now she's even more worried about him."

"Yeah, I was thinking the same thing."

"A lot of us were. I've seen half a dozen trucks heading towards the fire hall already. Most have four-wheelers in the back. I'm on my way out the door now."

"Has anyone made an official missing person report yet?"

"Connie said that was her next call. I'll follow up when I reach the station."

"Good. I'll swing by headquarters and pick up the search packet. There are certain procedures that have to be followed and verified. Mrs. Wilson gave me most of the information I needed last night. Then, I'll come to the fire station."

Scott hung up and looked down at Roscoe who sat at his feet. Ever since being told there was a job for him to do, he had been following Scott's every move. Roscoe did not take retirement well; he was eager to get back into action.

Scott wasn't sure at this point where he would send the searchers, but he knew where he and Roscoe would be. He also knew his choice of location might not be popular with the others.

When he had asked Connie the night before how her marriage was going, her answer had been vague. "Every marriage has its ups and downs," she had said.

"And where is the elevator right now?" Scott had asked. "On its way up or on its way down?" Connie had evaded the question.

Scott and Roscoe would be searching the area around the house and out-buildings at the Wilson farm. Did he suspect foul play from

Connie? No. He simply wanted to rule it out early. He didn't need any nagging doubts playing with his concentration.

Connie was a well-toned, attractive blond in a tomboyish sort of way, he had observed. Her face and eyes had suffered too many tears in the last couple of days, but that couldn't disguise his overall impression of the woman. She had a healthy, outdoorsy look about her. Her hair was long and tied back. Her fingernails were trimmed short.

She didn't strike him as someone who avoided hard work. Instead, she looked as though she could take her place in the rough-and-tumble world of farm life. Despite her anguish about her missing husband, she had been keeping up with the chores that needed to be done around their farm for the last two days. If he could believe Chief Cosh's story about George's binge drinking, this wouldn't have been the first time Connie handled all the work alone.

Rain still danced across the fire department parking lot in brief gusts, leaving ever-changing, wavy patterns like charging foot soldiers in the various puddles. Scott pulled his bright, yellow slicker close to his face and jumped from his Ford Explorer. He didn't know where this day would take him, but he wanted to have a set of wheels beneath him that would get him there and back. This SUV promised to cover the most territory. He trotted the few steps to the open doorway. Chief Brian Cosh waited to greet him, slamming the door shut as he entered.

"April showers…," Brian said.

Scott slid out of his jacket, gave it a quick shake and hung it on a nearby hook. "Not a lot of help for our search." He looked around the room. Several men and women were having animated conversations in little groups. A long table was covered with coffee urns, tea pots and a selection of sweets and sandwiches. Word of George's disappearance had spread through the community like a cold germ through a daycare centre.

Scott noticed one group of men at the far end of the food table away from the others. Shoddy clothes hung from their shoulders. Bloodshot eyes peered back at him. Their noses, red-veined and swollen, stood out on their faces. They stuffed sandwiches into their mouths like they hadn't eaten in a week. Those holding coffee cups clutched them in both hands to keep them steady. These, Scott concluded, were the drinking buddies the chief had described the night before. Everyone had turned out to search.

Conversations slowly ceased as the people noticed the uniformed Mountie. They drifted closer to where Scott and the chief stood.

"The APB came up negative," Scott said. "Ditto for the hospital admissions and drunk-tank lodgings. I don't suppose you've had any luck since we talked earlier?"

Brian lowered his voice. "None whatsoever. It's like he's disappeared into smoke. We have no real starting point for a search."

Scott looked at the others who were crowding closer, trying to pick up the conversation. *Why not?* he thought. They had legitimate concerns for the fate of their friend and neighbour. They weren't here in this ungodly weather at this early hour for the cold egg sandwiches. They wanted to know what was going on. Every element of the community was represented.

He held up his hands to get their attention. "Folks, I know you're all here to help and we greatly appreciate that and definitely need it. This is going to be a community effort, a successful community effort."

There were a few forced smiles and nodding of heads.

"When are we going to start?"

"Where do you want us to look first?"

"Are you bringing in some helicopters?"

"What about dogs?"

Scott held up his hand again. "All good questions," he said. "The chief, his officers and I are going to have a brief strategy meeting to plan our attack. Right now the ceiling is too low for an air search.

We'll see what happens when the rain clears up. As for dogs, we need a place to search first. We don't want to just go blindly running around. That is not an effective search strategy

"You, yourselves, know how big a search area we have and how spread out it is. Have some coffee and sandwiches and discuss any ideas you might have among yourselves. Most of you know George. Where might he be? We'll be looking for your input. We're going to do this together."

Scott, Brian, the deputy chief and two captains quickly moved into the chief's office. The others stood there for a second or two and then drifted over to the food table. The conversations became enlivened again as everyone expressed their agreement or disagreement with what was going on.

CHAPTER 5

THE FIVE MEN jammed into the chief's minuscule office crowded around a large, coloured topographical map spread out on the chief's desk.

Brian Cosh pointed to a blue line winding from the top left corner of the map to the middle of the bottom, Whitfield River. More precisely, his finger marked a spot where the blue line intersected a broken red line. The red line indicated a woods road crossing the river.

"Here's where George was working. Up by the Millicent property in Mary Jane Falls." His porter was found here." Brian's finger moved down to a solid red line, what passed for a main road. I guess this is the last place we know where he was."

Scott studied the map. His hand made a sweeping gesture to cover the entire area. "We'll start a road search," he said. "We'll walk every road in the area where George might have travelled. Beat the bushes. Check the rivers. His truck has to be somewhere. Find the truck and we have a starting point for our search." He looked at the rain beating against the office window. "Any tracks in his work area will be puddles by now. There will be no way of telling what is new and what is left over from last fall."

"That makes sense," the chief agreed.

"We'll set up a grid if a site looks promising. Then, it might be a good idea to have the four-wheelers transport some of the searchers to the deeper regions of the grid. Those guys brought in their machines; we'd better use them or we'll lose both man and machine. If this becomes a full-fledged search, we'll need all the bodies we can muster."

Brian gave the Mountie a thoughtful look and then slowly shook his head. "I'll tell you, some of those good ol' boys are not going to dismount their ATVs. Wherever we put them, the cheeks of their ass will not separate from the plush leather seat of their Hondas and Yamahas."

"Ah, the voice of experience," Scott said with a chuckle. "As the search area expands, the outer edge is going to grow in magnitude. We'll send those iron horsemen out to what we conceive to be the farthest extreme and let them work back towards the foot searchers."

"So that's the plan?" John asked. "We go to the work site and start searching?"

Scott looked up from the map with a surprised look on his face. "No, not yet. We have to determine where to search first. Tromping through the woods is tiresome work. We don't want to tire out the troops until we find a definite clue as to where to begin. That is our plan for when we get our starting point. For now, we concentrate on the roads where the porter is, around the farm and any place else George may have ventured."

"This rain is a pain in the ass," Brian said. "Anyone searching on foot will be soaked in minutes. We have to keep an eye on each other as well as looking for George. Hypothermia can set in fast in this type of weather."

Again the Mountie nodded in agreement. "According to the weather office, this rain will be finished before noon. The afternoon search won't be as dreary. I notice lots of food out there already. What we really need is something hot and fast for when the searchers come back. A big pot of hardy soup, a bowl of hot chili, something quick and substantial to fill their stomachs and warm their innards as soon as they walk through the door."

"Already simmering in the kitchen," Brian said. "Mary is looking after it." He patted his stomach. "I can guarantee it will do the trick."

Scott smiled. "Mary is your wife? I met her at Connie's place last night. Lovely woman. Is there anyone with Connie this morning?"

"The Red Hat Society ladies have filled that role. A bunch of them are at the Wilson farm making sandwiches and generally keeping Connie occupied while the search progresses."

"Red Hats? I would think Connie is too young to belong to that group."

The chief laughed. "Much too young. Still, she is the one who got the older women together and organized their initial meetings. This is their payback. Everyone in the community owes some sort of debt to Connie. That table of food is a testament to the high regard in which she is held."

Scott looked at the mountain of food. He hoped it wouldn't all be needed.

"I'm going to head out to the Wilson farm and look around," he said

"Look for what?" Brian asked.

"George Wilson. This is standard procedure. Verify that he's not somewhere on his own property before we start scouring miles of forest land."

"OK," Brian said. His voice transmitted an element of doubt about the Mountie's judgment. "How many men will you need?"

Scott stepped back from the desk so that he could see the other four men. "None. I have my dog in my vehicle."

"Your dog? You think he's dead, don't you?" John Haydon took an intimidating step towards Scott.

Scott held his ground. "That's one of the options we have to consider. He's been missing for two days."

"I prefer to keep a more positive outlook," John said. He moved back to the desk and looked down at the map. "There are a lot of places to find a man alive."

"There certainly are," Scott said. "That's the other option. The one we are all banking on."

Silence descended on the room while each man studied the map, looking for some sort of inspiration.

"Do we want to bring in the search-and-rescue teams from other areas?" John asked.

"I've alerted them," Scott said, "but for now, we have all the manpower we need. When we need fresh searchers, they'll be ready to step in."

They spent ten more minutes fine-tuning their grids and coordinating who would be team leaders before they returned to the larger hall. It was decided that John and the chief would check out George's vehicles to make sure they hadn't broken down and George had gone for parts. In the time they were organizing in the small office, the larger room had become a community social affair. The earlier grim looks had been replaced with smiles and laughter. The bickering over what should be done had been put aside. All that changed when Brian's office door opened.

Immediate silence filled the room. One hundred pairs of eyes focused on the chief, waiting for the word to spring into action. Brian spelled out the plan. They listened intently, then a few murmurs started to break into the silence.

"We've all done this before," Brian said. "If you have any questions or suggestions, let's hear them now."

David Gates stepped forward from the bleary-eyed, red-nosed contingent. "Do I understand you right, Chief? Are you talking about searching the roads on foot? I could cover ten, hell twenty, times the area on my big Honda in half the time. I don't mind paying for my own gas if the municipality objects to reimbursing me. I sure don't cotton to the idea of walking around in this downpour." His voice had the gravelly sound of a lifelong smoker.

There were sounds of agreement throughout the room.

Brian nodded. "You're right, David. We could do this a lot faster on our ATVs."

"Damn right," David Gates said. "That only makes sense."

Again there was general agreement from part of the crowd. Gates acknowledged the voices as if he had come up with some brilliant new discovery to save mankind.

Brian held up his hand for silence. "The thing is, David, we're not looking for speed. We're looking for accuracy. We only want to do this once and we don't want to miss anything. If George's truck slipped off the road and crashed through some alders or something, they might snap right back into place after he passed." The chief put his elbows together, spread his palms and then let them snap back together with a clap. "A person on foot could spot the truck better than a man on an ATV who has to keep one eye on where he is going.

"We have enough of us here that we can blanket the reasonable areas to search in a couple of hours. If we do it right the first time, we're not going to be repeating the whole exercise again in a couple of days. So, although your ATV is definitely faster, we've decided that a foot search makes more sense."

"Well, I think you've decided wrong. I ain't gonna be walking around in this rain." Again there was a contingent in the hall that expressed their agreement with Gates.

Brian looked over at Scott, an inquiring look on his face.

Scott stepped up beside the chief. "Well, sir, we thank you for coming out and I hope you'll keep yourself available if we don't find poor George during this phase of the search." He scanned the entire room with a challenging look in his dark eyes. "Right now we're doing a foot search. This, we feel, is the best approach to take for this stage. If some of you aren't up to walking a few hundred yards, we understand. You all know how physically fit you are and we don't want anyone risking their own health. It's been two nights. We can all look out the window and see what last night was like. I only hope that when we do find George, he's still inside his vehicle and not lying in a puddle somewhere.

"Anyone, like…" he looked at the chief with an inquiring look "…David, who isn't up to a foot search, we ask that you step outside so that we can divide the remainder of you into search teams and assign you an area of attack."

"Wait a minute," Gates said. "I didn't mean I wasn't going to help. I just was making a suggestion. I'm no cripple; I can walk with the best of you."

"Only with a bit more of a list," a voice from the crowd said. Tension-breaking laughter filled the room. The search quickly got organized and underway with all hands on board.

CHAPTER 6

SCOTT BOWEN MANOEUVRED his SUV into Connie Wilson's driveway. Several cars filled the yard, Scott noticed through his wipers slapping back and forth across the windshield. These would be the ladies unable to engage in a physical search, but who still wanted to lend their support to Connie. He parked close to the barn door.

Even though the ice had been broken the night before, Scott knew that his intention to search the farm might not be favourably received, especially now that the house was crowded with friends. He looked into the back seat where Roscoe could hardly contain his excitement. The dog's voice was quiet, but his eyes were barking wildly.

"Just a few minutes longer, big fella. I want to tell Mrs. Wilson that we're here and what we are about to do."

The expression on Roscoe's face was clear. "Don't talk about it; do it!"

Scott dropped from the vehicle and ran across the back yard. There was a slight overhang outside the back door that protected him from the rain. He tapped lightly on the door, waited, then tapped harder. Inside, the noise level dropped off. A lady in her mid-sixties opened the door. A large, floppy red hat was perched on her head. The look on her face was a cross between expectation and dread.

"Did you find George?"

"No, ma'am."

The look dissolved into one of disappointment. "Why aren't you out looking?"

"Could I speak to Mrs. Wilson please, ma'am?"

Connie Wilson materialized behind the woman blocking the doorway. "It's all right, Pamela. Corporal Bowen was here last night. He's leading the search."

"Doesn't look like it to me. George isn't here; I can tell you that."

Connie put a hand on her mother-in-law's shoulder and gently eased her out of the way. "Let the man in, Pamela. It's pouring rain out there."

Scott stepped inside the kitchen. Rain puddled on the floor at his feet. Several women were now staring at him. Most sported some sort of red hat on their heads. The debris from making several loaves of sandwiches could be seen lurking on the table and counter tops. Dirty tea cups cluttered up the sink. These people had been here for a while.

Scott hesitated briefly. "Could I speak to you alone for a minute?" he asked.

Connie's face quickly lost all elasticity. "Have you found something?"

"No. No, I just want to bring you up-to-date on what we're doing."

"You can bring us all up-to-date," the mother-in-law said. "We all want to know what you're doing to find George. You should have been here yesterday as soon as Connie discovered him missing. Waiting forty-eight hours to help a man who may be injured somewhere is stupid. Stupid, I say." She turned to face the room. "Don't you ladies agree with me?"

"You know you're right, Pamela."

"The law is an ass. Didn't someone famous say that?"

The others murmured their assent and, as a group, moved closer to the Mountie, crowding him back towards the doorway.

"Pamela, is it?" Scott asked, turning his attention on the mother-in-law.

"Pamela Wilson, I'm George's mother."

"I understand how you feel, Mrs. Wilson, but you'd be surprised how many people show up in that first forty-eight hours. They are usually pleased to have been spared the embarrassment of having the police involved."

"George is a hard-working family man. He wouldn't abandon his family if there wasn't a problem. Connie must have told you that."

"Of course she did."

By now Pamela stood mere inches away from him, glaring up into his face.

"I've heard the stories about his drinking and I'm sure you have too. They're not true. A bunch of jealous lies. Maybe when he was younger, he did have his wild moments, but that all changed in the last few years. He is a responsible farmer now. You've got to stop listening to garbage-mouth gossip and concentrate on finding my boy."

Scott reached out and took hold of the older woman's hands. He looked at her with what he hoped was a comforting expression. "I understand. We are doing everything we can. Now, I wonder if I could talk to Connie in private for a few minutes and then we'll bring you all up to speed on what is currently taking place."

Before any of the others could render their objections, Connie stepped forward and took Scott by the arm. "Step into the living room with me." She guided him through the assemblage of concerned neighbours.

"Elizabeth," she said to one of the younger women present, "guard the door and keep my mother-in-law in the kitchen." Connie forced a smile at Pamela. Please don't come barging in on us, Mother, the smile said.

Elizabeth Schofield did not fit into the Red Hat demographic. She had barely turned nineteen, had auburn hair, sparkling blue eyes and a body that could be described as pleasantly attractive. Her family lived on the adjoining farm. Strictly speaking, Elizabeth was a come-from-away. The farm had been in the family for generations, the result of a land grant from King George IV to her great-great-great grandfather. Her own father had moved back from Oakville, Ontario, to take over the running of the farm only ten months ago.

Paul Schofield had deserted the farm twenty-five years previously after graduating from Acadia University. He had taken his freshly minted degree to Ontario and then abandoned the four years of liberal arts schooling in favour of an assembly-line job at the Ford plant in Oakville. More money. With the downturn in the car industry, he had taken a generous buyout from Ford and rejoined his aging father in an attempt to make the farm profitable again. With his father's experience and Paul's money, they were succeeding.

Elizabeth appeared to be as concerned as both Connie and Pamela about George. Despite the age differences, Elizabeth and Connie had become fast friends. Perhaps Connie recognized a little of herself in Elizabeth. Connie was not a come-from-away, but a come-back-from-away.

As soon as she had thrown her graduation cap into the air at Tri-County Regional High School, her only goal was to get away from Raymond's River forever. She arrived in Halifax with big dreams, little money and few skills. Tim Horton's welcomed her to their corporate family. By sharing an apartment with two other girls, she was able to eke out an existence.

Connie was not a quitter. For three years she endured the aching feet and uniform-stripping glances from some of the male clientele. After a year of this lifestyle, she started going back to Raymond's River as often as she could get a ride.

Soon, Cal Lindsay started driving to the city on weekends to bring her home for the Saturday night dances. She and Cal had dated off and on during high school, but never anything serious. Cal was always a gentleman and they still got along well. Not so Cal and Connie's father.

"You know what he does for a living?" her father asked on more than one occasion, fire and brimstone blazing from his eyes. This would confuse Connie, because she didn't think her father was a hypocrite. He, after all, was a farmer, a worker of the land in the same way Cal's family were, even though Cal worked on other people's land and not his own.

"Yes," she would defiantly answer. "I know."

It turned out she didn't. She believed Cal worked in the woods as a machine operator. It turned out he was being groomed to take over the bootlegging franchise of Raymond's River.

Connie had been elected head girl in her senior year. She starred in the school play in both her junior and senior year. A lot of people expected to see her gracing the silver screen before too long. That was not to be.

Finally one day, her father, a confirmed teetotaller, could take no more. He spelled it out in complete detail. The Lindsay family were a disgrace to the good people of Raymond's River. They were corrupting the youth and leading some of the adults into a life of drunken wastefulness. He lay everything that was wrong in the small village at the feet of Cal's father.

Connie flatly refused to believe him. She confronted Cal that very weekend. Cal made no attempt to deny the charges or justify his line of work in the family business.

"It is what it is," Cal told her.

"It is what it is?" Connie was stunned. Reluctantly, she stopped seeing him. She could see no other option. The success the year book referred to didn't envision her as becoming the wife of the local bootlegger.

George Wilson jumped in to fill the gap. George caught her fully on the rebound. They had a whirlwind romance and before Connie realized what was happening, she was back living in Raymond's River as George's wife. The life on the farm that she had been so eager to get away from became her full-time occupation.

As time went on, her marriage had more downs than ups. To make matters worse, George turned out to be one of Cal's best customers. Alcoholic may have been a little strong in describing George's condition, but if there had been meetings held in the community, she would have had George attending them.

Over time, George eased back on his drinking. Connie didn't know if maturity had crept up on him or if he got tired of waking up sick and hung over. One thing about farm life, morning chores had to be done in the morning. They were no fun with a big head.

The fatal accident had been a life-changing event. He almost stopped drinking completely. Despite the serious cutting back, George still let loose with the occasional binge. Connie learned to accept that as a fact of life.

Their relationship was too bumpy for Connie to let herself become pregnant. This was not an environment to bring children into. As a result, she immersed herself into the life of Raymond's River in the same way she had immersed herself in all aspects of school life.

The kitchen full of women, including the young Elizabeth, were all her good deeds coming home to rest. Connie did her best to make sure Elizabeth was welcomed in her new community, introducing her to acting in a minor role in the group's latest theatre production. Now Elizabeth was returning the favour in Connie's hour of need.

"Don't worry, Connie," Elizabeth said, "no one will get by me." She struck a fake muscular pose that would intimidate no one.

CHAPTER 7

CONNIE LED SCOTT to the living room. Two chairs sat facing each other in a bow window with a low, narrow table separating them. It created a perfect spot to sit and have intimate conversations. Scott noticed the rings in the wood, left from steaming mugs of hot chocolate. White lace curtains were pulled back and tied with little pink bows to reveal the rain that streamed down the glass like giant teardrops, highlighting the sombre mood in the house. They sat.

"I have some questions for you," Scott said. "Some of them are not going to be easy to hear."

"Nothing has been easy these last couple of days." The melancholy look on her face tugged at Scott's heart strings. "Let's get it over with."

Scott's expression acknowledged the distress Connie was going through. "Last night you said your marriage had its ups and downs. Was George depressed in any way? Did he appear to be withdrawing?"

Connie's laugh contained no humour. "George was not a man to display his feelings, one way or the other. Food on the table, beer in the fridge, and gas in his truck. That pretty much sums up his wants in life."

Scott sat silently for a few moments, his head lowered while he tried to frame his next question. Then he looked up and engaged Connie's eyes. "Is it possible that he took his own life?"

Connie stared back at him as if she didn't understand the question. She gave her head a quick shake. "Suicide? Is that what you're asking?"

"We have to consider all possibilities."

Connie's voice rose in volume. "Let me assure you, suicide is not one of them. Committing suicide requires more of a commitment than George was prepared to make about anything."

Scott noticed a flush coming into Connie's face.

"I'm sorry," she said. "No, I don't believe George would ever contemplate suicide. I don't want you to get the wrong idea about George. He is a hard worker. He took over this farm when his uncle died. None of his cousins were interested in returning to Raymond's River to run it. There was too much work involved for his aunt to be able to do anything with it. She had been sickly for years.

"George stepped in, gave her a fair market price for the place, more than anyone else was prepared to offer. The place had become run down in the last years of his uncle's life. George knew that the appearance was only cosmetic. The underpinnings of the place were in great shape. He really laboured at making a go of the place."

She gestured with her hand to encompass the surrounding room. "He succeeded. We were getting by, but it wasn't a money-maker. The mad cow scare of the '90s just about did us in. George kept beef cattle as well as milkers.

"Suddenly, it was costing us more to keep the steers than we could sell them for. One friggin' cow in Alberta. That's three thousand miles away for God's sake. We were farther away from that cow than most of the farms in America. But that didn't stop the bastards from turning down our beef at the border. The whole damn thing was political, you know. It had nothing to do with a sick cow."

Connie's face had filled with colour. Her eyes were flashing lightning bolts. Scott could see a Connie who people wouldn't want to get on the wrong side of. He also saw a side of George that no one had presented to him before. He placed a reassuring hand on top of hers. She sighed and settled back into her seat.

"George didn't give up. That's when he bought the old skidder and porter and started developing the wood lot. He did it mostly by himself. Between the two operations, we are getting by. It was nice to have the money, but now George spends all his time working."

Her eyes misted over a little. She swiped at them with the back of her hand. "It was during the beef crisis that he started drinking again. Up until then, he had pretty much cut back to the occasional beer after work. So, to answer your question, Corporal, no, I don't think he would commit suicide."

Just then, there was a light tapping sound, the living-room door opened and Pamela walked in carrying a tray with two cups of tea and a plate of sandwiches.

Connie gave her an exasperated look. "Mother, please. Give us some privacy."

"I'm not staying. You need a cup of hot tea if you're going to have a serious discussion. It helps keep the mind clear and open."

"Are you listening at the door, Mother?"

Pamela's eyes narrowed. She threw back her shoulders and flipped her head in the air. "I'm just trying to be helpful. I thought you might want some tea."

"Thank you, Pamela," Scott said. "Some tea will be great. Thank you."

The older lady placed the tray on the small table. "Milk or sugar?"

Scott gave a wave of his hand. Connie glared up at the woman and added her own milk to her tea from the container Pamela had placed on the tray. She said nothing.

Pamela stood back and stared at the two people. "We are still waiting to be briefed on what kind of search is taking place. You promised to fill us in."

Scott's lips peeled back slightly in what could almost pass as a smile. "Just a couple of minutes more," he said. He turned back to Connie. "This won't take much longer." He looked back at Pamela. "We'll be out soon." The message was clear. Get out.

"Humph," Pamela said. She resented being dismissed by the Mountie, but nevertheless headed back to the kitchen. She stopped at the door and looked back. "Remember, we're waiting out here."

Neither Connie nor Scott acknowledged her statement. They heard the door shut heavily.

"As we speak," Scott said, "searchers are combing the neighbourhood on foot looking for any sign of George's truck. The chief and one of his men are checking out the forestry equipment in case there was a breakdown and George went looking for spare parts."

"He would have phoned me if that happened."

"Where would he have gone for parts if he needed them? Halifax? Truro? Windsor?"

Connie's eyes drifted towards the outbuildings in the yard. "Mostly, he would have tried a junk yard or a machine shop. Parts for those old machines are not always easy to find. Sometimes he had to have the new ones specially made. He's got a complete workshop out there in the garage where he does a lot of his own work."

Scott nodded. "I've been thinking about that. I'm going to search those outbuildings and the area around them myself."

Connie sat back. "Here on the farm? If he was here, I would know about it."

"I'm sure you would. Still, there are so many possibilities that we must try to eliminate them if we can. It's possible that his truck broke down somewhere and he had someone drop him off to get his tools. You do have two vehicles, don't you?"

Connie nodded.

"He may have planned to get you to drive him back to the truck and he fell or slipped into a hole or something. Did you search around the farm?"

Connie shook her head. "No, but we don't have any holes you can fall into."

"There may have been a weak spot in the barn floor." Scott pointed out the window. "It's been raining a lot this spring. Spots in the ground can give way and create holes big enough for a man to slip into. A lot of these old farms have dry wells hidden on them. These things do happen. I've seen it."

Connie wiped her hand across her brow in an attempt to ease her tension. "I never thought of any of those things. Where will you look?"

"I have my dog in the truck to assist me."

"You've got a search dog and you're going to waste time looking around our farm?"

Connie's eyes were flashing again. This time Scott was the target of their wrath. He lowered his voice as counterpoint to her increased volume.

"This is not a waste of time. This is an important place to look. I'm sure you understand."

"No, I don't understand. You and your dog could be much more useful someplace else. I know George is not here."

Scott shook his head. "No, not at the moment we can't. We have no real target area to search yet and the area around your farm has to be eliminated. Trust me on this. This is our best move." He leaned forward as he spoke to add credence to his statement.

Connie slumped down in her chair again. "If you really think so, go ahead." She looked up into Scott's eyes. There was a flicker of a smile. "You are the one who will have to tell George's mother what your plan is. She's not going to like it."

"No, probably not." Scott was distracted by movement outside the window. A dark blue, half-ton truck with a crew cab was discharging four people on the side of the road. They all wore fluorescent yellow and orange highway vests over their shiny yellow slickers. Searchers, Scott thought.

The night before, they had searched from their vehicles. Today, it was to be a meticulous foot-by-foot examination of anywhere a truck could have disappeared. They were devoting all their attention to the ditches on both sides of the road. Scott smiled inwardly. This is perfect.

He abruptly stood up and went into the kitchen, leaving Connie with a confused look on her face. As he passed through the door, all the women turned towards him in unison.

"Well," Pamela asked, "what's happening?"

Scott smiled. "We have searchers scouring the sides of the road throughout Raymond's River all the way to Mary Jane Falls and beyond. If you look out at the front of the house, you will be able to see some of them now. This is taking place everywhere. I myself am going to join them in the search right now." He didn't elaborate.

Everyone in the room crowded towards the rain-streaked windows. The fluorescent vests stood out in the dull, dismal day. Heads nodded their approval throughout the room. Finally, this was something concrete that they could see with their own eyes. Real action was taking place. Scott slipped out the back door.

CHAPTER 8

SCOTT JUMPED INTO the back seat of his truck. Roscoe's coarse tongue licked the side of his face. His big, front paws danced along Scott's upper thigh. Scott wrapped an arm around the excited dog's neck to contain him.

"Get into your vest, big follow. There's work to do."

Roscoe ducked his head and lifted one of his front paws while Scott helped the dog into a waterproof, orange jacket. The words "SEARCH DOG" were inscribed on the back. At one time, the writing had proudly proclaimed "POLICE," but no longer. Roscoe was a civilian that Scott contracted at no charge to the municipality. Scott assumed all liability for the dog as well. Even getting this much of an agreement from the powers-that-be had been a major battle. It had been a battle that Scott refused to give up on. The dog had too much talent to be wasted lying on a rug in front of a fireplace.

Scott's eyes surveyed the horizon. To the west, the sky appeared to be getting a little lighter. The storm was nearing its end. The search would begin inside the barn and other outbuildings. By the time they got outside, rain would no longer be falling. That would help visibility, but they would still get soaked. It would take hours of intense sun to dry off all the bushes and grass.

The pounding rain would clear the air, leaving that famous April fresh smell to everything. Everything that is, except a decomposing body if one was around. The clearer air would make that smell stand out even more clearly to Roscoe's well-trained nose.

Scott popped a Reactine allergy tablet into his mouth and dry-swallowed it. The commercials showed sufferers rolling in rag weed with no ill effects. He would settle for just being able to walk through a barn. Spring, in general, was a bad time for Scott's allergies. Red, itchy eyes were the norm. Spending time in a barn was tempting fate.

Dog and man jumped down from the Explorer and ducked through the rain to the barn door. Scott pulled it open and they slipped inside. Roscoe's nose immediately went into the air, sniffing out the various samples hidden there. Scott did a visual scan.

Against one wall, he spotted a pink and silver mountain bike. Mud diminished the shine on the chrome fenders. This confirmed his assessment of Connie's physical condition. He looked around to see if there was a mate for the bike. Deeper in, he spotted the blue version of the same model. It was laden with overalls and bits of harness. The front tire was askew as the bike slipped a little from the wall under the weight of its load. The tread looked like it had on the day the bike had been wheeled from the store showroom. The bike looked expensive. Poor George. The road to hell was paved with good intentions.

Roscoe checked every nook and cranny, crawled under every raised floor space, and struggled up to the overhead loft in one of the buildings. The results were consistent throughout. There was no body, dead or alive.

By now the rain had stopped and the sun was breaking through the band of clouds. Connie appeared in the barnyard with a bundle of sandwiches and cup of coffee.

"You're soaked," she said, stating the obvious. "I have a fire in the wood stove. Some of the older ladies are affected by the damp weather. It makes their rheumatism act up. You should come in and warm up."

Scott considered the offer. Connie had not asked him how the search was going. The look on his face must have transmitted that information loud and clear. She refrained from saying "I told you so" as well. Scott was thankful for that.

He looked out at the acres of cleared fields surrounding the house. Soon, they would be covered in hay. For now, they were starting to green up after the long winter. They would have to be searched before he could write off the place completely. A proper search would require more manpower than he and Roscoe could provide. That would come in the next phase of the search routine, the clutching-at-straws phase. After all other possible leads had been worked to their end, the searchers would simply blanket the community, hoping for a lucky break.

Pamela Wilson was still in the house. Scott would have to interview her. As George's mother, she might have information about where George might go to be alone or to let off steam. Now that Scott was soaked and muddy would be a good time to carry out that task. Pamela would not be questioning his dedication to the search.

He looked down at Roscoe. He was mud up to his knees. The orange of the jacket had taken on a definite brownish hue. His limp was becoming more pronounced. Scott reached down and ruffled the fur on the dog's head.

"Ready for a break, boy?"

Roscoe looked indifferent. He would rest or he would search. It didn't matter to him. He was just glad to be back in action. Part of that task was to follow the orders of his master.

Scott opened the truck door. A blanket covered the back seat. Roscoe jumped, didn't quite make it and placed his front paws on the edge of the seat. Without comment, Scott reached down and gave him a boost. Roscoe turned around a couple of times and then settled down into the blanket. His big tongue lolled in the corner of his mouth, slowly moving in and out with each breath.

"Old war injury," Scott said to Connie as way of explanation. Connie gave Roscoe a pat on the head. Roscoe accepted it, but did not respond in any way. He was working.

The interview with Pamela brought nothing new to light. Pamela viewed her son through rose-coloured glasses. Nothing she said jibed with the community view of George. To her, butter wouldn't melt in his mouth. Despite Scott's prodding to have Pamela name some places that might yield positive results, Pamela stuck to the litany that her boy was a God-fearing, home-loving, young man who would not take off and leave Connie alone. Something serious had befallen him.

Scott's wet, bedraggled appearance did impress her. In Pamela's eyes, a search was a physical thing. She didn't understand that the ultimate success came from the mental aspect of the event. The organization and efficiency were the things that would lead to the finding of her son. Blindly running around without any planning was a waste of time and resources. Scott did not waste any of his time or resources trying to explain that to this woman. He knew better.

He headed back to the fire hall, hoping, but not expecting, that Brian Cosh and crew had had better luck. Anything positive would have resulted in a phone call to the Wilson house; so would anything negative. Neither call had come through.

CHAPTER 9

SCOTT CHECKED HIS rear-view mirror as he pulled into the fire hall parking lot. Chief Brian Cosh's red truck followed him in and pulled up beside him. Several pickups and cars already occupied the spaces closest to the door. Now that the rain had stopped, that fact carried less importance. John Haydon stepped down from the passenger side of the chief's vehicle and waited for Scott to dismount.

"Both machines performed like finely tuned luxury cars," he said. "Even in the rain, they kicked over right away and after a couple of minutes settled into a rhythmic drone that would make any owner proud."

John was referring to George's porter and skidder, tools of his trade in the small-time logging industry.

Scott nodded. "It was a long shot, anyway."

Brian came around the truck to join them. "Still a few fresh cut trees back there to be yarded out, but basically everything looked to be in order. He seems to be selling it as fast as he's cutting it. What's our next move?"

"I've called up a helicopter to assist in the search. It looks like we're going to get a military one. That's an added bonus."

"Because they make better searchers?" Brian asked.

"They are trained in it," Scott said, "but their machines have OLIS on board."

"OLIS?" John screwed up his face in confusion. "Acronyms. Doesn't anyone talk English anymore?"

Scott laughed. "Doesn't seem like it. Anyway, it stands for Outward Looking Infrared Scanning. The same technology they use here in the fall when they're looking for marijuana."

A cloud passed over Brian's face.

"You're familiar with the weed searches?"

"Oh yeah. The bastards used my wood lot for one of their grow operations last fall. When that helicopter hovered over my house, I thought it was going to vibrate all the dishes off the shelves. Scared the bejesus out of Mary. Must have set up there for a full two minutes. I went out in the yard to have a look. I could have shaken the pilot's hand, they were that low."

A twinkle lingered in Scott's eyes. He had heard this story before from other farmers in the area. "We raided a number of grow-ops around here. You weren't the only victim."

"Victim? Hell, I just wanted my cut. Growing marijuana pays better than anything else I can get from the ground." He laughed. "I hope you caught them."

Scott's expression changed again. His eyes darkened. He changed the subject. "OLIS serves a number of purposes in the hands of a trained operator. They'll be looking for one of two heat signatures."

The chief gave him a grim look. "Living person or dead body?"

"You've got it."

"Let's keep our fingers crossed that it's the former. How long do we have the choppers for?"

"The rest of the day, for sure. They will cover the road from George's to the search site on the way in. If they don't have any luck at those two spots, they will check out around George's farm." Scott shrugged. "Then, I guess they will just broaden the pattern until they run out of light."

"Or find George."

Scott laughed. "That might not stop them. These guys have to get in a certain amount of hours a month to maintain their flight pay."

As if on cue, the sound of the rotors could be heard thrumming in the distance.

"I radioed them the coordinates they need," Scott said, "at the same time I was talking to headquarters. There's been no activity on George's debit card or any of his credit cards. That's not a total surprise. Connie said he used cash for most transactions. Always carried a wad of it in his wallet. Had the cards more as an ID or credit reference than for actual use."

The two firemen exchanged glances. Brian shrugged. "I guess that comes as no surprise. Outside of the milk sold to the dairies, most of the things done around here are on a cash basis. The underground economy is alive and booming."

"How much of a wad of cash would he carry?" asked Scott.

Brian hesitated before answering. He reached up with his left hand and slowly rubbed his chin. "Well, that all depends. He was taking firewood off the Millicent place. George cuts and splits it right on the spot. His gear was set up in a clearing there. We checked it out. No problems with any of it, either. He's got a dandy little rig that cuts, splits and loads the wood into the back of a truck. Owns an old gravel truck. It was parked in the clearing, empty.

"If he was selling the wood to city folk, he would probably be getting at least two hundred dollars a cord, maybe more delivered. Five cords would give him a thousand bucks. Two, three customers like that. You do the math."

"Everyone knows this?"

"George liked to make a show of paying for his round up at the pub. He'd pull out a bundle of cash about a half-inch thick. Barely be able to fold it over. He'd peel off a hundred. Laugh and say to the waiter, 'Got change for this?' Then put it back and pay him with twenties. It was almost a ritual."

A shadow of irritation flickered across Scott's face. "Great. Now we have another option. It may be a robbery that got out of hand. The table at the pub may have been filled with his friends, but the next one over could have had anybody sitting there. You've already checked out the pub?"

"George occasionally has his lunch there. The girls don't remember seeing him there this week. They said he hardly comes in at all anymore. Drinks fruit juice or pop when he does. That was one of the first places we checked."

"That doesn't rule out robbery. The thieves may have taken a few days to get organized. They may have waited for the chance to catch him alone. They may have been waiting for him to make some deliveries. If they called him pretending to be interested in buying some wood and George told them they would have to wait because he had three or four orders ahead of them, it would be worth their while to wait. They could bide their time and then hit him at the most opportune moment."

"George and our prime ministers were pretty close buddies," John said. "Especially Robert Borden on the hundred dollar bill and Mackenzie King on the fifty. I can't imagine him giving any of them up without a struggle."

A frown took hold on Scott's face. "Maybe that's the problem. If he had passed over his money, we might not be here today, at least not doing a search. His truck could have been an added bonus."

On that ominous note, the three men fell silent. Then, as a group, they started across the lot to join the other searchers. "If no one inside has anything else to offer," Brian said, "we'll start preparing for the grid search. Even if the military finds George right away, the experience will be good for future searches. These guys are too hyped up to do anything else of use today."

"I want to go out and look around with my dog before the area gets all tracked up. I'll let Roscoe start at the vehicles and see where he leads me."

As they entered the hall, a bowl of steaming soup was thrust into their hands. Each and every person turned towards them. Brian could read the unspoken question on everyone's mind. Any luck? Brian shook his head. This ritual had been repeated with the return of each search team. The room returned to its previous state of quiet murmuring. Already hope was draining away.

Brian brought a spoonful of the thick vegetable soup to his lips. Before the spoon even touched his mouth, he could feel the heat. He blew on it before carefully taking a sip. He spit this back into the spoon. John and Scott were watching him. "Might have to cool a little before we eat it," Scott said. He inclined his head towards the pot sitting on a gelled gas burner. Bubbles could be seen breaking around the edge of the pot.

Brian set the dish down on the table and gave a short whistle. Instantly, he had everyone's attention. Their casual attitude was a ruse. They were waiting for instructions of some sort.

"A Forces helicopter has joined our search."

This announcement was met with nods of approval. Brian could sense an increase in optimism. He turned towards Scott.

"Corporal Bowen wants four volunteers with ATVs and a passenger for each one."

Hands shot up around the room.

CHAPTER 10

THE AFTERNOON SEARCH PROVED fruitless. The helicopter combed back and forth, back and forth, in an ever-expanding area. Teams of men and women on foot came in and searched until dusk. The helicopter moved over to the area around George's house. It made short work of the cleared fields and then scanned the trees surrounding them. A visual search was still easy to do. The full glory of the foliage would not be displayed for a couple of weeks.

The next day, a fixed-wing aircraft from Greenwood expanded the air search. Experienced teams of searchers from other parts of the province came in and bolstered the army of men from the local area. A team of navy divers swam the river all the way down to the Bay. After four days, Scott was left with the difficult task of telling Connie that the search would be phased back.

"But he can't just have vanished," Connie said. "I don't believe in alien abductions."

Scott looked over to Brian Cosh for some support. The two men agreed it would be best if they told Connie together. Scott would provide the official face of the search; Brian would represent the community at large.

Brian rubbed the stubble of a beard sprouting on his face. The search cut deeply into his daily routine. He had to make some concessions somewhere and shaving fell by the wayside. He seemed to come to a conclusion about how to word his statement. "The fact that we didn't find him could be construed as a good thing. We have really scoured this area. If there had been…" he hesitated. This was not coming out the way he had planned.

"A body?" Connie finished the sentence for him. "Is that what you were going to say?"

A flush of red crept up Brian's face. "Well, yes. If there had been a body, we would have found it."

Tears that had been filling the corners of Connie's eyes started to flow down over her cheeks. "How is this a good thing?"

"It means he could be alive somewhere," Scott said. "I know that is hard to understand right now. Why would he simply disappear? I can't answer that." His eyes probed hers for an answer.

Connie held up a hand to stop him. A degree of hope showed on her face for the first time in four days. "He might have gone out to Alberta."

She let the statement hang in the air for several seconds. The men exchanged glances, but neither spoke.

"We had discussed George going out to work in the oil sands. Several people from Raymond's River are working out there. He thought he could go out, make some big money and come back and put the farm on a more secure footing."

Brian nodded. "I can think of at least six local people working out there right off the top of my head. I know there are lots more. If you listen to them, they are raking in the dollars hand over fist."

"That's what George kept saying. I didn't want him to go and I told him so."

Now it was Connie's turn to blush.

"You know what he's like, Brian. If he got out there living in one of those camps filled with men, making good money, he would soon go back to his old ways. He's been good about his drinking lately, but every day is a struggle. When it comes to booze, George is weak."

Brian glanced out of the corner of his eye to see Scott's reaction to that statement. They were airing the family laundry in front of the lawman.

Scott's expression never changed. "Do you think he would go out there without telling you, just to prove you wrong? Might he show up in a couple of weeks with his paycheque in his pocket?"

Connie looked out the window, avoiding both men. "The first part might be true; there's not a hope in hell for the second part."

Scott looked at Brian, raising his eyes into a question mark. Brian gave him an indifferent look and then nodded his head to agree with Connie's assessment. George wasn't an alcoholic in the sense that one drink would set him off. He was an alcoholic in the sense that given enough temptation, he would succumb to hitting the bottle again, big time.

Scott sat back in his chair. "This changes a lot of things. George has been gone for five days. Unless he pushed it day and night, it would take him that long to reach northern Alberta. If he slipped into the underground economy out there, he will be hard to find. We can only hope he found an honest company that asked for his Social Insurance Number. Even then, it will take a while to track him down."

"Given the option, he'll be taking the underground route," Brian interrupted. "That's the life he knows. People like George farm until they die. They don't retire and collect Canada Pension. They don't put their money into RRSPs. They put it in bottles and bury it in their back yards, stuff it under the floor boards in their bedroom or spend it as fast as they make it, especially when times are tough. The less the government is involved in their lives, the better they like it."

"George had a bank account for one reason," Connie said. "To cash the cheques he got from the dairy. He only kept enough money there to make his truck payments. He only did that because the dealership insisted he do it that way. The rest he carried with him.

"Once a month, he would drive around and pay our bills with cash. When the money ran out, that was all the bills he paid. Those he missed would be on the top of the list the next month. It wasn't elegant, but it's worked ever since we got married."

"I've heard stories about him carrying a wad of cash around with him," Scott said. "Was that ever true?"

"Just like I said. On the days he paid his bills, he started out with a wad of cash. We didn't always run short. When there was money left over, he still carried it in his wallet. That was how he kept track of how we were doing. He'd flip open his billfold and look in. Didn't need bank statements or spreadsheets. Instant reconciliation."

Scott looked down at the table and then back up at Connie. "What about you? If he kept all the money on him, what have you been living on for the last week?"

Connie gave the Mountie a surprised look and then laughed. Considering the topic of the conversation, it was pleasant, lilting laughter. "On payday, doling out the cash started with me. George didn't see why any fat cats should be living off his money while his family did without. I have a budget for food, clothes, whatever. George made me his number one priority. Despite all his other faults, it's hard not to love a man who puts you ahead of everyone else in the world. I've been getting by." She hesitated. "And as Brian says, there may be lots of money stashed around the place. If times get tough, I'll start lifting floor boards or looking for freshly dug up earth." She smiled. Scott couldn't determine for sure if she was joking or not.

Her eyes swept around the kitchen. An empty casserole dish soaked in the sink. A Tupperware container of cookies sat on the counter. A loaf of fresh home-made bread in a clear plastic bag perched on top of the cookies. "My only worry about food this week involved where to store it. The neighbours have been unbelievable. There's enough food in my freezer for me to put on my own church supper. In fact, that's probably where it came from, the cancelled supper.

"Some of the men have been showing up before going to help search to tend to the morning chores. Others have arrived in the evening for the same thing. It's like they have a roster set up. There's always someone, but never more than we need." Her gaze stopped on Brian. She gave him a searching look that penetrated his skull.

"Yeah," he said, "just like someone set up a roster."

"It's not that I don't appreciate the help, but I can do this on my own. Except for three silly years pushing coffee for Tim Horton's, I've spent my whole life living on a farm. I can do the work."

"I'm glad to see that things are going OK for you," Scott said. "Despite the fact that we're going to cancel the ground search, that doesn't mean we are abandoning the case. We'll have the members in Alberta follow up on whether George is out there. I'll keep following any leads that come up here. We'll have the police forces all across the country looking out for George's truck. Any time you have any questions, give me a call. In the meantime, I'll keep you informed of our progress."

He looked at Brian. "I've got to check in at headquarters and file some reports."

Brian nodded. "I'm going to stick around here for a while. Maybe I'll give Connie a hand with her evening chores. If a list exists, and I'm not saying it does," a smile broke across his face, "I think my name might be next."

They all shared a smile briefly before a more serious look clouded Connie's face.

"Who tells Pamela Wilson the search has been called off?" she asked, looking back and forth between the two men.

"Not me," Brian said. "I have barn chores to do."

"The search hasn't been called off. It's been scaled back." Scott fought to keep the edge out of his voice. In every unsuccessful search, there came a time when tramping through the forest becomes an exercise in futility. For George, that time had arrived.

"OK." This time the Mountie was the target of Connie's intense stare. "Who's going to tell Pamela that? I'd like to be a fly on the wall at that meeting where you explain the nuances of a scaled-back search and a called-off search to my mother-in-law. Believe me, Pamela is not too good at grasping subtle differences. I wish you luck, Corporal."

Brian said nothing. A smile flickered at the corners of his mouth. He simply offered Scott a thumbs-up.

CHAPTER 11

CALLED OFF OR scaled back didn't really matter. A gradual change came over the village. A few people showed up at the fire hall each morning to continue searching more remote areas of the community. These men intended to leave no stone unturned. Brian did his best to keep these things organized and to keep the searchers from tramping over old territory again. With each setting sun, he could see the hope diminishing. Each day, the numbers dropped as well. By the end of the second week, their numbers had dwindled to one team. The quest became more a social gathering than a real search, an excuse to get together and talk over coffee.

Connie noticed the differences around the farm. The degradation of support started with phone calls. The men who had been helping in the barn would call to see if she really needed them that day. Connie always said she could get by. Then the phone calls gradually stopped, along with the helpers. The two-a-day offers of support tailed off to two a week. Finally it was only Brian making the effort, and he, after all, was family.

The visiting ladies with their casseroles of food also dried up abruptly. Once the ground search ended without success and rumours spread that quite possibly George had vacated the area on his own, they simply stopped coming. They seemed to fear Connie's sadness would rub off on them. Elizabeth proved the exception. She still came over faithfully. And Pamela, of course, phoned every day to commiserate. But the others, not only did they stop coming, they avoided Connie when she went out shopping. They had run out of things to say to her, or so it seemed.

Connie didn't see this as a bad thing. It almost came as a relief. As long as she had a house full of visiting women, she felt she had to act as hostess. Now she could sit around in jeans and a T-shirt and eat ice cream or cry or do whatever she wanted. Elizabeth supported her regardless of her choices.

Corporal Scott Bowen also called regularly to apprise her of the department's efforts. He also wanted to know if she had heard from George. He still held out hope that George had gone to Alberta like the migrant farm worker in Ian Tyson's song *Four Strong Winds*. Despite that hope, the members in Alberta had been unsuccessful in finding George. Scott continued to offer encouragement, but Connie's faith started to waver as well.

After she had missed a couple of ladies auxiliary meetings at the church, Pamela reported projects Connie had been working on had come to a standstill. Connie couldn't believe her hard work to get these things up and running could slip down the drain. When Pamela explained the projects were discussed at the meetings but no one stepped forward to actually carry through on them, Connie realized the time for moping around and doing nothing had ended.

Was it a watershed moment? That description might be a little excessive. Still, Connie had to take a close look at where her life was heading. George might be dead. He might have run off forever. It didn't matter. The time had come for Connie to get back into gear and take control of her own life.

A palpable strain permeated the air at her first meeting back after making this decision. She walked in minutes before starting time and took her place at the head table. Why not? The president belonged there. At first, all conversation came to an abrupt halt. Then, people started questioning whether or not she should be there. At first, behind cupped hands while leaning into their neighour's ear and then, the brave few confronted her directly.

Connie met this resistance head on. She knew no other way.

"George is not home yet. I still have no idea what happened to him or where he has disappeared to. I can't live like a hermit waiting for him to come wandering back. Does anyone have a problem with me chairing this meeting?"

That broke the ice. In reality, everyone rejoiced at seeing her back. The stalled engine that kept these meetings going had restarted. Without Connie at the helm, they became bitching sessions about the lack of accomplishments. With her present, things got done. Raising enough money for the group to continue meeting stood as the main function of most of these meetings, regardless of the umbrella organization. Connie made this happen. She knew how to delegate. She also followed up to make sure the assigned tasks were completed. Before long, the people in attendance had put George out of their minds, at least temporarily.

In less than two months after George mysteriously disappeared into the vapour of the universe, Connie's life returned to near normalcy. At home, she began cooking for one, although Elizabeth frequently joined her for a meal. No one pulled the covers off her while she drifted off into dreamland. This brought some ambivalence. Most of the time, she saw it as an improvement. Still, sometimes in the dark of the night, she found herself reaching out to the other side of the bed, disappointed in finding only blankets with nothing under them.

And, of course, the job of maintaining a working farm fell squarely on her shoulders. She briefly considered hiring someone to help her. She quickly dismissed that idea. The farm business barely broke even. That explained why George had been out working in the woods on the day he disappeared. No, producing enough milk to maintain her milk quota would be her job, alone.

The firewood-producing machines — the porter, the skidder, the splitter and loader, the five-ton truck — could be looked at in two ways. Right now, they were an expense, decreasing in value as they sat rusting in the yard. Brian had brought them home for her. She could sell them, pay off what she owed, and have a little money left over to pour into the running of the farm.

Money only ever went towards the running of the farm. It never covered it. She recalled the joke about the farmer who hit it big on

Lotto 6-49. When asked what he would do with his winnings, he replied, "Keep on farming until it's all gone, I guess."

At the time, Connie had laughed at the joke. Now that she made all the decisions, it didn't seem so funny. Reality sucks.

The other option: hire someone to run the equipment for her. Unlike hiring help for the farming, this made sense. To break even would be an accomplishment. It would stop the drain on funds the payments took from her farm income. It demanded she hire the right person to do the job. Someone not afraid of hard work and, most importantly, someone who would not have their hand in her pocket. She only had room for one outside hand in her pocket and the bankers had theirs firmly entrenched there. Despite diligent searching, she had not located any hoards of cash George had hidden around the place. She needed another option.

Breaking even would not be her goal. This phase of the business should also be a money-maker. George had proven that. She needed someone willing to work as hard as George had. Despite all his faults, no one could say George avoided doing an honest day's work.

Then, out of the blue, Cal Lindsay surprised her with a phone call. How was she doing? Could he help in any way? The phone call followed the same course of several calls that had come in the last couple of months from other concerned neighbours. Connie presented a strong front and declined all offers. She could almost detect the relief coming across the phone wires when she did. Not that the offers weren't sincere. They were. Still, helping out a "widow" woman could become a long-term investment of time if George never returned.

Cal took the call one step further.

"You know I never denied selling liquor from my house," he began after a slight lull in the conversation.

"How could you?" Connie answered. "Everyone in Raymond's River but me knew you held the title of local bootlegger."

A slight chuckle came from Cal's end of the line. "I'm really sorry about that. I honestly believed you knew what I was doing. The whole basis of my business depended on everyone knowing where to come after hours. I never tried to hide it from anyone."

Connie didn't answer right away. The anger she felt after the revelation from her father about Cal's livelihood began to resurface. She fought it back. Cal told the truth. He had never hidden it from her. The subject simply hadn't come up. Connie, not being a drinker, never needed to know the name of the local bootlegger. In fact, she never even considered such an animal existed, a totally foreign concept to her. No one in her house used the devil's tonic. Her father saw to that.

She responded in a more subdued voice. "I guess I'm the one who should be sorry. I over-reacted."

"No. No. I'm not saying that. I understand your reaction. Especially now that I'm older and wiser. At the time, I bootlegged, and proudly. I honestly didn't think I was doing anything wrong. My father had convinced me the only reason the government opposed our selling liquor was because we challenged their monopoly. They lost money to us. It made sense at the time."

"But you still do it."

"I do." He paused. "In my own mind, I can rationalize it. I still don't pay taxes on the profit. The old man would roll over in his grave if I did. But neither do a lot of the other people in Raymond's River. You sell a cow for cash. You pocket the money. Same thing. Someone fixes the brakes on my car in their back yard. They pocket the money. George sells me a load of firewood; I pay cash. No GST." Cal paused to let all these examples sink in for a moment. He continued. "I sell you a case of beer or bottle of wine. It's all the same thing. Is it right? Probably not, but it happens. I'm not calling to tell you I've changed."

Connie was startled at that abrupt revelation.

"Why are you calling? You're concerned about my well-being?" A trace of sarcasm lingered in her voice.

"Yes, I am." Earnestness could be heard in Cal's voice. "You notice I never rushed off and got married after we broke up. I still think you're the greatest person alive." Before Connie could answer, he rushed on. "But I have another reason for calling. One that can benefit both of us."

"I'm listening."

"I'll be honest with you. Business is not as good as it once was. The government has put liquor stores in every little town and village in the province. Every hamlet now has a convenience store selling booze from a back room. When I do it, it's called bootlegging. Now that the government gets its cut, it's called offering a service to the rural population."

"You want me to start drinking to fill the gap left by George?" Cal could hear the irritation in Connie's voice. "I don't understand your point."

Cal laughed. "No, George has been a disappointment these last few months. He really seemed to have kicked the habit." Pause. "I'm sorry. I didn't mean that. I know how you must feel to have him suddenly disappear like that. It must be devastating."

"We all have our burdens." Her patience with this call was wearing thin.

"That is why I called. George runs a profitable firewood business. I've worked with him on occasion during the busy periods. I operated the skidder while he ran the porter. We put out a lot of wood in a short time. Some of my other clients would help with the splitting and loading."

The conversation had veered from the track Cal had laid out in his mind before calling. He had to get to his point in a hurry.

"The winter wood-burning season will soon be upon us. I admit it's a little late to be cutting wood to burn this fall, but there is a demand for it. A lot of people put off buying it until this time of year and most of the dry wood has already been sold to the early-bird customers. Wood cut now will be dry enough by January or February if it is split and stacked right."

Cal stopped to catch his breath and let his words sink in. "We could go into business together."

"Me, working with the local bootlegger?" Connie made no attempt to hide the contempt in her voice.

"No, you working with a local woodsman. Don't define me by my night job. I'm one of the best machine operators around here. Ask anyone."

"My, my. Aren't we modest?"

Cal's voice took on a harder edge. "Ask anyone. I'm not making an idle boast. Let me be totally honest, Connie. I need the money. I don't want to work for someone else. I want to go into business for myself. Well, not just myself, in business with you. You've got the gear sitting idle. I've got the ability to run it. It's useless waiting for my ship to come in unless I actually launch the sucker in the first place. Together we can make this work."

Connie remained silent. This was exactly the kind of offer she was looking for. She didn't have to ask anyone about Cal's skills. She knew he told the truth. George had proudly flashed the money the two of them had made during that spell they worked together. George had nothing but praise for Cal's ability. At first, she had chalked it up to Cal being his good buddy and supplier of demon liquor. But then, George had replaced her worn-out, leaky fridge and added a dishwasher to the complement of kitchen appliances. All paid for with cash. All coming from working with Cal.

Cal said nothing. He let the silence linger.

"We should get together and talk about this," Connie finally said. "I would want to put the terms in writing. We might even declare the income on our taxes."

"I wouldn't have it any other way. As it is, I run the risk of having people accuse me of taking advantage of poor Connie Wilson. I want everything on the up and up."

Connie laughed. "One thing I can assure you. Nothing in this arrangement will be influenced by what anybody else thinks about poor, old Connie Wilson. Business is business. Don't forget that."

Cal shared the laughter. "I'm quaking in my boots already. And I didn't say old; you did. When can we meet?"

CHAPTER 12

SEVERAL CARS FILLED the parking lot at the local seniors' hall in Raymond's River. The noise emanating from the building sounded like a daycare centre in full operation. Only the lateness of the hour belied that possibility. The monthly meeting of the Raymond's River branch of the Red Hat Society rocked the hall. The ladies, crowded around tables playing parlour games, cackled like a hen house at feeding time.

Crokinole boards filled two tables, with four boisterous players surrounding each board. Cries of "ow, my finger" rang out at regular intervals along with whoops of joy when someone dropped a checker into the centre hole and scored a twenty.

Card games occupied two more tables, one of auction forty-fives and one of cribbage. Gossip overruled card playing in importance. Finally, Scrabble took centre stage in a quiet corner at the back of the room. Here, four heads focussed on the seven tiles in front of them, each in deep concentration, trying to form point-producing words. Every so often someone would say, "I don't think that's a word, Emily." Emily had her own version of the dictionary going on in her head.

"Any news on your son?" Edna Hiltz asked Pamela Wilson during a lull in the cribbage game. The room around them became silent. Edna adjusted the crimson red boa around her neck while she waited for an answer. She looked around at the others who were eager to hear the answer but had been unwilling to ask the question.

Pamela gave Edna a pained look. "I really don't think anybody is looking anymore. I know the Mounties gave up. They call Connie every so often, but they never have anything new to tell her. They want to know if Connie has heard anything, to be doing their job for them. How could Connie hear anything from a dead man?"

There was an audible gasp in the room. Those who had not tuned in to the conversation looked over to see who was saying what.

"You think he's dead?" That question caught everyone's attention.

"Of course he's dead. If he wasn't, we'd have heard from him. He might run off on his wife without telling her anything." She looked around the room to measure the reaction to that statement. "But he wouldn't run off on his mother. It breaks my heart to admit it, but there can be no other conclusion." Tears welled in Pamela eyes, but she refused to let them flow.

Furtive glances were exchanged around the room. Few people argued with Pamela. Disagreement hid in some of those faces. To these people, George fleeing his marriage was exactly what happened. Another forty-year-old refusing to accept the reality of getting older along with a wife aging beside him. The Red Hatters were all twenty years or more older than George. They remembered him mainly as a rowdy drunken teen who did nothing but cause trouble. They disregarded the in-between years when he built up his aunt's farm to be the going concern it was today. Doing good things failed to provide grist for the rumour mill. Bad things re-circulated forever.

"I call them myself, every so often," Pamela continued. "They won't tell me anything. They say they are following all leads as they come in, but when I try to pin them down as to what those leads are, they clam up. The lazy bastards aren't doing a damn thing."

Edna blushed at that answer. Her face matched the colour of all the hats in the room. She regretted bringing the topic up. She thought she was being a concerned neighbour. Instead she had opened a well of venom.

"I see Cal Lindsay is using George's porter." Mable Booth said, turning the conversation to a new direction. "He's cutting firewood up behind my property."

"Probably ripping Connie off," Pamela said. "I tried to warn her about him. She wouldn't listen. Said she needs the money. Course she does. She's a woman trying to run a farm alone. We all know what farming's like these days, even for someone who knows what they're doing."

That statement was met with universal approval.

"I think he's after something else," Pamela went on. "You know men. They are all after the same thing. This isn't the first time he's been sniffing around Connie. He dated her before George came on the scene. He can't fool me. I know what he's after."

This brought another chorus of nods from many in the room.

"The same thing as us," 83-year-old Joan McNeil said in a low, snickering voice. Those near Pamela suppressed smiles. Those at the far reaches of the room let theirs have full bloom. Pamela didn't respond.

Now all the games had ceased and everyone listened to Pamela. "She insists it's strictly business. She might think that, but I know better. Cal Lindsay caused George's little drinking problem a few years ago. Cal led him down that path to oblivion. George was weak, I know that. Thank the Lord, he got over it."

More furtive glances. Old beliefs died hard. Not everyone knew of George's spell of sobriety. They all remembered the fatal car accident that had claimed a child's life.

"Ladies, I think it's time for lunch," Mable said, as she pushed back her chair, stood up and pulled down her purple dress that had ridden up her hips. She could see this discussion had taken a turn contrary to the motto of the Red Hats — girls just wanting to have fun. "The tea and coffee are in the kitchen. The sweets and sandwiches are under those cup towels on that table over there. Everyone help themselves."

A general scuffing of chairs across the floor sounded as everyone moved at once. They could finish their current game or rush to get to the front of the food line. Food carried the day. It had been less than three hours since most of these people had finished a big sit-down supper. Still, if food was being served, it must be time to eat.

Mable eased up beside Pamela in the line. She spoke in a low voice. "I know you're going through a rough time. If there is anything I can do to help…"

Pamela shook her head. "Thank you, Mable. I just have to take it day by day. Sometimes I hold out hope George will soon be home and then on other days, like today, I feel like he's gone forever. I shouldn't have been so blunt back there. I hoped these games would give me a break from thinking about him all the time." She gave her head a weary shake. "Nothing does."

Mable patted her on the shoulder. She appeared to be searching for the right words to say. Finally, she decided no right words existed and turned to load her plate with sweets and sandwiches.

CHAPTER 13

CAL LINDSAY REACHED into his pocket and slapped five crisp, brown, one-hundred-dollar bills onto Connie's kitchen table. Prime Minister Bobby Borden stared up from the top one, a good old down-home Nova Scotia boy.

"It's not much, but it's a start," he said. A smile split his face from ear to ear. "I've paid the landowner, taken my share, paid for the gas and oil, and set aside a reserve for repairs and maintenance. This is your share of the take."

Connie stared down at the money. It was more than she had expected to see this early. Slowly, she reached out and spread the bills apart. She looked up at Cal who was waiting for some sort of response. None came.

Cal fumbled a piece of paper out of his shirt pocket. "It's all here," he said as he held the paper out to Connie. "I've itemized every penny I've spent. Set up a bookkeeping program on my computer to handle things."

Connie realized Cal had misunderstood her silence. "Oh, Cal, this is great. I can put this money to good use right away. I didn't think it would be this much. Are you sure you took your proper share?" She reached out and took the paper. She turned it towards herself and scanned the figures. "How many hours did you spend in the woods? You don't want to overdo it in this summer heat."

Cal laughed. "I feel like a little kid playing with big boys' toys. I love doing this. I've been up cruising the Millicent place. George must have been just starting there. The woods look like they've been hardly touched."

The smile fell from Connie's face like a broken elevator.

"I'm sorry," Cal said. "I know talking about George must be painful. I wasn't thinking."

Connie gave a dismissive wave.

"Still, in all fairness to the Millicents, I should finish there before moving on to someplace new. They have a government grant for silviculture work. They'll lose it if we don't act on it quickly. Either that or they'll get someone else to do the work."

The government offered grants to wood-lot owners to keep their lines cleared, their roads up to a certain standard and to put in proper bridges. This served two purposes. It helped to continue a renewable resource industry and it gave firefighters access in case of a forest fire. In return, the wood-lot owners had to follow certain standards in doing their work. Cal had taken courses in the past to qualify him to do this work. Now he was getting to put his theory into practice as his own boss.

He sat quietly for a short while. "Maybe I'll just do the work and not tell you where I'm going to be. That way, no bad memories will be dredged up."

Connie shook her head. "No, I want to be an equal partner in this operation. Keep me informed. The Millicent place is a good place to work next. George must have thought so or he wouldn't have set up an operation there."

Cal nodded. The smile returned. "Good. That's settled. I'll start there tomorrow."

"You'll be working on the left side of the road? In case I want to go looking for you. Bring you a lunch or something."

"That's right, the left. You already know more about the operation than I thought you did. There should be enough wood in there to keep me busy most of the summer."

"Good," Connie said. She didn't elaborate.

"So, I can look forward to hand-delivered, home-made lunches?"

Connie gave him a coquettish smile. "We'll see. You never know what might happen."

Cal turned serious. "The word is out in the village that we've teamed up in this operation. Have you heard anything negative?"

"For the most popular man in town, a lot of people don't hold you in high esteem. I've had numerous warnings."

"The most popular man in town?" Cal looked confused.

"The local bootlegger. He's always the most popular man in town."

Cal laughed. "That's not as true as it once was. Now that the government has legalized bootlegging, it has lost some of its glamour. All their cronies are getting in on it."

"Maybe so. My mother-in-law warns me on a regular basis that you're only after one thing. George's father left her well provided for. She doesn't know what it's like to try to keep a farm afloat."

"The mother-in-law. That's to be expected. What about the others? What are they saying?"

"More innuendo than anything. They don't know how hard a worker you are."

"That's not entirely true. I've worked for a number of them. I've given every one of them an honest day's work for an honest day's wage. Because of who I am, some of them thought I should be working for less. I never let that happen. I never undervalue my services."

"George always spoke highly of you."

"George always paid me what I earned, too. Anyway, now I'm doing it for myself. I appreciate you giving me the chance."

Connie reached across the table and gave him a light-hearted tap. "Don't get maudlin on me. I've partnered up with a lumberjack, not a sissy boy."

Cal lowered his eyes. When he looked up, they were glistening. "We're going to show them. We'll prove every one of them wrong." The smile returned to his face. He pushed the money across the table. "Let me take you out to supper at a fancy restaurant. Our first pay day deserves some sort of celebration."

Connie hesitated. "That might give the wrong impression." She could see the hurt in Cal's face. She slapped her hand on the table, making Cal jump. "No, you're right. This moment deserves a celebration. We are business partners and we have nothing to be ashamed of. Let's eat in the village."

And they did.

CHAPTER 14

Early July

CORPORAL SCOTT BOWEN sipped from a mug of steaming, black coffee at the local Tim Horton's coffee shop. Across the table, he was joined by Detective-Sergeant Jim McDonald from the Major Crimes Division of the Halifax Detachment. This was a social call.

Scott had spent the previous three days at a dog-training facility with Roscoe. Even though the big shepherd was no longer officially on the force, Scott had convinced his overlords to allow Roscoe to keep his skills up to date with periodic refresher courses. Jim had happened by on the last day of training to check on some other matter and the two men had agreed to meet for coffee at the Elmsdale location. At least that is what Scott thought.

Despite this being a friendly visit, they discussed police business. Jim inquired about the missing person case from a couple of months back. He said he half expected to be called in on it when there failed to be a resolution.

"I thought about giving you a call," Scott said. The two men had worked several cases together. "But, in the end, I think Wilson ran. There were no signs of foul play. His truck has never shown up. I think he simply said '*Sayonara*' as the Japanese put it. Trouble is, he didn't actually say it to anyone in particular. That would have saved us a lot of time searching."

"What about his wife?"

"She was as baffled as anyone. She seems to be handling it all right though. That reinforces my opinion that things in the marriage may not have been the best. She was more concerned than upset about the disappearance."

"No other suspects."

"I briefly entertained robbery as a motive. He carried a lot of cash on him. I couldn't come up with any suspicious characters. George was well liked in the community. You know, the friendly drunk, life-of-the-party kind of guy. Somewhere along the line, any thieves would have been turned in by someone. The officers in the fire department were leading the search at the local level. They promised to keep their ears open for any suspicious comments. Nobody ever heard anything. It's hard to investigate an unreported crime, even if our federal government thinks they are rampant in the country. No, I think he just up and took off."

"Good. I'm glad to hear that. It's not like I don't have enough on my plate already. My desk is piled high with open cases. There's a small-scale war brewing between a couple of the local drug families. They keep shooting at each other, but honestly they all need to spend some time on the range. That way we could have one in the morgue and one in prison for a very long time."

Scott reached across the table and gave him a good-natured punch on the arm. "You thrive on having your plate totally full. These shootings are getting old. What are you actively working on now?"

Jim took a slow sip of his coffee and gazed out the window, watching the traffic heading towards the nearby Sobey's grocery store. He looked back at Scott.

"Some hikers found a body at the bottom of a cliff along the Bay of Fundy. Half-buried in the sand just above the high-water mark. Been there for a while. Did you hear about it?"

Scott perked up. "No. I've been out of touch for the last couple of days. I'm surprised no one called me. It could be George Wilson."

"It's not. The first officer on the scene identified the body. Low-level hooligan. Petty theft. Stolen cars. You probably know him." Jim reached into his pocket for his notebook.

"That's why I was called in. With his past record, foul play could have been involved." Jim flipped back a few pages, read a couple of lines, then looked up at Scott again.

"Jason Browne. Lots of drunk and disorderlies, DUIs, auto theft, drugs. Don't have his juvy record, but I'm sure it reads the same way."

Scott nodded. "Oh yeah, it does. I recognize the name. A real pain in the ass. Wondered what happened to him. Figured he had moved out west or something. I don't remember him being reported missing. Was he?"

"No next of kin that we can find. It appears you local Mounties knew him better than anyone." Jim smiled. "None of you filed a report. Pretty slack of you."

"I don't want to be crass, but he won't be missed by us. As I said, he was a royal pain in the ass. Does it really look like murder?"

"Too soon to tell. We'll have to wait for the coroner. He had a broken bottle of lemon gin in his jacket pocket. Lots of liquor bottles scattered around on the top of the cliff. Ring of rocks from a campfire. It looks like he staggered away from a party and dropped over the cliff, smashed in his skull. No one noticed him missing. Nice to be popular. Oh yeah, one other thing. He wasn't wearing any pants."

Scott raised his eyebrows. "No pants?"

"We found them snagged on a bush half-way down the hill. You know the man. Was he stupid enough to lower his butt over the edge of one of those high cliffs to take a crap?"

Scott laughed. "You think he was taking a crap and fell over backwards?"

Jim struggled to suppress a smile. "That's the consensus of those on the scene. When you gotta go, you gotta go."

The two men sat in contemplative silence for a couple of minutes. They were comfortable enough with each other that they felt no compulsion to fill the void with sound. Then Scott shook the absurd image from his mind and looked up.

"How long do you think the body was there?"

Jim rubbed his chin, giving the matter some thought. "Judging from the way he was dressed, or half-dressed, I would say a couple of months. He was covered in mud. Seems the Fundy tides covered him a couple of times. They can get pretty high around there at certain times of the month, I've been told."

"Highest in the world," Scott said. "It's a wonder he wasn't washed out to sea. For that matter, how do we know he wasn't washed in from somewhere else?"

"We're not completely sure, but all indications are that he came from the top of the bank. That will have to be verified for sure. One of his feet was jammed between a couple of rocks, keeping him in place."

"What was he wearing?" Scott said.

"Had on a spring jacket with a heavy sweater under it. I'd say it was after the cold winter days had ended but before the warmer nights had really taken hold. Probably around the end of April. Found his wallet in his pants pocket. Ten, twelve dollars in change. A couple of credit cards. No bills. Robbery hasn't been completely ruled out."

"Interesting timing," Scott said. "We had an aircraft up around that time looking for George Wilson. They made several passes along the shore. Strange they didn't see anything."

Jim shrugged. "I could be off by a couple of weeks. We'll try to find out when the party took place. The locals must have seen or heard something. That will give us a better time line."

"Maybe. Those parties aren't a rare event. They happen on a regular basis."

"Oh, so you know about them."

Scott didn't answer right away. "Do you want me to look into the party angle?"

"Only if you have time."

"In that case, I guess you don't."

Jim glanced out the window again and then back at Scott. He slowly smiled. "Actually, you do. I've spoken to Inspector Holland. He's opened up a couple of days in your schedule. Someone else will be covering your patrol duties." The smile took on more of the air of a smirk.

Scott shook his head in the negative. "Aw, come on. The way you describe it, it was just a drunken accident. Why the big deal? Why are you even involved? The Bay of Fundy must be way out of your jurisdiction."

Jim took a slow sip of his coffee before answering. "You'd think so. Budget cuts. Efficiency drives. Major Crimes is now provincial in nature. Centralize the expertise. We're always looking for new good men to join our cadre."

"No thanks. You still haven't told me why Major Crimes is even involved."

"You know we initially check out every suspicious death. I don't know about this one. Something doesn't feel right. I can't believe a person could disappear in the middle of a party and someone not be a little concerned about their whereabouts." Jim gave his hands a little wave in the air in front of him. "The one explanation is that someone threw him over the bank and, as you said, expected the body to be washed out to sea. Just a fluke that it wasn't. Spend a couple of days looking. See if anything turns up. This is more your territory than mine. You know the people. They'll talk to you easier than they'll open up to me. You've got a kind face."

The look Scott gave Jim had no suggestion of kindness in it. "I'd rather not. Every time you get me involved in one of your cases, headquarters starts pressuring me to join your little band of merry men. I don't want that and you know it."

Jim nodded his head, "I know, but please, have a look around. If it looks suspicious, I'll take over. In the meantime, you'd be doing me a big favour. I am up to my ass in alligators and it's such a time-consuming drive to come out here every day."

Scott scowled at the man across the table from him. "Do you have an address? I need a starting point." He knew it was senseless to argue with the sergeant.

Jim did. He passed Scott a folder with the current information from the case. This had not been an accidental meeting, Scott realized. He had been set up.

"There's not much here. The investigation is just getting underway. I walked the scene yesterday, but thought it best if you get in on it during the early stages. That way you won't have to play catch-up later if it turns out to actually be a homicide in your back yard." A good-natured grin sparkled on his face. "You wouldn't want to miss out on that."

Scott did his best to remain stoic, but couldn't maintain the facade. "OK, but just a couple of days," he said, "then it's back on your desk."

CHAPTER 15

SCOTT BOWEN PULLED his police cruiser into the farmyard of Günter Manheim. Günter owned the land adjacent to where Jason Browne's body had surfaced the day before. This name had come from the brief meeting with Sergeant Jim McDonald. Scott still viewed that meeting as a setup.

A white Samoyed dog came rushing from the barn towards his car. The barking could have awakened the dead. Well, maybe not. Browne had slept though it for a couple of months. When the dog reached the door of his car, it sat and stared up at him with deep blue eyes. The tail wagged back and forth, clearing the spot of dust.

Scott looked at the dog. Was this friendly demonstration an act or was the vicious way it had charged from the barn the act? He lifted the door handle and slowly opened the door. The tail beat harder against the ground. Scott stepped out. The dog jumped up and almost knocked him backwards into the car.

A harsh shout sounded from the direction of the barn.

"Wolf, get down. Get down, now."

The intention was to save Scott from being manhandled by the animal. Instead, Scott feared drowning in slobber. He placed his hand on the dog's head and gently eased him to the ground while briskly rubbing its ear with the other hand. Wolf leaned into the hand on the ear. Scott had made a friend for life.

Günter Manheim came running up. "Are you all right?" He sounded concerned for Scott's life. His image of the dog, a protector of his farm and family, and the reality of the situation were miles apart. He snatched the dog by the collar, pulled him away from the Mountie and held on tightly.

"Lovely animal you have there," Scott said. "I'm fine."

Günter's eyes looked apprehensive. "You're here about the body they found yesterday? I put up fences. I post signs. It does no good. Nobody listens. *Dummkopfs.*"

Günter obviously feared being held responsible for the man's death.

"I am, but you have nothing to worry about. I'm simply trying to figure out when the event may have taken place. Do you remember any parties or gatherings happening in that field?" He pulled a notebook from his pocket and stood with a pen in hand poised to write. Scott expected an answer.

"More than once. I try, but I can't stop them. Sometimes I see the glow of their campfires." He pointed to the west of his house. "As you can see, that hill prevents me from seeing into the field. I used to go over when I knew people were there. No one ever listened to me. It is useless to argue with a bunch of drunks in the dark. I threatened to call the police. They laughed at me. You people seldom came anyway. Now, I ignore them."

His eyes dropped to the ground, emphasizing the slump of his shoulders. He slowly shook his head back and forth. "One of them falls over the cliff and dies and I will be held responsible. It is not right."

The man, Scott realized, worried about the legal system holding him responsible. Scott saw even more. Günter held himself responsible. He took this death personally. He felt he should have done more to stop the intrusions onto his property.

"Sir, this was absolutely not your fault. There is nothing you could have done to prevent it." Günter eagerly nodded his head, clutching at any straw that relieved him of blame. Scott continued: "Do you have any idea who uses your field for these parties? On the occasions when you go over, do you recognize anyone? All I need is a name, one name, and I can take it from there."

Günter shook his head, appearing to clear the image of Browne's half-naked body from his mind. The hikers who had discovered the body had come to Günter's house to make the 9-1-1 call. Günter, himself, had rushed back along the shore to assist in the recovery of the body. Scott's words seem to reassure him. He raised his downcast eyes and held those of the Mountie's. His shoulders became a little more square.

"Two months ago the local high school kids held a party there. They promised me they would leave the area clean, stay away from the edge of the cliff. They know the risks. I didn't give them permission, but I knew they would be there anyway. I begged them to be careful."

Scott placed a hand on the man's shoulder. His heart went out to this poor immigrant.

"This is not the first time someone has tumbled into the Bay. The local kids know the risks. I'm sure they were serious about being careful." Scott let his eyes drift to the edge of the bank. "Sometimes the best intentions are not enough. Sometimes other factors come into play."

Günter's eyes followed Scott's. "There have been others fall off the cliff before? Others have died?" Günter had only owned this farm for the last five years.

Scott nodded. "Usually one a year somewhere along the coast. Not always fatal. It seems it has to happen once every spring to remind everyone else of the danger."

"Ya, ya. The local boys promised me they would be careful. I believed them." The relief coursing through Günter's body was palpable. He grabbed Scott's hand and for no reason started shaking it. "I don't think that man belonged with the kids. He is too old. Ya?"

Scott eased his hand from the farmer's grip. "It's been a while since he saw the inside of a high school. When did this party take place? Do you remember a specific date?"

"A Saturday night near the middle of April. I was working on my income taxes when they asked me. I filed on April 15. Somewhere around then."

Scott tried to hide his disappointment. That would have put the party before George had disappeared. If Browne had fallen over the cliff then, his body would have been spotted by George's search planes.

"You say there were other parties?"

"Ya, ya. Much later. Mostly this month when the weather got warmer and school was over. The nights were still cold back in April."

"School has only been over for a week."

"Ya, last week they had another big party there. It went on all night."

Again, this did not help Scott's time line. Browne's body had been exposed to the elements for more than a week. It had to have been at least a couple of months. It was possible the search plane had missed the body. Scott hadn't seen the corpse himself. He was only going by the description he had from Sergeant McDonald.

"You saw the body, sir? You were at the actual site?"

"Ya, I went in before the first policeman arrived. I thought I might be of some help."

The casual shrug of his shoulders was all the comment necessary to point out that Jason Browne was long beyond being helped.

"Was the body hidden in any way or was it in plain sight?"

Günter stopped to think before answering. "It was in a deserted part of the beach. Sand had blown up on it, partly covering it. Maybe once or twice the high tide had washed over it. It was a muddy red in colour." He stopped talking and seemed to be giving serious thought to his description. "But, once you were there, it lay in plain sight. His jacket was brown like the beach and he had no pants on." He looked at Scott to see if that was new information to him. "His legs sort of blended in with the dirt that covered them."

"So, if an airplane flew over, it would be possible they would not see him?"

"From above? The edge of the cliff may have shielded him. The cliff dropped straight down and the tides have undercut the top of the bank. Every year I own less and less farmland. Still I am taxed on the same amount."

Scott smiled. Beefs about taxes were universal. His thoughts went back to Günter's description of the death scene. Then he motioned with his notebook. "You know some names of people who might have been at the party."

Günter gave him the names of a few families around who had kids the right age. He couldn't say for sure if they had been at the party or not. He had not authorized the party. He was not responsible.

Good story, Scott thought. Stick to it.

He reached down and patted Wolf once more.

"I hate to impose, but could you show me where the body was found?"

A smile lit up Günter's face. He eagerly offered his assistance. He looked at his watch. "We must hurry. It will soon be time for high tide. The water comes right up to the foot of the bank. Makes walking impossible."

The scene disappointed Scott. That area of beach looked like any other. There had been a full moon the night before, causing higher than normal tides. Even the previous day's footprints made by the investigators had been washed away. There would be no evidence from a couple of months ago to offer any assistance.

When he looked to the top of the cliff, the bank dropped straight down. The body would not have been shielded from a plane flying overhead. The heat signature would have been detected by OLIS even if the body was camouflaged with mud. At least, Scott knew when the body wasn't there.

He thanked Günter for his help and moved on.

CHAPTER 16

FIVE MINUTES LATER, Scott located Tommy Watson. Tommy lived on the neighbouring farm, but on the opposite side of the road. He was a tall boy, approaching six feet, and weighed about one hundred and fifty pounds. He sported a blue baseball cap, bearing the high school crest, a golden sword and shield on a blue background. Otherwise, he was dressed for working in the fields: tan-coloured work boots, blue jeans and a black T-shirt with Mick Jagger's enlarged tongue filling up the front.

Tommy wielded a small hoe that he used to dig weeds from around a row of tomato plants. He didn't hide his eagerness to stop and talk to the Mountie, or anyone else who happened by and wanted to shoot the breeze. Sweat ran from under the brim of his hat and down across his forehead. His face and arms were the colour of coffee with only one cream. Tommy had spent many days working outside this summer.

"That dude wasn't at our party," Tommy informed Scott in answer to his inquiry about the previous day's discovery.

Scott studied the boy for a minute. Scott had asked if Tommy knew that a body had been found on the beach across the road. He hadn't mentioned a party.

"Tell me about your party," Scott said. Once again he had his notebook and pen at the ready. He raised his eyebrows to encourage Tommy to go on.

"Which one? In April, we held a fundraiser, and last week, a social gathering took place."

"The earlier one. When in April?"

"April 20th, a Saturday night. The Student Council organized that one. We raised money for a Safe Grad Prom."

Scott stopped writing. He looked at the boy with a look of incredulity on his face.

"All those liquor bottles we found were from the, what did you call it, the social gathering? The first one contained no alcohol?"

"I didn't say that. It was organized. We sold tickets. Like I said, it was a fundraiser. You couldn't get on the site with booze unless you had a designated driver with you or you lived close enough to walk home. We collected all the keys at the gate. The DD had to be sober to get them back at the end of the night. No exceptions. I was a designated driver."

"And this was to raise money for a Safe Grad program? Correct me if I'm wrong, but that means alcohol-free?"

"Teenagers drink, Sergeant. This party gave them a chance to get it out of their system. The prom was alcohol-free. We received funding from the Safe Grad program to help defer costs along with the money we raised here. It was a revolutionary idea and it worked. No one was hurt at either party."

"And who decided if you got your keys back?" Arguing with drunks who thought they were sober occupied much of Scott's time while patrolling. He referred to it as entering a battle of wits with an unarmed person.

"We had a couple of football players holding the keys. One had lost a sister to a drunk driver. He didn't take any shit from anybody. If he said you didn't get your keys, you didn't get your keys. Sometimes if you were drunk and unreasonable, he would assemble a committee to help him judge. He would then run you through those road-side tests that you guys administer. Touching your nose, walking heel to toe, reciting the alphabet. When you made a big enough fool of yourself, he'd tell you to get lost. Nobody was left stranded. Someone sober would always drive the car home. It was extra work, but nobody dies."

Scott liked what he heard. Finally he nodded. "Whatever works."

Maybe this generation would reduce the carnage on the highways from drunk drivers. He at least thought they deserved credit for trying something new.

"Tell me how you know the man who was found yesterday was not at your party."

"His name was Jason Browne, right?"

Scott nodded. The community telegraph had circulated the story about the grisly discovery throughout the village like cold germs whipping through a kindergarten class. Name of the victim, description of his body and a variety of possible theories had spread along with it.

"As the party went on, we had a few gate crashers. That's inevitable. Jason Browne was not one of them. We all know Browne. He would not have been welcome at our party. He hangs around outside the high school and tries to pick up girls. Thinks he's God's gift to women. The girls think he's a dirty old man. He's got to be crowding thirty. I think he's a loud, obnoxious prick. Just about everyone avoids him"

Scott made an entry in his notebook. This description pretty much agreed with his assessment of the man.

"Does he ever have any success with girls? Somebody I could talk to?"

"Success. Yeah, he has success. There are two girls at school who will go out with anyone for a price. Whatever you want for twenty-five bucks. You supply your own condom. Fast service guaranteed."

"Great. Do you know how I can get in touch with those girls?"

Tommy raised his eyebrows and snickered.

Scott looked up from his notebook. "Somehow that didn't come out right. If I want to interview these young ladies as part of this investigation, how do I reach them?" He then laughed himself.

"Don't worry, man." Tommy's smile broadened. "If the price is right, they'd do a cop." Then he gave Scott their names. He didn't know where they lived, only that they didn't travel on his school bus.

Scott recorded the names. The school could provide the addresses if any follow-up was needed.

"Were they at the party?"

"Oh yeah. They were both there. They considered the ten dollar ticket price as a business expense. They more than covered expenses before the night ended. They had what they called their virgin list. Your last chance to lose your virginity before you graduated from high school. Hand, mouth or the full-meal deal. A price for every wallet. They did their advertising before the sun went down. Everyone on the list got a flyer with some pretty graphic art work on it. There was no doubt what they were offering. Once it turned dark, the store opened its doors. Nothing like a few beers to loosen your inhibitions. Man, I'd rather remain celibate for the rest of my life than go anywhere near either of them."

Scott's head made an involuntary nod. He had no interest in Tommy Watson's sexual proclivities. "But you're sure Jason Browne wasn't with them."

"I'm sure. He wasn't their friend, regardless of what he thought. Just another paying customer. If he didn't have money in his hand, he didn't get a second glance from either one of them. He knew that."

Tommy chopped the head off a couple more weeds, then looked back at the corporal. "I don't have to tell you about Jason Browne. He was a thief and trouble-maker. We didn't want him at our party. He knew that, too. Like I told you, I was a designated driver. I remained sober all night. I know what was going on and who was there. Jason Brown wasn't. If he took a dive off that cliff, it wasn't during our bash."

"Any idea who might want to throw him off that cliff?"

"Sorry dude, not my circle. I'm sure there would have been a line-up to do it, a long line."

Scott grunted. Tommy was right. Jason Browne did not travel in any circles where hard work was involved. Scott could not picture Browne with a hoe in his hands. At least not the kind of hoe Tommy worked with.

He snapped his notebook shut and slipped it back into his pocket. He had hoped for a better start in this quest. Sergeant McDonald had suggested he spend a couple of days looking to see if this should be a homicide investigation. A drunken Jason Browne tumbling over the cliff while having a crap would debase that idea.

His failure to be in attendance at all only raised more questions. If he wasn't at the party, what brought him to that field? If it wasn't a party, who might have been in that field with him and why? The answers to these questions were crucial to Scott's ability to arrive at a conclusion of either murder or death by misadventure. Scott had more work to do before reporting back to the detective.

The time allotted to the investigation seemed to fall short as well. Two days. To reach an accurate conclusion, one way or the other, by tomorrow would require things to move along a lot better than they had today.

"You say Browne didn't travel in your circles. Can you give me the names of anyone who did associate with him?"

"Sorry. I never saw him with anyone that I can remember. He always struck me as a bit of a loner. His personality sucked. The school banned him from the grounds. He hung around across the street at a burger joint. A lot of the kids eat there at lunch time. Jason often played the big shot, trying to make an impression on everyone. Most people considered him to be a jerk."

A light came on behind Tommy's eyes.

"Actually, that's the last place I remember seeing him, maybe a week after our party. He flashed a roll of bills around, trying to buy burgers for some of the girls. Said he'd made a big score. They acted as though they might lose their lunch if he sat at their table. Some of the guys cashed in on his generosity. Jason was a sucker for anyone who appeared to be his friend. He bought a round of burgers and cokes for one table that I know of.

"Still there when I left, at a table by the door. The staff might be able to give you a lead. They make the best burgers around. The real thing, not like those fast-food joints in town. That, in itself, would be a good reason to go talk to them even if they can't give you any leads."

This bit of advice generated a smile from the policeman. "OK, I'll check it out. You're sure about the time line? It was after your party?"

"I'm sure. The prom-planning committee met there for lunch. We knew how much money we had to work with so it had to be after the party. Like I said at the beginning, that dude didn't die at our party. I'm positive he wasn't there."

Scott thanked Tommy for his help and climbed back into his cruiser. A hunger pang smacked him in the stomach. He looked at his watch. Lunch time crept up on him. He may as well check out the diner. If Tommy thought they made the best burgers around, Scott was ready to test his claim.

The food lived up to its advance billing. The information garnered proved to be useless. No one remembered seeing Jason Browne for several weeks. That came as no surprise to Scott, considering Browne had been soaking up the sun at the foot of a cliff on the Bay of Fundy for the last couple of months, bare ass exposed to the elements. The waitresses at the diner held Browne in the same high regard as Tommy and, for that matter, as Scott himself. They paid no attention to his comings and goings. They rebuked any advances Browne made and didn't realize he had not been around until Scott started questioning them. Browne was the kind of person who could leave a party of two and not be missed.

That explained his long absence from the community without ever being reported missing. If the Fundy tides had picked up the body and taken it out to sea, no one would have ever acknowledged his passing. In a way, Scott thought, how sad. That thought lived in his mind for less than a second. Some people improved the world when they went missing. Jason Browne fell into that category.

CHAPTER 17

B RIAN COSH NOTICED the Mountie car in the diner parking lot and pulled in beside the white Ford. Scott Bowen looked up from his computer screen on the dash beside him. He acknowledged Brian's presence and rolled down his window, spilling his cool air-conditioned environment into the warmth of the early July evening. Brian did the same.

"Any word on George Wilson?" Brian asked. He didn't have to wait for an answer. The dismal look on the Mountie's face said it all.

"Nothing. It makes you want to believe in alien abductions."

"Seems like. You've heard about the body found in the Bay?"

Again the look on Scott's face transmitted his answer. He nodded. "I've been assigned to determine the circumstances surrounding the discovery. Heard anything that might be of help?"

"Me? Sorry. I only know what's in the rumours floating around the community. Was he really naked when they found him?"

Scott smirked. "That rumour is only half true. No pants. No underwear. Might've been dumped while taking a dump."

Brian looked momentarily confused, then understanding showed on his face. "Oh, that's rough timing. Accidentally or on purpose?"

"That, my friend, is the $64,000 question. I've tried to trace his last steps, but not with a lot of luck. Did you know the victim?"

Brian shook his head. "Jason Browne, right? I know who he is, but I don't really know him, if you know what I mean. He broke into our fire station a while back. Did a bunch of senseless damage. Pleaded guilty when they caught him; got probation and time served by his day in court. What a fucking joke that system is. Part of his sentence included making restitution to us. Not a fucking, red cent has showed up in the last year."

A little red crept into Brian's face. Swearing did not come naturally to him.

"I didn't even waste my time going to the sentencing. I might have shot off my mouth, got myself in trouble. Would likely end up serving more time than that moron did."

Scott tried to keep his face neutral. He made no comment for a few seconds. Then he nodded his head. "That sounds like our boy. Gets away with this foolishness time after time and probably thought he always would. Looks like that myth ended at last. The big judge in the sky seems to have done what the local judges around here didn't have the intelligence to do. The man could only be described as a wart on society. He did spend a little time in jail for grand theft auto once. He stole cars and sold them to a local chop shop. Even then, they let him out before his sentence half ended. Needed the room, they said. What they need to do is build some more prisons."

"No arguments from me," Brian said. "They should build one on Sable Island. Put them there and let them fend for themselves. No need for guards. If they want to swim for the mainland, good luck to them. What is it, about one hundred and fifty kilometres, and that puts you in Canso, the most rugged and desolate part of the province."

Both men sat quietly for a minute or two. They had to rein in their emotions. Brian spoke first.

"Maybe I could help you. We've got pictures of him and some of the other chronic trouble-makers at the station. When they come into the community and we see them, we keep an eye on their doings. If he decided to break the law again, we intended to nab him in the act. No telling how much force might be required to hold him until your boys arrived."

Scott looked up. Alarm registered on his face. "I don't like the sound of that, Chief. Vigilantism is never a good thing. Someone might get hurt or even killed unnecessarily."

Brian detected the conflict in Scott's voice. He realized that despite Scott's frustration with the system, he would never condone violence on the part of Joe Citizen. His own face remained stoic.

"Maybe they could, but just about everything we have in that station was paid for with money raised in this community. A lot of long hours and hard work put that stuff there." His eyes narrowed and he fully captured the gaze of the Mountie. "Then, some asswipe comes along and destroys it just to get his kicks. I can understand why someone would want to shove him over that bank. Hell, I wish I came across him there with his balls to the wind. I'd gladly put my foot in his chest and push."

That image brought a smile to the face of both men.

"As someone else told me, there would be a line-up to do that. My job is to find the person standing first in line."

"To congratulate him, I hope." All humour left Brian's voice.

"Maybe," Scott said. "As far as I can find out, the last time anyone saw him, he was sitting in there." He indicated the diner with a flick of his head. "That sighting happened towards the end of April."

Brian rubbed his chin. His eyes pinched almost closed as if thinking was a great effort. "I saw him in early May, a couple of days after we cancelled the search for George. I'm sure of the date because to my surprise, Connie pulled into the drug store parking lot beside me. To my knowledge, she hadn't ventured into the village since George's disappearance. At the same time, Browne got out of an old blue truck. It belonged to someone who lives over on the shore. Let me think about it for a while and I'll probably remember who.

"Ordinarily, I'd have kept an eye on him, but seeing Connie in the village surprised me so much that I walked her into the pharmacy while she picked up some medications. We chatted for a while. She assured me she understood us stepping down the search. That turned out to be just Connie showing a good face to the community. When I went to help her with her chores the next morning, I found a different woman.

"Her bloodshot eyes indicated she had spent the night crying. She flitted from one thing to another without thought, you know, nerves totally shot and agitated by everything I said or did. It took me a couple of hours to get her calmed down. I guess she needed one good cry to get it out of her system. Ever since then, she's been pretty stoic about the whole thing. I swear, if that dammed husband of hers is alive somewhere, I'll kill him myself for what he's putting that woman through."

Scott winced at that statement, but he understood where the chief was coming from. "When we phase back a search, everyone involved finds it difficult. At least locating a body brings closure; simply stopping leaves so many unanswered questions. The family always takes it hard. Still, we can't keep going over the same ground forever. It's a decision that has to be made."

He looked down for a few seconds, lost in thought. "What about Browne?" he asked when he looked up again. "Where did he go when he got out of the truck?"

Brian slowly shook his head. "When I finished talking with Connie, he had disappeared. Must be hitchhiking, I thought at the time, but I'm not positive about that. Never saw him again. I'll ask around and see if anyone else remembers seeing him."

"I'd appreciate that, Chief. I have to visit the M.E. tomorrow to see if they have an accurate time line on his death, but for now around the first of May seems like the best guess."

He looked at the bustle of activity taking place behind the window of the diner. "Tommy Watson says this place makes the best burgers around. I can't say that I can argue with him. If you're hungry, give them a try."

Brian patted his belly and smiled. "They made the best burgers around long before Tommy Watson started eating them. The kids come to school for this food and as a bonus, they leave educated. I'll be in touch if I find anything that can be of help."

They rolled up their windows and went about their respective tasks.

CHAPTER 18

ELIZABETH'S PALE FACE had a sheen of perspiration covering it. She leaned back against the bathroom door off Connie's kitchen, one hand still holding the doorknob behind her back.

"This has been going on for two or three weeks now," she said. "Right out of the blue, I feel the urge to throw up. By noon, I'm feeling fine again."

Connie looked up from the morning Chronicle on the kitchen table. "Two or three weeks?"

"Something like that. I paid no attention at first. But then it began happening day after day. It's been at least three weeks, maybe a month or more."

"What about your periods? Are they still regular?"

The question surprised Elizabeth. She lowered her eyes and studied a spot on the floor in front of her. Then she looked up. "I think I'm a little late."

"A little late is no big deal. How late?"

Elizabeth hesitated. "Three months."

Connie gasped. "That's not late. Those are missed periods. Have you seen a doctor?"

"No, not yet."

"Come on, Elizabeth, you might be pregnant. You do know that, don't you? This is not a sickness. You're not going to wake up some morning and be cured. Well, at least not for another six months. You've got to go see a doctor and get this confirmed." Connie paused to catch her breath. "I don't want to pry into your personal life, but is pregnancy a possibility? Have you been with somebody? If you are pregnant, there are things you should be doing. If you're not pregnant, then we should have you checked over. Throwing up every morning is not normal, otherwise."

Tears popped into Elizabeth's eyes and started running down her face. She had struggled to avoid the word *pregnancy* since missing her first period. Now Connie had used it four times in fifteen seconds. The reality of her situation could no longer be denied. "My father will kill me if he finds out. What am I going to do?"

Connie got up from the table, put her arms around the girl and gave her a gentle hug. "Oh honey, this is not the end of the world. Your father might surprise you. Still, you've got to see a doctor. Some important decisions must be made and delaying any longer will only limit your choices."

Elizabeth pushed Connie back. She had a look of shock on her face. "There are no decisions to be made. I have only one choice. I am going to have this baby."

Connie reached out for her again and pulled her close. "OK, there's one decision made already. Are you sure you've considered all the options? Have you told the father?"

The tears started to flow again. "I'm not going to tell the father. He has nothing to do with this. It's my baby and I will take care of it."

"So, you have given this some thought. You did know you were pregnant. Now that you've openly admitted it, you can get busy with what has to be done."

Connie stepped back to arm's length and looked Elizabeth in the eyes. "I'm here to help you, not judge you. You might want to reconsider telling the father. He has a right to know, too. Unless this was an immaculate conception, he did have something to do with it."

Elizabeth sat down at the kitchen table. "Oh, Connie. This is all messed up."

Connie sat across the table from her. Elizabeth averted her eyes. "He has gone to Alberta. I don't even know how to get in touch with him if I wanted to. I loved him once, but it's all over now. It was over before I knew I was pregnant. I don't want him involved with my baby or with me anymore. It's best if I keep his identity a secret. I don't want everybody around here second guessing my decisions."

Connie decided not to argue with Elizabeth at this time. There were too many other things to do. Elizabeth had to see a doctor. Her parents had to be told. She might choose not to tell the father, but living at home and not telling her parents would be an impossible feat.

Connie studied the girl a little closer. She hadn't started to show yet, but her breasts were becoming a little fuller. Even under loose, baggy T-shirts, Connie could see that taking place. It wouldn't be long before other changes followed. In another couple of months or so, it would be obvious to anyone who cared to look that Elizabeth had either gone on an eating binge or that she was pregnant. Every woman in the community would know the latter was the case.

"Look at me, Elizabeth. First things first. Let's confirm what we both suspect. We could be wrong. If that is the case, we have to find out why you are missing your periods. Have you tried one of those drug store kits or anything like that?"

Elizabeth shook her head and averted her eyes again.

"Let's do that while you're waiting for an appointment with your doctor," Connie said. "I'll call and set up a date. If you are sure you want to go through with this, we have to get you into prenatal classes. Who do you see?"

Again Elizabeth shook her head. "I've never been sick since we moved back here. I don't have a doctor."

"OK." This presented a problem. Most doctors Connie knew were not taking new patients. Her own was overbooked most of the time, which led to long waits every time Connie had to see her. "What about your parents? Who do they go to?"

"Same thing. Once or twice, Dad went to the clinic in Truro to get a prescription for antibiotics. Otherwise, we're all pretty healthy."

Connie got up and walked over to the telephone. She picked up the phone book and tossed it on the table in front of Elizabeth. If

Elizabeth insisted on becoming a mother, she had to start looking out for herself. "Find a family planning clinic somewhere close. We'll call them and make an appointment. I think there's a couple in Truro."

Connie leaned back against the kitchen counter. Elizabeth leafed through the phone book. For now, Connie respected the decisions her young friend had made. She would not push her for answers. Still, she wondered who the father could be. Elizabeth had lived in the area for less than a year. Connie couldn't recall seeing her with any one man in particular during that time. That didn't mean a special friend didn't exist. Elizabeth had been parachuted into the area for a few weeks every summer for as long as Connie could remember. Maybe one of those summer romances had bloomed into the winter season before breaking up with the spring thaw.

One other person briefly came to Connie's mind. She shook her head and dismissed that thought before it could even take root. Elizabeth said the father had gone to Alberta. She would know if that were the case. How many men would she have slept with? Connie had to admit times had changed since she had escaped her teen years.

Who were the young men who had recently left the area for work in the west? That thought produced a long list of candidates. Once the first boy had ventured out to the oil sands, filled his pockets with money and then returned home to spread the wealth around, there had been a general exodus. And that was only in Raymond's River. The same thing repeated itself in all the little communities around. Go to Halifax, go to Edmonton. It made little difference. Unless you planned on being a farmer, and few of the current generation did, your only choice after graduation required you to leave the area to look for greener pastures.

This annual migration west had been taking place for six or seven years now. She laughed to herself inwardly. Six or seven years didn't even come close to this annual out-migration. Only the current destinations of Alberta or B.C. fell into that time frame. Her grandparents and great-grandparents had started the trend. The

Boston States were their destination of choice. Later, when Connie
was younger, Ontario served as the new Promised Land. Now the oil
fields of the west held the new Holy Grail. Guessing the boy's name
from the clues she had so far proved impossible. She would have to
convince Elizabeth to talk to her. She needed to know for sure who
had fathered this baby.

"I have a number."

Elizabeth's voice broke into Connie's thoughts. She pointed to a
spot in the Yellow Pages.

"Good, honey. Let's give them a call."

CHAPTER 19

"A MASSIVE, CRUSHING force to the head killed him. It looks like he tumbled off the cliff head-first and hit a rock."

Dr. Jane Melnick held up an X-ray film for Scott to study. She pointed to the white area at the top of the skull. Dr. Melnick served as medical examiner for the province. She had conducted the autopsy on the body of Jason Browne.

"Prolonged periods of being immersed in the muddy water make it hard to analyze the wound to any degree. Every time the tide came in, his head would be underwater, and then the tide would go out and it would be baking in the sun. Dirt, sand and rocks would abrade the area with every new high tide."

"But do we know for sure that this is where he died?" Scott asked. "He wasn't hit on the head before he went over the bank?"

"The injuries are consistent with a fall from that height. We never found the actual rock he landed on. The landscape changes with every tide. A few times, with the higher tides, he would be totally submerged. The only reason he wasn't washed out to sea is that his foot was jammed between two larger rocks."

Detective-Sergeant Jim McDonald leaned back in his chair. He had already had this briefing before Scott's arrival. "Tell him why you think our taking-a-crap theory is full of shit."

Dr. Melnick rolled her eyes at the wording of the request. "Two things," she said. "The contents of his large bowel were not at a level that required evacuation."

She watched Scott's face blanch as he visualized how the doctor had come to that conclusion. There were some things the public didn't want to have first-hand knowledge of.

"And the second?" Scott asked to move the conversation along.

"There were blunt-force injuries to the front of the head, indicative of landing on a rock. The stones there have a sandy quality about them and the wound was full of sandstone. This would suggest that he had been facing the Bay when he took his dive. If he had been in a standard squatting position for a bowel movement, the injuries would have been to the back of his head."

"Couldn't he have flipped over in the air on the way down?"

"Not impossible, but highly unlikely. The fall was too short to do a complete flip. The photos from the scene show his feet facing the bank. A back flip would have had the feet facing the Bay."

Scott nodded his understanding. "That doesn't explain why he was half-naked. His pants were found snagged on the stump of a tree that had slid half-way down the bank. If his clothes were down around his ankles to start with, that should have broken his fall."

"You would think so," Jim said. "Now Doctor, tell him what Mr. Browne might have been doing instead." There was an evil sparkle in the sergeant's eyes.

Dr. Melnick placed the X-ray back into a folder on her desk and withdrew a printed document. "We found pre-seminal fluid in his penis."

"Pre-seminal fluid?"

"Mr. Browne had his rudder fully extended to guide his trip to oblivion," Jim said.

"He was standing on the bank, whacking himself off?" Scott shook his head.

"We don't know that," Dr. Melnick said. "We only know he was in the late stages of arousal."

"Jumped-up Jesus," Scott said. "This case gets weirder by the minute. Death by misadventure takes on a whole new meaning with this one. What do we think? He was standing there beating his meat and the bank gave way under his feet? No, if that happened he would have slid down the bank and not done a face plant at the bottom." The others could see Scott running through the various scenarios in his mind.

"Unless half-way down, he hung up on the stump, flipped over and then fell the rest of the way head-first. How far would you have to fall to crush your skull?"

"Not far. It would depend on the angle that you hit." The doctor looked over at Jim before continuing. "There's a problem with this idea. We found no scratches on the victim's legs. If he hung up on the stump, there would have been some scratches as the branch ran up his leg and snagged onto his pants. The condition of the body suggests that he went from top to bottom without encountering anything on the way down. His only injuries were to his head."

"OK," Scott said. "What if he was standing facing the Bay getting his self-induced jollies? In a moment of excited delirium, he topples forward, feet apart. His body misses the stump, but his pants snag it and his feet simply slip out on the way down. Had he been drinking?"

Dr. Melnick looked down at the report. "His blood level was 0.21. He would definitely be unsteady on his feet. At that level, achieving an erection would require a lot of work on his part as well."

"Sounds good to me," Scott said. "Case closed. I've got to get back to my real job."

"Not so fast, partner." Jim put a hand on Scott's arm to keep him in his chair. "At least two other possibilities come to mind. Your scenario with him facing the Bay, pants around his ankles, works for me. But what if, instead of falling, someone comes up behind him and pushes him over the bank? We're looking at a homicide in that instance."

Scott shook his head. "I don't even want to hear these wild ideas. You homicide guys are always trying to complicate things. Not every death is a murder." He hesitated for a few seconds, a smile on his face, waiting for Jim to continue. "All right," he finally said, "what's the other idea you've cooked up?"

"A sign of a true detective. Always searching for the truth. This is the really simple one. He already had his pants off for some reason or other and someone threw him over the bank face first."

"No," Scott said. "That doesn't wash. There would have been signs of a struggle, other injuries. Why would he have his pants off?"

"Now who's complicating things? The lack of other injuries suggests he had help. A mere fall would have given him scratches and contusions. To completely clear the bank the way he did, he must have had some extra force pushing him out there, giving him momentum."

Jim looked over at Dr. Melnick. "Can you be sure the blow to the head didn't come before he went over the bank? Maybe somebody hit him first, then threw him over."

"That's not impossible. The site of the injury has been so degraded by the tides and sand that we can't definitively rule that out. All the sharp edges of the wound have been sanded smooth. The way he was hanging allowed the head to absorb most of the wave action."

Jim sat quietly, pondering this new information before speaking again. "Maybe he made a pass at a straight guy. Some men get upset by that. Dr. Melnick has determined there was no sign of sexual penetration in Browne's rectum. That sort of rules out a gay encounter."

Scott picked up the the report. "It does not, however, rule out the possibility that there was a woman involved and the boyfriend came along. The upset lover might have felt totally justified in dispatching the sexual attacker over the cliff. In that case, both members of the couple would feel it in their best interest to keep the matter hush hush. She being a possible rape victim; he being a potential killer."

Jim put his hand on Scott's shoulder, excitement in his voice. "Now you're thinking. Those are some ideas to get you started. As I said earlier, you know the people; you know the area. I'm going to need your help on this. I need you to pick through all these possibilities and find out what actually happened to Jason Browne."

Scott put down the report and picked up the X-ray and pretended to study it. Noticing his concentration, Dr. Melnick leaned in, ready to answer any questions Scott might have, or to see if the Mountie had come up with something she had missed. Instead, Scott looked over at the sergeant.

"You never give up, do you? I don't want to join your little cadre of detectives. I know you don't understand it, but I'm happy doing what I'm doing." He paused. "I'll help you out this time because I can see you will never solve this thing without me. And that means you'll forever be around here bugging me and keeping me from my real work." He waved a finger at the detective. "But this usurping of my position has to stop."

A smile lit up Jim's face. "All right. Just this one time."

Both men knew that wouldn't be true.

CHAPTER 20

ANTHONY PICNIC PARK had turned into an ocean of brilliant colour — in constant motion and yet not moving. Instead of white caps on blue water, it was red hats on green grass. Beneath the sun hats were all sizes and variations of purple T-shirts and blouses. Picnic baskets were being emptied onto tables. Drinks were being poured. Laughter and chatter filled the air. The Red Hatters were having their annual July picnic.

Slogans abounded on the T-shirts. "I still ride my bicycle, TOO" said one. The letters in TOO were larger and had a frenzied look about them.

"I don't understand what that means," Veronica Thompson said to Joan McNeil. "Why is there a 'TOO' at the end of the sentence and why is it bigger?" The picture lurking above the bold letters showed an elderly woman on a bicycle. Both feet were off the pedals and the legs were spread up and forward. The smile on the caricature's face was larger than the face itself.

Eighty-three-year-old Joan proudly thrust her well-developed but sagging bosom forward. "Honey, if you don't understand it, I won't be able to explain it to you. There are some things you never forget how to do once you've mastered how to do them." She elbowed Bertha Melanson sitting beside her and they both burst into laughter.

"That's true about riding bikes, too," Bertha said and they both let out another gale of laughter.

Veronica, a life-time spinster, sat with a confused look on her face. Finally she joined the laughter as well. Both women knew Veronica was still in the dark.

T-shirt slogans, however, were not the main topic of discussion at the picnic. Anthony Park stood a few miles down the shore from the area where Jason Browne's body had been discovered. The beach at the park was a continuation of the beach at the foot of the bank. It had been less than a week since the discovery.

"I've heard he was naked as a jay bird when they found him," Veronica said. A blush crept into her face at the mere use of the word naked.

"That's not all," Sarah Densmore said. Sarah sat at the next table over. She leaned towards Veronica, Joan and Bertha in a conspiratorial manner. She looked to her left and to her right before speaking. "I hear his pecker was cut off and stuck in his mouth." She gave an emphatic nod.

Veronica gasped.

The lady beside Sarah joined in the conversation. "It all has to do with drugs. What's that one the young people use at parties? They call it the love drug."

"Ecstasy," said Sarah. "People say he sold it at the high school."

"Pills," Joan said, disgust in her voice. "I sure never needed any pills when I was that age to reach ecstasy. Kids today can't do anything for themselves."

"No," Sarah said. "The boys buy them and slip them to the girls without them knowing about it. Can't be bothered to do a little honest courting to get what they want. Now when I was a girl..."

"When you were a girl, a caveman whacked you over the head with a club and dragged you off to his cave." Joan's shrill laughter rang out across the park. All eyes turned their way. A few more ladies drifted over to join the discussion.

"You can make jokes if you want to," Sarah said, "but I hear one of the fathers of a girl who had been victimized by the drugs killed him. He could be one of our neighbours."

"That's not true." A new voice entered the conversation. Margaret Stillman worked at the municipal office. She spoke with an air of authority. "It was a warning to other drug dealers to keep out of this area. There's a gang that operates up the shore and they think they are the only ones who can sell drugs in this area. Jason Browne tried cutting into their territory. He was a warning to all the others. Let them kill each other off, I say. It saves our tax dollars for more important things."

Joan looked across the field to another table several feet away. Pamela Wilson was holding court at that table. She could see Pamela's head bobbing up and down as she talked. No doubt she was setting everyone straight as to what had happened. She lowered her voice.

"The man was dead for a couple of months."

"End of April, I heard."

Joan nodded. "That's the same time that George Wilson disappeared." She looked into the eyes of the others at the table. "Does anybody but me find that suspicious?"

Veronica let out a small scream and then quickly covered her mouth. "You think George killed the man?"

"I didn't say that." Joan beat a hasty retreat. "He might be the killer or maybe he was involved with Jason Browne selling pills and got knocked off too. Maybe they just haven't found his body yet."

Margaret leaned into the centre of the table so the others could hear her lowered voice. "I know a number of the farmers are having trouble meeting their tax bills. Things haven't rebounded yet from the mad cow scare. If it wasn't for my job with the municipality, my Bill would have trouble making his payments."

There were nods of agreement around the table.

"But George, involved with drugs?" Veronica shook her head.

"We all know he's familiar enough with liquor," Sarah said. "Drugs are not a big leap from that. Desperate times; desperate measures."

The table fell silent.

The ladies at Pamela Wilson's table were indeed talking about the gruesome discovery. Pamela was describing the anguish that swept over her when she heard a body had been found at the nearby shore.

"The first I heard of it was on the radio. I was listening to Cat Country when the news came on. All they said was that a body had been discovered washed up in the Bay. They gave no name, no other details. Let me tell you, I almost fainted dead away on the spot."

Heads nodded in a sympathetic gesture.

"When I got control of myself, I called Connie to warn her. I didn't want her to get the same shock that I had. It was all I could do to see the phone pad through my tears."

"Did she have her radio on?"

"I'm not sure. She sounded surprised, but she asked me where the body was found and then assured me it wasn't George. At that point, she didn't know who it was either. She sounded so confident that I was able to relax a little. Someone must have called her before me. The whole thing aged me about twenty years."

"The cops would have phoned her as soon as the body was found and they knew it wasn't George. You came to the obvious conclusion. Naturally, you'd think it was your son. I would have thought that, for sure. So would Connie if they hadn't called her."

Another voice chimed up. "I knew about it before the radio broadcast the news. I thought about calling you both. Whoever told me said a stranger had been found, not George. They didn't know who, but the word of the discovery spread fast. 'Is it George Wilson?' is the first question everyone asked." She lowered her eyes. "I should have called you."

Sparks replaced the grief in Pamela's eyes. "It wasn't your job to call me. The police should have phoned. Those sons of bitches called Connie but didn't call me. His mother. Don't they think a mother has feelings? I can understand Connie being too upset to phone me. That damn Mountie should have made the phone call, not Connie. He never liked me from the time we met in Connie's kitchen. I told him to stop talking and get out and do his job. You all heard me. Now, he's trying to get even with me. Well, mister, let me tell you, I'm going to tell him a thing or two."

Pamela's face and hat merged into one solid colour.

One of the ladies reached out a hand and placed it on Pamela's shoulder. "Now, now dear. Just calm down. You don't want to have a heart attack over this. The good news is that it wasn't George's body they found. At least you can be thankful for that."

Tears burst from Pamela's eyes. Her whole body shook with the sobs. She pulled a tissue from her purse. "These last few months have been so hard. I just wish it was over. I wish George would come home."

The others at the table exchanged glances. You could read the message in their eyes. That would be a nice conclusion to the whole episode, but many didn't see that happening any time soon, if ever. Fortunately, Pamela was in no condition to read eyes and no one put their thoughts into words. Sometimes reality was too hard to face.

CHAPTER 21

Late September

CAL LINDSAY LEANED back in the Adirondack chair on his front lawn. The early afternoon September sun felt good on his milk-chocolate-coloured face. His life had settled into a calm, comfortable routine. Most days found him outside absorbing the rays of the summer sun. His dark complexion led some people in the community to speculate that there had been an Indian in the wood pile at some point in Cal's ancestry.

He had been up when the first red rays of the morning cracked over the horizon and in the woods to start processing that day's orders for firewood. This early start was necessary to beat the heat of the day and the worst of the black flies and mosquitoes. Routinely, he would put in a full morning working on the woodlot. When things went well, he would then relax over a brown-bag lunch before delivering a load to the client and collecting the money.

The money. That was the driving force behind the entire procedure. The exercise was good. The fresh air was good. But let's not try to kid anybody; both he and Connie looked forward to the financial rewards reaped by this regular routine.

Often Connie surprised him at his work site with a more elaborate lunch than the plain cheese sandwiches that he slapped together every morning. They would enjoy the solitude of the forest while eating, maybe discussing the business or maybe just philosophizing about life in general.

Connie believed she had an eye for scaling a stand of trees. Scaling was judging the number of usable cords of wood that could be taken from a particular part of the forest. Keeping in mind the principles of good silviculture, she would make recommendations as to where Cal might want to cut next when one area of trees become depleted. Her assessments were sometimes uncanny in their accuracy. At other times, her guesses were way out in left field. Cal seldom argued with her choices. He allowed her appraisals to influence where he cut next as long as her estimates promised a reasonable return on the time expended.

Afternoons, when the weather was fine, like today, would find Cal asleep in this chair outside. Sometimes, he slept for up to three hours at a time. This depended on how his other business had gone the night before. There were some nights when those clients wanted to hang around until two or even three in the morning. Cal never turned them away.

His bootlegging enterprise failed to bring in the money that his summer wood-cutting efforts had netted, but the occupation proved to be steady and reliable. It was steady because those in search of drink knew that they could depend on Cal to provide liquor when they really needed it. During the day, the same people would frequent the government-run establishments. They were seldom under stress when they made those purchases. When the night demons were chasing them and only a shot of strong spirits would save their soul, they came knocking on Cal's kitchen door. Cal stood out as their salvation and saviour. They were his faithful flock.

He was just beginning to nod off when the sound of a vehicle intruded into his subconscious. His eyes fluttered open and he leaned forward in his chair. A red half-ton wound its way up his driveway.

Cal looked at his watch to see if he had actually been asleep and didn't know it. He hadn't.

"Who in the hell is this and what do they want at this time of day?" he asked of no one. He practised his stern face. He wanted to transmit his annoyance without actually putting it into words. He didn't want to discourage business, simply to control the hours when it arrived.

The truck pulled up in front of the house out of Cal's sight. He didn't get up. He heard the door slam. Then the smiling face of Brian Cosh popped around the corner.

"Afternoon, Cal," Brian said, a smile lighting up his face. "One honey of a day."

Despite himself, Cal smiled back. "Yeah, Chief, it's a beaut. What brings you out here?" Cal felt positive Brian hadn't dropped by to be neighbourly; he got right to the point.

Brian smiled at the abruptness of the statement. You were never going to fool Cal with small talk. He had had too many people try to con him out of a free drink by trying to appear to be his best buddy. He had a way of sensing when people had something other than chit-chat on their mind.

"I was wondering about Connie. How's she doing?"

Cal's eyes opened wide. "Connie? Why are you asking me?"

"You're in business with her. You see her on a regular basis. How's she doing?"

"Chief, you see her almost as much as I do. You're forever over there helping out around the barn. Why not ask her?"

Brian nodded. "I have. All I get back are platitudes. 'I'm fine.' 'Things are OK.' That sort of thing. What's your take on how she's handling all of this?"

"Well, Chief. Her husband walked out on her without a word and no income unless she worked damn hard to make one. How would you take that?"

Brian shook his head. "I don't believe that's true. I've known George all his life. He drank too much. He could be self-centred. He might even be abusive from time to time, but I don't think he walked out on Connie." He paused for a few seconds; his stare penetrated the glare coming back from Cal. "He's dead. There's no doubt in my mind of that. Connie soon has to start thinking that way as well."

Cal said nothing, but didn't release the lock on Brian's eyes. His views of George differed greatly from those of the chief. Cal usually met George when he had had way too much to drink and was looking for more. Under those circumstances, people often said things they didn't say in polite company. Not only were their principles relaxed, but they often became morose and confided in their bootlegger as if he were their bartender, shrink or priest. Professions where confidentiality was expected. Cal usually obliged.

This fact left Cal with a moral dilemma of his own. Could he, or should he, breach George's confidentiality? It had been quite a while since George had staggered up to Cal's door, but it used to be a regular occurrence. George said he came to bury himself in a bottle because his wife had locked him out of their bedroom and he couldn't bury himself in her. That would bring a chuckle from the other drinkers assembled in Cal's kitchen. Most weekends saw all six kitchen chairs filled and sometimes folks sitting on the kitchen counters.

A little encouragement was all George needed to get him talking. He would describe in more detail than a husband ever should his bedroom athletics with his wife. The others would ooh and ahh at the appropriate spots. Cal could swear some of them were practically masturbating under the table at George's vivid descriptions. It often sounded like George was reading aloud from letters in the Penthouse Forum.

Every so often, George would look over at Cal and wink. Then he'd say something like: "You know what I mean, Cal. You had a go at Connie before I came on the scene and took her away. I'm the one who won the trophy wife."

At times like this, Cal struggled to remain in his chair. His instincts demanded he beat the crap out of this braggart. Then, he'd remember his father's words of advice:

"There are no percentages in getting into a fight with a bunch of drunks. Words may have power, but they don't break noses and they don't blacken eyes. Anything said in the wee hours of the morning will be lost in the alcoholic fog of lost memories the next day."

Cal would suck it up and say something like: "That just goes to show that the best man doesn't always win." George would stare at him, laugh and then continue with his narration. The others were oblivious to this by-play. They were too wrapped up in listening to George's stories, vicariously getting involved in the action themselves.

Maybe his father was wrong about no one remembering what took place in these alcohol-driven story sessions. Cal definitely remembered. Of course, Cal was the exception to the rule at these parties. He remained sober.

This resulted from another piece of advice his father had given him during his educational phase before turning the business over to him: "There's no gain in drinking up the profits. Stay sober, son, and you won't be giving anything away for free. The profits will be yours. This is a business we run."

Cal allowed himself a maximum of two beers a night. These he nurtured so as to always appear to be drinking along with the others. When anyone offered to buy him a beer, he simply thanked them and pocketed the money. With Cal, everything was cash up front. He didn't run a tab for anybody. His father had been a good teacher.

Now that Brian was forcing him to think back on these events, Cal wondered if someone else had remembered the stories George relished telling and retelling. Had they remembered some of the graphic details and the disharmony George complained about? And if they had, had these details somehow gotten back to Brian?

About ten months or so before he disappeared, George had stopped showing up for his regular spot at the table. There was never any explanation, not that Cal expected one. There had always been breaks of a couple of months at a time when he would climb on the wagon, but George always succumbed, until this last time, almost a year. If killing a kid hadn't totally stopped him from drinking, Cal wondered what had made him pack it in this time.

Had Connie clipped his wings because she found out she was the star character in the bedroom monologues? That was possible. Cal knew that Connie had no fear of George.

Cal measured his words carefully. He was not one to tell tales out of school.

"I'm not so sure of that, Chief. If things were going bad, he may have just thrown in the towel and moved on. He could be a real bastard some of the time. It was a side of him that he hid from the good citizens of Raymond's River. To those of us who didn't fit that description, he let it all hang out."

Now it was Brian's turn to be surprised.

"I'm not sure I follow you, Cal."

Cal shifted in his chair while he tried to find the right words to continue.

"They liked to present the image of hometown jock and high school queen getting married and living happily ever after together. That, my friend, was not always the case. You've got kids, Chief. Most married couples do. Not Connie and George. Ever wonder why?"

Brian shook his head. "To be honest, I never have."

"You know what I think? I think the idea of bailing out was always lurking somewhere below the horizon in George's thinking. Connie's too. Kids would be a complication. I think George looked on Connie as more of a triumph than a lifelong companion."

"A triumph?"

"Yeah, a triumph. 'Look at me. I've bagged the home-coming queen.' On more than one occasion, he referred to her as his trophy wife. Just my opinion, but you did ask for it."

"Did Connie tell you any of this?"

"Hell no, Chief, and I haven't told her what I think, either. I'd be surprised if she didn't suspect it some of the time. Connie's not a stupid woman."

He sat up straighter in his chair and pointed to a six-dollar plastic Wal-Mart chair nearby on the lawn. "Pull up a chair, Chief."

Brian retrieved the chair and sat facing Cal.

"You think you know George quite well," Cal continued. "Maybe you do. It's the sober George that you know or at least the nearly sober George. I've met that George. I've even worked with him. I'm not convinced that is the real George. The one I know best is usually half in the bag, sometimes totally in the bag. Many a night, I've tucked him into a spare cot because he was in no shape to go home. In the morning, he would be apologetic, couldn't remember anything he had said the night before and would be anxious to get home to Connie and become the George you knew."

Cal raised his index finger and gently waved it towards Brian. "The question is, Chief, which was the real George? The one you knew or the one I knew? More importantly, which one disappeared? If it is your boy, you may be right. He could be dead. If it's my version of the man, then he's drunk in some bar in some other part of the country, crying in his beer and pouring out his story to some disinterested barkeep on how life has treated him badly."

Cal gave a dismissive shrug of his shoulders. "Either way, he's gone."

"Didn't you work most of last summer for George operating his skidder?"

"I worked for your George, the sober one. He paid well. We got along together well. It worked out for both of us. He appeared to have stopped drinking at the time. I think of them as two separate men in the same body. He was a little schizo, maybe."

Brian shifted uneasily in his chair. "Maybe you're right. I've spent some time with his mother lately. She visits Connie a lot, as you know. She could make anyone a little schizo."

"You've got that right, brother," Cal agreed.

CHAPTER 22

"I'VE EXHAUSTED EVERY lead," Corporal Scott Bowen explained to Detective-Sergeant Jim McDonald. "Jason Browne last appeared in downtown Raymond's River on May 2nd, according to the local fire chief, Brian Cosh. Brian remembers the date because it ties in to a search effort we were having for another local resident. He also remembers Jason Browne because the man had destroyed a bunch of stuff at the fire hall. According to the chief, 'One minute he was there, the next he was gone.' No one else remembers seeing him after that."

"Right, I remember the search for the farmer. Did he ever show up?"

"Never. Disappeared without a trace. I'm suspecting alien abduction."

Jim looked up from the walnut cruller on his plate, a surprised look on his face at that revelation. Scott's smile spread from ear to ear.

"Gotcha," Scott said, then turned serious again. "Still, I can't really offer you any better explanation on either case. Both men disappeared without a trace within a couple of weeks of each other. I've spent a little better than two months talking to everyone who might know Jason Browne. A man from the Noel Shore dropped Browne off outside the pharmacy in Raymond's River. That's where the chief saw him.

"This man said Browne had been drinking and flashing some cash around. He picked him up hitchhiking. When you recovered the body two months later, there was no money on him, according to your report."

"No, his wallet was in his pants pocket, but it was devoid of cash. That's how the member at the scene was able to make the quick identification. He recognized the name on his ID and then, armed with that information, was able to identify the body even after it had been exposed to the elements for two months."

Scott nodded. He had read the reports, several times. "That was the second reference made to a sizable amount of cash in Browne's possession. Tommy Watson, a high school kid, saw him at the local diner trying to impress the girls with his money. That led me to believe robbery was the motive, but it didn't help me any in advancing the case. The money was missing, but there were a couple of credit cards still inside. Nowadays, just about anybody can get a credit card. I checked out Browne's. Both were maxed out, but a thief wouldn't know that.

"Besides the credit cards, Browne had a couple of gold chains around his neck. They were the real thing and gold is pretty easy to unload these days. Seems to lead away from the robbery theory.

"He must have met someone between the time he left Raymond's River and when he ended up at the foot of the cliff to whom he either owed money," Scott held up his forefinger. "Or bought something from." Up went the next finger. "Or a drug deal gone bad." The ring finger rose. "Who knows?" He raised both hands in front of his face and shrugged.

He took a sip of his coffee. "This fellow who had picked Browne up said another thing I found interesting."

Jim stared at Scott, inviting him to continue.

"Browne said more money would flow from this source. He owned a cash cow. But when pushed, he supplied the man with no further details. He dismissed the story as the idle bragging of a drunk. Browne, he said, was notorious for his story-telling. Always had some big deal just about to hatch."

Now it was Jim's turn to look thoughtful. "Did you ever discover where this small-time hood came into his windfall?"

"I had my suspicions. One of his actual convictions was for grand theft auto. He stole the car and sold it to the owners of a local chop shop. I interviewed them. They denied ever knowing Browne, even when I confronted them with the evidence of the previous conviction. 'That must have been the former owners,' they said. 'The business is now a legitimate parts supplier and junk yard.' Of course, that was a load of bull crap."

"Any cars reported stolen in the area?"

"None that I could find locally. That doesn't mean he didn't go farther afield. Like everything else in this case, it proved to be another dead end."

Scott bit into his doughnut, chewed briefly and continued. "Another theory I've unsuccessfully run into the ground deals with drugs. If Browne were peddling crack cocaine for some other source, sold it and blew the money on himself, that would account for both the wad of cash and his sudden fall over the cliff. Justice can be swift with some of those gangs. Again, I came up blank."

A silence fell over the two men as they sipped their coffee. Both were running possible scenarios through their heads, ruling them out and moving on to think of another possibility. Finally the sergeant broke the silence.

"Tell me again about the alien abduction theory."

"Crop circles were found on a nearby farm," Scott said, without skipping a beat. "Inside the area, we found numerous pointed cleft footprints left by the invaders. Problem was, the local farmer believed they were deer tracks. He was applying for a permit to shoot them out of season. But seriously, I hate to give up on this case because I find it intriguing. The thing is, there is no place else to go with the investigation. For now, it's going to go to the back burner. I'll keep an ear open in case I hear anything, but…" Scott passed a file over to the sergeant "…the ball is back in your court."

Jim reluctantly took the file and flipped it open. It had grown since he conveyed it to Scott in early July. He rifled though the various pages. Most contained interview notes; the page on top tied all the other pages together. At the bottom, typed in capital letters, stood the final summary: ACCIDENT OR HOMICIDE? NO CONCLUSIVE EVIDENCE EITHER WAY.

Jim dropped the folder on the table and made a dismissive motion with his hands. "I appreciate all the work you put into this. Sometimes a mystery is just that: a mystery."

"It wasn't a total loss. I got to meet a lot of people in the area in an unthreatening way. Everyone had heard the rumours about Browne's death and was eager to talk with me. I dispelled some of the wilder versions of the stories that were circulating."

"The satanic rituals and gang killings?"

"Yeah, those types of things. The one that really took hold suggested his penis had been cut off and shoved into his mouth. People liked to believe that story, especially when they tied it in to Browne selling Ecstasy pills or crack. They wanted to believe justice was served. I'm not sure I convinced everyone it didn't happen."

"Who knows? It may act as a deterrent to some up-and-coming pill pusher. Stories like these take on a life of their own and soon become urban legends. We'll have this story being repeated all over the country within a year. Everyone will swear they know a friend of the guy who actually killed the punk junkie, or the outraged father who dispensed justice for every other outraged father out there. That unknown man will become a folk hero."

"Jesus, Sergeant. Now you've got me believing it happened. Are you the one who starts these tales?"

Jim slid out of his chair and stood up. He tapped the file covering the death of Jason Browne on the table. With no family or friends to push for its resolution, these pages would join the ranks of other unsolved deaths in the cold-case file.

CHAPTER 23

P AMELA WILSON LEANED into the table and lowered her voice. "Connie, your young friend there is in a family way."

Elizabeth Schofield had disappeared into the bathroom for the second time since Pamela had arrived. Despite her loose-fitting, bleached cotton top popular in the sixties, worn over a billowing pair of blue shorts, hiding her condition became harder and harder with each passing day. To date, only three other people were in on her secret, four if you counted her doctor. Connie had insisted early on that Elizabeth bring her parents into the picture. To Elizabeth's surprise, they had been very supportive.

Her father, Paul, found Elizabeth's refusal to reveal the name of the baby's father the most upsetting aspect of the event. He believed the man should contribute to her expenses. He also believed the man had a right to know about his impending fatherhood. But the more Paul pushed for a name, the more stubborn Elizabeth became. She simply refused to cooperate.

Paul doted on his two children. He wanted only the best for them and the thought of having the sounds of little feet running around the farm house had him excited. He would be a good grandfather. Most grandfathers he knew claimed that if they had known being a grandfather would be so much fun, they would have had their grandchildren first.

Elizabeth had been both surprised and relieved at the reaction of her parents. Still, she had no desire to announce the news to the whole world yet. The timing of that announcement would soon be out of her hands. The developing baby growing inside her had its own schedule. Maintaining her secret would soon demand she stay completely out of sight from the rest of the community.

Elizabeth's mother had also been keeping a low profile around Raymond's River. Although the discussion had never actually been held by the family members, the possibility that Elizabeth might have a new sister instead of a new daughter loomed high in her parents' minds. The more Elizabeth refused to give up the name of the child's father, the more Paul thought it might be wise for him and his wife to claim parentage of the baby. Late forties might push the bounds of believability, but not beyond the realm of possibility.

Elizabeth's little visit to Connie's house would, however, wipe out the eventuality of that miracle of birth taking place. Pamela Wilson had never, even remotely, been described as a discreet person. For Pamela, secrets were meant to be shared. So much the better if she were the one doing the sharing. She enjoyed the power she received from knowing something that someone else didn't. She never held this power for long. Pamela was an extreme gossip.

Connie looked over at the bathroom door. She could deny what her mother-in-law had observed, but to what purpose? The truth would soon be out. Even if Elizabeth were to go back to visit friends in Ontario, have the baby, then return, Pamela would now spread the word among her own peers. These folks were the parents or grandparents of Elizabeth's friends. Raymond's River had a small-town mentality. Trying to cover up the birth would be a mistake, especially in these times when having children out of wedlock occurred commonly. Still, Connie said nothing. It was not her job to reveal Elizabeth's secret.

Pamela leaned closer. "You must know this is true. Who is the father? How far along is she? What do her parents think?"

"Slow down, Mother," Connie said. "You don't even know for sure that you're right."

"Of course I'm right. All the signs are there." She paused. "Never having had children of your own, you wouldn't recognize them."

Connie looked up as if she had been slapped across the face. Her green eyes burned into those of her mother-in-law. "Sometimes it's time to put an end to the deficiencies in the gene pool," she said.

Now it was Pamela's turn to look hurt. Anger surged in her voice. "Are you saying my George would not have made a good father?"

Connie struggled to get a grip on her own temper. She failed. "It depends on whether or not you want to raise children with a drunk as a father."

Connie could see that remark stung. Pamela's voice returned to its normal volume. "My George was not a drunk. True, sometimes he drank a little too much, but so does everyone else once in a while. Even you."

Connie took a deep breath and let it out slowly. She could see that even after all this time, Pamela was struggling to make sense of George's disappearance.

"I'm sorry, Mother. Whenever I think about George, I go a little squirrelly. I know how much you must miss him."

Pamela lowered her eyes. "We both do. I'm sorry, too."

She looked over at the closed bathroom door. "But that doesn't change what I said about Elizabeth. You'd have to be blind not to see it."

Across the room, the bathroom door opened. A red-faced Elizabeth emerged. "See what, Mrs. Wilson? That I'm 'in a family way'?"

Elizabeth turned sideways, offering her profile to the two women across the room. She pulled her cotton top down tight against her body-revealing her swollen abdomen.

"This is a miracle from God. I'm not ashamed of it."

Pamela's face flushed at the perceived rudeness of the young girl. Connie could see her hackles rise, again.

"Of course it is, dear," Connie said before her mother-in-law had a chance to make a retort. "It's just that you caught Pamela off guard with your condition. Isn't that right, Mother?"

Pamela glared over at Connie, then, following Connie's previous example, she took a deep breath before looking back at Elizabeth. A distorted smile fixed itself on her face. "You surprised me, my dear. How far along are you?"

Elizabeth's defiant look dropped off her like a mantle falling to the floor. She knew the eventual questions would all be asked. How far along? How are you feeling? Do you know if it's a boy or a girl? And the clincher: Who is the father?

"Six months, give or take a little. The doctor says I'm doing fine. She's done an amnio but I don't know if it's a boy or a girl. I don't want to know until it happens."

Pamela smiled at the last statement. "In my day, we never had the option of knowing. That was part of the excitement. Still, it makes buying shower gifts easier if you know whether to buy blue or pink." Pamela hesitated for a few beats. "What does the father think about not knowing? Men are usually anxious to know if they are going to have a son and heir."

Elizabeth looked at Connie. Connie had warned her this question would come up over and over again. She had done everything in her power to convince Elizabeth to bring the father into the picture. Connie gave her a knowing look, but didn't bail her out of the situation. Elizabeth would have to get used to dealing with her decision.

"I haven't told him. I'm doing this on my own."

Pamela's eyebrows raised up into her forehead. She slowly shook her head. "I know this is a new age when women are taking charge of everything. But there are still some things you can't do on your own. Having a baby is one of them. Somewhere back at the beginning of this journey, a man had to be involved. You don't have the right to exclude him. It's his baby, too."

Elizabeth was surprised at the forthright opinion expressed by Pamela. Others had argued with her — Connie, her father — but Pamela wasn't presenting her views as an argument. She was presenting them as a fact. What right had this old woman to dictate terms to her?

"You're wrong about that. This is my baby and I can decide who I will and who I won't tell." Her voice got shriller and higher as she reached the end of the statement.

Connie stood up, ready to intervene in the impending argument. To her surprise, Pamela remained calm at the challenge that had been thrust at her. Pamela lowered her voice.

"You can hide the name from the rest of us, but surely you can't expect the father to remain oblivious of the facts. Unless you are sleeping around with everything in pants," and here Pamela held up her hands in a placating manner, "which I know isn't true, he will do the same math as everyone else. He will know he is the father. Will he step up and do the right thing? I don't know. You are making it harder on him to do that by denying his existence."

Only the ticking of the kitchen clock broke the silence in the room. It counted off the seconds before Elizabeth responded to Pamela's quiet approach. Tears suddenly exploded from her eyes. She ran across the room and into Connie's outstretched arms.

"You know I can't tell him about the baby." Elizabeth looked down at Pamela to explain. "He's gone west and I don't know how to contact him. He doesn't even know the baby exists."

"Well, surely his family can tell you where he is. His family will want to share in the joyous occasion just like everyone else."

Sobs wracked Elizabeth's body. "No, I can't tell his family. They don't want to know about this baby. I can never tell them."

The two older women exchanged glances over Elizabeth's head. "Why not?" Connie asked. This was a new part of the story to her. She could think of only one reason why the family wouldn't want to know about a new baby. She didn't like the implication.

Pamela reached out and took Elizabeth's hand and looked up into her tear-filled eyes. "Excuse me for asking, but is he married?" Depend on Pamela to cut to the crux of the matter.

A new rush of tears escaped down Elizabeth's face. She slowly nodded her head. That was the best she could do. She could not put the indignity into words.

Connie pulled the young girl tighter into her grip. Oh, you poor baby, she thought. What have you gotten yourself into?

CHAPTER 24

PAMELA WILSON WAS beside herself with excitement. She had commandeered the front passenger seat, riding shotgun as the kids put it, in Mable Booth's old Pontiac. Two other women, decked out in red hats and purple dresses, occupied the back seat. The four were on their way to a supper meeting at a Truro restaurant.

As of yet, Pamela had told no one of Elizabeth Schofield's pregnancy. That news in itself would give her star billing as the gossip mill started churning at the Red Hat Society meeting. The additional fact that the father was a married man from the local or near-local area would make sure no one could top her exclusive reporting. She would hold that information back until the excitement of the baby news started to dwindle, then she would surge to the forefront again.

She struggled to fight back the urge to tell the others in the car with her. The words wanted to bubble out of her mouth.

She would have lots of time to develop the story to its fullest because Mable would never be confused with Dale Earnhardt or even with Dale Jr. when she got behind the wheel of her car. While most people considered the speed limit to be the posted amount plus ten, Mable drove the posted amount minus ten. Still, if Pamela spilled the beans to these women in the car, one of them might usurp her story before she could extoll it to the full membership over dinner. Reluctantly, she opted to wait.

Connie had been presumptuous enough to suggest that Pamela not mention the joyous occasion until Elizabeth herself had a chance to spread the word. Pamela had considered Connie to be a controlling person ever since she had latched on to her son. On more than one occasion, Pamela had pointed out to others that Connie would not serve on any committee in the community unless she had an executive position. Only a couple of people had bothered to try to point out to her that it was the other way around. If Connie served on a committee, the other members pushed her to take the leadership role.

Connie's admonition would not serve as a detriment to Pamela's exclusive. She counted herself lucky that she had a Red Hat meeting come up before any of Connie's various club outings. Pamela would be the first to spread the word.

"I've heard some exciting news this week," she said to Mable.

Mable glanced over at her and quickly returned her attention to the road. She had both hands on the steering wheel in the standard ten-to-two position. Her white knuckles continually sawed the wheel back and forth in short strokes. The steering on the Pontiac was loose enough that the passengers weren't constantly rocked back and forth by the action.

Her nephew, Ralph, tried to convince her the new hand position was nine and three, but Mable would have none of that. She had been driving for over forty years and her late husband, Gerald, had taught her this technique. It suited her fine.

"What's that, dear?" Mable managed to get out without losing her concentration on her driving. She didn't look at Pamela when she spoke.

"I can't tell you yet. I'm saving it for the full meeting."

Mable tightened her grip on the steering wheel. "OK, dear. I guess I'll have to wait."

Pamela frowned at the elderly driver. She had hoped for a more inquisitive reaction.

Joan McNeil leaned forward from the back seat. "Has one of our members gotten a new boyfriend? Some of them definitely need to get laid. It will improve their disposition." Her cackling laugh reverberated throughout the car.

Pamela turned and snapped at Joan. "It's not about any of our members."

"Whoa, somebody needs to get laid." Joan nudged prim and proper Veronica Thompson in the ribs. "Right, Veronica?"

Veronica's face flamed brighter than her hat, but she remained silent.

"Don't be so crude, Joan. There's more to life than sex." Pamela kept her eyes straight ahead, refusing to look at the smirking Joan.

Joan waggled her finger in Pamela's direction. "Spoken like someone who isn't getting any. Come on, tell us your gossip. You're busting a gut to get it off your chest."

Pamela turned again to scowl at Joan. Mable took a quick peek in her direction. "Why don't you tell us now, dear? We'll act surprised when you tell everyone else at the restaurant."

Pamela looked over at her and smiled. "Really I shouldn't. Connie doesn't think I should tell anyone at all."

From the back seat, Joan spoke up again. "Guess who's pregnant?"

Pamela wheeled around, hardly believing her ears. "Would you stop interrupting. I'm trying to have a discussion with Mable."

"My great-granddaughter, Sheila, is going to have a baby. I'll be a great-great-grandmother."

"A great-great-grandmother?" Veronica said. "How can that be? You don't look a day over fifty."

Joan nudged Veronica with her elbow again. "You're so kind, my dear. I do look damn good for someone of the plus side of eighty. Do you want to know my secret?"

The others groaned.

"It's no secret, dearie," Mable said. "Everyone knows how you do it. When is the baby due?"

"She should be born somewhere around Easter. I just hope I'm around to see it. They've promised to name her after me. Emma Joan. If I die off, her maternal grandmother is campaigning to have her name used. Madeline. I have to hang on just to prevent that from happening to the poor child. Madeline is such an old-fashioned name."

"We were talking about my news," Pamela said, her voice taking on an unintended shrillness.

"No," Joan said, "we weren't. You were saving your big announcement for the regular meeting. My news is for anybody who wants to hear it. Now, as I was saying…"

"Is your great-granddaughter married?" Pamela interrupted.

"Of course she is." Despite Joan's free-love attitude for her peers, it didn't extend to the younger generations.

"Well, having a baby is no big deal to young marrieds. It is expected. Now the person that I'm talking about, she won't even admit who the father is."

"Do you know someone else who is having a baby?" Veronica asked.

"Pay attention, Veronica. Getting pregnant is what we are talking about."

Veronica looked slightly confused. "I thought we were talking about Joan becoming a great-great-grandmother. People get pregnant every day, or is that every night, but a great-great-grandmother. Now that's exciting."

Mable nodded her agreement. "We'll have to arrange to have a great, great party for you when the time comes. We'll do that for our April meeting of the Red Hatters. I'll start planning it now. We'll tell the others as soon as we get to the restaurant and see what ideas they have. This will be fun."

Pamela slumped back, seething, in her seat. Being one-upped always upset her. Being one-upped by Joan McNeil was doubly annoying. She had missed her chance by being coy. Now her breaking news would just be an add-on to the talk about having babies. She'd have to jazz it up a little for the full meeting.

CHAPTER 25

CORPORAL SCOTT BOWEN directed his Ford Explorer into Connie Wilson's driveway. Roscoe, from his place in the back seat, detected the decrease in speed and opened one eye. He noticed he was on a farm. Both eyes came open and he struggled to his feet to check out any animals that might be about.

It was the sixth-month anniversary of when the search for George Wilson had begun. Scott wanted to bring Connie up-to-date on the activities that had taken place during that time. To the untrained eye, it would appear that once the neighbours stopped running their four-wheelers up and down the trails where George might be found, all searching had come to a halt. That was not the case. Scott had the bulging folder to prove it.

Connie appeared in the doorway with a tray containing an insulated coffee pot, two mugs and a tray of muffins and sweets. She had been forewarned about this visit by Scott. She paused briefly at the top of the steps and gazed up at the cerulean sky. At the outer reaches of the horizon, a few wisps of high cirrus clouds could be seen, but otherwise, there was an uninterrupted panorama of blue.

The hum of an electric window being operated drifted up to her as Scott's face replaced the reflection of herself in the Explorer's side window. His smiling face almost allowed her to believe this was a social call from a friend. It wasn't.

Connie lifted the tray slightly in his direction. "I thought we might have this meeting outside on the lawn. We're not going to have too many more of these days before the snow starts to fly again."

"Fine by me, but I hope you're wrong about the snow, at least for another two or three months." He indicated the back seat of his vehicle with his thumb. "Do you mind if my dog gets out for a run? He loves it here in the country."

"Not at all. Every farm house should have a dog in the yard. I've been thinking about getting one myself."

George one, the sober George, agreed with Connie about having a dog. George two, the drunk, severely mistreated the first two dogs that joined their family. After giving the second dog away to a family in Mary Jane Falls, Connie vowed that she would never let another dog become a victim of George's wrath. The mere fact that Connie was entertaining thoughts of acquiring another animal suggested she may be giving up all hope after six months.

"Then again, George didn't really get along with animals that were simply house pets. Maybe I won't be getting one."

Scott crawled down from the front seat and opened the back door of his SUV. Roscoe ungracefully hopped down to the ground. He sat looking at Scott, waiting for instructions.

"Go play," Scott ordered and Roscoe took off at a three-legged gait around the yard. Scott watched for a few minutes to make sure Roscoe understood his boundaries, then joined Connie at a picnic table under the shade of a large sugar maple.

The smile left his face as he sat down. "I wish I had some good news to present to you, but I don't. Let's get that out of the way right from the beginning."

He studied Connie's reaction to his statement. She appeared ambivalent, showing neither disappointment nor surprise. "We have been working your case hard," he continued, holding up the folder. "I have reports from every part of the country where we've had a BOLO on George's truck."

Connie gave him a confused look.

"Be on the lookout. Sorry, no more acronyms. We've monitored government records to see if there has been any activity on his Social Insurance Number. We've kept a constant watch on his bank account."

At Scott's suggestion, Connie had opened her own bank accounts so that George's could be monitored for any usage. "To date, they've all drawn a blank."

Connie toyed with the apple-bran muffin on her plate before looking up at the Mountie. "I know you've done everything you can, but in my heart I can feel that George is still alive." A little pink came into her cheeks. "That sounds stupid, I know. It's just a feeling I've got that I can't shake."

Scott reached across the table and placed his hand on one of Connie's. "It's not stupid. It's called hope. Hope is what helps most of us get from one day to the next. On the local level, we hope that we're going to stay healthy; nationally, we hope that the economy is not going to go down the tubes; internationally, we hope that George Bush is not going to do something stupid and ..." He struggled for a thought. "Well, with Bush, hoping for that is enough. And universally, we hope that some supreme being is looking over us and guiding our ways."

Connie forced a smile. "Thanks for the encouragement. I don't think philosophy is your forté, but I appreciate you trying."

Now it was Scott's turn for a full-fledged blush. "Some people have a knack for saying the right thing at the right time and sounding so full of wisdom. I guess I'm not one of them, no matter how hard I try. I had a sergeant who once told me the secret to doing this was to say something that sounded profound. It didn't have to make sense as long as it had the ring of deep thinking. I don't think he ever stepped outside the classroom with his theories."

Connie moved from a smile to a full laugh. "Profundity is not what people either want or expect from someone who wears your uniform. They want action and I see you have been doing that." She slipped her hand from under Scott's and touched the folder.

"There is something else I should tell you." Connie chewed on her lower lip for a few seconds before going on. To Scott she looked like she was debating whether or not to go on at all. "I've talked to a psychic."

Scott showed a brief "give me a break" look and then fought his expression back to neutral. He sat quietly for a few long seconds. He stared deeply into her blue-green eyes. He hoped he hadn't rolled his own, but knew he probably had. "Many people in your circumstances do," he finally said. "What did this psychic have to say?"

Connie looked like she wished she had said nothing. Scott gave her a nod of encouragement. Her voice came out tentatively. "She agreed with me that George is alive. She says he is living in a wooded area by a lake. She says he's healthy but in turmoil. He wants to come home, but he doesn't know how the people of Raymond's River will receive him."

Scott nodded. Considering the amount of effort the local community had put into the search, that would be a valid concern. "And did she tell you where this lake is situated?"

"She's not sure, but no farther west than Ontario. She could see a wood stove and a pile of firewood stacked outside. George always stacked his firewood. He said it dried better that way than simply leaving it in a loose pile."

"Well, that clinches it," Scott said and immediately wished he could retract the words. "I'm sorry," he said. "Everyone hears about how these psychics help solve any number of cases. I've been in this business a long time and I have yet to speak to the officer who actually got the final big break in a case from some mystic. Most of them appear out of the woodwork after the fact and expound upon how some vague prediction they made can be tied to the resolution of the case. Their predictions are so general that any number of solutions would fit into what they said."

Colour slipped up from under Connie's collar and rose to her hairline. "She seems so sincere."

Scott pointed to an area beside the barn. "Look over there. You have row upon row of firewood stacked up for the upcoming winter. George enjoyed working in the woods. Did you tell her that? Once you get beyond the Ontario-Manitoba border, cabins in the woods become more and more scarce. On the other hand, you'd be hard-pressed not to be on a lake if you were in northern Ontario or Quebec. The place is loaded with them." Scott paused. "Just don't get your hopes up based on what this lady had to say."

"It's not just that. Have you ever heard of woman's intuition?"

"I'm not telling you to give up hope. We are still looking. Silver-and-black Dodges are pretty popular trucks. There are thousands of them on the roads. Members across the country have pulled over any number of them. Licence plates are easy to change. If George is on the run, he may have taken plates off a similar vehicle. In the process, we've managed to capture a number of drug dealers."

"Drug dealers? What has that got to do with George?"

"Nothing. Nothing. But as long as we have them pulled over, it doesn't hurt to check for other things. We can't randomly pull vehicles over for no reason at all. Looking for your husband's truck gives us a valid reason for our actions."

Now it was Connie's turn for a sarcastic retort. "Thank God, someone is benefiting from his disappearance."

Scott scrambled to reword his statement. "No. You're getting the wrong idea. What I'm saying is that just about every truck that answers the description of George's vehicle is being pulled over. We are sincerely searching for your husband."

This revelation brought no smile to Connie's face. A different tact was required. "If your psychic is correct and George has gone to ground, it may take us months to track him down. There are thousands of kilometres of back roads where he could be holed up. If he takes even rudimentary precautions to evade us, we may never find him."

"I understand. George never wanted anyone in authority involved in his life. I've told you that. That included banks, government, anyone who could hold sway over him for any reason. Living off the grid would not present him with much of a challenge."

"That may be true around here, but eccentricities like that in a strange town or village would attract attention unless he had someone in the area to ease him into the local population."

Scott took a plain piece of paper from the folder. "I know that I've asked you this many times before, but are there any people anywhere that George might be in contact with? Any new names that you've thought of since the last time we talked?"

"I've given you all the names from our Christmas card list, all the names from my e-mail address book, all of our business contacts. Short of giving you George's high school year book and the Raymond's River telephone directory, I don't know what else I can do."

"We've already checked out those two sources." Scott kept a straight face when he made that statement. Connie didn't know if he was joking or not.

CHAPTER 26

THE WAITER HAD yet to finish filling the water glasses when Pamela spoke in a voice that carried the entire length of the long table in the banquet room of the Flying Dagger Chinese Restaurant.

"Ladies, guess who has gone and gotten herself pregnant?"

She gave Joan a scathing look which Joan translated as meaning Pamela was not talking about anyone in Joan's family. This was pure Pamela getting the first word in.

An open question like that did not solicit any answers from anyone gathered in the room. Veronica and Mable rolled their eyes at each other. There were questioning looks all the way down the table from the others before Joan piped up. "Tell us, Pamela. Who got knocked up?"

Pamela pulled her red shawl up around her shoulders in a grand look-at-me gesture. "Little Elizabeth Schofield." She firmly nodded her head to confirm the truth of that statement, then leaned towards the assembled ladies. "And that's not all." Again she paused dramatically, waiting for someone to ask the inevitable questions to keep this discussion going.

Joan McNeil clasped her hands together in an exaggerated gesture. "Do tell us more, Pamela." Her voice deepened into a passable imitation of Paul Harvey. "What is the rest of the story?"

This response earned Joan a few snickers from some closest to her and a withering glare from Pamela.

"Go on, Pamela," Mable Booth encouraged. "You've had us wondering about your news all the way from Raymond's River."

Pamela smiled at Mable. "Thank you, Mable." She looked up and down the table at the others. "She's keeping the father's name a secret." Pamela abandoned the idea of holding back this information for a more dramatic moment.

"A secret? Why would she do that?" someone asked.

Pamela's face swelled with pride that she was the only one present who could impart this gem of information. "He's already married."

"Married?"

Now some of the faces in the crowd took on a worried look. Raymond's River was not that big a place. There were no six degrees of separation from anyone at this table to anyone else in town; there were at most two degrees.

"Married to whom?" The questions were coming from all over the room.

Pamela preened at the attention. "That's just it. She won't tell anyone. Not even her parents."

"Why not? He has a right to know."

"That's the best part. He has packed up his family and headed out west. He's out of her reach." Pamela had no way of knowing if any of that last part was true. Elizabeth had not mentioned anything about the man's family. Furthermore, the man was not running from his responsibilities; he was totally oblivious to his new-found fatherhood. Those facts did not make for as good a story, however.

Now she could see the room dividing into little groups. Each was going over the names of people who had recently left Raymond's River to work in the oil patch of Alberta. Voices were being kept intentionally low. The names being referred to were sons or grandsons of others present at the table. Occasional furtive glances were aimed at Pamela.

"I've tried to tell her that she has to let him know he's a father," she said to the few who were still listening to her. "But, oh no, she won't listen to me. Kids today think they know everything."

"Are you sure about this, Pamela?" Mable asked. "I saw Elizabeth at the drug store last week. She didn't look pregnant to me."

"She's just starting to show. Six months along, I would say. Did you notice the loose-fitting clothes she wears? Kids today don't dress like that. The tighter and skimpier, the better. Elizabeth was no different from the rest of them. That's why she's in this predicament in the first place. There's no mystery any more like there was when I was a girl. Now, if you've got it, flaunt it. If you haven't got it, enhance it, and I don't mean with a few tissues like we stuffed in our bra."

That comment brought a titter of laughter from some of the ladies present. The others were still counting relatives and trying to remember their whereabouts and how long they had been out of the province.

"I know she dated Bobby McNeil two summers ago when she was visiting her Granddad," Muriel Singer said. "I haven't seen Bobby around lately. Didn't he marry that Henderson girl from up around Mary Jane Falls?"

"Bobby is living in Halifax, thank you very much," Joan McNeil said. "He's got an important job with the government and he's not running away from any parental responsibilities." Joan was sitting five people away from Muriel, but even at eighty-three, there was nothing wrong with her hearing. Bobby was her great-grandson.

"All I said was that I hadn't seen him around lately," Muriel retorted. "Who knows what kind of influence a great-grandmother who sleeps with any man she can coax into her bed has on a young, maturing boy?"

Joan threw back her shoulders. "I don't coax men into my bed. They line up to come voluntarily."

Before Muriel could respond, Betty Shaw spoke up. "I can think of at least three young married families that have left the area in the last six months. Many of you here know who I mean. You are related to them."

"I know that Fisher boy from Mary Jane Falls is working in Vancouver."

"He's not married."

"Not to a woman anyway. I hear that's what he likes so much about Vancouver. The lifestyle."

The chatter went on and on. Names brought up, defended, rejected or hung onto as possibilities. For now, what Connie would say when she found out Pamela had blabbed Elizabeth's news failed to concern her. She relished in the glory.

The hot dishes of food started to make their way from the kitchen. It had been all pre-ordered — various kinds of fried rice, egg rolls, beef and chicken mixed with a variety of vegetable combinations and warm Saki for everyone.

With the opening of each steaming dish, the conversation level dropped a little lower, until after three minutes, Elizabeth Schofield's pregnancy appeared to be of no interest to anyone at the table, except Pamela. That appearance was an illusion. A lot of sons and grandsons were going to be drilled about their extra-marital activities during the next week or so. Everyone who had moved west searching for work would be getting letters from home. Some would be blunt and to the point. Were you sleeping around with Elizabeth Schofield? Did you get her pregnant? Others, more subtle. Are there other reasons why you left home besides seeking employment?

Every mother, grandmother, great-grandmother wanted to be able to attend the next Red Hatters meeting with proof that their offspring were in the clear. Only then could they truly immerse themselves in the mystery of who fathered Elizabeth's baby. If asked, most would agree it wasn't really any of their business. But still…

CHAPTER 27

"A PSYCHIC?" DETECTIVE-SERGEANT Jim McDonald asked. "Anyone we know?"

"She wouldn't give me a name. Said as a non-believer, giving me the details would be a waste of her time. I tried to convince her I was open to being proven wrong, but she didn't buy it. There are some things you just can't fake."

Corporal Scott Bowen sat in the sergeant's west-end Halifax office. His work there concerned another matter, but eventually the conversation always came around to any cases the two had open.

Jim served with Major Crimes — robbery and homicide. Over the years, many of his cases had taken him out into the area covered by Scott's regular patrolling. Often they teamed up to solve cases where their interests overlapped. Scott enjoyed the diversion of working with the detective branch, but not to the point where he wanted to do it full-time. Jim, impressed with Scott's analytical skills, endeavoured at every opportunity to get Scott out of uniform and into the investigative branch populated by the force's detectives.

"Is this a free psychic or is this someone working for a fee?"

"Connie refuses to discuss any details of the arrangement, but the advice is ongoing. I get the impression the psychic initiated the contact. Connie called me this morning to report the lady had a vision of George fishing off a riverbank in the rain. He had on a green raincoat and a Tilley hat. Could I check the weather across the country?"

Jim looked out his own window. There were a scattering of low clouds in the sky, but not the type that would produce any moisture anytime soon. Scott followed Jim's gaze.

"There are bands of rain from B.C. to Quebec with localized showers in northern New Brunswick. Those clouds are the leading edge of a system moving our way."

"So that narrows the vision down to the rest of the country. Not bad for building up your accuracy if this case is ever broken. What about the Tilley hat? Did George own such a thing?"

"Connie didn't even know what a Tilley hat was. When I explained it was a floppy, broad-brimmed hat like you picture an Australian wearing, costing in the seventy-dollar range, she assured me he never wore such a thing. Baseball and trucker caps were his signature headgear."

"Interesting. That would mean that George is altering his appearance. He is taking steps to avoid being found."

"What?" Scott gave Jim a look of total disbelief. "You're not buying into this bullshit?"

Jim did not answer right away. Instead, he got up from behind his desk and went over to a four-drawer filing cabinet against one wall. A ten-cup coffee perk was perched on top of it, half full. Jim refilled his cup and offered the pot to Scott. Scott looked into his own mug and gave a slight shake of his head. Jim returned the pot and sat down again.

"Tell me, what open leads are you following right now?"

"We've got a BOLO on his truck everywhere in the country."

"That's been what, six, seven months without a hit? What else?"

Scott looked down into his coffee cup and swirled the liquid around. "OK, we've got nothing going on right now. The case has come to a complete standstill." He looked back up into Jim's dark eyes. "But that doesn't mean I'm going to listen to every loony-tune who comes along with some cooked-up, half-ass theory."

Jim's white teeth flashed in a smile. "You are wrapped up in this case. You're not developing a thing for the little lady involved, are you? I've never seen you so touchy."

"I don't believe in psychics. It's that simple. You give them so much as five minutes publicity and when the case breaks after hours and days and weeks of work, they claim some tip they gave solved the case. Some tip so far off the mark you hardly remember it yourself. And if the outcome of the search goes bad, they accuse you of ignoring their superlative leads."

Jim sipped from his freshly poured coffee. He waited to be sure Scott had talked himself out on the subject. "The trick is to not ignore this person, but to nail her down to specifics. She says George is fishing in a river. Ask her the name of the river. Ask her what province and what part of that province. Don't let her get away with generalities."

"Why? Why bother with her at all?"

"Because some day we are going to find George. From what you have told me about him — woodsman, hunter, fisherman — everything this psychic is saying will turn out to be true. I could make those same predictions myself with a high expectation of accuracy. That's because they are so general as to be useless. You have to get out in front of this. Eventually it's going to make the news. These things always do. For every statement she makes, you have to point out the uselessness of it. The trick is to make it look as if you want to use her advice, but she refuses to offer anything specific. We have to look like the good guys here."

Jim sat back in his chair and smiled. "This time, things are in your favour. The subject is not some lovable, ten-year-old kid, but an adult male who has a reputation of binge drinking. A man who has left his poor, struggling wife in the lurch trying to run a beef and dairy farm all by herself. You are taking time out of your busy schedule to try to find this lout and bring him back home. The public will be on your side. If you demand specifics from this psychic, they will demand specifics. When she can't provide them, and when we find George, it will be honest, hard work on the part of the force that brought the search to a successful conclusion." He gave an emphatic nod. "We both know that will be the truth."

He pointed a finger at Scott. "It will be a public-relations coup."

"Right," Scott said. His demeanour lacked the enthusiasm that went with that agreement. He wasn't looking for any coup; he just wanted to bring George Wilson back home or at the very least, he wanted to bring this case to a conclusion. What he didn't want was to have some unknown psychic second-guessing his every move.

CHAPTER 28

Late December

SNOW SWIRLED AROUND the Schofield farm house, home of young Elizabeth. The wind rattled the windows. The walls of the hundred-year-old building seemed to be vibrating in the embrace of a massive early winter nor'easter that had snuck up on them from the Atlantic Ocean.

A three-foot gap of clear ground showed between the house and the nearest drift, which stood level with the middle sash of the first-floor windows. Beyond that could be seen an unbroken plain of nothingness, like an empty sheet of paper waiting for a writer to type "Chapter One" at the top and then fill in some details.

Outside the back door could be seen the front bumper and grill of Connie Wilson's Toyota Landcruiser. A square of blue framed this post-modern artistic rendering. The rest of the vehicle was lost in the sea of white. A six-inch hump above the mean level of the snow indicated the location of the vehicle's roof.

Connie had traded in her sensible, grey, four-door Camry for this slow-moving, powerful four-wheel-drive vehicle when she found herself spending almost as much time in the wood lots as in the barn. She had discovered that a car just didn't cut it on those rutted, back roads.

Cal had been initially surprised by Connie's interest in their forestry enterprise. He had quickly embraced it, however. Connie, it turned out, could handle a skidder or porter with the best of the men in the area. Being a part owner of the business gave her that extra incentive that hourly employees seemed to lack.

The presence of Connie's Landcruiser in the Schofield yard, however, had nothing to do with the logging industry. Paul Schofield had called Connie at one o'clock that morning to report Elizabeth's water had broken. The fury of the storm, firmly established by that time, caused Paul to doubt the wisdom of taking his two-wheel-drive half-ton to the hospital in Truro. Could Connie bring over her powerful four-wheel-drive Toyota?

Connie hadn't hesitated for a second. This was a week earlier than the expected due date for Elizabeth's offspring, but numbers on a calendar had little to do with the exact timing of a birth. Within a week of the predicted date was close enough for Connie to jump out of bed, throw on some heavy, winter clothes and venture out into the raging blizzard.

The five-minute excursion from her driveway to her next-door neighbour's driveway eliminated any thoughts about heading out for a hospital and all the services it could offer. When Connie parked at this back-door location, the wind had blown it clear. The presence of the Landcruiser would alter the wind patterns enough to cause the entire backyard to fill with at least five feet of solidly packed snow blown in from the surrounding fields.

That was the last thing on Connie's mind as she jumped from her vehicle into the face of the storm. She had to hold on to her door with both hands to keep it from flapping flat along the front fender of the Toyota. Relief stood out on Paul Schofield's face when she entered the warmth of the kitchen. His wife insisted she couldn't deliver the baby without help. Paul happily turned that function over to Connie.

Although Connie could have said, "I don't know nothing 'bout birthing babies," she exuded a sense of excitement.

"Thank God you made it," Paul said. "I was watching your struggle out the window. Every so often, the wind would die down for a second or two and I could see your headlights inching our way. I'm sorry to have gotten you out in this."

"Wouldn't have missed it for the world," Connie said. "Once I started, I was committed. I had no intention of abandoning Old Blue anywhere near where a snowplow might run her into a ditch. Has anything happened yet?"

"No, Elizabeth's been resting fitfully for the last hour. Every five or ten minutes, she lets out a groan as she cramps up. We may have lots of time, according to her mother."

"Maybe," Connie said and ran up the stairs to Elizabeth's bedroom.

This was Elizabeth's first child; Connie had yet to experience this joy of nature; and Elizabeth's mother was nearly two decades away from her own two brushes with childbirth. She had had an epidural for both. As such, there was not much experience cluttering up the landscape of the room.

"Relax," Connie reassured Elizabeth. She held up a Red Cross first aid book. "I've taken the standard first aid course many times and it's all spelled out, step by step in this book. See. Page 142." She forced a smile. "I've always wanted a chance to put the theory into practice."

A sorry excuse for a smile touched Elizabeth's face. She let out another groan of pain.

"Besides," Connie continued, "the Indians used to crawl off behind a bush by themselves, deliver their own baby and then report back for their tribal duties all in the same day. It's just a natural, everyday occurrence of life. It's going to happen with or without our help."

Elizabeth grimaced as the contraction wracked her body. Connie wiped off her forehead with a damp facecloth.

"You're a true country girl now. It's only city folks who think babies can only be born in hospitals."

Elizabeth grimaced. "I'm still a city girl at heart."

Paul had brought in a chair from his bedroom and then left the women alone. Connie sat on one side of the bed, dozing every now and then. Elizabeth's mother sat on the other, stroking her daughter's hand and mumbling words of encouragement.

"How long has it been?" Elizabeth asked, after a particularly long contraction.

Connie's eyes popped open. She looked at her watch. It read 6:35. "Not long. Everything is proceeding according to schedule."

The contractions closed to less than two minutes apart. It was time to get the show on the road. Paul Schofield had put in a call to the transportation department to have them send out a plow to the area. They had not been very reassuring. The intensity of the storm was overwhelming their equipment. They were not even keeping the main roads open. The wind was filling in the highways behind the snow blowers before the big trucks were out of sight. They promised to do their best.

Connie had stationed Paul in the kitchen, boiling water. One ear listened for an approaching plow, the other concentrated on the cries of pain from his only daughter. He would like to get his hands on the man who had done this to her. Elizabeth still maintained her silence on the matter. Suddenly, he heard a new sound — the sound of a new life. He rushed up the stairs to Elizabeth's bedroom.

It had all happened so fast, Connie had almost missed the catch. One moment, she stood beside Elizabeth while she screamed in pain. The next, her hands closed around the crowning head, giving the shoulders a light twist and in the blink of an eye, the baby slid out the birth canal. Connie had a towel ready and closed her hands around the slippery, little boy just in time. With no encouragement from anyone, the little fellow spontaneously let out his first cry. And, just like that, the population of Raymond's River grew by one.

A full mane of flaming red hair grabbed everyone's attention. The blue eyes, the red patchy complexion, the ten fingers and toes were all dwarfed by this feature.

"Wow," Paul said. "It doesn't matter what name you lay on this lad, you know what everyone is going to call him."

"Red," Connie said. "That will inevitably be his nickname as he grows older."

By now, "Red" had been cleaned up and lay on Elizabeth's chest. "No," she said. "I won't let that happen. I'm going to call him Tim."

"Tim?" Connie's voice caught in her throat. She knew of two Timothys who lived in the Raymond's River area. She couldn't remember their marital status or where they currently lived. She studied Elizabeth closely. "That's a nice name. Any reason why you chose it?"

Elizabeth nodded. "After Timothy Dalton, the actor. My boy's going to grow up to be suave and sophisticated like him."

"Uh huh." Connie looked at the Schofield parents. Neither of them seemed to think anything was out of the ordinary. They had only been back in Raymond's River for a little over a year. They didn't know all the boys in town. Apparently they knew of no Tim who had been calling on their daughter.

"The water's ready," Paul said and indicated the direction of the kitchen where the pots of boiling water waited.

"Thank God," Connie said. "Who else wants a cup of tea?"

CHAPTER 29

C AL LINDSAY RAMMED another cork into a bottle of crystal-clear red wine. He placed the bottle into the final slot of a twelve-hole cardboard box, slapped a strip of packing tape over the flaps and slid the case back against the wall of his underground wine cellar.

This was case number fifty. Fifty of seventy-five of a very special product. A product where revenues dropped entirely into his own pockets and none into the eager, grabby hand of the tax man.

The snowfall of the previous week had brought his wood-cutting operation to a complete halt. There was simply too much snow in the woods to even consider trying to get around. It did free up a large block of time for this necessary bottling task. It also gave his mind time to wander to things that might have been, if his father had been involved in some other occupation.

He did enjoy the bootlegging business, the camaraderie and the money, but working with Connie these last few months had him thinking of Robert Frost's road untravelled. There were times, when his mind was on the edge of sleep, that he thought this new partnership might expand to include farming. He had been heavily involved in this year's hay crop production. Many of his afternoons had been spent making hay instead of sleeping in his backyard.

As he edged further towards sleep, the partnership moved from the barn and into the house and, dare he dream it, into the bedroom. Mrs. Connie Lindsay. He liked the sound of that name.

This scenario contained one major problem. Connie already carried another name: Mrs. Connie Wilson. How long would George have to be missing before Connie could drop that burden from her lovely, slender neck? Cal didn't know.

To date, Connie had expressed no interest in Cal's dreams. To her, the operation remained strictly business.

Wine splattered on the floor as the bottle he was filling overflowed. Cal quickly pulled the filling tube from the bottom of the container, cutting off the supply. Pay attention to what you're doing, he admonished himself. This is no time for daydreaming.

He poured a little of the beverage from the too-full bottle into a nearby glass before inserting the cork and wiping off the spilled residue. He raised the glass and smiled.

"To future partnerships," he said. "May they be bountiful."

CHAPTER 30

CORPORAL SCOTT BOWEN sat at his desk, one of six similar oak monstrosities, all army surplus, in the office area of the small, rural RCMP detachment. No barriers, no half-walls, no cubicles. By simply looking up from his desk, Scott was free to seek help and inspiration from his fellow officers at any time. Any time that is, except now. He was alone on this Saturday morning. The other duty men and/or women were out patrolling. The office staff were not in. They lived in the nine-to-five, Monday-to-Friday world. Any calls would be diverted to the 800-number in Truro and then, if necessary, back to the appropriate cell phone or radio manned by the local officers.

He was studying the final forensic reports from the autopsy of Jason Browne. Browne's body had been found at the beginning of the previous summer, six and a half months ago, at the foot of a cliff along the edge of the Bay of Fundy.

Accident or homicide had yet to be determined. Browne appeared to have no next-of-kin and no one was pushing for a conclusion. The forensic testing had slowly wound its way through the system, often being pushed to the bottom of the pile as more pressing cases emerged. Now, a little over six months later, Scott had the last help Jason Browne was going to get from the system in his hands. Like the rest of the information he had, nothing was conclusive.

As a surprise to no one, there were indications that Browne had been drinking at the time of his death. His condition could have been described as impaired, although the time between his passing and the discovery of his body made an exact reading impossible. Examination of his hair also brought no surprises. Browne was a regular drug user, right up to the time of his death.

Scott had already made these assumptions and conducted his investigation as if these things were truths. It was slight consolation that he had no reason to reinvestigate matters in the light of these findings.

What was new, but still no surprise, was that Browne was infected with low-level STDs — sexually transmitted diseases. This may open a new avenue to check out. Tommy Watson, a local high school student, had informed Scott that Browne was often seen hanging around the school trying to pick up the female students. If Browne failed to practise safe sex and had passed one of these little hitch-hikers along to some girl, revenge may have been the motive, especially if the girl had continued the chain and infected her boyfriend or some other male partner.

Scott shook his head. He wanted to avoid going down this road. He flipped through the papers on his desk. Tommy Watson had given him the names of two girls who would service anybody if the price was right. Scott had talked to both girls. They had both been forthright and upfront. They had slept with Jason Browne. In return, he had given them certain gifts to show his appreciation. Damn right, they had taken all the necessary precautions. No, they didn't know of anyone else at the school who had been so accommodating. Some girls were just too full of themselves, they concluded.

At the time, Scott had not pursued the matter any further. Now, so many months later, would it be worth his while? Would anyone admit to dating this reject of a man? It was a long shot, at best. Couple that with the fact that if indeed revenge was the motive, anyone who had carried out the act would be loath to acknowledge even knowing Jason Browne. He would have to treat every girl in the school as a hostile witness. That would not fly with anyone.

Although high schoolers seemed to be Browne's first choice, that didn't preclude affairs with women his own age. In searching for next of kin, Scott had come up completely empty in the friends and family department. Browne was your archetypical social outcast. It was like he was raised by wolves and then set free on the residents surrounding Raymond's River. Revisiting that area would be a waste of time.

That left prostitutes. A definite possibility. However, Browne was more likely infected by these women than him infecting them. STDs were a hazard of their trade. Revenge would not be high on their agenda. If some pimp had killed Browne, word would have gotten out. There is no sense in making an example of someone and then keeping it secret.

Scott closed both folders. The passage of time had given him no new insights.

Maybe he should consult Connie Wilson's psychic. Perhaps she could give him a lead on what happened to Browne. If ever there was a candidate for a lost soul to be stuck on this side of the great curtain, or whatever the dividing barrier was, Browne seemed to fit the bill. His spirit should be roaming the fields along the bay seeking justice for a life that had gone totally wrong. Any psychic worth her salt should be able to tap into that power.

Scott got up from his desk and walked into the kitchen alcove. He was scaring himself with these thoughts. He took a coffee mug down from the cupboard and filled it with the strong black liquid. Tentatively, he brought it to his mouth. It tasted like corn flakes. He dumped the pot and made a fresh brew.

The plan laid out by Sergeant McDonald had not come to fruition. Connie still refused to give him the name of her medium friend. Because of this, Scott had not been able to directly push for specifics. He had tried his best to do it through Connie. The results had been spotty. Sometimes Connie agreed to firm up the speculations with facts; other times she insisted that the lady was providing all the information she had available. In the end, nothing concrete came from his efforts. He was no closer to finding George and unable to pin the psychic down.

Connie did keep him up-to-date on the woman's ramblings. Lately, she had claimed that George was becoming more and more depressed. Christmas had been particularly rough on him. She could see a dark aura surrounding him and with each sighting, the emanation became darker and darker until it was almost black. The psychic feared George was near suicide.

As before, everything she said could be applied to just about any man separated from his wife. Regardless of who initiated the break, certain feelings would bubble to the surface from time to time. Suicide would surely be among these emotions. Although interesting, none of this proved of any use to Scott's investigation.

Sergeant McDonald had not dismissed the insights of the psychic outright. Scott wondered what his superior's reaction would be if he closed the file with a finding of suicide and his only source of evidence came from this delver into the occult.

This tempting thought danced through his mind, caused a chuckle and passed on. He hadn't completely given up on this case yet. Another avenue of investigation might be opening.

Scott had noticed the presence of a new man at the farm when he dropped in for his periodic updates. Brian Cosh had told him this person was the local bootlegger who had since gone into business with Connie producing fire and pulp wood. In answer to Scott's questions about the man, Brian had been totally forthcoming with his thoughts and concerns.

Brian had noted the man's presence more and more often. Brian still went over to Connie's on a regular basis to help with the farm work and to generally keep an eye on her. He noticed Cal doing a lot of the work that Brian had previously done.

This could be interpreted as both good and bad. Good in that it freed up Brian to do other things. Brian had a boat load of commitments in the community. Bad in that Brian wondered what Cal's intentions might be. He knew of their dating history. He understood their partnership in the forestry endeavour. Both made money from that. The extra money helped Connie.

However, the free services Cal offered around the farm caused Brian some unease. Their close business association naturally made them closer friends. Despite his long-time bootlegging occupation, Cal remained a good guy in Brian's estimation. He had offered as much information as he could to help in the early stages of the search for George and faithfully pounded the woods with the rest of them during that first week. Still, Brian kept an eye on how things were developing.

Brian had passed all this information on to Scott. Now Scott, the ever-suspicious cop, wondered how long-range Cal's thinking might be. Might he have had something to do with George's disappearance? Cal's help early on could merely have been a diversion to lead any investigation away from himself and on to others in the community.

Scott gave his head a shake. His frustrations over his lack of success in these two cases had him dreaming up fantasy solutions. With or without their history of dating, it was natural for a man of Cal's age to be attracted to a woman as becoming as Connie Wilson, especially since they were being thrust together as business partners. He had even wondered what would have happened if he and Connie had met under different circumstances. He could see himself enjoying Connie's company. Cal was not doing anything abnormal.

That aside, the casualness with which Brian had identified Cal as the local bootlegger took Scott slightly aback. Brian added no more significance to the remark than if he had said Cal was the local blacksmith or banker. The criminal aspect of the vocation seemed to escape Brian completely and Brian was one of the leaders in the community.

This attitude no doubt dated back to when government-run liquor stores were a rarity outside the major centres in the province. The local people considered the bootlegger to be providing a necessary service to which they had as much right as their city and town friends. Maybe once upon a time, but no longer. Government-run stores were everywhere.

At the moment, bootlegging stood low on Scott's list of concerns, but he couldn't outright dismiss his other thought: Cal as a murderer. It wouldn't have been the first time a love triangle had evolved into something more diabolical. This might be an avenue for Scott to look into. Besides, he had no other leads. It was either this or pack up the case.

CHAPTER 31

THE LADIES OF the Red Hat Society were all atwitter. Elizabeth's baby became the talk of Raymond's River. Not just because it was a new life in the community, but because of the flaming shock of red hair the young lad sported on his head.

According to Gregor Mendel's law of genetics, red hair came from a recessive gene. Most of the ladies could remember back to the distant days spent in elementary school when they drew the four squares marked black hair, blond hair or blue eyes, brown eyes and then figured out the possibilities of hair or eye colour for their offspring. Genes came in pairs. The dominant gene would determine the colour in a mixed combination. The only way a recessive colour could come to the forefront was if both genes were from the same pool.

Various shades of brown hair and the inclusion of hazel eyes made practical applications just about impossible for the lay person, but they had all dutifully filled in what the possible genetic combinations would be.

From school, most of these women moved on to become farmers' wives. Although the old monk, Mendel, had based his studies on the growing of garden peas, these women had seen his laws in action in the raising of herds of cattle. They knew about keeping the line pure and which breeds to cross to increase production of milk while preserving some other desired quality.

They had never applied the science to people. People just happened. At some point in everyone's life, someone would say "he has his father's eyes" or "that's the Hennigar nose on his face."

People seldom related these quirks of fate to Mendel and his garden peas.

But now they could. Here was real-life red hair. Not a variation of red. Not auburn. Not strawberry blond. But red, really, really red. Somewhere along the line, two recessive red genes had been passed along through the successive generations of two separate families until they collided during a night of passion to produce little Timothy Schofield.

The detectives of the Red Hat Society were determined to track down those families.

The evening had started out as a games night, a night that followed the pattern of the many other nights pursuing the same passions. Several tables were set up in the hall with the various games — crokinole, scrabble, auction forty-fives, cribbage or bridge — being played by the participants. That was the intention, at least.

At one table, play had ceased altogether. The score sheet had been flipped over and the four players leaned studiously over the scratches Lisa Tingley made on the back.

Lisa was a life-long resident of Raymond's River. She not only lived and worked in the community, but she was the liquor store clerk — she made it her business to know everything that was going on, always had.

"I remember when I was a little girl, a farmer from outside the edge of town had really red hair. Most people referred to him as 'old carrot top' when he wasn't within listening range. Otherwise he was simply known as 'Red.' His last name was Haydon or Hasting or something like that."

"John Haydon. He was my grandfather," Roberta Haydon offered from the next table. She came over to have a look at what was taking place. "My brother-in-law, Basil Schofield, still owns the old place. He and his son Paul are still farming it after all these years."

"That's right." Lisa said. "Elizabeth is your grandniece."

"Yes, I guess she is. I've sort of lost touch with that part of the family since my sister Mary died. Basil was living on his own for a while, but he insisted he didn't need any help from us. Called me and my other sister, Elsie, a couple of busy-bodies."

"As I recall, you and Mary were never what you would call close." Joan McNeil joined the conversation. "When was the last time you were over to see her before she got sick?"

"That's family stuff, Joan. It's not public business." Roberta looked from one person at the table to another. All were dying to hear the story. Roberta wasn't actually averse to telling it, again, with her own peculiar slant to the events.

"My brother, Robert, never did get along with Basil. Robert always thought the farm should have gone to him. Elsie and I agreed. Somehow Basil convinced Daddy he should be the one to get it. I don't know what tricks or chicanery he used. Robert had worked on the farm from the time he was a little boy. We all did, I guess. But Mary was the oldest and Robert was the youngest. He was the only boy. Somehow Basil used the age factor against Robert, and Mary went along with him and so did Daddy. So you're right, Joan. I never felt welcome there after Daddy died. Even before if the truth be known."

"I thought Robert left the farm of his own accord. Joined the navy or something."

"He was in the navy for three years. Fought in Korea, saving the world from Communism. When he got out, there was no place on the farm for him anymore. Mary's kids were using his bedroom. Elsie and I were already married at the time. He lived with me for a couple of months and then got a job in the city. He never went back to the old homestead, not even when Daddy died."

This part of the room became silent for a couple of minutes. No one could think of anything to say about those events. Then one of the crokinolers yelled, "Yes, twenty. We win."

That broke the silence. The attention was back on Lisa's chart. She had filled in the information provided by Roberta.

"So, we know where Elizabeth's part of the red hair came from. Her great-great-grandfather. Now the hard part. We have to figure out who the father is."

"In this community, it's not hard to come up with a starting point," Joan said. "Let's face it, when I was a young lass looking for dates back in the forties, your choices were pretty limited. When two young people got serious about each other, you didn't ask if they were related. You asked 'How closely related are they?' Old 'Red' Haydon is probably our apex on the other side of the family tree as well."

There was a general nodding of heads. Most of these women had lived in Raymond's River or its surrounding area all of their lives. The older ones in the group knew to whom Joan referred. Now that they were reminded, most of them remembered "Red" Haydon. He had been a conspicuous sight when he showed up in town for groceries or to attend the barn dances and annual picnics. He had died around the time the Second World War was breaking out.

"How many kids did Red have?" Lisa asked Roberta. "They would have been your aunts and uncles."

Roberta thought for a minute before answering. "There was Aunt Hilda and Uncle Tom. They moved down to Boston so we never saw much of them. There was Aunt Mary. Her full name was Mary Jane. The falls outside of town are named after her. She was married to George Wilson, Pamela's father-in-law. There was Dad. He was the only boy. That's why he got the old homestead and why my brother Robert thought he should get it, too."

"That was the usual way back in those days," Mable Booth said. "The daughters would get married off and go live with their husbands and the sons would stay home and look after the business. Things have changed these days. Sons can't wait to grow up and get away to the city. My place will probably go to my nephew Ralph. He's the one doing the work there now that Gerald has passed."

Some of the others crowded around the table gave Mable a sympathetic look. Gerald had "passed" when he was shot and killed by his neighbour, who had mistaken him for Ralph. The neighbour thought Ralph was having an affair with his wife. At the time, he hadn't been, but now they seemed to be spending a lot of time together. The neighbour had taken up residency at a penitentiary in Ontario for at least twenty-five years.

Lisa looked up from her listing of the names and scowled at Mable.

"Let's stay on topic here. Were there any other kids?"

"There was Aunt Elizabeth. She never had any children. She died from TB when she was twenty-three. Consumption they called it in those days."

Lisa had started to write down Elizabeth's name. She crossed it off the list with two bold strokes of her pencil. Roberta winced. Even though she had never known her aunt, there was still a family connection. Proudly Lisa held up the sheet of paper.

"Here's our starting list. Hilda, Mary Jane, Robert and Marion. All of these people would be carrying the red-hair gene. Roberta, you're a candidate for the gene. How many children do you have?"

"Wait a minute. Wait one freaking minute here. You are trying to accuse one of my grandchildren of being that baby's father?"

Silence descended on the room like an express elevator dropping from the twenty-second floor.

Lisa looked from Roberta to the others and then back to Roberta. "I'm not accusing anybody of anything. We're just trying to get to the bottom of this mystery. Solving a puzzle, that's all."

"Your solution accuses one of our family members of fathering that bastard child and then running away to avoid responsibility. I'm not the only one in this room who is descended from John Haydon. Just about everyone here is a first or second cousin. It could be anyone of our grandchildren you are accusing. Mary, you are named after your mother and my Aunt Mary Jane. Betty, you were named after Aunt Elizabeth."

These two women nodded in agreement.

"Do you want me to go around the room and tie in everyone here to either John himself or to John's father? He had to have the damn red-hair thingy too or he couldn't have passed it on to John. There were only a half-dozen or so founding fathers of Raymond's River back around 1800 and they were already related to each other when they arrived here."

"Roberta is right," Mable said. "Let's forget about this foolishness and get back to our games. The food will be ready soon, anyway."

Before Lisa had a chance to object, the others quickly returned to their own tables. They could all see where this investigation was going and they all knew Roberta was right. Any one of them could be the great-grandmother of young Tim Schofield. Their curiosity had suddenly abated.

Maybe the younger generation cared little about who jumped into bed with whom, but to these Red Hatters, the sanctity of marriage was still sacred. Most had spent thirty-plus years devoted to the institution. To them, it was a lifelong commitment.

CHAPTER 32

CONNIE SLID THE door to the barn's milking parlour shut and shivered as she stepped out onto the snowy path leading to the house. The drifts were slowly abating in the daily winter sun. Still, the area had an eerie moonscape quality as the outside lights lit up the peaks and bathed the valleys in darkness. Everything was still at least two feet higher than the normal landscape height and the plains between the peaks and valleys had a windblown flatness. The whiteness of the snow gave everything a clean, pure look.

The glow of a set of headlights could be seen above the huge banks flanking both sides of the main road. Connie watched as they swung into her driveway. Cal Lindsay's four-wheel-drive truck pulled up beside her. Cal had a sheepish grin on his face.

"Sorry, I'm late. I got to reading Stephen King's latest book while I was eating my supper and the time just evaporated. He does that to you. One more page becomes five more which turns into ten and that into twenty and, well," he gave a shrug of his shoulders, "your chores don't get done."

"No need to apologize. I don't expect you to be over here every night helping with the milking. I'm more than capable of handling it on my own. George always did it, even when he had a massive hangover."

"Of course you are, but many hands make light work and as long as we have all this snow hanging around, I'll not be doing any wood cutting. Once you start doing physical labour every day, you become hooked on it. I have to do something to keep busy."

Connie put an artificial pout on her face. "That's all I am? A diversion?"

A slight blush stole into Cal's winter-white face. "That's not what I said. Don't go putting words into my mouth."

He reached through the seats to the floor in the back of his truck and produced a bottle of wine.

"Lindsay's finest. Three years old. Full-bodied, slightly fruity on the front of the tongue with a touch of maple and a hint of nuts on the back. Leans towards dryness but doesn't make your mouth pucker. A peace offering."

Connie reached out and took the bottle. She examined the homemade label which revealed nothing about the maker. It simply said "Blueberry Wine, Estate Grown. From Nova Scotia's Finest Blueberries" along with the year.

"You're modest. If this is Lindsay's finest, you should be taking credit somewhere. Fine wines are something to be proud of."

"True, but as it says in Proverbs: 'A man's pride shall bring him low.' There are too many government agents out there who would be more than willing to make this bit of Biblical advice come to life. Competition is simply something they play lip-service to. Giant monopolies are what they really believe in."

Connie stepped back as Cal swung his vehicle's door open. She still did not condone Cal's alternate profession, but she was now willing to try to at least live with it. Through many discussions over the past few months, Cal had tried his best to show her it wasn't he who had led to George's drinking problem.

He admitted he had often sold him liquor, but availability was not the question. Government-run stores were open every night until ten except Sunday, and even they were open on that afternoon these days.

When Connie lived at home with her parents, demon rum had never darkened their doorway. Now, she had to admit a glass of wine with a meal added to the ambiance. She realized the control was in her own hands. George had been a victim of his own weaknesses and had not been put upon by evil sellers of booze like Cal, despite what her father and Pamela Wilson preached.

She passed the bottle back to Cal.

"Come on inside out of the cold."

"I missed the milking, but at least let me help clean up the barn and change the straw."

"Too late. Everything is done. Come on into the house."

Cal looked back at the barn. He had to admit Connie could look after the farm as well as or better than most of the men he knew. She had a work ethic second to none. When she wanted something done, it happened, no questions asked. He followed her to the back door leading into the kitchen.

Once inside, he unzipped his nylon parka and pulled off his Kodiak boots. A pair of leather slippers waited on the boot tray. He slipped into them. They were a pair Connie had bought for George. George considered them too fancy to wear around the house and instead used an old pair of blue corduroys. Connie didn't pass that story on to Cal when she first offered them to him. He, in turn, didn't question the providence of the new, unused footwear.

"I have some apple pie in the fridge," Connie said. "As you know, I usually save my dessert for when I'm finished the barn work. I put the coffee on to brew right before I went out. It should be perfect by now."

"Both sound good to me." Cal comfortably lowered himself into a chair at the kitchen table. "Maybe a slice of cheese would go good with that pie. Medium cheddar?"

"My favourite," Connie agreed from in front of the fridge. "I'll give the pie a few spins in the microwave." She took two mugs down from the cupboard and filled them to the brim with black coffee. She knew Cal didn't use milk or sugar.

She retrieved the pie from the microwave, added the cheese and joined Cal at the table. He waited for her to be seated before taking his first sip of coffee.

"Not too strong. Not too weak. Just perfect."

Connie smiled. "I aim to please in everything I do."

Cal cut off a bite of pie with the fork and brought it half-way to his mouth where he hesitated. "I've had a request for a load of firewood."

Connie looked up, interested.

"Problem is, the stuff we cut last September and October is still too green to safely burn. It should dry for at least another couple of months more."

"Who wants it?"

"Some city folks who moved into the old Johnson place up the River Road. Real-estate agent told him he could get by on four cords of wood for the winter and that's all he bought."

"It's been a cold winter. Who sold him the first batch?"

A sardonic smile played across Cal's lips. "Dwight Jessop."

"Jessop? I doubt our city slickers got anywhere near four cords. That slime ball would short his mother, except she'd beat the shit out of him if he tried it."

"My thoughts exactly. Selling them green wood would be almost as bad. I tried to tell him that."

Connie cut off a wedge of the cheese and placed it on her bit of pie. She transferred both to her mouth and washed it down with a drink of coffee.

"I have enough wood in the woodshed to see me through this year. There's some stuff George cut last spring piled out behind the barn."

She paused as a look of sadness swept across her face. She unconsciously wiped a tear from the corner of her eye. Cal was caught off guard by the emotional display. His own feelings were ambivalent on the subject. While he appreciated Connie's sadness, his own life had changed for the better with George's departure. He thought he had been living happily before, but now he knew he had just been marking time. He looked down at the table and said nothing.

Connie continued with a slight hitch in her voice. "There's at least ten cords of wood there, but it's still in log lengths. It was to be my next year's wood. I could let a couple of cords of that go."

Cal looked up again, his face brighter. "I knew you would have a solution. A couple of cords should be all they need for now. At the same time, we'll have them for customers of our own, especially when they see our two cords are pretty close to Jessop's four cords. I'll come over tomorrow morning and start to process it." He looked towards the window. "I suppose it's under ten feet of snow."

"No, the westerly wind keeps that area behind the barn pretty clear. It will be frozen solid, though."

Cal nodded. "I run my saw hot and sharp. I can handle it. Whenever I worked with George, we used to cut and split the wood on site. Leave the mess there. I'm surprised he would bring his own home in log lengths."

"George was a business man. The other stuff he was selling for a profit. He would handle it as quickly and efficiently as possible. Our wood, he would slowly dabble at it in his spare moments. Half an hour here, half an hour there. It was always ready when we needed it and didn't cut into the business end of things."

Cal gave her a knowing smile. "I can appreciate that. I do the same thing with my wines. I make their preparation a sort of relaxing hobby, a hobby that pays dividends."

"Speaking of wine, let's pop the cork on some of Lindsay's finest. Let's see if this guy is all talk or if the product backs up the bragging."

"No fear here."

Cal pulled a corkscrew out of his shirt pocket.

CHAPTER 33

CORPORAL SCOTT BOWEN slowed his police cruiser as he coasted past the Raymond's River Fire Department. Chief Brian Cosh's red half-ton truck was in the parking lot. It stood out in stark contrast to the dirty white snow banks defining the outer perimeter of the lot. With no new snow for almost three weeks, the piled-up snow was losing its lustre. Now all the sharp edges had dark lines of dirt outlining them. Climbing temperatures had been slowly whittling away the height of the piles, and the brooks and streams were starting to flow again with the runoff. The January thaw was in full bloom. Only in Nova Scotia could you get spring weather in the dead of winter.

Scott wheeled around and parked beside the chief's truck. George Wilson's disappearance investigation had come to a complete halt. The only things new Scott had to contemplate were the weekly updates from Connie's psychic. These had been getting darker and darker in tone as the winter wore on. The latest had George sitting alone in a dark cabin playing with a length of stout rope. He had been tying and untying hangman's nooses. It did not take too much imagination to figure out the implications of these images.

Much of this information had come over the telephone from Connie. Scott wanted to talk to her face-to-face. In that way he would be able to determine how much Connie was buying into the psychic blather.

Seeing Brian Cosh's truck had caused him to detour. Brian seemed to be keeping a close eye on his cousin's health, physical and otherwise. Scott wondered what Brian's views were on this supernatural searching. He would have to try to remain neutral in his questioning. If his own contrary views were too much out front, Brian may hold back on what he really thought. Much to Scott's dismay, otherwise intelligent people seemed to buy into this psychic fiction.

Brian looked up from his desk as Scott tapped lightly on the window glass separating the office from the truck bays. He waved Scott in.

"Just catching up on some paperwork," Brian explained. "Even when business is slow, there seems to be no end to it."

"Tell me about it. It's the bane of my profession. We have to fill out reports to explain why we have nothing to report."

Scott sat in one of the hard maple chairs across from the chief. He hesitated a few seconds before asking: "Heard from Connie lately?"

"I stopped in for a late breakfast a couple of days ago. I had finished up my chores early and thought I'd give her a hand. Turns out she didn't need it, but the trip still earned me a meal. Two farm-fresh eggs, country-cured bacon, homemade bread, toasted. Strawberry-rhubarb jam." He lightly patted his stomach. "I turned down the home fries. Watching my waistline. It was well worth the trip."

"My mouth is watering just listening about it. How was she?"

Brian showed surprise at the question. "She was fine. Has been for several months now. It seems unkind to put it so bluntly, but she appears to have gotten over George's disappearance and moved on with her life. The period of mourning is long over."

Scott contemplated this analysis for a few seconds.

"Do you think she has accepted he is dead or that he simply left her and moved on with his own life?"

Brian shrugged. "Does it really matter? Gone is gone."

"One way offers hope of reconciliation."

Brian let out a short, gruff, non-humorous laugh. "Not in this case. In retrospect, I think there were problems before George disappeared. I don't see her welcoming him back even if he did have the nerve to show his face in Raymond's River again."

Again, Scott let this information sink in.

"Has she talked to you about this psychic she is seeing?"

"Psychic?" The question was laced with incredulity. "Connie Wilson? I don't think Connie buys into that crap. What have you heard?"

Scott gave his hand a dismissive wave. "That's what I was going to ask you."

Brian straightened up the papers he had been working on. Jogged them on the desk and then set them aside. "I've been in close contact with Connie ever since it all went to hell last April. This is the first I've heard of any psychic. Even if one of those whackos had contacted her and she told them to go to hell, I'm sure she would have told me about it. Is there someone out there harassing her?"

Scott studied Brian without answering. His concern was obvious. The underlying threat to anyone trying to take advantage of his cousin stood out as well. Scott was surprised Brian was in the dark about the psychic.

Connie had been giving Scott almost weekly updates on the information she had supposedly been receiving from the other side. Brian was related, but only a cousin. If Connie had chosen not to take Brian into her confidence, it was not up to him to break her faith. He had trusted Brian to know what was going on in Connie's life and had based many of his own decisions on what he had learned from discussions like this. Now it appeared Brian may not have been kept in the loop to the extent Scott had believed.

"It's quite common for people like that to come out of the woodwork in situations like this. I see it all the time. Publicity seekers, nut cases, true believers. I thought Connie may have said something to you."

Brian relaxed again. "No, nothing. I said she was doing good. One of these shysters could set her recovery back with their wild stories. Let me know if you hear anything. I promise you, I'll nip it in the bud right away."

"As you said, Connie is a bright, intelligent woman. I'm sure she can handle the situation if it arises."

"So I guess this means you're not having any luck otherwise? Have you been in contact with soothsayers? Did they contact you or did you call them?" The way Brian's eyes were laughing suggested he was kidding the policeman. The laughter disappeared from them when he saw a vein pop on Scott's forehead. "Only kidding," he quickly added.

Scott shook off any suggestion of wrongdoing. "Of course you are. They often call us when we have cases like this. So far, no one has bothered

"In answer to your first question about having any luck, the answer is none. George has disappeared off the face of the Earth. People disappear from time to time and don't get found for years. When they are running away, it becomes a lot more difficult. They still get found. It's his truck that mystifies me. If George didn't take off on his own, as a lot of people suspect, what happened to his truck? Trucks can't drive away by themselves."

"I'd say you answered your own question." Brian became momentarily silent. He had a pen in his hand and was doodling on his desk pad. He looked up at Scott again. "Connie and I have always been close. Over the last few months, the bonds have grown even tighter. She's never gone into any great detail, but, as I said, I get the impression their marriage was foundering. I don't think she even admitted that fact to herself until George was gone for a while. If the truck drove away, in my opinion, George Wilson was hanging on to the steering wheel at the time, his feet firmly on the pedals, the right one hard to the floor. That's how I see it, for what it's worth."

Scott nodded. That was definitely one option he could not dismiss.

CHAPTER 34

S COTT HAD PHONED ahead to see if Connie Wilson was going to be home. She had assured him her day did not include any travel plans. He could drop in anytime. If she wasn't in the house, she'd be in one of the outbuildings working on some equipment that needed repairs.

Scott had said nothing at the time, but this visit coincided with the nine-month anniversary of George's disappearance. He regretted having nothing new to bring to the table.

Before leaving the office that morning, he had checked all the overnight postings to see if there had been any new action on George's truck. There was none. Members in other parts of the country had long ago stopped searching every black Dodge half-ton they saw. Scott couldn't blame them. It had been a long shot at best.

Still, that was one thing about the case that haunted him. What had happened to that truck? If it had left the province, a computer check of the VIN should have found it being re-registered in some new location. The Nova Scotia plates had expired at the end of December. Even if it was still in the province, there should have been some record of it.

That left three possibilities. He had them recorded on a small section of white board hanging beside his desk.

1. It could have been shipped overseas. Half-ton trucks were popular everywhere in the world.

2. It could have been dismantled. There would be a strong market for second-hand parts from a truck of that age.

3. It could be using stolen tags from some other vehicle. A simple screw driver would be the only tool needed to accomplish that task.

There was one other possibility. It could be sitting in the bottom of a lake, river or ocean somewhere with George Wilson still sitting in the driver's seat. Not exactly as Chief Brian Cosh described, but with George's skeletal hands clinging forever to the steering wheel, the bones of his right foot resting lightly on the gas pedal. George had served as fish food if the window was down, a grotesque reverse aquarium if the windows were up.

Scott shuddered at the thought. He had seen that scenario on a few occasions. Both the swollen, gas-filled, unrecognizable bodies of the long-ago drowned and the picked-clean-to-the-bone bodies which had spent several months or years underwater. Neither was pretty. He tried to clear his mind as he pulled into the driveway leading to the Wilson house. These were not the images he wanted dancing through his head as he greeted Connie Wilson with no news, good or bad.

As he stepped from his car, he glanced over towards the various outbuildings. No sounds emanated from inside of them. He walked up the back steps to the kitchen door and tapped lightly. When no one answered after thirty seconds, he looked back at the outbuildings. They still looked deserted. He knocked again, this time harder.

He detected movement inside and could see someone emerging from the doorway he knew led to the living room. Connie Wilson slowly crossed the room and opened the door to him. Her eyes were red-rimmed, her skin pale. Her hair had the disarrayed look of someone who had been running her fingers constantly up the sides of her head until the path of each finger stood out like an irrigation ditch through a hay field.

"Oh, Corporal. I was just about to call you." Her voice sounded distant. This was not the same person he had been talking with not two hours previously.

"Mrs. Wilson, are you OK?" Her distressed look seemed to call for a more formal interaction.

"Fine," she answered instinctively. "No, no, I'm not fine. My psychic friend called me an hour ago. The news was not good."

Oh, for Christ sake, Scott thought. "What did she have to say?"

Connie's eyes took on a far-away-look. "It's over."

Scott waited for her to continue. When it became apparent she had no more to say, he asked: "What's over? What did this person tell you?"

He took Connie by the arm and guided her towards a chair at the kitchen table. He then hurried back to the door to remove his rubber toe caps.

Connie waved a hand in his direction. "Don't worry about those. A little snow won't hurt this floor. It's seen a lot worse than that. George used to think nothing of tracking all through the house with his barn boots on." A fresh gusher of tears poured down her face. "I don't have to worry about that anymore."

Scott ignored the comment and neatly placed his rubbers on the boot tray beside the door. He noticed the pair of men's, leather slippers already there. He joined Connie at the table. Briefly the thought of taking her hand passed through his mind. The idea was rejected. It would be best to keep this formal until he found out what exactly was going on.

"Mrs. Wilson, tell me what has happened."

Connie brushed the tears from her face with the back of her hands. She took a deep, calming breath and seemed to regain a little of her composure.

"George is dead. He hung himself last night."

Scott struggled to control his reactions. "How could you possibly know that, Mrs. Wilson? What did this woman tell you?"

Connie forced a smile onto her face. "I thought we agreed you were going to call me Connie. Pamela is Mrs. Wilson." A new look of anguish took control of Connie's features. "Oh damn. I have to call Pamela. I have to tell her what happened."

Scott let out a sigh and immediately regretted doing it. Connie's eyes narrowed as she gave him a cold look.

"I know you don't believe any of this, but what have you given me?" She paused, creating a dramatic effect. "Nothing. Absolutely nothing."

Scott fought back an urge to smile. The words to the old Edwin Starr protest song of the seventies had popped into his head, unbidden. Starr believed war was good for absolutely nothing. Scott placed psychics in that same category as Starr did war. They had absolutely no value. He held up his hands as if warding off an attack.

"I apologize. Give me another chance. What did the lady say?"

The disdainful look remained on Connie's face. "She called me this morning just after you did and said it was over. George had hung himself through the night. He left a note on the table in his cabin."

"A note?" Scott shook his head. "What did it say?"

Once again the tears started to flow. "It didn't make a lot of sense. He wrote: 'I can't stand the guilt anymore. I never intended for any of this to happen. I'm sorry.'"

Scott waited for Connie to go on. When she didn't, he asked: "Sorry about what?"

"I don't know." The tears gushed from her eyes. "It makes no sense to me."

"I'd like to talk to this lady. She might be able to give me some details that will assist in the investigation. Give me her phone number."

Connie gave a harsh grunt. "Like you're suddenly a believer. Don't try to con me, Corporal. She doesn't want to talk to you. She says she's not doing this for publicity. She's only trying to help me out. She had been through a similar experience in her earlier life and she knows the anguish I feel."

"I can check your phone records and get the number that way." He smiled at the end of the statement in an attempt to take away some of the combativeness it threatened.

"That's what you'll have to do. I don't know her number. She always calls me."

"Don't you have call display?"

"The number and name are both blocked. I'm sorry, Corporal. I want to get to the bottom of this as much as you do. I feel obligated to respect the lady's wishes." Connie wiped the drying tears from her face. "On an intuitive level, I feel she is right. I think George is dead. I don't how he died. I don't know if he hung himself. I don't know what he would feel guilty about. I just feel something has changed and he is now dead. Call it women's intuition."

Connie brushed some invisible crumbs off the table before looking back up at Scott. "On the bright side, if that is the right choice of words, I will now be able to get on with my life. It's been hell for the past year with this hanging over my head. Every time the phone rang, I would wonder if this was the call that would tell me where he is or," a hitch came back into her voice, "if he was dead. Now I know."

Scott stared at her, not knowing how to respond to that statement. If this was going to bring her some sort of closure, what right did he have to rain on her parade? He didn't believe a word of what the psychic had said. On the other hand, he wasn't the one who had to live every day with the wondering and doubt. And furthermore, he had nothing to offer to contradict the psychic's story. The case had gone so cold, it could be used to keep an icebox functioning. This time he reached out and covered Connie's hand with his. Connie smiled.

"Well, that's one way to look at it," he finally said and let the subject drop.

CHAPTER 35

"SHE SAID HE'S dead. Committed suicide."

Detective-Sergeant Jim McDonald studied the face of Corporal Scott Bowen before responding to those two statements.

"Who said he's dead?"

"The psychic. Who else would know stuff like this?"

The two policemen were once again sipping coffee at the Tim Horton's coffee shop in the Elmsdale mall. These periodic get-togethers had become a ritual. Although Jim's area of operation was Major Crimes, he liked to keep his finger on the pulse of what was taking place in the area surrounding the metropolitan centre.

Many of the people he ended up dealing with had come into the city from these nearby towns and villages. Often naive, sometimes bad from the start, some of them found themselves caught up with the criminal element always looking for fresh blood at the grass-roots level. People unknown to the city police who could avoid immediate suspicion when a crime took place. All big-city police forces had their lists of known suspects to match up with their particular areas of expertise. It took a while for these newcomers to earn a spot on those lists.

Scott did his best to keep track of the comings and goings of the local thugs in his jurisdiction, passing any information on their movements on to Jim when appropriate.

With this cooperation, a lot of these newbies to the city crime scene were caught sooner rather than later. Scott had already passed on a couple of new names and descriptions to Jim at this meeting. These two had not reported back to the school system after the

Christmas break. By talking to their friends and associates, Scott learned their new residence was in Halifax and not in Alberta, as most people had suspected. His initial reaction was good riddance; then he felt a pang of guilt and decided he had best pass the information on to Jim. It was the least he could do, as his problems moved on to become someone else's.

Neither boy had committed any serious crimes. They were involved in vandalism at the school, suspected of petty theft by some of their neighbours and were a terror on the roads with their beat-up clunkers. Scott deemed them prime candidates for recruitment by some of the organized city gangs. Jim agreed.

Now the conversation had moved on to unsolved cases. George Wilson's disappearance always sat near the top of Scott's mind. For the past ten months, he had run down every lead, no matter how vague, that had come along. These leads had been few and far between in recent months, except for the ranting of a psychic who could see into the ether.

"She claimed he left a note about not being able to stand the guilt anymore." Scott leaned back in his chair. "Some crap about being sorry for what happened. No other details."

"I thought I had advised you to go head-to-head with that woman and destroy her credibility before she got herself too established in the case."

"You did. It didn't happen. Connie protected her identify like a father defending the honour of his virgin daughter. I couldn't even get so much as a name. It's hard to believe a woman who seems to have such a firm grasp on reality in all other aspects of her life can buy into this crap. It's almost like she is filling some gap left by George's disappearance with this virtual image of her husband. She shares his mind but not his body. At least up until now. This latest revelation puts paid to that connection."

"So tell me about the death. Did she give you any clues you might be able to work on? Location? Method? Time?"

"Only method and time. Hung himself one night a week or so ago. The best I could do on a location was a cabin in the woods. That narrows it down to somewhere in the boreal forest."

"What did the cabin look like?"

"From previous descriptions, it was your typical hunting camp. Rough-hewn walls, clunky wooden furniture, built-in bunks and an old wood stove in the centre. There are thousands of them out there matching that depiction. Hell, I know of at least ten right around here."

"You've checked them out, I trust."

"More than once, including this last week. Chief Cosh organized some snowmobilers to do a ride-by. Didn't give them any details, just had them take a look. The last thing we want to do is feed the ego of this psychic."

Jim took a bite of his walnut cruller and slowly chewed it. "That's a lot of effort for a non-believer." A slow grin spread across the sergeant's face as he watched Scott react to statement.

"When a case is genuinely as cold as this one, you have to follow up even when you know the whole exercise is a waste of time." Scott sipped his coffee. "Strange thing, though. She's been exceptionally quiet in the media. Probably waiting for a body to be found so she can blend her version of events into reality." His shoulders had a slump to them, telegraphing his frustration with his lack of success. It was apparent he felt he had let Connie Wilson down. Now he was overcompensating by going against his better judgment and following Connie's flights of fancy.

"The good news is," Jim said, "if there is any truth in her vision, next year when hunting season opens again, someone may open their cabin to the withered remains of your victim. Then you'll finally be able to stamp this case closed. In the meantime, you'll have to keep it on the back burner along with the Jason Browne investigation in case something useful comes up."

Scott scowled. He firmly held up his forefinger. "A, I still don't believe this shit, and B," his big finger joined the first to form the peace sign, "what if he owns the cabin himself? If it's in an isolated area, it may never be checked out." Scott paused. His face took on a perplexed look. The second part of the sergeant's statement hit his conscious mind.

"Jason Browne? That clown who fell, jumped or got pushed into the Bay? Hold the phone, buddy. Stop the bus. I was only doing some leg work on that case. The last time I saw that folder, it was on your desk. By the way, how are *you* coming along with it?"

Jim laughed. "Thought I might be able to slip it back into your bivouac. I've interviewed the previous owners of the junk yard where Browne was arrested for car theft. They vaguely remember him as a hanger-on who was always trying to ingratiate himself with more powerful people. Couldn't give me any new leads or information about family. Oh yeah, they assured me the new owners were as honest as the day is long. They would never consider running the yard as a chop shop. I'm preparing a search warrant so we can go in and have a look. It's taking a while for it to grind through the court process."

Jim shrugged. "But that's police work for you. If it was easy, everyone would be doing it." His radiant smile lit up his face.

Scott responded with a half-hearted smile of his own. It had nowhere near the brilliance of that of his fellow officer. He, after all, was the one working the open, missing-person case with a live wife, live friends and definitely a live mother. When Jason Browne dropped off the face of the Earth, almost literally, there was hardly a shudder in the time-space continuum. Scott's interest in the man had ceased with the passing of the file back to Major Crimes. No one else had shed a tear for the passing of Jason Browne; neither would Scott.

CHAPTER 36

THE CALL CAME into the depot before seven a.m. Scott, always an early riser, was there even though he was not on duty for another hour. He instinctively reached out and answered the phone. A drunken ATV driver was terrorizing Raymond's River's main street. He was doing wheelies, smoking his tires until clouds of nose-irritating smoke made the street impassable and generally interfering with the progress of all those commuting citizens who had to get to work in the city before eight o'clock.

There was no doubt of the identity of this besotted buffoon. Every caller identified him as David Gates. Scott searched his memory for some sort of recognition. He knew the name had a familiar ring. Then it came to him in a flash. He was one of George Wilson's drinking buddies, the guy who didn't want to participate in the search unless it was from a perch atop his red-and-blue Yamaha four-wheeler. He recalled the bulbous, red-veined nose of a heavy drinker. Drunk at seven in the morning would not be foreign to the likes of David Gates.

This was not some immature, coming-of-age prank of a teenage boy rebelling against authority. Scott placed Gates' age somewhere on the plus side of forty. What kind of bee had gotten into his bonnet? Scott would find out soon enough. He grabbed his hat and headed for his cruiser.

He hit his lights and siren and eased down on the gas pedal until he was cruising along at about 120 km/h. At that speed, his senses had to especially heighten to the possibility of someone pulling out of a driveway on the twisting, winding Highway 14.

His goal was to catch this clown still in the act. He didn't want to have to go looking for him down some back road. He wanted it all on video tape.

Sporadically, he met pockets of cars who must have risked passing Gates. Most of their speeds matched his. This was not a good situation.

As he crested the hill above the little village, dark clouds of tire smoke drifted his way. Even above his siren, he could hear the roar of the engine of the mighty machine. He checked to make sure his in-car camera was recording the outside events.

Gates had his front wheels locked into a tight left turn, forcing the machine to circle continuously in the middle of the road. Black, brackish smoke poured from the back tires, alternately obliterating the view of the drunken man and then giving strobe-like views of the stunt, depending of the fluctuations of the wind blowing down the road. Gates appeared to be oblivious of events around him. Scott could see Gates' greasy, black hair trailing out behind him. No helmet.

The challenge for Scott would be to get control of the man without getting involved in a high-speed chase. He knew the ATV could almost match his cruiser's top speed. He also knew how dangerous it would be to have a drunken fool hanging on to the handle-bars of a machine going that fast over the rough, bumpy roads around this rural village.

Through a break in the smoke, he noticed another flashing red light. One of the village's fire trucks pulled across the road on the opposite side to Scott, effectively blocking any egress Gates might have in that direction. Scott changed the pitch of his siren to a bassier rat-a-tat sound. From this close, it would be impossible for Gates not to hear this new, louder, more penetrating warning.

Gates' eyes locked on the approaching police car. His head seemed to swivel on his shoulders as the ATV kept up its rotation and the head appeared not to be turning. He let go of one handle-bar and gave Scott the universal middle-finger greeting. Then he wrenched the handle-bars to the right.

The front wheels of the Yamaha straightened and the vehicle reared into a sudden wheelie like a stallion getting ready to bolt. The machine was sideways in the road. When the wheels dropped, it shot forward, straight at the nearby ditch. Gates yanked, too hard, on the handle-bars in an attempt to spin past the blocking fire truck. In the blink of an eye, the right-hand wheels left the ground. The machine flipped on its side and disappeared over the hard, crusted snow bank. Just as suddenly, it reappeared, bouncing and rolling across the adjoining field. First the undercarriage came into view, followed by the empty seat and then the undercarriage again. Once, twice, three times before landing upright on its four wheels. Gates no longer sat in the driver's seat.

Scott jumped from his vehicle. He noticed Brian Cosh coming from the other direction. Brian had been driving the fire truck. Both men met at the point the ATV had momentarily disappeared before rolling back into sight minus its rider.

David Gates lay in the bottom of the ditch covered in mud. He was about six feet down the embankment. The indentation at the bottom of the trench was narrower than the spread of the quad's handle-bars. With the luck only drunks seemed to exhibit, he had avoided being crushed by the dropping machine. The handle-bars had hit the top of the gully and bounced the machine away from Gates, rolling out into the field. The startled Gates was left behind in the narrow ditch, spitting mud and water from his mouth, but otherwise unharmed.

"Don't move," Brian called down to him. "You might have a neck or back injury."

"We can only hope," Scott said under his breath.

Brian turned to face him. He had heard the comment. "It may take us a while to determine how injured he is. He will have to stay in that mud until we do." He winked at the policeman.

Gates had landed in the ditch with enough force to sink him into the mud. When he tried to get up, he discovered he couldn't. Unknown to him, the suction of the wet muck was holding him down. Fear replaced the drunken bleariness in his eyes.

"Help me. I can't move. I'm paralyzed."

"That water's got to be freezing cold," Scott said. "It won't take long for hypothermia to set in. We've got to get him out."

"I suppose so," Brian said. "The snowmobile suit should keep him warm for a while. Wouldn't want any of my men to get injured clambering down that bank."

Scott nodded. "You know best."

Gates was sobering up fast. "Somebody help me." Fear was evident in the plaintive scream.

"Hold still," Brian said, still from the top of the bank. "An ambulance is on its way."

"I can't move. Get me out of here."

The more he struggled, the more he settled into the mud that was engulfing him. His broad shoulders and bulky snowmobile suit filled the width of the narrow channel and stanched the flow of water on the uphill side of him, the side where his head rested. Now his face was almost at water level. His ears had turned dark red.

"Help me. I'm going to drown."

Brian looked at Scott's clean uniform. "You stay here. He might really have head and neck injuries. We shouldn't move him until we get a backboard and collar here. It's not going to be easy to extract him from that mud. Even if he isn't hurt, it will be good practice for my team. You can't pass up opportunities like this."

Scott thought for a moment. He looked down at his neatly pressed uniform pants. "You're right, Chief. I don't think he's going anywhere. I'll wait until you bring him up."

From down below, Gates screamed up at them: "Get me out of here, you bastards. I'm going to drown." He raised his head slightly and spit out a mouthful of water.

"Relax," Brian said. "You're not drowning. The water is as high as it's going to get." This last statement was true. Two little rivulets of water were flowing past each of Gates' ears, over his shoulders and into the front of the suit. From their position above Gates, this was obvious. From Gates' perspective, with the water lapping at his ears, drowning seemed inevitable. "Keep your mouth shut and stop moving your neck."

Gates started to respond but got another mouthful of freezing cold water. He kept his mouth shut as ordered.

A small crowd was gathering on the village's main street. People who had been disgusted by the antics of the ATV driver were feeling a sense of satisfaction that justice was being served for once with one of these drunken yahoos.

Within a minute, more volunteer firemen arrived. They got Gates loaded onto a backboard and dragged up the bank.

To be safe, Brian insisted he remain strapped to the board until the paramedics could come and have a look at him. Someone like Gates would never miss an opportunity to initiate a lawsuit if he thought there was a buck to be made. Brian wanted to head that off at the pass.

Scott took advantage of the intervening time to conduct an interrogation of his prisoner.

He started by advising him of his rights to a lawyer and to remain silent. Gates was interested in neither, especially the part about remaining silent.

"Let me up off this fucking stretcher."

"Not until a doctor checks you out. You've been involved in an accident. You were driving drunk and recklessly out on the main street. You may be injured."

"I'm not injured. Let me off this thing." A string of words that would make George Carlin blush followed that statement. Scott let him go on until he ran out of steam.

"OK, that's out of your system; now let's answer some questions."

Gates gave him a smouldering look. "What do you want to know?"

"Seven in the morning is a bit early to be as drunk as you are. Mind telling me what the occasion is?"

To Scott's surprise, Gates' eyes misted over. An actual tear formed in one corner.

"I was at a wake for a dear, departed friend."

Scott waited, a look of impatience on his face.

"Didn't you hear? George Wilson killed himself."

Scott and Brian exchanged looks.

"When? Where?" Brian had heard Connie's tale about the physic, but had discarded it.

"Last week. He hung himself at a camp in the woods."

A look of disappointment replaced the look of surprise on Brian's face.

"Who told you this?"

"Right from the horse's mouth. George's mother told Alwin Downey's sister, who told Alwin, who told me. A bunch of us got together at Cal Lindsay's place last night and had a farewell party for George."

"You were at Cal's place until six o'clock this morning?" Brian asked. "I find that hard to believe."

"We started at Cal's. Then we went back to Alwin's until his mother kicked us out. We jumped on our rigs and drove over to my place. We were going to take a sunset drive along the river to celebrate George's life. The other pussies are passed out on my living room floor. I was just taking a farewell ride for George when you assholes showed up. Everyone deserves a tribute of some sort. His bitch of a wife wasn't doing nothing."

Scott noticed the muscles in Brian's face tighten. His fists bunched up.

"Look bad to hit a man taped to a backboard," Scott cautioned.

Brian glared across at him.

"Not too many people around here would care one way or the other. Mr. Gates has put on these road demonstrations before. Many times before. Today, he claims to be commemorating the death of a friend. On other occasions, I think he was celebrating the opening of a pack of cigarettes. It doesn't take much to get him out. The only reason you were called today was because he was keeping honest people from getting to work. He's not usually up this early."

Scott nodded his understanding. He looked back down at Gates.

"Takes a lot of booze to keep you drinking until sunup. Where'd you get it?"

Gates looked at him warily. "What difference does it make? Ultimately it came from a government liquor store somewhere. It's people like me that keeps this province going. The taxes I pay on booze are what pay your salary."

"I wish," Scott said. "They don't pay me that much. You personally could keep a whole detachment going."

"So the visit to Cal's didn't involve buying any liquor?" Brian asked. "You think we just fell off the turnip truck?"

"You might have. I have nothing to say about Cal Lindsay or anybody else for that matter."

Again Scott looked across Gates' prone body at Brian. "Lindsay is the local bootlegger?"

Before Brian could answer, Gates interrupted. "I didn't say I bought anything from him. I didn't say nothing."

"Afraid Cal's going to cut you off? He's going to know you spent an hour or so in here talking to the PO-lice. Word will get back to him."

"Let it. He knows I wouldn't say nothing about where I buy my booze. He knows me. I can keep my mouth shut."

Scott laughed. "If only. I guess I can take that as a confession. Good work, Chief."

CHAPTER 37

THE FEBRUARY MEETING of the Red Hat Society had the ladies displaying their athletic skills at a nearby Truro bowling alley. Raymond's River was too small to support such a facility. That fact didn't diminish the popularity of the sport. The talent level ranged from "I kept that one on the alley" all the way up to "How do you mark a strike on a spare?"

Bowling, however, was not on the top of everyone's mind that day. Lisa Tingley had been doing her homework. Red-headed baby Tim Schofield was a challenge she couldn't ignore. She had already traced the maternal side of the family back to Tim's great-great-great-grandfather John Haydon. Now she was working on the paternal side.

This was more of a challenge. She had no ending point as she did with Elizabeth. That didn't slow Lisa down. In her opinion, she had the starting point: the same John Haydon.

Lisa had lived all of her seventy-five years in Raymond's River. Until Tim's arrival on that cold, stormy December night, there had been no other flaming red-heads except John Haydon in the village. She wracked her mind to think of any strawberry blonds. None came to mind. John had to be the source of that recessive red-hair gene.

Lisa acknowledged the possibility some outsider had moved into the area and contaminated the gene pool. On a massive leap of faith, she concluded that didn't happen. Her reasoning: she said so. That was good enough for her.

First on her agenda was a trip to Halifax and the Nova Scotia Archives. She spent several days rolling through the microfilm tracing John Haydon's family tree all the way to the present. Over half of

Raymond's River seemed to have some tentacle of their family that somehow or other managed to work its way back to "old carrot top." Lisa was undeterred.

Next she talked to all the older people who dropped into the liquor store where she worked. What did they remember about some of the older families?

At this stage, she had to cut through the faulty memories of some of the people she talked to. Lisa knew some of these people had no idea what they were talking about. Lisa, herself, remembered the families in question and knew the chain of relationships. She remembered who had married whom. In most cases she had been at the weddings. In some she had been a bridesmaid.

She was the classic example of always a bridesmaid and never a bride. Men were a bunch of chicken shits. Back in her marrying days, they had been afraid of a strong-minded woman, a woman who took nothing off anybody. Any man who thought he could order her around was in for a quick lesson on what was to become the new order.

Lisa never felt the need to burn her bra, but those Janie-come-latelies were following in the deep footsteps she had long ago stomped into the earth. She was a classic feminist before the word had ever come into existence.

Still, she wasn't about being bullheaded just for the sake of bullheadedness. If she thought someone could help her quest, she was not too proud to ask them. Some of those asked gave her legitimate leads; others sparked her own mind to remember long-forgotten events.

She even grabbed a couple of bottles of sherry off the store shelves and set out to visit some of the older people in the community. Initially, she had started with a clipboard. That grew to a file folder. Now she carried a briefcase. Every bit of remembrance was filed away for future study.

Lisa eliminated those who had blond-headed children and all their descendants. The blond gene was also recessive. The two genes,

Lisa decided, would not combine. That cut her list in half. Gregor Mendel might have thought she was taking liberties with his laws of genetics, but Gregor didn't intimidate Lisa anymore than any other man. She was a woman on a mission and she was not to be stopped.

She took her notes to the liquor store with her. She studied them during the slack periods. She showed them to the older customers who might have some insight. She turned off her television at night. No sacrifice there. All the good shows had been replaced by inane, bitchy reality shows. With the flick of the on-off switch, her interest in who got voted off the island, the boat, the house, the street, wherever, disappeared. She felt better for it.

Very quickly, she became an expert on every family in Raymond's River and surrounding area. She knew who was related to whom and how. She could rattle off how anybody in the community could be traced back to old John Haydon or not, if that was the case.

She never lost sight of the prize. Who was the father of Tim Schofield?

Her lists were honed over and over until she reverted back to one clipboard with a few definite possibilities. These people had one thing in common. Several people recalled there were a couple of dark-haired men sporting red beards when they let them grow out. Lisa jumped on these names. The red recessive gene was alive and well in these men. The final path to success had do go through them. Lisa declared it to be so.

Scientific methodology be dammed. Woman's intuition was leading this search and the search was almost over.

CHAPTER 38

SCOTT SCOWLED AT the ringing phone on his desk. He was trying to catch up on his paperwork and had scheduled some office time to make this happen. He leaned over and looked at the call display.

Blocked name. Blocked number.

Scott sighed. Telemarketer or another police force. He didn't want to talk to either.

Reluctantly, he picked up the phone. "Corporal Bowen."

"Good news, Scott."

Scott recognized the voice of Detective-Sergeant Jim McDonald. With Jim, the words "good news" did not always mean Scott should get excited. He hesitated for a few seconds.

"Great, let's hear it."

Jim laughed. He could hear the lack of enthusiasm in Scott's voice. "I've gotten word on one of your investigations. The warrant to search the junk yard where Jason Browne did business has come through."

Scott leaned back in his office chair. An audible sigh could be heard going across the wires to the Halifax office. "I care about this, why? I dumped Jason Browne back in your lap a long time ago, remember? Frankly, I don't care why or how he died. He was a scourge on society. Good riddance to bad rubbish."

Jim faked a shocked tone of voice. "A statement like that from a true humanitarian. I don't believe it. This warrant has been almost eight months in the making. I finally had to go to the auto theft division to get some help to push it through.

"They set up a sting operation. They took a list of recently stolen cars and sent in some undercover operatives to try to purchase parts for a similar vehicle. It took a few tries, but they succeeded. As a bonus, we have an inventory of used-car parts from the legitimate buys. If you need anything, give them a call."

Scott could tell he was kidding, but refrained from even a small smile. Even though he was alone at his desk, he didn't want to get caught up in the sergeant's scheming. He had spent too many hours trying to figure out what had happened to Jason Browne, with nothing to show for his efforts but a slight February tan from his time spent interviewing several party-goers last summer. He was determined not to get involved again.

Jim continued as if Scott had responded positively to his attempt at humour.

"It may not help us much in the Browne case at this point. We'll grill them on any knowledge they have of Browne. Who knows, they might slip up and reveal something. By now they may be feeling complacent. Someone must know what happened to the man.

"At any rate, if they are a chop shop, it will give us an excuse to shut them down again. That can be the Jason Browne legacy."

Scott scoffed. "His legacy consists of him being found bare arse to the wind at the bottom of a cliff. The reason for his death eludes us, but whoever sent the message knows and so, I would imagine, do the people for whom the message was intended."

"True. But if there was some sort of connection to the chop shop, we may be able to make the link. Do you want to be in on the raid when it goes down?"

"Me? Why would I?" Scott hesitated. Even to himself, that question didn't sound convincing. Both he and the sergeant knew Scott couldn't extricate himself from this case after all the hours he had logged on it last summer, despite his outward reluctance to get involved again. Jim remained silent, waiting for the capitulation. Scott didn't bother trying to outwait him. "OK, what the hell? Give me a call when you get the date and I'll clear my calendar."

"Tomorrow morning at dawn." The words carried a sense of urgency. "We want to catch them still in bed if we can."

"You're not wasting any time."

"We don't want to risk any chance of a leak."

"Makes sense. Who are we?"

"The Emergency Response Team will lead the charge. If the junk yard owners killed Browne, any other deaths may be considered freebies. We want to deter them from opening fire on us."

"That makes sense as well. I'm in favour of anything that keeps me safe."

"I agree. There will be some officers from auto theft. I'll represent Major Crimes. You'll be part of my team. We've got some cadets to paw through the parts bins. One or two guys from the drug squad may tag along."

The scuttlebutt on the streets suggested this junk yard distributed drugs to the street-level sellers. No sales to individuals were suspected at the site, but some believed many of the boxes said to be containing second-hand carburetors or tail lights or even large items like fenders also contained baggies of white powder or bottles of coloured pills. At the same time, despite exotic names like Mustang, Pinto and Jaguar, these same people believed many of the wrecks hauled onto the lot were actually mules. Secret stashes of drugs found new temporary homes while hiding in these vehicles.

To date, the drug squad had not been able to gather enough evidence to warrant a search. They were now standing by, with a prosecutor at the ready, in case the quest for stolen auto parts revealed evidence of drug dealing.

The current warrant wouldn't allow them to start tearing cars apart looking for drugs. Still, if they spotted anything in plain view during their own search, they would be allowed to act on it. The judicial system, which often seemed to tie one of their hands behind their back, had given them permission to be all over the site. It would be a shame to waste such an opportunity.

Spot one thing out of the ordinary and the ERT members would secure the scene until the new search warrant could be drawn up to include drugs and drug paraphernalia. This could be a two-for. Actually, a three-for if they could tie the owners to the death of Jason Browne.

The upcoming search would be thorough.

CHAPTER 39

"JOE WILSON HAD a red beard? Are you sure? I always remember Joe as being clean-shaven." Mable Booth stifled a laugh. "Pamela would have it no other way. Beards were undignified."

"Not back in the sixties. Every kid who could grow facial hair had either a beard or a mustache," Lisa Tingley said.

"And that was before Pamela came on the scene," Veronica Thompson offered. "I remember Joe's beard during his hippie phase. It was dark at the top of his face and got redder as it went down. The mustache was all red. The first thing Pamela did was make him shave it off."

"Lisa, what are you saying?" A shocked look came on Mable's face as the reality of what Lisa was suggesting sunk in. "Joe has been dead for better than ten years. He's not Tim Schofield's father. Are you saying George Wilson is the father? That's why he disappeared?"

A hush dropped over the table like someone had asked for a volunteer to organize the clean-up committee. The other two women looked at Mable and then at Lisa. The significance of her accusation settled over the rest of the foursome like a falling parachute. George Wilson had been having an affair with the kid next door. George, who was twice Elizabeth's age. More than twice, in fact.

Veronica was the first to speak. She lowered her voice, but still spoke with passion. "No, Lisa. You've got it wrong. Not George. He wouldn't cheat on Connie. Not with the neighbour's kid; not with anyone. The idea is absurd."

Joan McNeil leaned over from the next table. She had picked up Veronica's whisper with her newly acquired computer-powered hearing aids. "Did someone say George Wilson was cheating on

Connie? Men. None of them can keep it in their pants. Who was he doing it to?"

"Stop this. Stop this right now," Mable said. She waved her hands at her table mates. Her voice was also held to a whisper. "This is a Red Hat meeting, not a gossip session. We're here to bowl and have fun. Stop and think about what effect these unfounded accusations will have on the people here."

She turned and looked further down the allies to see where Pamela Wilson was sitting. Pamela was at the far end talking with Edna Hiltz. Neither lady was paying the least bit of attention to what was being said around them. Their attention was focused on the score sheets. The game must have been close.

"The facts are the facts," Lisa said. "I've done a great deal of research on this and George is one of three possible candidates."

"Well it has to be one of the other two," Veronica said. "Who are they?"

"No," Mable said. "This is not the place to be discussing this. This can only lead to hurt feelings and resentments. That's not why we are here."

"Candidates for what?" Joan asked. She came over from the neighbouring alley. So far she was the only outsider interested in the discussion. She had just bowled a spare and her turn was over. The others on her lane kept bowling.

"Get your head out of your friggin' ass, Mable. Not talking about it is not going to change anything. There is a possibility George Wilson is Tim Schofield's father. Pamela can try to will that away, but that won't make it happen."

"What!" Joan's voice carried throughout the building, even above the sounds of falling pins. All eyes turned towards her.

"Go back to your games," Mable said, an edge to her voice. "Joan just heard about a new man who might be interested in sleeping with her. We all know how excited that gets her."

There was a little titter of laughter and a lot of smiles as everyone resumed what they were doing.

"God will get you for that," Joan said. "Still, if you know someone, introduce me. All the regulars are running out of gas, even with the little blue pill to give them a boost. It does no good to have a hard pecker if you don't have the horsepower to drive it. I don't mind doing some of the work, but I'll be damned if I'm going to do it all."

Veronica blushed the colour of the red hat perched on her head, a familiar condition when she sat anywhere near the outspoken Joan. "Joan. How can you talk like that?"

"I just tell it like it is, dearie. I don't gloss over nothing. Now tell me about George Wilson and Elizabeth Schofield. Give me all the dirt."

"There is no dirt," Mable said. She lowered her voice so those at the other tables couldn't hear her. "Lisa is into wild speculation about little Tim's father. She doesn't know enough to keep her nose out of other people's business."

Joan looked over at Lisa, a gleam in her eye. "Shame on you, Lisa. Fill me in with all the details. Who saw them where?"

Lisa sat up primly in her chair. "No one actually saw them. This is all scientific. George's father, Joseph, was the son of Elizabeth Haydon, who was John Haydon's daughter. Elizabeth married Joe Wilson.

"Ironically, Elizabeth Schofield is named after her great-great-aunt Elizabeth who was George's grandmother."

"So George and Elizabeth are related. How creepy is that."

"They would be second cousins, once removed. That's not really very close. They probably didn't even know about it. The Schofields didn't associate with the rest of the family. Some dispute about the property back before the War when Red died."

"And how was Elizabeth related to Red Haydon? I knew Red when I was a young girl, not in the Biblical sense mind you. I just knew him when I was a teenager."

"Elizabeth's grandmother Mary was Robert's daughter. Robert and Elizabeth, George's grandmother, were brother and sister. They were both Red's kids. The red-hair gene passed down through both branches of the family until it merged again in little Tim."

"Lisa. You don't know that." Mable could barely contain her anger. "You can't just make an accusation like that in public. Think of the hurt you are going to cause all concerned."

Again the room went silent. Some of the ladies left their seats to come closer to see what all the excitement was about. Pamela Wilson was among them.

"Ladies, go back to your seats," Mable said, a note of pleading in her voice. "This is supposed to be a games night. Let's enjoy the game."

It was too late. The stopper had been removed from the bottle of perfume. There was no putting the fragrance back inside. To some, the gossip-mongers among the group, the scent had a pleasant feel. To others, Pamela for sure, the odour was pure toilet water and not the French version.

Those closest to the discussion eyed Pamela as she came closer. She had been bowling poorly and was not in any mood for hijinks. Then they looked back at Lisa, wondering if she was going to make the accusation right on the spot. Before either woman could speak, Veronica stood up.

"You said there were a couple of other names, Lisa. Who were they?"

Lisa looked defiantly at Veronica. Pamela Wilson didn't intimidate her. Then she looked at Mable. Mable still had the pleading look on her face. She didn't want the Red Hat meeting to deteriorate into a feud between the various families. Lisa sighed.

"There's the obvious one, John Haydon. He's a great-grandson of Red; named after him in fact."

Those in the know about the discussion nodded their heads. It wouldn't have taken a whole lot of research to come up with that connection. John, however, had black hair and when he grew his beard in the annual beard-growing contest, it came in black as well.

"David Gates is also a direct descendant. David's mother was the granddaughter of William Soley, who was Marion Holdon's son. Marion was a sister of Elizabeth and Robert. His beard has a red tinge, as we all know, since half the time he roams around unshaven."

"David Gates and Elizabeth Schofield? Not in a million years." Joan McNeil shook her head as if she was the definitive expert on the subject of who might couple and who would not. No one doubted her qualifications.

"What are you talking about?" Pamela asked. "You're not going on about young Tim Schofield again. Give that topic a rest." Initially, Pamela had been eager to discuss young Tim. That was when she had all the knowledge and the others hung on her every word. Since then, Pamela had been able to find out nothing new and the others had lost interest in her speculations.

"Pamela's right," Mable said, almost too eagerly. "Lisa, it's your turn to bowl. You're holding up the game and it's almost time to eat." She made a sweeping gesture with her hands: "Everyone get back to your allies and let's get the bowling finished. The meal is ready to be served."

For Mable, food almost always trumped any other activity. She wasn't alone. The others moved back to their lanes. If Pamela noticed a certain section of the Red Hatters was avoiding her, she said nothing.

The restaurant attached to the bowling alley had a buffet dinner being served. The Red Hatters ate for a special low rate as part of their bowling experience. For many of them, the food was the most enjoyable part of the outing. Bowling was too much effort at their age.

CHAPTER 40

A REDDISH TINGE bordered the eastern sky as the sun slowly struggled to make its appearance for the day. It would be another ten minutes before the brilliant, yellow ball actually crawled into sight.

A half-mile from Duggan's Junk Yard sat a line of dark police vehicles. Their occupants were leaning over the engine bonnet of the lead SUV. A blow-up of an aerial photo held all their attention.

"There are two gates." Sergeant Jim McDonald pointed to two spots in the photo with a tight-beamed flashlight. "Both have heavy chains holding them shut."

Sergeant Ron Tingley of the Emergency Response Team (ERT) followed Jim's beam of light. Jim was telling him nothing he didn't already know. Ron had committed the contents of the photo to memory. He knew where every building set in relation to the other buildings. He knew how many rows of junked cars and trucks there were, and in which direction the streets and alleys of these vehicles flowed. He could name the year and make of the first car in each row.

This knowledge didn't only come from the photograph. The previous afternoon, under the pretense of buying a used part for his old Ford clunker, he had toured as much of the yard as he possibly could without arousing suspicion from the staff. When they said they did indeed have rims that would fit his car, he followed them from building to building to the remote location of a trailer full of such rims. Ron knew a car as old as his would have the parts stored further away from the generally asked for newer parts.

By combining the knowledge from that tour and the overhead view of the aerial photo, Ron felt as prepared as possible for the upcoming assault on the yard. The presence of the members of the ERT in their dark body armour, with automatic weapons at the ready, suggested more than a routine search was being prepared for.

While everyone hoped there would be no violence, that the owners and workers would quietly stand to one side, perhaps muttering about their civil rights being violated, preparations for the worst-case scenario were firmly in place.

Finding the murderer of Jason Browne stood high on the list of expectations of the raid in the eyes of both Jim and Scott. To everyone else, that aspect of the plan remained off the radar screen. Ron Tingley, however, was aware he might be dealing with suspected murderers. Although his team required no warnings about being careful, he did pass the information on to them. That only strengthened their resolve to quickly put down any resistance. They would not wait to be fired on before responding themselves.

"Chains are no problem," Ron said. "We can either pop the lock, cut the chain, or pull down the entire gate. It depends on how much of an impact you want to make on entering."

Jim contemplated the choices. The decision had already been made at the pre-dawn meeting to just crack the locks. Still, ripping the gate off its posts would set the pace for the rest of the day.

"We'll follow the plan. I want to be in the main offices before they know what hit them. The faster we get inside, the less chance there will be of violence. I can see them shooting across the yard at us; I don't see them pulling a gun five feet away from one of your men. The helmets and armour make a pretty imposing sight."

"Not to mention the rifle pointed at their heads and laser beams dancing around their chests."

"Exactly. We'll let your guys in first and secure the site. Then we'll follow up with the searchers. You've got your copy of the search warrant?"

Ron patted a pocket on the front of his Kevlar vest. "Right here. Mine and theirs. If he's reluctant to take it, I'll shove it up his nose."

"OK, sounds like a plan. The sun will be up in about three minutes. You'll be moving in from the east. Even if someone is looking out the window, he'll be squinting into the sun. Let's get into position."

Ron gave a radio signal to his men. A man on a well-muffled motorcycle pulled away from the others.

On a parallel road on the other side of the junk yard, a similar machine left another group of vehicles ready to assault the back gate. These motorcyclists were assigned to snap the locks. When the bulk of the party hit the yard, the gates would be standing open for them. There would be no slowing down. The first stop would be two feet in front of the buildings.

From overhead, the sound of a helicopter could be heard. It would pass over thirty seconds ahead of the attack. If there was anyone out in the yard, their positions would be pinpointed. The dogs, two Dobermans and a big black shepherd, that roamed the yard freely at night, would also be located. Previous research showed the dogs were slackards. They were usually asleep by sunup. Six men were assigned to quickly subdue them before moving on to other tasks. Drugs were the weapon of choice against the animals. Pistols would be used as backups. A bullet in the head would be a blessing for the abused dogs. Keeping them hungry and mistreating them is what some people believed made for good watch dogs.

Jim stuck his hand out to Ron. "Hit 'em fast and hit 'em hard." They bumped fists.

"There's no other way."

Ron climbed into the lead SUV. The convoy moved out as quietly as possible. They would not over-rev their engines. The first sound heard by the junk yard staff would be their doors crumbling under the hammering of a handheld battering ram. If that failed on the second swing, a hydraulic ram would extend from the truck parked in front of the office door. No door, no matter how well it was reinforced, would withstand the force of a two-ton, 400-horsepower battering ram. The steel-plated truck could drive right through the wall if called upon to do so.

As it turned out, the office was empty at sunup. The attack force quickly spread out and contained the unoccupied building. They would hold their positions until the officers serving the search warrant had completed their tasks.

The units coming through the back gate were assigned the task of capturing the house and its occupants. They simultaneously came through the kitchen and front entryway doors. An older man and woman were sipping tea at the kitchen table. The shock of the door crashing in caused the man to topple over backwards in his chair and spill coffee down the front of his shirt. He let out a scream of pain, coupled with a cry of surprise. His wife held her ground at the table, but her eyes became the size of the saucers.

"Stay down," the first armed man through the door ordered. He aimed his weapon at the man's head. The old man ignored the order and rolled over onto his knees and pulled at the buttons of his steaming hot shirt.

The cop recognized the situation and as soon as the old man had the last button undone, the cop pulled the shirt off his shoulders.

"Get down again," he ordered.

"Who do you think you're ta…" the old man started to say, but the barrel of the gun had returned to within an inch of his forehead. He lay back on the floor.

The wife looked from one invader to another and slowly raised her hands. She obviously thought resistance would be futile.

The second wave of men ignored all this activity and brushed by the first cops. Their destinations were the two bedrooms at the back of the house.

The men coming through the front door were assigned the living room, empty, and dining room, also empty, before heading for the bedrooms on the second floor. A naked man pulled open the door of the first bedroom at the top of the landing as the black-clad figures scampered up the steps. He stumbled back into the room as two heavily armed ERT members pushed him back with the barrels of their rifles. A naked woman on the bed grabbed at the blue sheets and pulled them up over her ample breasts.

"Who the fuck are you guys?" the man demanded. Somehow, standing there with a limp dick drooping in front of him, the question didn't carry the force he had intended.

Two more members of the force joined them.

"Sit on the bed and don't move." The cop indicated where with a flick of his head. The rifle barrel never wavered from its location in the middle of the man's chest.

Down the hallway, an ear-piercing scream reverberated throughout the house.

"Don't shoot. Don't shoot." A high, keening voice pleaded for clemency.

"Stay down on the floor with your hands behind your head." There was no pleading in that voice. It was all authority. "Make another move for that pistol and the next shots won't come from a Taser."

Back in the first bedroom, the lead cop looked at his naked captive. "You too. Down on the floor."

The man quickly complied.

The second cop took a man's cotton housecoat off a hook on the wall and threw it over to the girl. "Out of bed, ma'am. Put this on and then sit on the floor."

"Turn away first," she said, venom in her voice.

The cop shook his head. "Not going to happen. Either slip into that thing and get on the floor, or just get on the floor. Those are the only choices."

The woman stood up facing the officer. She stuck out her chest as she slowly slid first one arm and then reached back to slide the other into the housecoat.

"There," she said, "is that what you wanted to see?"

"They're breasts, ma'am. One looks pretty much like all the rest. Sometimes a little bigger, sometimes a little smaller. But, in the end, they are just breasts." There was no humour in the man's eyes. The rifle never wavered. It was pointed into the valley between the two breasts, equally as indifferent as its holder.

"Go to hell," she said and dropped to the floor beside the bed.

CHAPTER 41

SERGEANT JIM MCDONALD sat at a desk in the junk yard's main office. Across from him sat the man from the first bedroom, no longer naked. He was listed as the owner and president of the operation on the company's charter. Corporal Scott Bowen was roaming freely around the office looking at the various documents on the wall. Jim explained the parameters of the search warrant and the cooperation he would be expecting to the junk yard man.

Oliver Kaulback sat shaking his head. "That is not right. We are a private company. Our books are private. We don't have to show them to you." He made a sweeping motion with his arm to include his entire operation. "None of this is right. That is why my family came to Canada, to escape the evils of a police state. In Canada, you can't do this. I know my rights.

"My lawyer is on the way. He will put a stop to this. You must stop until he gets here."

"Besides searching all the buildings on the premises," Jim went on as if Kaulback had never interrupted him, "we will be checking all the VIN numbers on the vehicles in the yard and you will provide numbers of vehicles that have been dismantled. We will also want to know the origin of each vehicle and see the documentation of where you obtained them."

Jim had been scanning the papers in front of him. He stopped and looked up at Kaulback. "Do you have any questions about anything I explained to you?" He pointed to a sheaf of papers on the desk in front of Kaulback. "That is your copy of the warrant. I'm sure your lawyer will want to see it when he arrives. He will then inform you everything we are doing is legal. You might want to have him stick around. If we find anything violating any of our laws governing the running of a business like yours, we will want to interview you, probably down at police headquarters."

Jim looked out the window where a half-ton truck had entered the yard under the direction of the officers at the gate. "We will also be detaining your staff for questioning as well. Once they turn onto the street leading here, there will be no turning back. How many staff do you employ on a daily basis?"

Scott drifted over to the window and peered through the open curtains.

"That's the third half-ton to come in. Five people in all."

"You're holding my staff? What about my customers? Are you holding them as well?" Kaulback's disgust with the day's events was evident in the tone of his voice.

"We have a list of customers who may be of interest to us." Jim smiled. "Both customers who buy from you and who also sell to you."

"That's crazy. You'll ruin my business if you harass my client base."

"Let me ask you about one man in particular. Does the name Jason Browne ring any bells with you?"

"Jason Browne?" Jim could see the man trying to make a connection to the name. Then his face brightened. "The dead man? Your partner there already asked me about him last summer." He pointed a finger at Scott. "I knew nothing then. I know nothing now."

"His name won't show up in any of your records? I understand he sometimes sold wrecked vehicles to you."

Kaulback's face took on a worried look. "Is that what this all about? The death of that low life? I don't know a thing about it except what the corporal told me last summer and what I read in the newspaper after I talked to him."

Scott came over and stood by the desk.

"When I interviewed you last summer, you said you had never heard of Browne."

The junk yard owner squirmed in his chair. "And at the time, that was the truth. My brother looked after that part of the business. I must have told you that. Last summer, he was in Europe. You were to return to talk to him when he got home."

Scott said nothing. He stared down at Kaulback.

Red crept up from Kaulback's collar and into his face as he talked. "We are not murderers. Don't try to stereotype us because of where we come from. We came to Canada to get away from all that."

He made a dismissive wave of his hand. "We may have bought a vehicle or two from that man. I don't personally know. You told me my predecessors dealt with him. It is possible we did too. It's only natural he would have continued to bring his business to this location. But if he did, we did not do anything illegal. He would have to have had papers for anything he brought us. We wouldn't take anything without the proper proof of ownership."

Jim held back the surprise he was feeling. He and Scott exchanged looks. This was more information than he dreamed that simple question would generate. In the summer, when Scott had last interviewed Kaulback, the company president had denied ever having heard of Jason Browne. At the time, Scott had thought it was a long shot. He was just covering all the bases.

Now that Kaulback's business was under siege, he admitted there may have been a connection, a legal one of course, but still a connection.

"So anything he sold you would be registered with the Department of Motor Vehicles?"

"No. No. That's not what I'm saying. If a vehicle was going to be junked anyway, there would be no reason for going to all that hassle with the government. He would need the signed permit transferring ownership. He would then give it to us. That way, we knew the vehicle wasn't stolen. That was our only concern. We are a legit business. I keep telling you that."

He added emphasis to the last part of his statement, hoping the tone of his voice would make it so. In his own mind, he seemed convinced he was doing nothing wrong.

"We would then send in the paperwork to the Department of Motor Vehicles signifying the car or truck had been junked and taken out of service."

"You do this with all your junked cars?"

Kaulback hesitated for a second or two too long.

"Well, not on an individual basis. We send a bunch of permits in at the same time. I'm sure there is an envelope of them around here somewhere."

He looked around the room as if he actually believed he would spot such an envelope.

Jim followed his eyes to see if he focused on any area in particular. He noticed a slight hesitation on one cabinet before he turned his attention back to Jim.

Scott walked over to the cabinet and pulled out the top drawer.

"I'm sure there is," Jim said. "We'll find it. We're going to be looking at every piece of paper in this place, checking VIN numbers to our data base of stolen cars," He looked out into the yard. "Even as we speak, someone is making a record of every vehicle on your lot." He pointed to a group of men dressed in dark blue coveralls who could be seen through a window leading to the back shop. *Police Cadet* was lettered on their backs in gold print. They are checking VIN numbers on every piece of glass and part that carries identification. We may have to charge you for doing inventory for you."

The smile Jim flashed was not returned.

Kaulback's attention centred on Scott and the open drawer. He spoke to Jim without looking at him.

"A lot of this product came with the business. We can't be responsible for every old wreck out there. All I can tell you is we've been running a legitimate business since we took over."

The door to the office opened and Ron Tingley stuck in his head.

"Bingo, Sarge. Get the additional paperwork."

Jim gave him a thumbs-up. He turned his attention back to Kaulback, who sat there with a confused look on his face.

"Mind if I use your phone?"

Kaulback made a disgusted gesture towards the phone.

"Why not? You're trampling over every other part of my business."

"Thanks." Jim pulled a business card from his jacket pocket and dialled the number on it.

"We need that amendment to the search warrant we discussed earlier," he said when the other party answered. He listened for a few seconds and then smiled. "Don't worry. We'll hold the fort until you get here."

"Holy jumped-up Jesus!"

Both Jim McDonald and Oliver Kaulback turned in Scott Bowen's direction. Scott was still standing by the filing cabinet. In one hand he held a bulky 8½ x 11 Kraft envelope. In the other was a blue-and-pink vehicle permit.

CHAPTER 42

"WHAT DID YOU find?"

Scott slowly raised his eyes from the permit and looked over at the two men at the desk.

"An envelope of permits. Mr. Kaulback may have been telling the truth."

Kaulback nodded vigorously. "I told you. We run a legitimate business here. Now you can take your men and leave."

Both men ignored Kaulback's statement.

Scott held up the permit in his hand. "It's the vehicle permit for George Wilson's truck."

"Your missing guy?" Jim got up and walked over to the filing cabinet.

Scott looked at the sergeant. "Yeah, and look at this. It's signed by George Wilson."

Again Kaulback tried to immerse himself into the conversation. "I told you. We run a legitimate business here."

Again the others ignored him.

"The truck never left the county. Wilson sold it to these guys before he left."

Now the sergeant did look back at Kaulback. "A silver and black Dodge truck. Last April. What happened to it? The truck was in working order. You wouldn't junk it."

"Last April. How would I know? I can't remember every vehicle going through here. It may have been an insurance company write-off."

Scott walked over to the desk and threw down the brown envelope. "These permits go back for a year. This is hardly what I would call a legitimate way to run a business. This looks more like you have something to hide."

The uniformed Mountie seemed to have more of an effect on Kaulback than the plain-clothes sergeant who resumed his position behind the desk.

"No. Nothing to hide. Those permits must have been overlooked. In a busy company, that can happen sometimes. I will personally take care of it later today. I will take it into the registry office myself. That's a promise."

"The truck," Jim said. "What happened to this truck?"

Kaulback took the permit and studied it, hoping for divine intervention. Then, enlightenment shone in his eyes. "Yes. Yes, I remember this truck." His voice became excited. He waved the permit at Scott. "We were not allowed to resell it. That was one of the conditions of us buying it. It could only be junked.

"My brother handled the negotiations. He got the truck for a tune."

"A tune?" Scott and Jim gave each other confused looks. Scott smiled. "You mean a song."

"Yes. Yes, a song. Talk to my brother."

The sergeant called out to an ERT member standing guard at the door. "Could you send someone over to the main house and have the brother brought over here." He looked at Kaulback. "What's your brother's name?"

"Rudolph, but everyone calls him Rudy."

The man at the door acknowledged the name and fingered a mike. He spoke a few words too low for the others to hear, then looked back at the sergeant.

"He's on his way."

"OK. You can see my business is run on the up and up. Call off your search teams and let me get back to work. I can't afford to have my customers go elsewhere."

"Not going to happen," Jim said. "Even as we speak, a new warrant is being drawn up to include drugs and anything that goes with the drug trade."

Once again Kaulback's face reflected the rollercoaster of emotions he was riding. "No, no, no," he stammered. "Any drugs you find do not belong to me. If some of my employees smoke marijuana, I can't control that. I am not their father or their mother. If I catch them in the act, I fire them. I don't have time to be chasing them around. I have a business to run. A legitimate business." He looked up at Scott, who was once again looking through the brown envelope. "See. He has all the paperwork. It just has to be filed with the government."

Jim laughed a short, gruff laugh.

"We're not interested in a couple of tokes of marijuana. We both know this goes a long ways beyond that. We think you are an importer."

Kaulback's dark face took on an ashen colour.

"Importer? Never. You are stereotyping again. Again you are wrong."

"Well, again you have nothing to worry about. We may have discovered you are not running a chop shop; you are just sloppy in your dealings with the government. We will apologize if that turns out to be the case, after you file all the proper paper work, of course.

"The same with the drugs. If we are wrong, we will apologize. No harm done."

"No harm done?" Kaulback's voice rose a couple of octaves. "My customers will be afraid to do business with me. They will not believe I'm an honest businessman if they see all your police vehicles in my yard. They will believe the worst."

Before Jim could answer, a dark-complexioned man appeared in the doorway.

"Oliver, what is going on? Nobody will tell me anything. Have you called our lawyer?"

Rudy appeared to be a couple of years younger than his brother, but was taller and heavier. He wore only a white undershirt and light-brown, twill work pants. His jet-black hair was still tousled. On his feet, he wore a pair of steel-toed work boots.

"He is on his way. Don't worry, I think I can work this out with these men. There has been some sort of mistake made."

"The mistake was letting them on our property to begin with. We have our rights."

Scott had been pacing around the room, vehicle permit in hand. This could be the major break he had been waiting for. He confronted Rudy with the permit from George Wilson's truck.

"I have some questions for you. Take a seat." He pulled a chair away from the wall and placed it beside Oliver's.

"I'm not saying anything until our lawyer gets here."

Scott shot Jim a frustrated look, then returned his attention to Rudy. "Your choice. The longer we sit here, the more business you're losing. We have road blocks set up. It may take a while for your lawyer to get through them. We are restricting who we let in until we finish our search."

"You can't stop our lawyer. He has a right to be here."

"Only after we are sure he is, number one, a lawyer and, number two, representing your company. Anyone can make claims just to get in here. Some reporter could claim to be a lawyer so he could get in and get the scoop on this story. It would make a big splash in the local papers. You don't want that to happen, I'm sure."

Oliver pointed to the chair beside him. "Sit down, Rudy. They want to know about a truck you bought last April. Everything is on the up and up. Just answer their questions."

"Last April?" Rudy tried a look of indifference. "Do you think I remember every piece of junk we buy?"

Oliver tried to smooth the path. "You remember. The one we were not allowed to resell. It was part of a poker game prize."

A flicker of a smile danced across Rudy's face. "The Dodge. I do remember." He laughed briefly, but became serious again when he took in the red vein throbbing on the corporal's neck.

Jim took in the way Rudy was dressed. "Oliver says you conducted the negotiations. No offence, but do you do that often?"

"I buy most of the vehicles people want to sell on an individual basis. You are looking at my clothes, yes. You can't crawl under a car or truck dressed in a suit. We are a junk dealer, but we don't buy junk. We have to be able to resell the parts to make it worthwhile."

"Who'd you buy this truck from?" Scott asked, cutting right to the chase. He offered the permit to Rudy. "Did you buy it from George Wilson?"

Rudy reached out and took the permit from Scott. He smiled.

"No. This man Wilson lost the truck in a poker game to the man I bought it from. His name was Browne." Rudy rubbed his forehead to help him think. "Jason Browne. He tries to sell me stuff from time to time."

An audible gasp escaped from Scott's lips. "Jason Browne?"

"Yes, I am sure that is it. Jason Browne. Like I said, he brings us in stuff from time to time."

Scott pulled another chair from the wall and sat down. The ramifications of this news rushed through his mind. At one time he had tried to link the two deaths. He had abandoned that idea and although the word coincidence was not prominent in his vocabulary, he conceded it did happen once in a while. Now it turned out that was not the case.

"Jason Browne sold you this truck belonging to George Wilson?"

Rudy pointed to the signature on the form. "It is all legal. George Wilson had signed it over to Browne. Browne won it in a poker game. He gave us the details of the game several times. I think he was slightly high at the time, or maybe just excited by his big win." He paused and pointed at the permit again. "It is all legal."

"Where would Jason Browne get vehicles to sell to you?"

Rudy shrugged dismissively as if that was not his problem. "He claims he buys old, no longer used, cars and trucks from the farmers around the area and then resells them to us. He always has signed transfers of ownership. Everyone wins. The farmer gets the junk out of his yard. This makes the neighbours happy. Jason Browne makes a little money, to spend on drugs and women, I think. That makes him happy. We strip the vehicles and resell the parts. This makes everyone happy. We are protecting the environment through recycling at the highest level. We are a good company, yes?"

Scott ignored the world-saving claim. "You give Browne enough money to make this worthwhile for him?"

"He keeps coming back. In most cases, he probably simply makes a deal with the farmer to haul the vehicle away for free. Whatever he gets from us is all profit, less his towing costs."

Scott took the permit and waved it in Rudy's face. "You believed that was the case with a 2008 Dodge truck in perfect running order?"

"No. I believe Browne won it in a poker game. That's what he told me. He had the signed permit. It was all legal. He wanted to get rid of it in a hurry before the loser could come after him to get it back. He didn't want it being driven around the area because he thought that would just cause problems for him with the man.

"I didn't care what the story was." He took back the permit. "I had legal ownership. Browne had no idea what the truck would be worth when you started selling it for parts."

Jim looked over at Scott. "Ever heard about these poker games?"

Scott shook his head. "Subject never came up with anyone I talked to. I'll definitely follow up on that angle, but I'm sure Brian or Connie would have said something about them."

Rudy held up his hands in a defensive move. "The poker games have nothing to do with me. I have the proper paper work. That is what matters. I questioned Browne about the truck. I was suspicious. That was his story and it made sense to me."

"You knew Jason Browne," Jim said to Scott. "Do you think he could concoct a story like that?"

Scott nodded. "Ordinarily it wouldn't be much of a story. We could easily check it out with the other players. With George missing and Browne dead, we don't know who the other players were supposed to be. I could ask around and prove it to be true if I had those names, but there is no way to disprove it. The game could have taken place anywhere."

"Also, it gives us a reason for George's disappearance. Who wants to go home and tell their wife they lost their truck in a poker game? If he's heavily into gambling, that could explain why they were having financial troubles on the farm. Like most gamblers, he probably planned to come home as soon as he won the money back. He may be still chasing that dream somewhere."

"Or, if that was the case, he could have shut Jason Browne up to keep the story from getting back to Connie. Browne was not one to keep his mouth shut. Once George killed him, there was no going home. That would explain a lot of things."

"That's a possibility, but I would think some of the other participants would have spoken up by now. It would be hard to keep something like that quiet."

"I guess I had better have another chat with Connie. I find it hard to believe she was holding out on me. It's possible she didn't even know about the poker games herself."

Jim held out his hand to Rudy to get the permit back. He studied it for a few seconds. "Let's get this signature checked. Make sure George is the one who signed it."

He passed the piece of paper over to Scott. "I guess I'm officially handing the Jason Browne file back to you. There's no denying it belongs in your bivouac now."

CHAPTER 43

AGAIN SCOTT FOUND himself driving through a late winter snowstorm as he approached the farm of Connie Wilson. Big, soft flakes fluttered down onto the road in front of him. He adjusted his speed accordingly.

As soon as the drug squad had arrived at Kaulback's junk yard, Scott had excused himself. Shit luck played a big part in police work, but even Scott was taken aback by this revelation. The search for George Wilson had taken an entirely new turn. The connection to Jason Browne added an upsetting component to the mix.

He had already talked to Fire Chief Brian Cosh. Brian denied any knowledge of large-scale poker games in the area. There were a few Texas Hold 'Em games played on weekends. These were mostly tournaments where there was a twenty or fifty dollar buy-in. Nothing that would have a reasonably new truck on the table. Brian wasn't even sure George ever took part in any of these poker games. Brian didn't and to his knowledge, George didn't either. By the same token, to Brian's knowledge, George wouldn't up and leave his wife to fend for herself in the operation of dairy and beef farm supplemented by a wood lot operation. There were aspects of George's life Brian wasn't familiar with.

The snow had a high moisture content to it. The temperature was hovering around the freezing point. As Scott stepped from his vehicle into the three inches that had accumulated to date, he could hear a squeaky, crunching sound.

He smiled. Late winter snow looked nice, covered the dirty snow piled in all the ditches, but promised not to hang around for a long time. It was one last fleeting glance of what had been and a reminder winter would hang around for as long as it chose. No calendar date would influence it.

A snowball whizzed by his head and splattered over the side of his vehicle. Scott instinctively ducked and his hand went to the butt of his service pistol.

"Don't shoot. Don't shoot." This was followed by a gale of laughter.

He turned to see Connie with another snowball in her cocked right hand.

"I've got you covered," she squealed and let the snowball fly.

Scott reached out, caught it, quickly reformed it into a solid ball and threw it back at her. A direct hit in the centre of her chest.

"Ooh. Nice shot. You must practise."

"This is perfect snowball snow. Great for snowmen as well." Scott hesitated. Connie looked like a kid in the first snowfall of the season. Her exuberance was infectious. He hated to be the one to take the kid-like smile off her face, but it had to be done. That was why he was here. To bring up the subject of her husband and any bad habits she might know about.

Connie sensed the change in his demeanour. The smile slid from her face like a snowball on a hot engine bonnet.

"I'm not going to like this, am I?"

Scott formed a handful of snow into another ball. He gently threw it in her direction. "Just a few more questions. Perhaps we could go inside and sit down."

"I've got a pot of coffee brewing."

As Scott headed towards the house, he noticed a slight indentation in the snow. Another vehicle had recently left the yard. Coming from the kitchen door were the traces of footprints buried under the freshly fallen snow. These had been made only a short time ago, perhaps after Scott called to say he was coming out. He hadn't wanted to make the trip in the snowstorm if Connie was not going to be home.

In no time, they were in the kitchen, each with a steaming mug of coffee in front of them.

"To drive out here on a day like this, it must be important. What's happening?" Connie's green eyes were wide open in questioning mode. Her eyebrows were slightly raised.

Scott put down his coffee. His face became serious. "We've found George's truck."

The change in Connie's appearance was metamorphic. A pallor dropped over her skin.

"You found George's truck? Where?"

Scott reached out a hand to take hold of Connie's. Concern replaced the look on his own face. "Connie, are you all right? Do you feel faint?"

Connie struggled to pull herself together. Succeeded slightly. Her skin found its colour again. She pulled back her shoulders. Her voice took on its usual strength.

"I'm sorry. Your words shocked me. Where did you find George's truck? What about George? Did you find him?"

Scott kept hold of Connie's hand. "There's no word on George. Not exactly, anyway."

He let go of her hand and took the vehicle permit from his pocket. "We found this during a raid at the Kaulback Auto Salvage Yard. Apparently, they bought George's truck last April. They have stripped it for parts."

Now confusion registered on Connie's countenance. "Bought it from whom?"

Scott hesitated. "This is where it gets strange." He slid the piece of paper across the table.

"Is that George's signature?"

Connie picked up the permit and studied it carefully. She looked back at Scott.

"Yeah, that's his fancy W. Takes up half the signature line. I don't understand. Where would they get a signed copy of George's transfer of ownership?"

The words were no sooner out of her mouth when a look of understanding replaced the look of confusion. She shook her head from side to side.

"No. No. You're saying George sold them the truck. I don't believe that. Why would he sell his truck, even if he was going to leave me? He would still need transportation."

Scott reached out for her hand again. She pulled it away.

"Is there something you're not telling me, Corporal? Stop beating around the bush. Tell me what's going on here."

"Did George gamble?"

"Gamble? What's that got to do with anything? He bought 6-49 tickets like everyone else around here. He bought 50-50 tickets at every event he went to. Is that gambling? Is that what you mean?"

Scott shook his head. "Jason Browne sold George's truck to the Kaulbacks. He claimed he won it in a poker game. Would George be in that kind of a poker game?"

Connie didn't even hear the last question. All the blood drained from her face and she tumbled sideways off the chair. Scott sprang from his, stumbled on a table leg, arriving too late to prevent Connie from cracking her head on the kitchen floor.

No sooner did she smack the floor than she regained consciousness again. Scott had her head in his hands watching a small bump materialize in front of him.

"What happened?" Connie looked up at the kitchen from her position on the floor. "My God, I fainted." She struggled to get up.

"Stay down," Scott said in a firm voice. "Let me look you over, first."

Connie pushed his hands away. "I'm all right. Let me up."

Short of using the kind of force one uses to control a suspected criminal, Scott realized he was fighting a losing battle. He took her hand and pulled her to her feet.

"At least sit down while I examine your head."

Connie's hand went up to the bump. Surprise registered on her face. "Did I fall that hard? I don't remember a thing. You told me something about Jason Browne. What were you saying?"

"Do you know Jason Browne?"

Connie took a second before answering.

"I know who he is. Everyone around here does. He fell over the cliff last summer and killed himself. What has he got to do with George's truck?"

Scott went to the refrigerator and removed a tray of ice cubes from the freezer. He grabbed a cup towel from the rack by the sink, made up a cold pack and applied it to Connie's head. Meanwhile he was answering her question.

"He claimed to have won the truck in a poker game. He sold it to the Kaulbacks to be junked. He was afraid George would come after the truck if he kept it."

"I don't believe that. George would never lose his truck in a poker game. He didn't even play cards."

"Are you sure? Could he have been playing without your knowledge?"

"I don't know how to answer that question, Corporal. I'm telling you he didn't play poker. If he did it without my knowledge, then I have no knowledge of it. Let's say he did lose it. What happened next in your vision of things?"

Scott shook his head and looked down at the table without answering.

Connie waited.

Finally, Scott looked up. "Would he be too ashamed to come home if he gambled away his truck? We can only assume all his money would have gone first."

"If that happened, where else could he go?"

"That's the $64,000 question. How upset would you have been?"

"How upset? I'd have killed him." Connie immediately realized what she had said. "Not literally. That's only a figure of speech. I'd have been damned upset. We've been struggling to keep the farm going. We were getting ahead of the curve. He wouldn't simply throw everything away on the turn of a card. George was too practical for that."

"If he was gambling, who would it have been with?"

Connie shook her head. "No one around here. The people in this community couldn't keep their mouths shut that long. Someone would have spilled the beans long before this."

Scott thought about that statement. It was similar to what Brian Cosh had said. The logic of it was so obvious, it couldn't be questioned. The alternative suggested he got involved in a game in one of the bigger towns or even in Halifax with a bunch of strangers. He may have been considered a mark from the country. They got all his money; George was known to carry thousands of dollars at times. Jason Browne could have gotten the truck as a reward for bringing him in. The truck could be considered more of a nuisance than it was worth, especially if they wanted to keep these games quiet and unknown to the police. That scenario was only one option. Scott hoped there were better ones.

"One last question: Could George have killed Jason Browne?"

Connie gasped at the mere suggestion. She lowered her voice. "I don't know. If any of this other stuff is true, then I didn't really know the man." She shrugged. "I don't know what to tell you. The man you are describing is not the George Wilson I lived with for all those years."

CHAPTER 44

"I'M GOING TO raid his bootlegging operation," Scott explained to Detective-Sergeant Jim McDonald. "I've checked our records and to my knowledge, he's been given a free ride for years, possibly forever. He first came to my attention a few months back, but at the time I thought he had given up the business and moved into legitimate enterprises. It was my impression he had gone into partnership with Connie Wilson. I know there are lady bootleggers out there, but I can't picture Connie as being one of them."

"Bootlegging is not a full-time occupation," Jim said. "He could easily be doing both. It could be a lucrative sideline to keep him in tobacco money."

"You haven't priced cigarettes lately. It takes a full-time job to supply that habit."

"How true."

"Still, you're probably right about doing both. That episode with David Gates a couple of weeks ago made me realize it was time to give Lindsay a reality check. We can't have drunks disrupting early morning traffic. Half-asleep commuters and drunken ATV drivers sharing the same stretch of highway can be a lethal combination."

Jim sipped his coffee and took a contemplative bite of his walnut cruller.

"Are Lindsay and Connie Wilson still in business together?"

"As far as I know. Wood harvesting slacks off during the worst of winter. Now that that period is drawing to a close, Brian Cosh told me they are setting up a maple syrup tapping operation. He still helps her with her farming chores and they are still selling some firewood."

"Does he sleep in his own bed every night?"

"That's an interesting question," Scott said. "The implications are far reaching." Scott had to stop and think before continuing. "I don't know for sure. When I went out to question Connie about George's poker-playing habits, someone else had been there shortly before I was. I saw the remnants of their footprints in the snow. It could have been Cal Lindsay."

"Check it out," Jim said. "If you find anything suspicious, we may have to assign someone from Major Crimes to come in and help you."

Scott's mouth dropped open. He held up his hands in a stop-sign motion.

"No, no, no, no. If we suspect Cal Lindsay as being a murderer, someone from Major Crimes should be involved in the case right from the start. Someone who already has knowledge of what has taken place to date. By someone, I mean you."

Jim ignored that comment. "What about the wife? You've checked her out? I remember you suspected marriage difficulties."

"Connie Wilson?" Scott shook his head. "The spouse is always on top of the suspect list in any investigation — murder, disappearance, whatever.

"On the first day, Roscoe and I searched all the outbuildings on her farm. The planes and helicopters checked the surrounding fields. Nothing. I conducted a thorough investigation and came up with nothing. Since then, I've gotten to know her pretty well. Unless she is one hell of an actress, I don't think she has any involvement."

"Good enough. So you think Lindsay is working on his own. Keep me informed."

Jim started to get up from the table.

"Sit down," Scott said in his most official voice. Others in the coffee shop turned to look at the two men. You could see the questions in their eyes. Who was this man the uniformed Mountie was being so stern with? Should they maybe be finishing up their coffee and heading out about their business? Should they stay and watch in case an arrest was about to go down?

A smile radiated across the face of the man in the suit and sparkled in his eyes. The uniformed Mountie returned the smile, equally radiant. The standing man sat and leaned forward. The voices dropped to little more than a whisper. No matter how hard anyone tried, and everyone did, they could not follow the gist of the conversation. They could only tell it was serious.

CHAPTER 45

T HE KNOCK CAME at about 9:30 in the evening. Cal had heard the sounds of snowmobiles outside, but thought nothing of it. The dirt road leading to his house was always snow-covered during the winter. Snowmobiles were more common than cars in this more remote part of the neighbourhood.

The weather had turned cold again, as it often did in March, especially the nights. Inside his kitchen, Cal Lindsay was comfortably warm. He had a small wood fire smouldering in his air-tight stove, enough to fend off the attacks of old Jack Frost, but not enough to drive Cal from the kitchen.

On the table in front of him were advance orders for firewood. Firewood for next season, not the current one. He was making sure he had enough stumpage purchased to cover the demand. With the escalating price of fossil fuels, more and more people were turning to the renewable resources of the forest. Cal had spent much of the last month cutting his current crop in advance of the spring rains that would turn the woods roads into quagmires. He had hauled what he could to the clearings he had created to act as servicing depots. Places he could cut, split and store his wood until the delivery date arrived.

He slid back his chair and ambled over to the door, squinted through the window and then held it open. Two men stood on the front step, rubbing their hands together to keep warm.

"Can I help you?" Cal asked. He looked over their shoulders into the yard where two blue-and-white Yamahas were parked.

The two men shot him bright, too big smiles. "Thought we might be able to get us some whiskey here," the one closest to Cal said. "Nothing like a shot of Canadian Club on a cold night to warm up the innards."

Cal looked at them, confused. "I'm sorry. I don't understand. Are you asking me if I can give you a drink of whiskey?"

The smiles disappeared from the men's faces. They looked at each other and then back at Cal.

"Actually, we heard we could buy a bottle from you."

Cal shook his head. "You heard wrong. Sorry fellas." He looked at his watch. "The liquor store in Raymond's River is open for another twenty-five minutes. You should be able to get there in lots of time."

He started to close the door.

"Raymond's River is quite a drive on a night like this. We're staying in Billy Martell's place up the road. We work with Billy out in the oil fields. He said we could use it for a week or so. Do some snowmobiling." The man looked back into the yard as if to verify his statement by the presence of the two snow machines.

"Besides we can't take those into town. They don't work too well on paved streets."

"Billy Martell's place?" Cal said. "Haven't seen good old Billy around for a few years. I heard his place had gone for taxes."

Cal had not heard that, but at the same time he had never heard William Martell called anything but William. Billy was a child's name, Martell claimed, and he was no longer a child. It had been over five years since Cal had seen the man around at all. To the best of Cal's knowledge, the place was sealed up tighter than the Kingston Penitentiary. The water pipes had been drained, the doors and windows boarded shut. William was saving the place for his retirement, but that was a few years off yet.

Now the two men exchanged serious glances. They had heard nothing about a tax sale. Their research showed the place had been owned by one William Martell for over twenty years. It also showed Martell lived out of the province. He had been one of the early deserters of the province in favour of the big money that could be made out west.

The man doing the talking forged ahead. "Billy must have paid the taxes himself. He gave us the keys, gave us directions and told us to enjoy." The smile came back to his face. "A few shots of whiskey on a cold night would make that last part easier."

Now the second man stepped into the conversation.

"We stopped at the fire hall in Raymond's River to firm up our instructions on how to reach the place. Talked to the chief there, Brian Cosh. Friendly man. Told us about all the amenities in the surrounding area, places we might want to explore this time of year. He also assured us if we needed some refreshments, you would be only too happy to supply us."

He gave an emphatic nod of his head to hammer home the last part of this statement.

"Ah yes," Cal said. "Chief Cosh. Probably told you he was one of my best customers, didn't he? Hard man to get away from when he starts spinning stories about Raymond's River. Knows everybody and everything about them. Probably told you some dandy tales."

"Well he didn't say he was your best customer, just that you never let him down when he needed to find a bottle after hours. He only had good things to say about you."

"That's the chief. Always a good word for everybody and always a practical joker."

The visitors nodded as if they knew that was true.

The smile left Cal's face. His eyes darkened and he leaned into the closest of the two men. The man stepped back to a lower step, almost as if the intensity of the stare had forced him backwards. Cal's voice took on a low, menacing tone.

"I don't know who you assholes are, but get the fuck off my property. You've never worked with William Martell. The chief never told you I'd happily supply you with booze.

"I've got a 4-10 shotgun hanging above this door. Out here we tend to shoot prowlers first and ask questions later. That's because we can never get a cop out here when we need one. We handle our own justice, swiftly and efficiently."

Now, both men were scampering backwards down the step. The lead man turned an ankle and fell into his partner. They landed in a heap on the hard-packed snow, scrambled to their feet, appeared to think about saying something, thought better of it and kept silent. They jumped on their machines and roared back towards Raymond's River without even a glance towards the property of William Martell.

Cal closed the door and went back to his table. Any thoughts of wood lots and firewood customers were swept from his thinking. There was no doubt in his mind these two men were undercover cops trying to set him up, but why? His father had been raided by the police on a couple of occasions. Cal had never been and for good reason.

One of the principles Cal's father had pounded into his head was to never, ever sell to strangers. If he needed the business that badly, it was time to look for a new vocation. There were enough potential customers in and around Raymond's River to more than keep his business afloat. Even with these known quantities, he should exercise extreme caution. Cal always followed his father's advice.

What had changed? He had always had a live-and-let-live relationship with his neighbours. He discouraged people from drinking and driving. If he really believed someone had had too much, he would either arrange for another means of transportation or offer them a couch to sleep on until they sobered up. There had never been a drunken accident on his road.

That's not to say Raymond's River didn't have its share of drunks running up and down the highways and byways. David Gates was not unique. Most of these yahoos bought their booze from the government outlets. Cal's customers were more refined drunks, who preferred drinking in comfortable, friendly surroundings over terrorizing the neighbourhood. There were exceptions. There were always exceptions. David Gates immediately came to mind. Even Gates usually took his liquor home to drink when he bought it from Cal. At least he took it to someone's home. Gates understood the importance of staying on Cal's good side.

Cal had heard about the debacle that had occurred early one morning a few weeks back when Gates held up the early-morning traffic before ending up in the ditch. It was true booze from Cal's enterprise had fuelled that event, but Cal had made sure Gates had been taken safely home first. Once he got there, Cal couldn't be responsible for keeping him behind those closed doors. Gates was an adult, sort of.

After Cal's father had been raided, he always scaled back operations for a while. "Why tempt fate?" he would say. He thought the laws surrounding liquor sales were as stupid now as they had been during prohibition, but he wasn't a crusader. Neither was Cal. He would get the word out to his more faithful customers that they should seek alternate sources for a while. He would explain about the visit from the two suspected cops and why he was taking precautions. They would understand. They would also try to find out who tipped off the police. Cal cutting back would seriously interrupt their way of life for a while. Lisa Tingley at the liquor store did not always welcome their custom, especially if they had had too much to drink already.

These precautions on Cal's part would make any new attempts at purchases even more obvious. The chance of a car load of cops arriving when Cal's kitchen was full of customers would be eliminated. The only thing the authorities could do now would be to arrive with search warrants. Cal would make sure they had no grounds to do that and if by some quirk of fate, they succeeded in obtaining a warrant, nothing illegal would be found when they did search.

CHAPTER 46

"How INCOMPETENT CAN you be?"

Corporal Scott Bowen was pacing back and forth outside Detective-Sergeant Jim McDonald's small cubicle in the west-end Halifax headquarters. His venom was not aimed at the sergeant, but at two plainclothes younger detectives.

"All you had to do was purchase a single bottle of whiskey from a man who makes his living selling the stuff. I didn't ask you to infiltrate the mob. I didn't expect you to become Donnie Bosco. I wanted you to buy one goddamn bottle of booze."

"Well, maybe you sent us to the wrong house," one of the men said, defiance dripping from his voice.

Scott stopped and wheeled on the man. "There are three houses on that road. You were to go to the second one. How hard can that be? Yellow clapboard siding, remember? They were white, yellow and white. The next house was another mile in. That's where you were supposed to be coming from."

"Well, Mr. Smarty Pants, that house was sold for taxes. It wasn't even owned by Billy Martell anymore."

"William Martell," Scott snapped. "Don't tell me you were improvising on the name. He went by William and the place wasn't sold for taxes. That was just Lindsay testing you. What other embellishments did you throw in on your own?"

"Nothing. We told him we had talked to the fire chief and he had assured us we could buy liquor from this guy."

"The fire chief didn't tell you that. William Martell did. For Christ's sake, we gave you a simple, tight script. All you had to do was follow it. Everything you were supposed to say was researched. We know it was accurate. Brian Cosh has never purchased a thing from Cal Lindsay in his life. They were simply schoolyard friends. You were to drop Brian's name to show you knew other people in the community. Nothing else."

"We had to go with the flow. Make it sound convincing. Then, for no reason, he threw us off his property. It wasn't our fault."

"Right. Go with the flow. When you left, did you head back towards the house you were supposed to be staying at? No. You headed for the main road. You've tipped him off and have nothing to show for it."

"For Christ's sake, it's only a bootlegging bust. Don't get you knickers in a knot. We might have been going into town. He told us the liquor store was still open."

Scott got right in the young man's face. "You were on snowmobiles. I know you're a city boy and think we sent you way out into the boonies on a wild goose chase, but the streets of Raymond's River are still paved with asphalt. They don't drive on them with snowmobiles."

Scott made a visible effort to rein in his temper. He lowered his voice so that the men had to listen hard to hear him. "We are investigating Lindsay for a suspected homicide. Right now all we have are suspicions, nothing we can act on. All we wanted you two to do was buy a goddamn bottle of whiskey. The liquor bust was to give us an excuse to bring him in and interrogate him. To see if we could swing the conversation around to a man's disappearance and from there to the possibility of a murder. You blew that easy opening."

He gave his hand a dismissive wave and turned his back on the men. "Go on. Go back to your regular duties. Write parking tickets or whatever it is you can do."

The sergeant gave his head a flick, indicating the men should leave. He turned to Scott.

"That didn't go exactly as planned. Things seldom do when you're trying to be sneaky."

Scott started to object, but Jim held up his hand.

"We both knew it was a long shot to expect him to make a sale to two strangers, no matter how good their cover story was."

"The man sells booze for a living. How hard can it be to make a purchase?"

"Real hard, it seems. We did learn something. Cal Lindsay is a cautious man. He looks at the long-term picture and not just the quick, easy buck. If he did kill George Wilson, we're not going to be handed that information on a silver platter. He is going to have taken precautions to cover up the deed. That in itself is worth knowing. It will keep us from storming in like a bunch of horny teens on a panty raid."

Scott winced. "It's been a long time since I've been mistaken for a horny teen."

"Now the question is: Is Cal Lindsay a horny teen? Is he doing this for the money or is he trying to make a play for Connie Wilson? You tell me they dated in the past. Connie moved on. Lindsay never married anyone else. Was he biding his time, waiting for the right opportunity to come along, or did he get tired of waiting and make his own opportunity?"

Scott sat down in one of the office chairs and rubbed his forehead as if fighting back a tension headache. "We're creeping up on a year since George disappeared and so far, it appears to be all about money between Lindsay and Connie. Both of them seem to be doing quite well in this business arrangement. From what I can determine, they are simply business colleagues."

"What's a year if you've already waited fifteen?" Jim said. "He's obviously not a horny teenager, but a very mature, patient man."

"That's why we have to stop him cold before he ingratiates himself into Connie's personal life."

Jim nodded, giving Scott a knowing look. "You came down hard on those two constables. You're not getting emotionally involved in this case, are you? You know you can't run an investigation if you lose your objectivity."

Again, Scott's eyes turned to cold steel. "I came down hard on those two because they were not taking the assignment seriously. They thought coming out to the country and buying a bottle of booze was a joke. It wasn't.

"I've been dealing with Connie since last April on a regular basis. She looks tough on the outside, but she is hurting like anyone else would in this situation. Sometimes when I'm interviewing her, I can see the tears just on the edge of flowing. A little push and I know she'll be over the edge.

"At first, I thought the business relationship with Cal Lindsay was a good thing. It was taking her mind off George and him walking out on her without a word. It gave her something else to concentrate on. Now, I'm not so sure. Especially if Lindsay has set this up. I don't want to see Connie get hurt again. Right now, as we come up on the first-year anniversary, she is vulnerable. Finding that truck raised more questions than it answered. We still don't know if George took off on his own or became a victim somewhere. How is this Jason Browne character involved in the whole thing? These questions have to linger in Connie's mind the same way they do in ours.

"A couple of kind gestures from Lindsay and he could be, as you said, in her bed. That's fine, if his intentions are honourable and the whole thing is happenstance. If it is some evil scheme on his part, I'll nail the bastard to the wall."

Jim gave a short, gruff laugh. "You are an old softie."

"No, I'm a humanitarian, remember? I look out for my fellow man and don't you damn well forget that. I'll kick your ass all around this office if you do."

Scott leaned back in his chair and smiled. He realized he was becoming morose. By now, he had hoped to have been able to offer Connie some closure. To date, he wasn't even close. He shook off the sad feeling. "Let's meet in Raymond's River tomorrow. I'll treat you to lunch."

CHAPTER 47

S COTT AND JIM SAT in the burger joint across from the school, eating what they had begun to call the best burgers around. Since that day last summer when young Tommy Watson tipped Scott off about this place, he had enjoyed the cuisine here on a number of occasions. The sergeant was a recent recruit to the place, but didn't argue with the designation.

The burgers, however, are not why they were here today. Despite knowing Jason Browne had sold George Wilson's truck to a junk dealer, neither case had made a huge jump forward. The sale accounted for the money Browne had been flashing around before his disappearance. Scott had talked to the wrong brother during the summer. If he had talked to Rudy instead of Oliver, things might be decidedly different now. But he hadn't and now almost a year had passed.

George Wilson could be considered the prime suspect in the Jason Browne case. Anger and revenge always rated high on the motive scale. Thousands of hours and hundreds of thousands of dollars had been spent searching for George. All to no avail. At least they could stop spending time looking for his truck. What was left of it was either driving around the province attached to numerous other vehicles or stored as individual parts on the shelves at Kaulback's junk yard.

Cal Lindsay was the closest thing Scott had to a suspect in the George Wilson disappearance and he was a stretch. Frankly, that was going nowhere. The odds were still better than fifty-fifty George had simply walked away from his former life, although with a wife like Connie, Scott found that option hard to believe.

The two policemen were now trying to figure out where to go next when Scott noticed a shadow looming over the table. He looked up at the elderly lady standing there. His mind sorted through his data banks of facial recognition. Then it clicked in. This was the lady from the liquor store. He had talked to her on a couple of previous occasions about George's drinking habits. As he recalled, once the information tap was turned on, there was no shutting it off with Lisa Tingley.

"Good afternoon, Ms. Tingley. Can I help you in some way?"

"It's Miss Tingley. Never married, never needed to. I survived quite well without some man sniffing around all the time. Don't need any of those new-fangled words to confuse the issue either."

Jim turned his head and smiled as a trace of pink crept up into Scott's cheeks.

"Call me Lisa; everyone else does."

"OK, Lisa. Is this a social call or can I help you in some way?"

"Neither. It's me that can help you. Everyone tells me to mind my own business, but I don't believe in that. If I can help out the police in some way, that is their business as well as mine."

Scott looked around and found a vacant chair at the next table. He reached over and grabbed it, slid it up to his table.

"Have a seat. We will accept all the help we can get, right, Sergeant? This is Detective-Sergeant Jim McDonald from Major Crimes, Halifax."

Jim got to his feet and offered his hand to Lisa. Her handshake was firm in his. A lifetime of handling cases of liquor had toughened her up.

"A detective, huh? You must be working on the Jason Browne thing. I've heard the rumours about George Wilson's truck. Let me save you some time. George didn't do it."

Both officers were taken aback.

"I've been doing some detective work on my own. Figured out what happened to George Wilson. He was long gone by the time Jason Browne was killed."

Lisa's voice was sharp and loud. Others in the diner were looking their way.

"Maybe we should discuss this someplace else," Scott said. He looked at Jim for backup. Jim was nodding his head.

"Right here is fine with me. You are both still eating your lunch. But if you want to be driving me all over the place, I'm willing to go. I'm just trying to do what's right, that's all."

Scott looked around, considering his options. Across the street was the high school. He could probably borrow an office there for a couple of minutes. They could drive back to his headquarters, but if Lisa's information turned out to be frivolous, that seemed like a waste of time. The fire hall stood a few hundred yards down the road. Brian Cosh would let him use his office, no questions asked. Well, Brian might ask, but he would accept not getting any answers.

He wrapped his hamburger in the napkin beside his plate. There were no Styrofoam clamshells for the food here. They came on plates, reusable ceramic plates. Jim looked at his burger, took one last bite and abandoned the rest.

Both men got to their feet. Both reached out to assist 75-year-old Lisa. She shrugged off both offers.

In less than a minute, they were in Brian's office at the fire station. The two or three firemen who were hanging around playing pool gave them a curious look, but then went back to their game. Lisa pointedly ignored them. She was here on official business, not wasting time playing games.

Lisa spoke first as soon as they were seated. She was going to control this interview.

"You've seen Elizabeth's Schofield's baby?"

Both men looked confused.

"The little red head, lives next door to Connie Wilson. Flaming red hair. Can't miss it."

A smile played across Scott's face. He had met Elizabeth and Tim at Connie's house on a couple of occasions. Jim gave his head a shake.

"I know who you mean," Scott said, wondering where this conversation was heading.

"George Wilson is the father." There was no hesitation in Lisa's voice. This was not an opinion she was offering. This was a fact she was stating.

"George? You know this, how?"

"It's all very scientific. Mendel's Laws. Are you familiar with them?"

Scott gave her a wary look. "Blue eyes, brown eyes; blond hair, black hair. I studied it in school."

Lisa pulled a sheaf of papers from her purse. "It all goes back to old Red Haydon. John was his christened name, but everyone called him Red. I remember him when I was a young girl. Had a head of hair the colour of Tim's right up until the day he died."

Scott looked at the sheet of paper she was showing him. He was glad they had opted to get out of the diner for this exercise.

"John was Tim's great-great-great-grandfather. Tim still carries the red-hair gene."

Lisa pointed to Tim's name at the bottom of a long chain of names.

"OK," Scott said. "And how does George Wilson tie in to this?"

He could see George's name on the line above Tim's joined by a line to Elizabeth's.

"John was George's great-grandfather. Elizabeth and George were second cousins, once removed. They probably didn't know it because there was a rift in the family back before either of them was born. A dispute over land around the time of the war. Split the family right down the middle. Such a shame. The genes didn't split. George still carried the recessive red-hair gene."

"I'm not sure I follow you," Jim said. "That's still a bit of a stretch to having George be Tim's father. Several other people in the community would have the same relationship, I would think. Do you have anything else?"

Lisa gave him a scalding look. "Of course I do. When George was younger and had facial hair, his beard came in red. One thing about working in the liquor store, you eventually get to meet all the young men in the community. None of them had a red beard like George's, except maybe his father before him. George started frequenting the liquor store while he was young and came pretty regularly. I guess you know that with all your questions when he disappeared."

"It's pretty circumstantial," Scott said. He sat back in his chair. "Did anybody ever see them together?"

"Have you ever had a secret affair, Corporal? You do it in out-of-the-way places where people won't see you. That's what makes it a secret. They were neighbours. There would have been lots of opportunities to get together on the sly." She used a tone of voice suggesting she was explaining the two-times table to primary school students.

"The timing is the key thing. Elizabeth probably just found out she was pregnant. Maybe she used one of those home tests you buy in the drug store, although I bet she didn't buy it around here. She must have told George, expecting him to do the right thing. But good old George lit out of here like a cat with his tail on fire. He hasn't been seen since. Men can be a bunch of assholes. The baby was born in late December. Do the math, gentlemen."

Scott looked over at Jim. He could see the fingers on one of Jim's hands going up and down like a piano player as he counted the months. He watched for the confirmation of Lisa's calculations. Jim looked up and nodded.

"There's quite an age gap between George and Elizabeth. George is literally old enough to be her father."

"Of course there's an age gap. Middle-aged men are always eyeing the fresh, young meat." Her voice dripped with contempt. "A woman their own age is too much for them to handle. George was a good-looking, life-of-the-party type guy. Elizabeth would be flattered to receive attention from him. Everyone was. It would make her feel older and more mature."

Scott looked out the office window at the men playing pool. None of them showed any interest in the conversation taking place forty feet away from them.

"Have you told any of this to Connie?" he asked. He was wondering if the same thoughts had crossed Connie's mind, if this was the cause of the dissension he had detected during the early interviews. Probably not. Elizabeth and Tim spent almost as much time at the Wilson house as they did at home.

"No. I'm not some meddlesome gossip. I did this to help you, the police. I had knowledge you didn't have. Not everyone knows the history of the community like I do."

Sure you did, Scott thought. Morbid curiosity about the identity of the father had nothing to do with it. He looked over at Jim, a questioning look on his face.

"You've put a lot of work into this, ma'am," Jim said. He picked up Lisa's chart and studied it. "It definitely could be one motive for George's disappearance." He looked at Scott. "It's not hard to check this out. A DNA test will confirm it one way or the other."

Scott gave him a noncommittal look. "Or we simply ask Elizabeth Schofield. She would know."

CHAPTER 48

S COTT WAS IN a quandary. After months of an investigation going absolutely nowhere, he became bombarded with new information. First, the discovery that George's missing truck, which he had scoured the country for, had barely left the community. Not only that, but George's signature showed up on the transfer of ownership. Now, the possibility existed George had fathered a bastard son with his next-door neighbour's daughter.

This last item had yet to be confirmed. Lisa Tingley's methods, despite her description, could hardly be called scientific. That said, they did have a ring of truth about them. Connie and George's marriage appeared to be on a roller-coaster. The timing of George's disappearance rang true with the moment of realization that a baby had been conceived. And good old Mendel's Laws. The flaming red hair could not be denied. George would not be the first man to be spooked at the thought of fatherhood. Especially if the mother, a kid half your age, lived next door. Then, add in the fact George shared a bed with a woman as strong as Connie Wilson. George may have simply chosen the path of least resistance.

Another factor demanded to know how willing a participant Elizabeth had been. Sex between two consenting adults is one thing. Rape is something else entirely. Elizabeth's silence leaned more towards non-consensual sex than it did a loving relationship. She seemed to be trying to forget the whole thing ever happened, a difficult task when you had a little red-headed baby demanding your undivided attention.

Scott had worked cases where he had a lot less evidence to get him started. Lisa Tingley claimed to have a more intimate knowledge of the history of the area than he did, and with good reason. What Scott referred to as history, Lisa remembered as current affairs.

Still, as compelling as this evidence appeared, did it give him the right to pry into Elizabeth Schofield's life? Elizabeth, who had spent almost a year covering up the identity of the father, had a right to privacy. And if Lisa Tingley's *scientific assessment* proved incorrect, a lot of people could be hurt by the accusation. Scott needed some confirmation and he had to believe Elizabeth hid information relevant to his case. More than relevant, it had to be necessary for the public good. He couldn't go on the same kind of witch hunt as Lisa Tingley had, just because of curiosity about the name of the father.

That kind of digging was the preserve of the neighbourhood busybody.

After some discussion with Sergeant McDonald, they had decided that honesty was the best policy. The next problem was how to interpret that statement. After careful deliberation, it was agreed Scott would arrange for an interview with Elizabeth regarding the events leading up to George's disappearance. As a frequent visitor to the Wilson household, this interview could easily be justified.

Scott wasted no time. He contacted Elizabeth that same afternoon.

Had Elizabeth noticed anything unusual in George's demeanour? Had she noticed any extra tension around the Wilson household? Had she heard the rumours about George's gambling and could she shed any light on that subject? All honest questions with the discovery of George's truck at the local junk yard.

Despite the care used in selecting the questions, Elizabeth refused to divulge any information about the Wilsons. Most questions she answered with a shrug of the shoulders and a shake of the head. Her attention was focused on little Tim who was enjoying his lunch during the questioning.

Elizabeth had asked Scott if he was all right with her feeding Tim in front of him. Scott answered no problem. Baby Tim was soon nestled up to his eyeballs between Elizabeth's swollen breasts, his lips firmly clamped on Elizabeth's left nipple, sucking away, oblivious of his role in the conversation about to take place. The scene was one of contented motherhood. It didn't make an aggressive interview style seem proper.

Scott used the opportunity to make the transition to the subject of the baby's father. Elizabeth clammed up completely. Scott could feel a sense of self-loathing building inside himself. Nevertheless, these were questions that had to be asked. The whole investigation might hinge on the answers to this one fundamental question.

"Was George Wilson the baby's father?"

Shock registered on Elizabeth's face. She pulled Tim from her nipple and hugged him protectively close before shaking her head in vehement denial. Scott gave her a wistful smile. The denial had come too late. Scott knew the truth. Another piece of the puzzle fell into place with a resounding clunk. Now, what could he do with this new-found knowledge? Did it give George another reason for running? Most definitely. Did it give someone a reason to murder George Wilson? Definitely, maybe.

While Scott conducted interviews on the outskirts of Raymond's River, the mystery of the red-headed baby had taken on a life of its own. Lisa Tingley was holding court in the downtown area. She was working the 3-to-11 shift at the liquor store. Her first customer of the day turned out to be Mable Booth. Mable needed some wine for a family get-together coming up on the weekend.

"The police were more interested in my research into young Tim Schofield than the Red Hat Ladies were," she told Mable.

Mable let out a long sigh. "You didn't go to the police with your conjectures?"

"I sure did. They were pleased to listen to me. Saved them a lot of time on the case they were working on. They thought George might have been involved in that Jason Browne murder. I straightened them out on that in a hurry."

Two other customers came over to the counter.

"What information did you have for the police?" Mark MacDonald asked. "Do you know who killed Browne? It was a friend of mine who found the body last year."

"No, but I know who didn't kill him."

Mark laughed. "So do I. I didn't do it. Mable didn't do it. You — well, I'm not too sure about you."

"Don't be a smart ass. They thought George Wilson might have been involved. He was long gone from the area before that happened." Lisa lowered her voice and looked around the store. "He's the father of Elizabeth Schofield's baby. That's why he took off. Didn't want to take the responsibility."

"Lisa!" Shock and disbelief filled Mable's face. "You don't know any of that is true."

"So that's what happened," Mark said, ignoring Mable's objections, sarcasm dripping from his voice. "I wondered why he disappeared. Makes sense to me. He's too old to take on the responsibility of a baby. Another ten years, he'll be looking to retire. Fifteen years, the baby's mother will be looking for college tuition for the little tyke. George did the smart thing."

Lisa's mouth dropped open. "You men are all alike."

"So are you women," Mark shot back. "Always jumping to conclusions that can ruin a man's life. Once accused, you're assumed guilty, no matter what turns out to be the truth. How do you know any of this? No one else in town knows anything about it. What makes you such an expert?"

"I did my research."

"Research. You're making wild guesses and unfounded accusations."

Another customer came into the store and stopped to listen to this exchange. She agreed with what Lisa had to say after Lisa spelled out the whole story.

Mark grudgingly conceded Lisa might have a point, but he doubted it. George was too smart to be playing around in his own back yard. That assessment did not stop him from discussing the matter with his wife over supper that night. She allowed that Lisa Tingley had her fingers on the pulse of the community. If Lisa said it, it was probably true.

It took Connie a day and a half to hear the story. She was livid. The version she heard had no ambiguity. Elizabeth Schofield had been sleeping with her husband. Young, red-headed Tim was the by-product of their union.

Everyone in Raymond's River seemed to know about the affair. Connie was in the process of picking up a prescription at the drug store when Edna Hiltz expressed her sorrow at Connie's situation.

"What situation are we talking about, Edna?" Connie asked. Edna had a way of confusing things people said to her. There was no confusion this time.

"Why, the affair your husband was having with the little girl next door. Some men can be such animals."

Connie felt like she was slapped in the face with a wet floor mop. She staggered back from the statement.

Edna looked surprised at Connie's reaction. Surely Connie must know about the affair. Everyone else in town did.

"Lisa Tingley said the police told her George was Tim Schofield's father. That's why he skipped town. One would have thought they would have told you first. That's the police for you. No sense of decorum."

Connie reached back and found one of the chairs provided for people waiting to pick up their prescriptions. Her heart was beating so fast, she was afraid she would have a stroke. She looked at the innocent face of Edna Hiltz now displaying horror at Connie's reaction. There was no point in arguing with her. Edna had definitely heard something. How badly she had misconstrued it would be fodder for another conversation.

Bob Landry, the pharmacist, hurried out from around the counter. He hadn't heard the dialogue between the two ladies, but Connie's reaction demanded immediate attention.

"Are you all right?"

He knelt down beside her and subtly took hold of her wrist, feeling for a pulse. His eyes opened wide at the rapid thrumming he felt under his fingers. He peered into Edna's now stricken face.

"What did you say to her?" His voice had an accusing tone.

Edna started to get flustered. She waved her hand back and forth in front of herself, not sure what she had done to trigger such a reaction in Connie.

"I was extending my condolences to Connie. I thought she knew. I don't understand why she doesn't."

Connie pushed off Bob's hand. Her colour was returning to normal. Her heartbeat was slowing. She reached out and took Edna's hand.

"It's not your fault, Edna. Calm down. You did nothing wrong."

Edna was not so easily consoled. "But I thought you would know."

"I'm sure there is some mistake."

"I don't think so. When I mentioned it to Billy Smith over at the grocery store, he said he saw the Mountie car at the Schofield place. Then Chris Dover, who was in the same aisle buying some bread, said he was at the fire hall when the police were talking to Lisa Tingley. It must be true."

"What must be true?" Bob asked, baffled by the conversation going on over his head. He stood up straight again, glad that Connie was returning to her normal self. "What are you ladies talking about?"

"Nothing," Connie said. She wanted to nip this rumour in the bud.

"Connie's George had an affair with that little girl next door," Edna said. "That young Mountie who has been hanging around the village for the last year or so told Lisa." No nipping would be taking place with this story. It had all the elements to blossom into a full-grown hydrangea bush with enough colour to appeal to everyone's interest.

Bob looked from Edna to Connie and then back to Edna. "Why would the police be telling Lisa Tingley any of this? Why would they tell anyone? I think you've got your facts confused, Edna." His voice had an understanding quality about it, as if Edna wasn't to blame for her confusion. As the dispenser of prescription drugs in the area, he had an intimate knowledge of most people's medical problems, both physical and mental.

Edna looked indignant. "I do not. I know what I was told." She turned and stormed out of the pharmacy.

Bob watched her go and fought back a smile. "She'll be back. She needs her prescription." He looked at Connie. "I'm sorry about what she said. She does get confused sometimes."

Connie nodded. "I know. I've had these wildly rambling conversations with her before." Connie looked towards the door where Edna had disappeared. "But something is going on. She may confuse the facts, but she doesn't manufacture them whole. I don't know whether to go over to the liquor store and confront Lisa Tingley or give Corporal Bowen a call. I have to get into the loop on this story."

"If you want the truth, I'd call the cops. If you want to confront the source of the story, I'm betting you will find it at the liquor store. Lisa, I seem to recall, has been talking to everybody in town about any red-headed ancestors they may have had. Now, I guess I know why."

"Red-headed. Great. George never had red hair, but he did have a red beard if he let it grow for a while. Surely that's not what this is all about."

"Many dark-haired men have red beards. That's why they don't let them grow."

Connie placed her purchases on the counter. "I'll give the corporal a call. See what he knows about this."

The bell over the outside door gave a tingle. A red-faced Edna Hiltz came walking back in. "I forgot my insulin."

CHAPTER 49

A T FIRST, SCOTT expressed surprise at Connie's call. To his knowledge, no one except Lisa Tingley and Elizabeth Schofield were privy to the information being discussed.

He was still working on the significance of his new-found information and how it impacted his investigation. George being the father of his neighbour's baby gave him one more in an ever-growing list of reasons to pack his bags and head for the hills. As the evidence piled up, this seemed to be the logical choice. Still, it did not preclude George from being the victim of a homicide plot. It also supplied one more reason why someone could kill him and feel confident they would get away with it. Scott was not yet prepared to abandon that theory. If it were true, the trail had been cold for much too long already. It was time to follow this path to a conclusion, one way or the other.

The anger coming over the phone lines at first took him aback. It only took a few seconds consideration to make him realize this should be the expected outcome. Lisa Tingley would never be confused with someone who exercised discretion over her opinions. He silently chastised himself for not making a call to Connie. Apologies would not be accepted at this late date. He didn't insult Connie by offering one. He could only offer the truth.

"Lisa Tingley confronted the sergeant and me at the diner with her story. We whisked her away to somewhere private to have her spell it out to us. I should have realized telling us was only one small step in a larger spreading of the tale."

"So what is the tale?" The anger in Connie's voice came through the phone undisguised.

"As I'm sure you've heard, she has linked George's disappearance to the birth of Elizabeth Schofield's baby. Something about them having the same ancestor several generations back who was well-known for his flowing mane of red hair."

"George and Elizabeth had an affair?" Now the full impact of Edna's wild story hit her. "Are you serious?"

"That's how Lisa tells it."

She changed the phone receiver to her other ear. "Can't you do something to stop her?"

"That would be like trying to push water uphill. Once the floodgates are open, nature is going to take its course. From what I know of small towns, there is no way of stopping the rumour mill at this stage. The best we can hope for is to get the truth out there to overcome any wild speculation."

Connie was silent for a few beats. "I hear you also talked to Elizabeth. What did she have to say?"

Scott considered explaining that any interviews he held with anyone involved could not be discussed with others. Instead, he decided Elizabeth's defence of the Wilsons might be what Connie needed to hear right now.

"She told us nothing. Regardless of what Lisa Tingley is saying, you have a staunch friend in Elizabeth. It was like talking to a brick wall." That was true. Elizabeth never admitted to having an affair with George. It was only a conclusion Scott had reached from her reaction to the accusation.

Connie gave a harsh grunt. "She's not much of a friend if she was sleeping with my husband."

Now it was Scott's turn to be silent. He wished this conversation was taking place face to face and not over the phone. There are too many nuances lost in a phone dialogue.

"Do you think that is possible?"

Connie's answer came out with a slight hitch. "I don't know what to think. No. I can't believe Elizabeth would do that to me." A pause. "At the time, I did suspect George was having an affair.

Women know things like that. They can sense it. But not with Elizabeth. I can't believe that is true. Elizabeth is over here every day."

"That could explain why he took off. He couldn't face you when Elizabeth told him she was pregnant. You're neighbours. He couldn't hide from her." Scott would try to ease into what he believed was the truth about the events of last spring.

"No. George had his faults, but I don't think he would have run." Then she quickly added: "Although that version of things does make a lot more sense than the poker game theory." Relief seemed to come to her voice.

Scott was taken aback at her quick change in attitude. This was not a turn he had anticipated. "Are there any male friends he would have talked this over with before leaving?"

Connie laughed. "What world do you live in, Corporal? Men don't talk over things like that. They just react."

She walked over to the electric kettle on her kitchen counter and plugged it in. Almost instantly, the water came to a boil. She made herself a cup of instant coffee.

Scott pushed on. "Maybe so, but who would he have gone to if he decided to break the male mould?"

"I don't know. Some of his former drinking buddies. Cal Lindsay, maybe. Cal and George got along real well."

"How are things with you and Cal?"

"Me and Cal? We're still in business together. Doing quite well."

"Didn't you date each other at one time?"

Connie laughed again. Her mood had greatly improved since the beginning of the call. She took a sip of coffee before answering.

"That was a long time ago, Corporal. Water under the bridge."

"Does Cal think that way?"

"We're friends, Corporal. That's all there is to it, good friends."

"Were you surprised when he suddenly reappeared in your life after George's disappearance? It was rather sudden, I understand."

"Maybe a little at first. He had a business plan. We discussed it; both saw possibilities for ourselves, benefits we both wanted, and we acted on it."

"And that's all it is, simply business?"

"At first. Now, like I said, we're good friends. I guess we always were. There was never any disharmony in our relationship. I would see Cal every so often when he was working with George. We were always cordial."

"There's no possibility Cal is looking for something more?"

Connie's voice took on an edge. "Where are you going with this, Corporal? Do you think Cal had something to do with George's disappearance? That's foolishness."

"You brought it up, not me."

Connie stared intently at the phone. Her eyes widened. She abruptly, but shakily, lowered the coffee cup in her hands back down to the table, spilling a little in the process. She changed the phone from her left hand to her right hand.

"You're suggesting Cal murdered my husband." She was at a momentary loss for words. "That absurd, absolutely absurd." She gave a shaky laugh. "You're way out in left field with that one. Cal and George were friends."

"More like rivals is what I hear."

"You flatter me. That was years ago. We've all matured since then. Cal and I are business partners who get along real well together. That's all there is to it. He had nothing to do with George disappearing. Case closed."

Scott let that statement sink in a bit before responding. "Cal is involved in some other business in the community, I understand."

Connie did not rise to the bait.

After a period of silence, he went on. "He's the local bootlegger."

"Is that right? I've never used the services of such a person."

"No, but George did. That's why they were good friends."

Connie sat down at the kitchen table. This conversation's course became like a winding river, new twists and turns around every corner.

"No. Cal worked for George. He operated the skidder. He's very proficient at it."

Scott became silent. He and Sergeant Jim McDonald had discussed Cal's involvement in George's disappearance. It had always revolved around liquor — the purchase and the consumption. Never had the subject of them working in the woods together come up. Cal could have been with George the day he disappeared.

"Were George and Cal working together when he disappeared?"

"No. Cal was preparing John Haydon's fields for planting. He was also well-known for his ability to operate farm equipment."

"John Haydon the firefighter?"

"Firefighter, farmer, one and the same."

Scott thought that over. That explained why Cal's name never came up when they were discussing who might have been with George that day. John knew where Cal was. He was paying him to be there. But a highly proficient operator could hide how much time he spent in the field. He wouldn't constantly work at top speed. He could do it in spurts and cover a period of absence without anyone knowing. One thing about farm work. Most of it was a solitary endeavour.

"Is Cal working for you today?"

"He's working for us. We're partners. He's skidding out some logs while the ground is still frozen."

"Where?"

Connie hesitated. "I'm not sure. Why don't I have him call you? That is if I can get him to stop laughing when I tell him what you think."

"That's all right. I'll call him. It's better if I approach him about this matter. Do you have his cell number?"

"Somewhere. I'll have to look for it."

Scott gave the business card rolodex on his desk a spin. "Never mind. I have his card here. Brian gave me a copy of it."

Connie didn't respond.

"I'm really sorry about Lisa Tingley. I should have called you as soon as she laid her story on me. I should have realized she would not keep it to herself. I'll talk to Elizabeth Schofield again. Now that the story's out in the community, she'll have to respond to it."

"Don't bother, I'll talk to Elizabeth myself."

Scott's voice took on a concerned edge. "That's not a good idea. Leave it for me to do."

"As you said, Corporal, the story is already out in the community. Elizabeth will expect me to talk to her about it. She didn't come over yet today, but I'm sure she will."

"Connie, this is a bad idea."

"Maybe, but it has to happen sometime, one way or the other. I'm in control of myself now. The shock has passed."

Scott could only hear the words. He could not see her hands fidgeting with the spilled coffee. Connie looked like she was anything but in control.

CHAPTER 50

SCOTT DIALLED THE number on the business card. The phone rang a couple of times and then went to voice mail.

"Damn," he muttered under his breath. "He must be out of range."

Scott thought for a few seconds and then broke off the connection.

No sense in tipping him off.

That thought no sooner hit his mind when a light clicked on in his brain. That was exactly what was happening. Cal was being tipped off. He called Connie's number again. It also went immediately to voice mail. Connie was on the phone. Connie had got through to Cal before him. She wouldn't have had to look up the number.

Young lovers, he thought. Doesn't matter how old they are, they still act foolishly. For Connie's sake, Scott hoped he was wrong about Cal. Hoping would not be enough. Scott would need proof.

He flipped his rolodex again and got the technical services number at the RCMP Headquarters in Halifax.

"I need a fix on a cell phone. Can you do that?"

Scott read off the number of Cal's phone. In less than a minute, he had a fix on the location and was told the phone was currently in use. He thanked the tech and pulled a topographical map from a nearby shelf. With a little fumbling around with a ruler, he was able to apply the coordinates to the map and mark Cal's exact location. Surprisingly, it was in the same area George had disappeared from a year ago.

"I think Roscoe and I should go for a stroll in the woods," he said. "He hasn't been getting enough exercise lately."

Less than an hour later, Scott parked his Ford Explorer beside Cal Lindsay's truck. He had put in a call to Sergeant Jim McDonald to bring him up to date on his plans. The sergeant was away from his phone. This time Scott did leave a detailed voice message. Jim had called back five minutes ago.

He had suggested Scott wait for Jim to come and back him up before going into the woods. Scott assured Jim that Roscoe would be all the back-up he needed, but suggested it would be good to have Jim along for the questioning later. Jim's car was roaring down the road on his way to the site, lights flashing, but no siren.

As Scott stepped from his vehicle, he could hear the rumble of the tree farmer through the barren trees. The ground in the forest sparkled as the early spring sun turned the snow cover to diamond-like ice crystals. This was old snow, snow that had been around all winter. It had gone through a number of freeze and thaw cycles and was as hard as ice. Pockets of this snow would still be here in early June unless the heavy rains broke it up.

In the clearing beside the two vehicles, a mountain of sixteen-foot logs was growing. Cal was working hard to beat the spring breakup of the ground when this road would be nothing but a quagmire. Connie's call had not stopped him from continuing with his work. Scott wondered if that was a sign of innocence or a sign of Cal's confidence in his ability to fool the police.

The sounds of the diesel engine diminished in intensity, indicating Cal was heading back for another load. Jim debated whether to wait for him to come out or to aggressively follow him. Roscoe made the decision. From the back seat, he let out a sharp woof. He had been promised an outing in the woods and he wanted to get it started.

Scott opened the back door. "Let's go big fellow."

Roscoe jumped down, stumbled, and sprang to his feet again as if the stumble was a routine part of disembarking from the high back seat. He sat at Scott's feet waiting for further instructions, but his eyes were already showing the excitement a romp in the woods would bring. Scott didn't make him wait.

"Let's go," he said. No orders. No commands. Roscoe was free to run around and soak up the ambiance of the wide open spaces. He bounded fifty feet down the road as fast as his three good legs would take him. Stopped, looked back at Scott and came running back to encourage him along. Scott patted him on the head and the two partners set out side by side along the road, beaten down to solid earth by the heavy machinery.

Ten minutes later, the mechanical sounds emanating from the forest changed. Scott knew Cal had reached his destination. Heavy logs were now being piled into the back of the porter for another trip out to the main road. Scott knew the big-wheeled vehicle crawled along at a pace not much more than a fast walk over this rough terrain. He started to plan how to conduct this confrontation that was now imminent.

Connie's warning phone call had limited Scott's choices of approach. He could not make this seem like an innocent meeting, although that would have been a stretch under the best of conditions. At the same time, an outright accusation would probably serve no useful purpose, either. Finding George's truck had brought the case actively back to life. Scott had to make it seem like he was eliminating all possible suspects.

Cal and George had a close relationship on a number of levels. It was logical for Scott to approach him early in the renewed investigation. He would have to suggest Connie had taken his questions about Cal a little too much to heart. He could suggest maybe Connie was thinking her relationship with Cal was ready to move to the next level. If Scott's theory of the murder was correct, that is information Cal would be anxious to hear.

If Scott was totally off base, and there was no murder, it would be interesting to see how Cal reacted to the suggested romantic involvement with his business partner. Whether he was dead or still alive, George's last visit to anyone in Raymond's River could well have been to Cal Lindsay. It was time to find out what Cal knew and what he and George may have discussed. Scott still didn't believe Cal's intentions towards Connie were strictly platonic.

A man couldn't have an extended relationship with a lady as fine as Connie and not want to take it further. Merely having those thoughts pass through his mind caused a blush to come to his cheeks. He could feel the increased heat and had to smile. Many believed you couldn't blush if you were alone. You couldn't embarrass yourself. Well, you could if you tried hard enough.

Up ahead, he could see the big claw of the porter swinging a load of rough logs into its cage. It neatly stacked them into place to form a tight, solid load. One tree canted at a cross angle to the rest. Like picking up a toothpick with a pair of tweezers, Cal grabbed the offending log from the load, aligned it with the rest and dropped it in place. Scott had just gotten there in time. That was the last log for this trip.

CHAPTER 51

CONNIE COULD SEE Elizabeth, Tim in her arms, making her way along the path between the two farms. This was the moment of truth. Connie didn't want to believe Lisa Tingley had solved the mystery of Tim's father. Connie believed Elizabeth had the right to her privacy. That was why Connie had never pursued the subject. She especially didn't want Lisa Tingley to be right about George. She was still trying to wrap her head around that tale of misadventure.

Not the part about George having an affair. Connie was sure that had taken place. A man can't be in close physical contact with a naked woman and not acquire some of her smells. George had carried those odours back home. He was unaware of them, but not Connie. That was her first clue. From there, she became more and more suspicious and more and more positive her husband of fifteen years was being unfaithful. But with Elizabeth? That was much too close to home. Elizabeth was too much of a friend. It couldn't be true.

Connie had never been one to avoid confrontation. In fact the opposite was true. She had a reputation for tackling all issues head-on. That was why she chaired so many committees in the community. Connie made things happen. When Elizabeth had missed her usual morning visit, Connie had called her and invited her over. Elizabeth had made excuses, but finally relented to Connie's insistence.

Connie heard Elizabeth's feet scraping the snow off on the mat outside the back door. She heard the click of the door latch releasing. Elizabeth no longer knocked. She simply let herself in. Is that what happened? When George showed an interest, and Elizabeth was the kind of young woman men would notice, did she simply let herself in, right under Connie's nose? Connie still refused to accept that possibility.

"Say hi to Auntie Connie," Elizabeth said as she waltzed through the door in an exaggerated effort to appear normal. Connie's heart dropped a little. Elizabeth was trying too hard.

Elizabeth would not have heard the rumours. Her family were not ones to socialize with the people of Raymond's River. It was not a snobbish thing; they shopped in the bigger towns and cities around from force of habit. In Ontario, they did all their shopping in the large shopping centres. Nothing had changed when they moved here.

Corporal Bowen had talked to Elizabeth. Had he broached the subject of paternity? He hadn't actually said one way or the other. He only said Elizabeth had refused to discuss Connie and her situation. Her situation. If George was Tim's father, it was Elizabeth's situation up for discussion. Still, the corporal had said the rumours flying through the community were unfounded. They were based solely on the speculations of neighbourhood gossip Lisa Tingley, and she had no hard evidence to back up her claims.

Connie hoped in her heart that was the truth. The bell, however, had been rung. The time for secrecy had come to an end. Elizabeth didn't have to reveal the father's name. She still had her right to her privacy, but with one notable exception. That privacy didn't extend to Connie's husband. If George was the father, it was time to fess up.

Connie reached out for Tim like she did every morning when they came over. She pulled back his bonnet and rubbed his nose with her own. The shock of red hair danced before her eyes.

Elizabeth sensed the change in the room. "Connie, is something the matter? You look strange."

Connie indicated one of the kitchen chairs. "Sit down, Elizabeth. We have to talk." Connie held on to baby Tim and took the other chair. Elizabeth was not going to walk out on her, at least not with her baby in her arms.

"Did I do something wrong? Is this about the policeman who was here the other day? I didn't tell him anything."

Connie started to have doubts. Surely if George was Tim's father, Elizabeth would know what this confrontation was about. Had denying the father's existence for a year wiped any memory of who it was from the girl's mind? Not even Connie would buy into that. When a man slipped his penis into you, you tended to remember who he was. Especially if a baby started growing inside you shortly thereafter.

"I have one question for you, Elizabeth. I want an honest answer. Yes or no and then we'll move on from there. Will you do that for me?"

Elizabeth shifted her eyes down to the table. An almost imperceptible shaking gripped her shoulders. A tear landed on the table. She looked up, streaks running down her face.

"Oh Connie. You don't know how much I wanted to tell you. I knew it was wrong right from the start and I tried to fight it off." She paused and took a big sniff. Mucous rattled in her nasal cavity. "But it just happened. I don't know how. It just happened."

"It just happened?" Connie's voice took on a shrillness, causing Tim to stir in her arms. She looked down at the baby and cuddled it closer. "That's the best you can do? It just happened?"

Elizabeth made a swipe at her eyes with the back of her hand. That merely redirected tears across her cheeks before they flowed down again. "It was only the once, honest. I wanted to tell you, but when George took off, I knew you'd blame me. You're the only friend I have around here. I'm so, so sorry."

Connie struggled to regain her own control. Knowing George had cheated on her somehow brought her a sense of relief. She had suspected it for a long time. Now, all the doubts were removed. Did it really matter with whom he had done it? Did it really matter if Elizabeth was not the only one? She had fallen for George's lines many years before. Elizabeth had bought into the same bullshit.

She reached out and took Elizabeth's hand. "Thank you for telling me. Now, it's time to move on. Can we both do that?"

The relief on Elizabeth's face was palpable. Again she stabbed at her tears with the back of her hand. "I know I can." She tightened her grip on Connie's hand. "I hope you can. I'm just so sorry about what happened."

"He's a bum. We're not going to let him break up our friendship."

Elizabeth gave a little shake of her head. "He never knew about the baby. I never told him. That's not why he took off. He was afraid of hurting you. We both felt we had let you down."

Connie blanched at that statement. That was not what she wanted to hear at this moment. "Let's forget about him. We've got a little baby here to care for." She brought Tim up to her face and kissed him on the cheek. "You're so cute."

Yes he is, Connie thought. He looks just like a little version of George. This was the first time she was able to admit that to herself, even though she had known it for months. A burden seemed to fall from her shoulders.

CHAPTER 52

CAL LINDSAY SETTLED his bucket on top of the pile of logs and turned to face the front of the porter. From his position eight feet above the ground, he spotted the approaching Mountie and his dog. His arm shot up in a wave, a disarming smile on his face. He didn't look like a man who had been warned the police suspected he was a murderer.

He grabbed the handles over his door and swung out onto the steel ladder which took him down to the ground.

"Cal Lindsay, I assume," Scott said.

Cal extended his hand. "The one and only. I've been expecting a call from you, Corporal. I didn't think I'd rate a personal visit." He offered an engaging smile.

Scott smiled back. "I just happened to be in the neighbourhood walking my dog."

Cal reached down and patted Roscoe. "What a lucky break that I happened to be here."

Both men laughed.

"I would have come to you," Cal said. "That's what Connie suggested. She said it would make me look innocent. Now, since you came all the way back here, I guess I look guilty, but I do have to get this wood out before the thaw comes."

Scott looked around at the trees lying in neat rows throughout the area. "Makes sense," he said. "I do have some questions for you." Scott's voice took on a serious tone. "I'm sure you know we found George Wilson's truck at the Kaulback Salvage yard, at least evidence it had been stripped for parts there."

"I would say it's safe to assume everyone in the community knows that by know. Jason Browne was somehow involved. There are competing versions out there about his role. That information is a little more sketchy." Cal raised his eyebrows and his voice at the end of that statement.

"Is it?" Scott asked. He didn't elaborate.

Cal looked at his watch. "I was just about to break for lunch. I always bring more than I can eat. You never know when I might still be here at suppertime. Pull up a stump and we'll talk." He pointed to a cleared area. "Those trees have been down for a year or more. They are less likely to get sap or stuff on your uniform."

Scott looked around at the trees that had been fallen. Most of their branches had been trimmed off and their tops removed. Their butts all pointed into the same area of the clearing.

Cal followed Scott's line of sight.

"I try to fall them in such a way that when I go in with the skidder," he pointed to another huge machine off to one side, "I can grasp onto as many butts as possible in one pull."

"I notice you're not clearcutting."

"I'm here for the long haul," Cal said. "By taking some of those taller trees, it opens up the lower ones to more sunlight. Their growth rate should take off for the next few years. They'll get much bigger, much faster. I'm just careful to leave some of the better quality trees for seed stock. High-grading is almost as bad as clearcutting. Some people think it's worse."

"High-grading?"

"Taking the best. Leaving the less-desirable trees behind. Soon your whole forest is made up of the less-desirable stock."

Scott took a bite of one of the sandwiches Cal had offered him. It was sliced Canadian cheddar on whole-wheat bread. Instead of mayonnaise, the condiment was strawberry jam. To his surprise, it was a tasty combination.

Roscoe lowered his nose and sniffed at a nearby stump. He made a tentative pawing near the base and sniffed some more. Then he looked up at Scott and barked.

"Quiet Roscoe. You know better than to be digging up animal holes. You never know what will bite your snout."

Roscoe took a couple of more digs and barked again. He sat and looked at Scott with an expectant look on his face.

Scott looked at the stump a little closer. It had a diameter of sixteen inches or more. "This must have been a beauty before it was cut down. Kind of a shame, in a way. Would have been a great seed tree, I would think."

Cal looked over at the stump. "That was probably a blow-down. Maybe from Hurricane Juan, more likely its aftermath. Juan weakened a lot of trees that have fallen down in heavy windstorms every year since the event. This one looks more recent."

"Not high-grading, eh?"

Cal shook his head. "You can tell by the stump. Notice how flat it is all the way around. No notches. No tear-out of wood down the side."

Scott stood up and studied what Cal was pointing out to him. "I'm not sure I follow you."

"When I'm cutting a tree, I notch it in the direction I want it to fall. If it's done right, the weight of the tree collapses into the notch and the tree ends up where you want it." He pointed to the trees waiting to be hauled out by the skidder. "That's how those trees all ended up in a neat line. This tree has no notch. If you cut a tree without a notch and let it randomly fall, it usually tears a strip out of the trunk when the weight of the tree gets to the point where it's going to topple over. Or worse, it settles back and jams your saw. You don't get to cut all the way through before the weight of the tree reacts in some way."

That made sense to Scott. He nodded his understanding.

"This tree would have been lying on its side, supported by its roots and branches. Someone, probably George, would have zipped through it in a nice clean cut, leaving a perfect table top or seat for you."

"But why is it back in the ground?"

"The roots would have been still covered in dirt and mud. Once the heavy tree was severed from the trunk, the weight of the roots could pull the stump back into the ground."

Scott looked around at the ground at the base of the stump. All the snow had been melted by the sun shining into this cleared area of the forest. Roscoe got to his feet and started digging again. Scott reached down and patted his dog. "Stop digging, Roscoe. You don't want to tangle with any creatures who might be living under there. Behave yourself."

Scott circled the stump, studying the ground around it. "This ground looks pretty natural to me. I can't see where the roots were torn up."

Cal came over and stood beside Scott. "This one settled in particularly well. It almost looks like it was tramped down into place and covered with leaves. You can usually see the gap and the disturbed earth to some degree." He looked at the top of the stump again. "It has to be a blow-down. They don't cut off that smoothly when they're still standing."

Scott knelt by the stump. "Everything is covered. I can't even see where the dirt was torn up." Roscoe nosed in front of him, sniffing where Scott was looking.

"Could be natural," Cal said. "The tree wasn't down for long before the trunk was cut away. The roots would have had most of the dirt still attached to them. The weight would make it settle in quite deeply and the wind and rain would fill in any gaps that existed." He knelt down beside Scott and Roscoe for a closer look. "Then again, someone may have gone to a lot of trouble to make it look this natural." He pointed to a couple of indentations on the top of the stump. "Those could have been made with the claws of a porter. Someone might have given it a good push to make it settle in better."

Scott ran his hand along the depressions. "It is suspicious."

"You think something is under this stump?" Cal asked.

"Maybe. Roscoe is trained as a cadaver dog. He finds bo…"

Cal held up his hands. "I get the picture." He studied the stump again. His eyes narrowed and he grimaced. "Do you really think there is something under there?"

Scott gave a slight shrug of his shoulders. "I don't know. It would be a bit of a stretch."

Roscoe barked two more times and made another pawing motion at the ground. "Still, you say George was cutting in here last year?"

"Well, I don't know that for a fact. George was cutting on the other side of the road. It all belongs to the same landowner, Laurie MacIsaac. I figure George may have cruised this section before he started over there, saw these blow-downs and decided to take them out first. There would have been some good timber in those logs. No sense letting them rot."

"Where does this owner live? I'd like to talk to him."

"Ontario. Still owns this part of the family wood lot. He was down for Easter to visit his relatives. He always strolls through his property when he comes back. Master of his domain type of thing. He lives on a city lot with thirty feet of frontage on the outskirts of Toronto. Likes to get out and stretch his legs on property belonging to him as far as the eye can see."

Cal let his eyes sweep around the forested area. "A lot of these trees are over-mature. Their centres are probably rotted out. It's either cut them down now or have them die as they stand. Most of them are only good for firewood. He gave me a call to see if I could clean it up for him."

Scott rubbed his chin in a pensive manner. "I remember the search. There wasn't much wood taken off the other side of the road either. The consensus suggested George was just setting up in the area. We did have searchers on foot go through this side of the road. By then, the rain had beaten everything down. Removed or filled in any tracks."

"Yeah, George had only started cutting over there in late March or early April. I finished doing the work on that side last summer and fall. I only recently moved into this area when I got the call from Laurie. He may live in the city, but he practises good work policies on his wood lots. He's a good guy to work for. Money is not his main motivating factor."

Scott looked back down at the stump. Roscoe was still pawing and sniffing at the base.

"Can you lift that stump?"

CHAPTER 53

"COME IN, SERGEANT," Scott responded to the crackle of his walkie-talkie. He glanced at this watch, surprised at the good them Jim had made.

"I'm out by your car. How are things going?"

"I don't even want to speculate. It's about a fifteen, twenty minute walk back to here. Are you up to that?"

"Speculate about what?"

"What are you driving? Can you bring it back that woods road?"

"Not on a bet. I'm in my regular, everyday Ford. Six inches clearance at most. I don't suppose you left the keys to the Explorer where I can find them."

"Yeah, I did. You can find them in my pocket. Start hiking. I won't start until you get here."

"Start what?"

"Hiking. Come as quick as you can. Over and out."

Cal had been standing beside Scott listening to this by-play. "Connie tells me I'm a suspect. I do have an alibi for the day George went missing."

"She told me."

"Well, it's true. I wasn't alone. John Haydon was with me. We were both working in the same field. He wanted to get it done before any more heavy rains came. If you recall, the day the search began, it rained with a vengeance. The heavens opened up that night and morning."

Scott thought back to the first day of the search. He nodded. It couldn't have rained any harder if someone had been controlling a faucet directly over his head.

"As for our relationship, it is strictly business. Connie had the machinery not being used. I had the knowledge to use it, but could not afford the capital investment to buy it. It was a match made in heaven as far as we were both concerned. We both needed the money."

"And now? How are things going now?"

"We're friends. We have a business in common. We see a lot of each other. I don't have designs of climbing into bed with her, if that's what you mean."

"She's an attractive woman."

Cal winked. "You're an attractive man."

Scott looked at him, not knowing how to respond.

"I don't have ambitions to climb into bed with you, either. Just trying to show you that you shouldn't be jumping to conclusions. Especially in your line of work."

"OK, point taken." Scott paused. "She does like you though."

"We're friends. I had my chance years ago and let it pass. Let's leave it at that." Cal hesitated for a few seconds. "Did she say something about me?"

Scott smiled and tapped Cal in the chest. "See, there is still a spark burning."

"As you said, she is an attractive woman. Even more so as she matures."

Roscoe let out a sharp bark and looked up at the two men.

Cal looked down at the stump where Roscoe was still sitting. His face lost a little of its colour. "What happens if we find something under that stump?"

"Let's see what we find first. Then, we'll take it one step at a time."

"What would a year-old body look like?"

"All you have to do is move the stump for us. You don't have to come any closer than that."

"If it's George, someone will have to identify him. I don't want Connie to have to do that. I knew him as well as anybody around here. Will there be enough of the old George left for me to recognize?"

"One step at a time. Identity may have to be made by dental records or DNA. You can relax. We'll let you know if we need you for anything."

A little colour came back into Cal's face. "I'm not a wimp. I could look."

"Everyone is not cut out for this sort of thing. Why subject yourself to it if you don't have to? It could visit your nightmares for years to come. It might not even be human. Roscoe smells the products of decomp. It could be something else."

Both men turned as they heard footsteps running up the road. Scott looked at his watch.

"Good afternoon, Sergeant. You made good time."

"My curiosity was piqued." He held out a hand to Cal. "Detective-Sergeant Jim McDonald, Major Crimes."

"Cal Lindsay, forestry worker and suspected murderer."

Jim gave him a strange look. "At this stage of the investigation, several people fall into that category."

"Oh, who else?"

"I can't divulge that." Jim looked at Scott. "What didn't you want to speculate about?

Scott indicated Roscoe with a nod of his head.

"Roscoe?" Then he noted the intense interest the dog was showing in the stump. He looked at Scott. "You think he found something?"

"I don't want to speculate. Cal says he can move the stump. It's the result of a blow-down. It's not firmly anchored in the ground."

"I can either grasp onto it with my porter bucket and try to lift it straight up, or I can hook on with the skidder and pull it over in the direction the tree originally fell. You can still see the chain-saw sawdust where the cut was made."

Jim walked over and looked at the stump. "Looks like it belongs here to me. Are you sure it's a blow-down?"

"You can tell by the way the top is cut," Scott said. He looked at Cal and winked. "Should I go on with more details or will you take my word for it?"

"That's all right, Einstein. I'm sure you know what you're talking about."

Jim took a digital camera from his pocket and started taking pictures of the surrounding area. "This ground doesn't look like it's been disturbed for quite a while. I'd like to get an overall shot from high up."

"How high?" Cal asked. "I could lift you up about twenty feet in the bucket of my porter."

Jim looked over at the machine. "I don't need to get that high. I'll just take the picture from the cab."

When the picture-taking was finished, Jim studied the two machines. "I think it's best if we peel the stump back to the position it was in before the top of the tree was cut off. If this is a murder scene, that is what it would have looked like before the murder."

Cal looked down at the traces of remaining sawdust mixed in with the dead, rotting leaves making up the layer of humus surrounding the stump. He positioned his hands as if holding a chain saw, adjusted them slightly to line them up with the line of chipped wood, and looked in the direction away from the stump.

"That would be the top of the tree over there," he said, pointing to a skeleton of branches seventy feet away. I'd have to get the skidder onto this path here to get a straight pull." He indicated a line between the stump and the crown of the tree.

Jim looked at the rough terrain. "Can you do that?"

"Do bears poop in the woods? You've aroused my curiosity about that stump. I can make it work. I hope you're wrong about George being under there. I don't know how well Connie will be able to take it. To think, he's been out here all this time. I can't imagine how he could have cut the tree off and got in the way of the stump at the same time. Anything is possible, I guess."

The two cops exchanged glances. Cal still didn't understand the implications this turn of events indicated. He had not bought into the murder theory.

Cal climbed up into the cab of the skidder and stepped on the starter switch. The diesel engine chugged into life. The big tires rode up over stumps, straightened out hollows and generally showed little difficulty finding the position of the perceived bed of the tree trunk. The removed branches, lined up like ribs along the path, snapped under the weight of the skidder, offering no resistance. Cal made a couple of adjustments and then jumped down from the still-running machine.

"This will give us a straight pull," he said. He grabbed the hook on one of the cables protruding from the back. He threw a folded eight-foot-chain over his shoulder. As he pulled, the cable reel spun easily, unfolding a trail of steel between the skidder and the stump.

"The trick will be to keep the links from sliding up the side of the stump," he said as he placed a coil of chain around the trunk. "This bark may simply peel away."

He pulled tightly on the shackle and snapped the ends to the hook on the cable. He gave a reassuring tug on the complete unit.

"Might work," he said. He looked over at the two men and their dog. "You'll want to stand clear just in case something lets go. If that happens, you don't want to be anywhere near the whipping steel cable."

Both men moved back behind the stump. This would also give them the first view of what might be under it when the lifting hatch revealed what was hidden there.

Cal made his way back to the skidder, making sure the laid-out cable was clear of any impediments along the way. Slowly he engaged the lever to start winding in the wire cord, first taking the strain, then speeding up the engine to actually pull.

The stump held its ground, still firmly frozen into its surroundings. The cable started to remove bark and slide up the tree.

"Whoa, whoa," Scott yelled to Cal. "It's going to slide off."

Cal reduced the power and came back to take a look. "Frozen more solid than I thought it would be." Chunks of the heavy bark lay on the ground around the stump, revealing a smoother, slippery tree surface.

"What if you took your chain saw and cut a grove to hold the chain?" Scott said. "You know, like the notch you use to determine the direction a tree falls."

Cal smiled. "You catch on fast, officer. I'll get my saw."

Five minutes later the chain was firmly ensconced inside a notch in the back of the stump. Sliding would no longer be a problem. Now the question was: Could they break the frozen connection of the roots and earth?

Cal gave a gentle laugh when Jim expressed that concern. "Don't worry about that, my son. I can snap the roots if I have to."

Jim shook his head. "That won't work. I do not doubt you have the power to move the stump. We have to have the dirt come with it. We need the same opening created when the tree originally blew down."

Cal stomped his boot into the frozen surface. "The roots should be stronger than the soil, at least around the trunk where they are thick. Any breaking would take place near the ends. If something is buried under here, this is where it will be." He indicated the space directly under the tree. "Let's give it a try. If it's not working, wave to me and I'll stop."

Both cops followed suit with the ground-stomping. "It is getting well into the spring," Scott said. "The ground should be breaking up under there. Let's at least give it a try."

"Pull gently," Jim said, "and watch for our signal." He had not spent as much time devoted to this case as Scott had. If they had to wait a couple of more days to bring in the proper digging equipment, he could wait. Scott was less patient. He wanted some answers now.

CHAPTER 54

ONCE AGAIN, THE wire cable became airborne as Cal took up the slack. This time, instead of the chain around the trunk sliding up, it settled into the groove carved out by the chain saw. The top of the stump started to lean in the direction of the rumbling skidder.

The engine noise grew in intensity as Cal increased the power. The ground around the stump started to vibrate. Jim and Scott stepped back farther. They were in the zone that was starting to lift.

Cal gave the diesel another boost of power. The stump leaned even more towards the direction of the cable and then, with a sudden ripping sound, a large circle of ground lifted into the air, hinged at the edge nearest Cal and the skidder. The smell of decomposing vegetation wafted from the hole. It had a pleasant woodsy smell, not that of a human body.

Roscoe didn't share that view. With several thousand more smell receptors than his human handlers, Roscoe could smell the odour of death. He started to bark and pull on his collar. Scott had a tight grip on him, not as a restraint, but to keep him safe from the lifting soil.

He let go and Roscoe bounded forward. He stopped directly under the stump, made a couple more pawing motions, sat down, looked back at Scott and let out a sharp woof. "Right here, stupid," was the message it transmitted to the cop.

Cal had taken up the slack on the cable again to keep the tree from settling back. He started forward to see what all the barking was about.

Scott could see the approaching head over the top of the upturned stump. "Don't come any further. This may be a crime scene."

Cal stopped. He was about to protest when he remembered what would make it a crime scene. He didn't proceed any further.

Jim and Scott moved in to where Roscoe was sitting. They expected to see a corpse mangled under the roots. Instead there was a coating of rotting leaves. A piece of black plastic shone through in one spot.

"What the hell?" Jim said. He moved some of the leaves aside. "A body bag." He screwed up his nose. He could now smell the decaying remains of a human being, or was that just his imagination now that he knew one was here?

"A body bag?" Scott said. He leaned down and ran his hands over the surface. "It seems to be serving the purpose for which it was intended. This hardly looks spur-of-the-moment. Not many people drive around with a spare body bag in their trunk. We have a great deal of premeditation with this one. If this is George, someone wanted him dead in a bad way."

Jim stood up. Scott joined him.

"We'll make sure what is in there was human," Jim said. "If it's a body, we'll stop contaminating the crime scene and call in the experts. Wanta flip to see who looks?"

"No," Scott said. "You're the senior man. I'll let you have the honour. Murder is your specialty."

"Thanks. Want to stand back out of the smell zone?"

"I'd have to go out by my car. Once you pull on that zipper, this area will be enveloped in that rancid odour."

Jim knelt down again. "Let's make it quick." He pulled on the zipper. Bits of twigs and leaves kept if from sliding open. He looked up at Scott, who was hovering over his shoulder. Smell or no smell, Scott wanted to see who or what was in this bag.

Jim brushed the debris from the path of the zipper with his gloved hand. This time when he pulled, the zipper stuttered along its track, allowing the two sides to separate. Both men recoiled from the smell. It no longer took a cadaver dog to know what was inside.

Jim folded back the flap to reveal the darkened head of a person. The cheeks were sunken, making the milky eyes and teeth look even larger than normal. He scrunched up his nose and held up his camera for a quick picture. A dark-haired male, with a flush of lighter-coloured whiskers stared up at him. No one could doubt this was a murder scene. Jim needed nothing more. He quickly pulled the covering back into place and slammed the zipper home. He got up, clutched his stomach briefly, then forced a smile onto his face.

"Thank God, that's over. Let's call the ME and crime scene specialists. They can have the fun of extracting the body from that bag." He backed out from under the overhanging stump. "A true identification is the next important thing."

Scott shook his head. "That shirt fits the description of what George was wearing when he disappeared. I've studied these reports so often, I've practically got them memorized."

"Jesus, what is that stink?" Cal Lindsay looked over the top of the extended root. He had worked his way closer so he could hear what was being said. He got more than he bargained for. "That smells like a batch of wine that's gone bad."

"Thanks," Scott said. "There goes my enjoyment of wine."

Cal stared down over the stump. "Is that a body bag?"

Jim nodded.

"Son of a bitch," Cal said. He barked out a short, gruff laugh. "He bought that himself."

Both cops gave Cal a surprised look.

"Care to elaborate?" Jim asked.

"Every summer, we have a 75-mile yard sale around here. Goes along the Fundy Shore, down to Kennetcook, inland to Raymond's River and then back to the shore at Maitland."

"Been there, bought the T-shirt," Scott said. "Go on."

"Three, four years ago, back when George was still drinking, he came out to my house one night raving about the unique buy he had made at the yard sale. The others were all curious about the way George was going on. He had them guessing for a while. Those fools would do anything George told them. None of their guesses were right, of course. Who ever heard of buying a body bag at a yard sale? But George had. Paid two bucks for it. He had no idea what he was going to do with it. Said it was too good a deal to turn down."

Cal slowly shook his head. "Look at him now. Who'd have thought?"

Jim looked up at him and then back at Scott.

"I don't suppose there's any way we can keep this quiet until we determine exactly what happened."

Scott looked at Cal. "I don't know, what do you think?"

Cal shook his head. "Not unless you're going to bring your experts here in unmarked cars in the middle of the night when no one is around. There's probably already a buzz in town about the presence of your vehicle out here at the search site." He turned to Jim. "A stranger heading down these back roads in one of those big, generic, dark cars detectives tend to use will have been noticed by a few more people. Add a couple more vans and the whole county will know something is up."

"He's right," Scott said. "I know my presence out this way always starts the gossip mills churning. We can assume the word will get out, maybe even before we do."

"In that case, we have to act quickly." Jim pulled his cell phone out of his pocket and started putting the investigative wheels into motion. He looked at Cal.

"Care to answer a few questions?"

Cal didn't answer right away. Then he said: "I do have an alibi for the time George disappeared. It is George, isn't it?"

"That has yet to be determined. If you have an alibi, you've nothing to worry about."

"I thought that before we knew for sure that it was a murder. Now, I'm a little more worried."

"If you're innocent, you shouldn't be."

"Does the name Donald Marshall ring any bells? What if there's something else for me to be concerned about when you start questioning me?"

Jim studied the man for a few, hard, long seconds. Then enlightenment came to his eyes. "I'm a homicide detective. What you do in your spare time, how you make your spare cash, if it has nothing to do with this murder, is of no interest to me."

"I'd like to believe that."

"Believe it. Is there anything you can tell us that is pertinent?"

"I didn't do it. John Haydon didn't do it. We were both working sunup until sundown in his fields in the days leading up to George's disappearance. John's a market farmer. He had to get his fields prepared. That's where he was when he got the call from Brian Cosh on that first night. I was still working. Only got home minutes before the chief came to my house inquiring about George and his friends."

Jim looked over at Scott.

"I know John," Scott said. "Officer in the fire department. I'll check out Cal's story, but, for what it's worth, I believe him. Brian Cosh says good things about him."

Cal looked surprised. "You've talked to the Chief about me?"

"We've been making some discreet inquiries. I'll be honest with you. I didn't come way out here for the exercise. You were being considered as a possible suspect. You have a pretty solid alibi. Your story is too easy to check out to be a lie. And frankly, you looked as surprised as we were to find a body under that stump."

Cal's shoulders dropped into a more relaxed state. Some of the tension drained from his face. He said nothing.

"Well, the wife is off the hook," Jim said. "It would take a man to handle all the equipment required to pull this off." He indicated the heavy machines used in the lumbering business.

A stricken look swept over Cal.

"What?" Jim asked. "Do you suspect Connie Wilson?"

"No. Connie wouldn't kill George."

"Something passed through your mind a second ago. Your body language shouted it out to us. What were you thinking?"

"You're wrong about it having to be a man. Connie, for one, can handle all this equipment as good as or better than a lot of men. I'm sure there are other women around who can do it too. Unpaid help is not easy to find. Sometimes you have to be married to it."

Jim looked over at Scott. "Did she have an alibi for the day of the disappearance?"

Scott paused to search his memory banks for that information. "As I recall, she spent the day cooking for a community supper to be held the following day, alone."

Scott pulled a notebook out of his pocket and flipped back through the pages until he was almost at the beginning. "The supper was cancelled because of the search."

"So, no alibi."

Scott shifted on his feet uncomfortably. "I can't see Connie doing this. She was too broken up about it. She'd have to be a hell of an actress to carry that off as well as she did."

Again, Cal looked concerned.

"Now what?" Jim asked.

"Connie is one hell of an actress. She starred in our school plays. I mean she really stood out head and shoulders above everyone else. She still performs in a community acting group in Halifax. She puts on a couple of shows a year here in the community." He shook his head. "I agree with the corporal. She loved George too much to kill him, even when George was acting like an asshole, which was a lot of the time."

Both cops perked up at that statement.

"Care to elaborate?"

"There were two George Wilsons. The happy-go-lucky one who drank a tad too much. Most people knew him. And the morose, heavy-drinking asshole that spent a lot of time at my place." He hesitated. "This is all off the record, right?" Cal prided himself with keeping people's private lives private.

The two cops exchanged glances.

"Explain what you mean."

"The second George failed to paint a happy picture of his home life. Was it just the booze talking? I don't know. I can assure you these were not stories Connie would want to have out in public. You are the first people I've ever mentioned them to, but I wasn't the only one with George when he talked like this. God knows what other shoulders he cried on."

"You never told any of this to Connie?" This side of George had eluded Scott in the last year of investigation.

"Especially not to Connie. Connie and I were friends. George and I had working relationships. Sometimes my line of work, sometimes his. To be honest, half the time I hated the man. I detested the way he talked about Connie when he got stinking drunk."

Jim made an entry in his own notebook.

Scott looked back down at the top of the body bag protruding from the rotted leaves. "I know we still need a positive identification, But I'm going to go over and tell Connie what we've found. I don't want her hearing this from some busybody making wild speculations."

"I'll go with you," Cal said. "She'll need a friend close by when she gets this news. I'm pretty sure she's given George up for dead, but still..." He let the sentence trail off.

Jim caught Scott's eye and gave his head a slight shake.

"No," Scott said to Cal. He understood Jim's reluctance to have Cal along. All the rules changed with the investigation of a definite murder. In a death like this, the spouse always jumped to the head of the line as a suspect. Despite Cal's alibi and the reassurances given to him by the two policemen, he also rated as a suspect. Protocol demanded keeping the suspects separated at this stage of events. Scott didn't really think either of those two was guilty, but protocol gave you a starting place until a real break came in the case.

The only other, and best, suspect at this stage was Jason Browne. He had had possession of George's truck. He had claimed to have been involved in a poker game with George that had not gone well for George.

If true, George may have started making waves for Browne or for the owners of the chop shop. The raid the other day had shown running a chop shop was not their principal line of business. They, instead, were a major link in the drug-smuggling trade. Having George making waves could bring them unwanted attention. They may have wanted to silence George's complaints, permanently. Unfortunately, Browne wouldn't be very forthcoming with any answers to this line of investigation. With his own possible murder still unsolved, proving him guilty of George's death would be harder than finding an as yet unthought-of killer.

"No?" Surprise showed in Cal's voice.

"We'll need you here when the crime-scene guys show up. They should be here within the hour. They may need your help."

Jim nodded his agreement. He knew Robin West, the forensic expert, would not let Cal anywhere near the scene, but on short notice, he thought Scott had come up with a great explanation.

Cal reluctantly agreed to stay, if he was needed. Anything to help find George's killer.

The sergeant walked part-way down the woods road with Scott. "Remember, this is a murder investigation now. The wife can't be completely ruled out as being a part of this."

"I know," Scott said. "But you've never met the lady." He held up his hands to ward off any rebuttal from Jim. "I promise, I'll keep an open mind. In the meantime, you keep probing Cal Lindsay. He may not have done it, but he knows a lot more about what is going on in this community than he lets on. His motto seems to be 'What happens in Raymond's River stays in Raymond's River.'"

Jim nodded. "Seems like, but don't worry, I intend to dig deeper into this. That's one of the reasons I wanted him kept here with me."

"And the other?"

"Finding a corpse in a body bag buried under a stump is a pretty unusual set of circumstances. I would like to hold that information back from the public. Let's keep this between us for now."

Despite a year in the ground, the corpse didn't look that bad. It had not been buried deep enough to keep it from freezing, but the body bag had protected it from frost damage. It had been a cold winter. The photo Jim had taken looked enough like George Wilson for both of them to make that leap of faith. That was the death they were investigating.

The murder was pre-planned and deliberate. As Scott had said, body bags were not something people kept in their back pockets in case they needed one.

Scott stopped and looked down at the ground for a few seconds before looking at his fellow officer again. "You're the homicide detective and I don't intend to tell you how to do your job, but I think I'd put some resources on investigating the Kaulback brothers. If George was floundering around inside their drug operation trying to get his truck back, they may have decided getting rid of him was the easiest option. They had a lot more on the line than most of our other suspects. Maybe there was more than one body bag sold at that yard sale."

Jim smiled and tapped him on the shoulder. "There you go again. Thinking like a true detective. Transfer over to my department and I'll let you lead that investigation personally."

Scott gave him a disgusted look. "I've got to go see Connie. It's important I tell her exactly what's going on before she finds out through the gossip mill. That already happened with the naming of George as the father of Tim Schofield."

"OK, but no details and keep your cell phone on. There are too many scanners out here for me to be calling you on the car radio."

"No problem. Keep me informed when the forensic guys arrive."

CHAPTER 55

SCOTT WAS RELIEVED to see Connie's Toyota Landcruiser when he pulled into her driveway. That meant she had probably been protected from hearing any gossip that might already be floating around the small community.

Everyone in town knew George's truck had been found at a nearby junk yard. They were all champing at the bit to be the first to spread the story that George, himself, had been located. This time the speculation might prove to be true. Scott definitely believed that was the case. He had never laid eyes on the man, but had lived with him for the past year. All his instincts told him the search for George Wilson was over.

Connie emerged from the barn as Scott pulled into her yard. A smile immediately flashed across her face. Her hand raised in an automatic wave. Then she appeared to notice Roscoe standing on the back seat of the Explorer. Her smile faltered a bit. Knowing Roscoe's specialty and perhaps noting the serious expression on Scott's face, she seemed to sense bad news was on the horizon.

"Got a minute?" Scott asked as he stepped down from his vehicle. He tried to keep his countenance as neutral as possible. Despite the fact Connie had already accepted George was dead — she had been informed of that by her psychic friend — Scott did not look forward to giving her the actual news. In reality, he was just giving her a heads-up that a body that could be George's had been found.

The look on Connie's face changed to reflect that of the policeman. "You did come all the way out here to see me. I guess I can spare a few minutes. Come in and we'll see how old the coffee in the perk is. I think it might be time for a fresh brew." She forced a smile.

Her gaze drifted over Scott's shoulder and into the Explorer. "I see you have your dog with you. Looking for something? Did you manage to get hold of Cal?"

Roscoe wagged his tail. He had pleasant memories of previous visits here.

Scott looked back at his dog and gave him the stay command. "Let's go inside," he said, "if you don't mind." He wanted to get this over with.

The smile on Connie's face faltered for a second. She looked at him warily before moving toward the kitchen door. They made small talk about the weather and the upcoming growing season while Connie prepared a fresh pot of coffee. She placed a plate of homemade cookies on the table. When they were both seated, Scott led off.

"We've found a body back in the woods near the original search area."

Connie let out a gasp. Her finger was hooked in the handle of her cup. The coffee spilled over the clean, white table cloth.

"Damn," she said as she jumped up to avoid getting the hot liquid in her lap.

Scott leaped to his feet and quickly retrieved the cup, placing it upright again. He grabbed a napkin from the centre of the table and made some ineffective swabs at the mess on the table.

"I'm sorry," he said. "I didn't mean to sound so blunt."

Connie stood holding the back of her chair, shaking her head. She struggled to pull herself together again. "No, I'm sorry. I over-reacted. I thought I had accepted George was gone. Hearing it from you seems to make it more official."

She got a dishcloth from over the sink and wiped up the remaining coffee before looking up at Scott again. "Where was the body? How did we miss it during the initial search? Are you sure it's George?" The questions tumbled from her mouth.

"We still have to make a positive ID. I hurried over here as soon as I could. I didn't want you to hear this from anyone else but me."

"So, it might not be George?" A spark of hope appeared in Connie's eyes.

"The medical examiner is on his way to the scene." Scott looked at his watch. "He may even be there by now."

Connie remained silent for a few minutes. She took a sip from her newly filled coffee cup. She pushed the untouched plate of cookies towards Scott. He smiled for the first time and took one.

"You still haven't told me where you found the body. Is it near where Cal is working?" Connie asked. "That area was searched quite thoroughly at the time. I don't understand how you could have missed him."

Scott shook a couple of crumbs off the cookie and popped the rest into his mouth. Slowly he chewed it. Connie impatiently stared at him, waiting for him to answer her question.

"There are some unusual circumstances involved. If this is George, we think he may have been murdered."

The colour drained from Connie's face like water from a ruptured backyard pool. Her hands shot to her mouth to contain the audible gasp that escaped. Her whole body started to tremble.

"George, murdered? I can't believe that." The words were hesitant and shaky.

"We think George may have inadvertently gotten himself involved with some unsavoury characters. We think they may have killed him."

Connie let out a short, harsh grunt of a laugh. "George was a simple farmer. He didn't involve himself with unsavoury characters." She seemed to rethink that statement and added, "at least none I knew of."

Scott raised his hands in front of him, palms up. "Maybe you didn't know your husband as well as you thought. The gambling, the truck," he hesitated for a few beats, "the baby. Did you talk to Elizabeth?"

Fire flashed in Connie's eyes. She pointed a finger at Scott's face. "George may have been a womanizer, but don't bring that beautiful, little baby into the same conversation as thugs and murderers."

Scott was surprised by the vehemence of the attack on his statement. He was searching for the right response when his cell phone rang. He looked at the display. The caller's name was blocked. Probably the sergeant, he thought. He flipped open the phone.

"Yeah," he said.

"Yes or no. Are you with the wife?" It was Jim.

The question caught him off guard. "Ah, yes," he answered.

"Don't say anything. Just listen."

"OK."

"The M.E. just opened up the body bag. The back of the man's head was severely bashed in. Probably what killed him." Jim let that sink in before continuing.

"OK," Scott said.

"We found the probable murder weapon under the leaves beside the body bag. It's some kind of pick used for moving logs around. Light, but extremely sharp, a little hook in the end for picking up the wood. Cal calls it a pickaroon."

"OK," Scott repeated.

"There were numerous knife wounds to the front of the body. M.E. says they were all post-mortem"

Scott didn't respond. He knew what Jim was suggesting. A crime of passion.

"A bone-handled steak knife was found extruding from the genital area. Cal Lindsay says there is a set just like it hanging in the Wilson kitchen."

"What are you saying?" Scott let the words slip out before he could stop them. Connie's head snapped up. Now she was listening more intently.

"You're in the kitchen," Jim said. "You tell me."

Scott let his eyes slowly and unobtrusively drift around the kitchen walls. Despite his efforts to conceal any emotion, his face went pale. Fastened to the cabinet near the sink was a brown wooden knife holder. It had slots for twelve knives, three rows of four. A bread knife, a carving knife, a filleting knife and a small cleaver filled the top row. Seven steak knives filled the next two rows. One slot was conspicuously empty. He let his eyes move further along the kitchen wall away from the knives.

"That's affirmative," he said.

Connie noticed the reaction. She looked back in the direction of Scott's gaze which by now had moved to the end of the cupboards.

"What's going on?" she said. She continued to follow the direction of his stare. The kitchen clock came into her view. She looked at her watch to confirm the time was properly set.

Scott held up a hand to hold off her questions. He had to control this situation.

"There's dried blood on the handle of the knife," Jim said. "It will be pretty conclusive evidence to match any suspect to the murder. The murderer probably cut themselves."

"OK, I guess we'll wait and see."

"I'm on my way over. Don't do anything until I get there. The level of violence at this scene is scary. You are going to want backup."

"I understand," Scott said. "Do what you have to do." He flipped his phone shut.

"What's going on?" Connie repeated.

"The medical examiner has arrived. He said they will need more tests to determine who the victim is. It looks like I may have been wrong."

Connie let her shoulders sag. A sigh of relief escaped from her lips. "If it's not George, who could it be?"

Scott shook his head. "I'm not sure. The body may have been placed there after George disappeared. That would explain why we never found it during the search."

"Where was it?" Connie asked for the third time.

"Hidden in some brush well off the road," Scott said. He watched Connie for a reaction to his little, white lie. There was a spark of relief in her eyes. He had hoped Jim was wrong in his conclusion. Now he wasn't so sure.

"I've got to call Pamela and tell her it's not George," Connie said. She was becoming more animated with each passing moment. She walked over to the kitchen phone. "She's sure to hear the rumours and jump to the wrong conclusion."

"Hold on," Scott said. "I haven't ruled George out yet. We have to run some more tests."

Connie smiled. "Call it woman's intuition. I'm sure it's not George. He committed suicide last January. Remember?"

Scott fought for time. Despite her words about George's suicide, Connie was becoming buoyant. "Perhaps it would be better to let a police officer go talk to Pamela. He could answer her questions, and you know she'll have lots of them."

Connie let out a light, lilting laugh. "There's only one question that counts. It's not her little boy they found in the woods. She won't care about anything else at the moment." She dialled the number.

Scott gave her a resigned look and took another sip of his coffee. He would deal with Pamela later. Right now, that was the least of his worries. The two women would talk until the sergeant arrived. He glanced up at the knife holder with the incriminating empty slot. How could he have been so wrong? There had to be some other plausible explanation.

CHAPTER 56

MINUTES LATER, SCOTT spotted Sergeant McDonald's black Ford pulling up beside the house. A white police cruiser drove in behind it. Two uniformed officers joined the detective. They chatted briefly before one of the men peeled off from the group and went around to the front of the house. The sergeant was taking no chances.

Scott went to the back door to let them in.

Connie stood facing the wall while she talked to her mother-in-law. She turned when she heard the door open. Her eyes opened wider at the sight of the two additional men. A confused look flashed onto her face and then just as quickly disappeared. She looked back at Scott.

"You lying bastard," she said. Her attention turned back to the phone. "Not you, mother. Disregard what I just told you. I've got to go." Without waiting for a reply, she hung up the phone.

The third policeman came in from the living room. He had let himself in through the unlocked front door. He looked from the detective to Scott and then to Connie. A look of defiance had settled onto her face.

Scott did the introductions. Connie remained silent for a few seconds.

"That was George's body you found, right?" She stared at Sergeant McDonald. "The husband is dead. It must have been the wife who did it. That's the way you homicide detectives think, isn't it? Pick up the wife and check it off as being solved."

Her gaze shifted to Scott. "I don't know what you think you know, but I'm innocent." She walked over to the kitchen table and sat down. "Serve yourselves coffee if you want it." She made a gesture towards the pot on the side counter and said nothing more.

Jim looked over at Scott and raised his eyebrows. "She's good."

Connie looked shocked at the statement. "You don't really think I had anything to do with this? I loved my husband."

"I'm sure you did," Jim said, "I don't know the details, but I know you're into this up to your pretty green eyes. It may not have been intentional; sometimes things just happen. Some little thing sets us off and before we know it, somebody is dead. We understand that."

"Well, I don't. You come in here and tell me my husband is dead and then accuse me of being involved. I think that is despicable."

"We're giving you a chance to tell your side of the story."

Connie's rock-hard exterior was beginning to crack. Jim was not giving her the benefit of any doubt. He was actively accusing her of murder. Suddenly a look of enlightenment came onto her face.

"You think it's about the baby?" She looked from Scott to Jim. "You think I killed my husband because he got another woman pregnant. Of course, a man would think that. That's not what happened. I talked to Elizabeth today. She explained everything to me. I forgave her. We're going to raise the baby together."

"Elizabeth told you about the baby?" Scott asked. "She actually told you George was the father?"

"She told me everything. It was all a mistake. She and George got carried away one night. He was bottling his homemade wine. Elizabeth was helping him. I had to leave to go to one of my stupid committee meetings. As often happens at these bottling sessions, they were sampling the product too much. George didn't rush the bottling process. His wine tasted good right out of the carboy. A sip here, a sip there, things got out of hand. It could happen to anyone. It was just the once. Elizabeth assured me it was never going to happen again."

"Score one for Lisa Tingley," Jim said to Scott. "I thought the old doll was as crazy as a loon. Maybe her scientific methods were accurate."

Connie's voice took on a hard edge again. "That meddling busybody. She has no scientific proof, just like you have no scientific proof I killed George," Connie said. "You can't have. I didn't kill my husband. Elizabeth told me he didn't even know about the baby. I knew nothing about Elizabeth's involvement until a couple of hours ago."

"But you did know George was seeing someone else," Scott said. "You knew he was having an affair behind your back. Raymond's River is a small town. Word would eventually get out. Someone like Lisa Tingley would find out and then everyone in town would know. You couldn't let that happen. You had to stop him. Didn't you?"

Connie's voice became even harsher. "It's true I knew he was having an affair. The son of a bitch was cheating on me, but that doesn't add up to murder. Thousands of men are running around on their wives, cheating, but you're not trying to solve thousands of murder cases. The two don't go hand in hand.

"George was a good provider. He was a hard worker. Do you think I enjoy doing farm work every day, morning and night? Sure, we were having problems. I could do without his sweaty body crawling all over me when I was in bed. If he wanted to stick his dick in some other woman, she was welcome to have it. I could have any man I wanted." She glared at Scott. "Even you."

Scott's face turned a deep red.

"Don't deny it. I've seen you looking at me. I knew what you were thinking."

"I was thinking what a wonderful person you were," Scott said. "I was impressed at how well you were standing up to life with your husband off in the wind."

"Ha, I bet you were. I don't need any man in my life. Elizabeth and I are going to raise our baby together. I may not be as sorry as I should be about George's death, but you'll never pin it on me. Someone else did me a favour and you can't prove otherwise."

Jim lowered his voice to be in counterpoint to the venom Connie was emitting. "You're wrong, Mrs. Wilson. We can. Even as we speak, the steak knife you stabbed him with is being tested for DNA traces. You left blood on the handle. What happened? When you stabbed him in the chest, did you hit a bone and have your fingers run down the knife blade? That happens a lot. I'm sure DNA tests will show the blood is yours. We do have proof, Mrs. Wilson."

Connie glared into Jim's eyes. Jim didn't flinch. "Steak knife? I don't know what you are talking about." She said it with such a positive feeling, it was hard to doubt the veracity of her statement.

Jim pointed to the wooden knife holder hanging on the wall. "Your missing steak knife? We found it stuck in your husband's genitals."

Connie looked up at the knife holder. The look on her face was one of confusion. Some of the harshness dropped from her face.

"You don't remember stabbing your husband, do you?" Scott said. Connie may have been a good actor, but Scott didn't think she was that good.

She shook her head. "There's nothing to remember. I didn't do it." This time she didn't sound so sure.

"That's not all we have," Jim continued. "The signature on the transfer of ownership for George's truck is being examined by experts. It will not only show George didn't sign it, but it will show you did. We have lots of documents with your signature on them. Unfortunately for you, you had to sign the same last name on both of them. Despite your efforts to copy George's style of writing, to an expert, your own style will shine through.

"Finally," Jim let a smile cross his face, "and this was a master stroke on your part, there was the mysterious psychic. That person, real or fictional, and now most likely fictional, had kept George alive for an additional nine months. Then, she had conveniently had him commit suicide in some isolated, out of the way, hunting camp. Even left a note.

"We had checked your phone records in an attempt to get a lead on who was conning you. We were trying to prevent you from being bamboozled by some fraud artist. The calls all came from one of those prepaid cell phones. The cell towers were always in this area. We suspected someone local, but now we see it was all part of your cover-up plan. It was genius."

Scott shook his head in disbelief that he had been sucked into that web. From the start, he said the idea was preposterous, and still, he had spent countless hours and resources following up the leads from those stories.

"I really believed in you," Scott said. "It scares me to think I could be that wrong about somebody. It makes me question my ability as a police officer.

"You had me convinced about everything. You could get angry at my innuendoes and then stand there and lie right to my face and make me feel like a jerk for even making any suggestions there may have been trouble in your marriage.

"At the drop of a hat, you could turn on the tears and make me feel guilty for questioning you. Questioning you is my job. Tears shouldn't bother me."

Jim looked at his fellow officer. He could share his disillusionment. Every officer had been fooled at one time or another. "Remember," Jim said, "Cal told us she was a natural actor. Everyone at her school thought she would go on to star in the movies. A woman that can generate tears at will already has a man over a barrel."

Scott tried to force a smile onto his face at Jim's attempt at commiseration. He looked back at Connie. "There's more to it than your tears. I liked you. I wanted to believe you."

"Well, I tried to warn you about that," Jim said. He was trying to get Scott back on side. They didn't have a confession from Connie yet and you could play the good cop angle too far. Scott was slipping into that realm. "A policeman's best weapon is detachment. You can't get involved with the people you're dealing with."

Connie's features softened a little. Her emotions were swinging back and forth like a pendulum from animosity to solicitude, from anger to cooperation. She placed her hands on Scott's. "I did appreciate all you were doing for me. I still do. I have to depend on you to see the truth here. This big-city homicide detective is convinced I'm guilty from a bunch of circumstantial events. He doesn't know me like you do. You know the truth. I couldn't kill my husband."

Before Scott could respond, the kitchen door crashed open. Brian Cosh came charging in. He looked at the people gathered around the table, Connie holding on to Scott's hand. One of the Mounties standing by the door grabbed him by the shoulders. Brian started to shake free, looked at the cop and seemed to accept the restraint.

"It's true, isn't it? You've found George's body?"

Scott was the first to speak. "It looks that way." He freed his hand from Connie's. "You'd better sit down."

Brian freed himself from the Mountie's grip and rushed over to Connie. He reached down and hugged her. "Are you all right? What have they told you?"

"Only that they've found a body they think might be George. They don't know who did it. At least they have no proof." She pointed to Jim. "This man thinks it was me."

Brian stared at Jim for a few brief seconds. "No they don't. They've arrested Cal Lindsay."

"What?" Scott, Jim and Connie all said at the same time.

"David Gates was out there on his ATV. He saw all the police cars around Cal's truck. They've got Cal back in the woods where the body is. Gates tried to go in, but the police stopped him and made him leave. He says he sneaked in anyway."

"Don't worry about Cal. He has an alibi." Connie was back to her self-assured self.

"Not according to Gates. They've got him in cuffs."

Connie turned on Scott. "You told me you were checking out his alibi."

Scott looked at Jim, who was looking at Brian Cosh. The two men had met a few years earlier during the investigation of another murder case in Raymond's River.

"Cuffs?" Jim said.

"That's what Gates said. He couldn't get that close. They threatened to arrest him, too, if he didn't get out of there. Said it was a crime scene."

Scott looked back at Connie. "I guess the alibi didn't work out. As you know, Cal was my first suspect."

Jim's gaze shifted from Brian to Scott and then back to Connie. He followed Scott's lead. "Looks like we've solved this one. A check on the ledger, that's all we care about. Right? We've got our killer."

"No," Connie said. "You know Cal didn't do it."

"Doesn't matter. We have enough proof to convict him."

"What difference does it make to you?" Scott asked. "You're only business partners. There are other men around here who can run a porter and a skidder. In fact, I've been told you can even do it yourself."

"That's a little harsh," Brian said. "She just found out her husband is dead. Show a little compassion."

"I don't think she just found out," Scott said. "I think she's known it for a while, quite a while." There was an edge in Scott's voice. He had taken over the role of bad cop from Jim, who now sat quietly and listened.

Connie glared at Scott. The pendulum was making another swing.

"Tell Brian how well you were getting along with your husband. He doesn't know anything about your marital troubles. I've asked him."

Connie's glare wavered. "Honestly answer one question for me. Where did you find the body?" Her eyes implored Scott for a straight answer.

"Stuffed in a body bag, stashed under a tree stump. Roscoe found it."

Connie looked down and studied her hands. When she spoke again, her voice was low and controlled. "The bastard deserved to die. You're right. I knew he was being unfaithful." She looked up. Her voice returned to its usual well-modulated tone with a touch of resignation in it. "I didn't know with whom and, honestly, I didn't care. Then, I began to suspect he was trying to make a play for Elizabeth. Innocent, little Elizabeth from next door. I never knew if he succeeded, but I knew he was trying. I've seen him flash his charm too many times not to know when he's making a move. I had to stop him." She slowly shook her head. "Turns out I was too late. The bastard got her pregnant."

Connie's shoulders sagged as the reality of her situation settled onto her.

"The day he died, I had taken him a hearty meal out to the wood lot — steak, potatoes, turnips, carrots, all the things he liked. I kept it all hot in an insulated bag. He had been coming home too tired to eat. Said he wanted to make as much money as he could as fast as he could." She gave a derisive laugh. "I thought it was for us. Tried to tell him to slow down a little. What a fool I was."

Connie paused and stared into her coffee cup as if it were a crystal ball with the images of that day flashing in front of her.

"I admit I might have been neglecting him of late. Sometimes a woman just gets tired of a man satisfying his own needs and ignoring hers." She looked around at the roomful of men. "You guys probably don't understand that. I wanted to make up for all that, start over again. I wanted him to leave Elizabeth alone.

"The poor kid was having a hard enough time adjusting to rural life as it was. Him sniffing around wasn't helping her any. I could see she was eating up the attention though, and I had to get him to stop.

My only intention when I ventured out there was to bring his concentration back to me. We had had some pretty good times in the past. We could have them again. All it would take was a little effort on my part. I truly believed that."

Again Connie paused. Her eyes lost their focus for a brief second, then she looked up again. Sparks seemed to be snapping in her eye sockets. "I know you won't believe this, but I had wiped the entire incident from my mind like it never happened. The whole thing was a total blank to me. Now I remember it all like it happened yesterday. When Elizabeth told me George was young Tim's father, the memories flooded back into my mind like a dam had broken. It shook me to my core."

Connie paused, looked down as if her mind had gone blank. Then, she looked at the Mounties with a new vengeance in her eyes.

"That bastard laughed at me. Asked why he would be interested in a frigid has-been like me when he could have a hot, horny, young chickadee like Elizabeth. Those were his actual words. According to him, she said he was the best lover she had ever experienced. Elizabeth denied that.

"He said he and Elizabeth were going to blow this burg and head out west where the good money and the good life were. Elizabeth hated living in this backwoods hamlet, he said. There was nothing I could do to stop them. I had held him back for too long."

Now the tension in Connie's voice was transmitting itself to her body. Her arms and hands started to shake. "Then the son of a bitch turned and walked away from me as if I wasn't even there. I spotted his wood pick sticking into a stump beside me. Without even thinking, I grabbed it and sunk the hook as far as I could into the back of his head. Grey matter spurted out with the blood. I knew I had killed him."

She slumped into her chair again, looking at her hands. Then she looked up again. "It was over. Just like that. George was dead."

The silence in the room was palpable. For a long time, no one said anything.

Connie looked over at Scott again.

"Cal had nothing to do with it. You knew that, didn't you? Accusing him was part of the game." She looked at Brian. "I can't believe you went along with them. I trusted you. Of all men, I trusted you the most."

Brian looked from one person to the other. "Connie, I don't know what you're talking about. I don't know what any of you are talking about. I hear George's body has been found. Cal has been arrested. I rush over to be with you and you're confessing to murdering your own husband." He looked thoroughly confused. "I honestly don't have a clue what is happening here."

Scott gave Jim a perverse look. He stood and beckoned towards the sergeant. "Come outside for a minute, will you?"

"Keep an eye on her," Jim told the uniformed officer in the doorway. He followed Scott out the back door.

"You know we can't use any of that," Scott said. "We should have read her her rights before she started."

Jim gave a shrug of his shoulders. "We don't need her statement. We have more than enough evidence to convict her. I just wanted to hear it with my own ears."

"I'm not so sure we do," Scott said. "You heard her story. Maybe manslaughter. Definitely not first-degree murder."

Jim's glance at Scott said it all. She still has you wrapped around her little finger.

"Manslaughter? I don't think so. It might have been manslaughter if she had come forward at the time. It's not manslaughter with the elaborate cover-up that followed. Manslaughter doesn't explain the body bag or George's truck ending up at Kaulback Brothers Salvage Yard or the long hours of searching you put in."

Scott nodded. "That's true, but I don't think it is all cut-and-dried." He shrugged. "Let's take her in. See what happens."

As they re-entered the kitchen, Connie's attention was focussed fully on their faces. Their brief departure seemed to have had an unnerving effect on her.

"I panicked," she said, without any encouragement. All eyes turned to her. "It all happened so fast, I didn't know what to do. I wanted to call the police, but with George running around with other women, I knew how it would look." She centred her attention on Jim. "And you guys always suspect the wife of murder right away. Isn't that true?"

Jim's face remained neutral, neither agreement nor denial.

"So here's what I did," Connie said.

"Wait," Jim said. Connie was surprised at the command, but stopped talking. Confusion was evident in her eyes.

Jim put his hand on Connie's shoulder. "Mrs. Connie Wilson. You're under arrest for the murder of your husband, George Wilson. You have the right to remain silent…"

CHAPTER 57

SCOTT LISTENED AS Jim droned through the familiar phrase. One more question nagged his mind. The cover-up was one thing, but how did the death of Jason Browne tie in to all this? If Connie had forged George's signature on the transfer, how did Jason Browne get hold of it? Scott waited for Jim to finish.

"Do you wish to have a lawyer present for this questioning?" Jim asked.

Connie's features had taken on an ashen hue. With the actual charge being laid, the fight had drained from her green eyes, making them appear more of a faded pastel than a real green. "Why bother? I'll wait until I get to the city. I assume that's the next step."

"We will want to take you in for a more formal questioning, yes. You can have a lawyer at that time if you so wish."

Scott couldn't wait that long. "How about answering a couple more questions for us?"

"Sure," Connie said. She didn't wait for the questions to be asked. She wanted to get it all off her chest.

"George already owned the body bag. He bought it at a yard sale. I begged him to get rid of it, but he wouldn't do it. He thought owning it was a big joke. I thought it was gruesome. The mere presence of it in our house disgusted me. How ironic. I struggled with how I was going to get rid of the body at first. Then, I remembered the body bag. I threw a couple of branches over George. We were still on the opposite side of the road at the time. I left him lying there while I went home for the bag."

Her eyes got that faraway look again. "When I came back, he hadn't moved. He was lying face down on the road. That's when the reality sunk in. He hardly bled at all. I opened up the body bag, but he was too heavy for me to wrestle him into it. The porter stood right there, so I used that to lift him onto the open bag. I remember jumping down to zip it up.

"I threw any dirt that might have had any blood mixed with it into the bag on top of him. Then I spotted the lunch I brought out for him. It was spilled all over the ground. I think he might have knocked it out of my hand before he turned away. I don't really remember."

Connie's eyes drifted up towards the knife rack in her kitchen. She noted the empty slot.

"Oh my God," she said. A surprised look came on her face. "The knife *was* lying there beside the body. I grabbed it and stabbed him and stabbed him and stabbed him." She looked down at her hand. "You were right. I think the knife slipped at some point and I cut my hand." Her eyes engaged Scott's. "I didn't remember doing that until just now. Honestly, I've looked everywhere for that missing knife. I left it in George, didn't I? I zipped up the bag with the knife still sticking in him. I remember taking him his dinner and I remember hiding the body. Everything in between was a blank until today."

Scott nodded. "I believe you." He looked up at the other two uniformed Mounties for confirmation.

"She sounds convincing," one of them said.

Brian got up from the table. "I don't believe any of this. The whole thing is a nightmare."

"I don't know what to tell you," Connie said. "I must have blocked the entire stabbing incident out of my conscious memory. Even the part about his affair with Elizabeth seems unreal. I still think he made most of that up." She paused. "Or he may have believed it happened in his own mind, but I think he exaggerated what really took place."

Jim looked at Brian, surprised that he was still there. He motioned to one of the other officers. "Please take the chief into the living room until we finish with this."

Brian shook his head. "No, I won't say anything else."

Jim nodded towards the door. Brian allowed himself to be reluctantly escorted out of the room.

"Continue," Jim said. "You stabbed him with the kitchen knife."

Connie looked at the knife holder with the empty slot, shook her head and went on. "I still had to get rid of the body. The porter was running. I climbed into it and scooped up the body bag with George in it. It was aimed down the road, so I went in that direction. When I came to the main road, I kept on going, no destination in mind. The road on the other side was more solid. It hadn't been used for quite a while and had grass growing in it. I drove until I noticed the stump and thought, 'What an ideal spot.'"

Connie shifted in her chair, getting more comfortable. She was holding nothing back. The whole story was coming out. It was like a catharsis, cleansing her soul after a year of inner turmoil.

"The first couple of stumps were too small to hide him under. Further off the road was a big tree that had blown down. It was perfect. I just had to clear a path. There was a chain saw in the porter, so I cut up the logs and stacked them in the back." She smiled at the memory. "'One last load,' I remember saying."

"I dropped the body bag in behind the upturned roots and threw the pick in with it. I didn't want to ever see that murderous thing again." She paused and her eyes become more alert. "You have to believe me; I never intended to hurt him. I was trying to win him back."

"I do," Scott said. "What happened next?"

"I fired up the chain saw and cut the stump from the rest of the tree. It settled back in place with a big whoosh and that was the end of it. George was gone forever. I can't believe you found him. I did my best to keep Cal from cutting in that area. If Laurie MacIsaac hadn't come home for Easter, I would have succeeded." She shrugged. "But Laurie wanted that area cleared of dead falls and Cal agreed it was the best thing to do. I didn't want to create a fuss, so I stopped arguing with him. By then, I figured George would never be found."

"So," Jim asked, "you're saying the stump just settled back into place and covered the body? It was serendipity we ever found him."

"I took the porter and gave the stump a little push to seat it securely, but otherwise, that's all there was to it. I figured the leaves would soon blow in around it and hide any disturbed ground. I cut up the rest of the tree and lugged it back to the other side of the road.

"Next, I had to get rid of George's truck. If he was going to disappear, the truck had to go with him."

Scott became more alert. This part of the puzzle had baffled him for the better part of a year.

"That's where Jason Browne gets involved," he said. "How did that happen?" He hesitated, struggling to find the right words for his question. "Did his death have anything at all to do with George's disappearance?"

The lights flashed back on in Connie's eyes. The green once again gained the colour of the waves pounding ashore in a North Atlantic storm. "Jason Browne, that little slime ball, got exactly what he deserved. I didn't kill him, although I gladly would have. He died in an accident."

Both policemen recoiled from this renewed acrimony.

"I had met that piece of shit through one of the outreach programs our church ran," Connie said. "It didn't take much of a genius to realize no outreach was going to help that thug. He was a waste of breath, a waste of a soul. He was only involved in the program because it kept him out of jail. Some judge, in his wisdom, thought Browne could be turned into a productive citizen. What an asshole he was. Jason Browne would never be rehabilitated into a productive citizen. That was never going to happen.

"As I said, I knew I would have to get rid of George's truck as well as his body. That was the only way to make it appear he had taken off. He wouldn't have gone anywhere without taking his truck with him. The two were more married than George and I were.

"I knew Jason Browne had been convicted of selling stolen cars to a chop shop. I also knew how to contact him in case I thought there was any chance he could be helped. A criminal proposal would be the only kind of help he would be interested in.

"I called him and made him a generous offer. I would give him George's truck with a signed transfer and all he had to do was take it to one of his buddies to be destroyed. They would pay him and so would I. I didn't really want to part with any of the money that was in George's wallet. That was what I was going to have to live on for a while. I mistakenly thought I could buy Browne's silence. He was going to win all the way around. The only stipulation was the truck be destroyed. It had to disappear right away."

Connie took a sip of her coffee and spit it back into her cup. "Can I get anyone some fresh coffee?" Neither man had any interest in coffee at this moment. They were caught up in this story. Connie refilled their mugs anyway.

"A couple of days later, I called Brian and started the wheels of the search in motion. As far as I knew, Browne had carried out his part of the deal. The truck was nowhere to be seen and you were searching all across the country for it. Everything was perfect." She allowed herself a self-satisfied smile.

Scott looked down at the table. He was thinking of all the officers all across the country who had been pulling over silver-and-black Dodges. What a waste of time that had been.

Connie's demeanour changed again. The story wasn't over. A new tension filled her voice. "A week later," she continued, "the day after the search was officially scaled back," she managed a small smile at Scott, "I was at the drug store in town. When I got back into my car, Jason Browne was in the back seat with a knife.

"He said he had heard the news stories about the search for George's truck and he wanted more money. I could smell the alcohol on his breath and let me tell you, I was scared. Even so, I was not going to give him any more money. I knew if I did, it would never stop."

She stopped to take a sip of coffee. Scott could see her hands were shaking. The retelling of the story was bringing back the fear she had felt.

"When I told him to get lost, he got angry. He insisted he needed something more from me. I told him I didn't have any more money to give him. I was trying to run a farm all by myself and I was losing money every day. There was nothing I could give him and that was that."

Connie became silent for a few moments. She stared into her coffee cup and then looked up again. "That's when he got really creepy. He told me to drive towards the shore while he thought. I was scared. I looked around for someone to help me. Brian had been right there seconds before. When I looked around, he was gone. Then, I felt the point of the knife touch my neck. Even though I knew it was a mistake, I had to drive.

"When we reached one of those fields running along the shore, he ordered me to pull over and get out of the car. He said he'd take it out in trade. He ordered me to take off my clothes. Well, that pissed me off. To think this punk thought he was going to have his way with me. That would never happen.

"I laughed at him and told him he wasn't man enough to do it with a real woman. Young kids were more his style and only if he paid them. I had heard all the stories while he was part of our program. I knew all about his deranged life and his prostitutes. He dropped his drawers and had this raging hard-on. He must have been working on it all the way out the road. He snapped his cock against his belly and told me to get down on my knees. It was pay-off time. Not for me. I took off running in the dark.

"He was struggling to pull up his pants and trying to catch me at the same time. Then I guess he kicked them off. I found them in the field afterward. At the time, I was just running as fast as I could, running blindly with no destination in mind. My only thought was to get away from this bag of shit. Then, I could hear him panting right behind me. He was so close to me, I could almost feel his breath on the back of my neck. He was yelling things like 'Stop bitch, you know you want it,' which only made me run faster. Suddenly, I realized I was almost to the edge of the bank. I don't know how. I noticed the change in the lighting or something. I'm not sure what, but I dropped down onto the grass.

"When I dropped, he tripped over me and went headlong over the bank. I didn't even look to see what happened to him. I jumped up and ran back towards my car. On the way, I found his pants. I grabbed his wallet from the pocket and fished out the money remaining from what I had paid him and what he had sold the truck for. It was mine anyway. Then I threw the jeans and underwear over the bank where he had disappeared. Without even looking, I turned and got the hell out of there."

Connie remained silent for several seconds, a far-a-way look on her face. Then she spoke again.

"I lived in terror for days, expecting him to show up. I was afraid he would shoot off his mouth and blow everything. A couple of months later, I heard he had been found dead at the bottom of the cliff. I rejoiced, gentlemen. That's what I did. I felt no remorse for that son of a bitch. He got exactly what he deserved as far as I was concerned."

She paused to catch her breath and take another sip of coffee. "He would have raped me if he had caught me. I know he would."

Connie turned to face Scott. "I should have gone for help with George before all this blew out of control. Marriage counsellors aren't popular here in Raymond's River. I was too proud. That's one of the big ones, isn't it? Pride."

A peaceful look slipped onto Connie's face. "That pride is an old sin with me. It goes back at least fifteen years. When my father told me Cal Lindsay was a bootlegger, I should have told my father it didn't matter. Cal was the man for me. Things would have been so much better for everyone."

She looked at Scott. "Cal had nothing to do with this. If you arrested him, you should set him free."

Scott nodded. "Small towns. Nothing moves through them faster than a rumour. You don't have to worry about Cal. I think he was the victim of David Gates' overactive imagination and need to be at the centre of things."

"That's good. I'll need him to take care of this place for me for a while. I won't be in jail forever, not when the jury hears my story about how George abused and neglected me, how he screwed the little girl next door. Baby Timmy with his flaming red curls will make a great silent witness on my behalf. One look at him sitting on his mother's knee in the front row of the court, a pretty young thing who was half George's age, will bring me all the sympathy I need. I may even get away with probation and time served."

Jim rolled his eyes at Scott. Her story was convincing. *She's probably right,* he thought.

Scott seemed to read his partner's mind. His head nodded negligibly. He could see a jury setting her free. He almost had.